Prais

"Dynamic, often exceptional work

"The best original science fiction anthology published this year." —Gardner Dozois

"By far the best original anthology of 1998." —Mary R. Kelly, *Locus*

"As editor Nielsen Hayden points out in his introductory paragraph, it is difficult to cleanly separate science fiction from fantasy. His second compilation of original short fiction illustrates that point with great style. . . . This baker's dozen of exceptional tales goes beyond the enchantment-versus-technology dichotomy and allows readers to simply enjoy some of the best new writing in speculative fiction." —*Booklist*

"*Starlight 1* generated a whole passel of award-winning or award-nominated stories, and itself won the World Fantasy Award in 1997. Now, with *Starlight 2,* Nielsen Hayden gathers another thirteen stories (one more than in the first volume), and it is just as likely to gather multiple award nominations. . . . It shows us the extraordinary versatility and range that can be encompassed by SF and fantasy when it moves beyond conventional genre boundaries: it shows us a way out." —*Locus*

"Nielsen Hayden's growing reputation as an editor probably rests, at least partly, on his avoidance of the genre clichés: some SF fans might be disappointed at the absence of interplanetary derring-do, while a certain kind of fantasy reader might feel outnumbered. Nevertheless, if you're simply looking for a recommendation, read no further: Just go out and buy the book." —Gwyneth Jones, *The New York Review of Science Fiction*

"An excellent, ambitious, and above all, highly polished science fiction and fantasy collection." —*Vector*

"The stories in *Starlight 2* play wonderfully off each other and off narrow definitions. There isn't a poor story in the bunch, and some are masterful."—*Edmonton Journal*

STARLIGHT 2

EDITED BY

PATRICK NIELSEN HAYDEN

A TOM DOHERTY ASSOCIATES BOOK

NEW YORK

This is a work of fiction. All the characters and events portrayed in this anthology are either fictitious or are used fictitiously.

STARLIGHT 2

This book is printed on acid-free paper.

A Tor Book
Published by Tom Doherty Associates, LLC
175 Fifth Avenue
New York, NY 10010

www.tor.com

Library of Congress Cataloging-in-Publication Data

Starlight 2 / edited by Patrick Nielsen Hayden.
p. cm.
"A Tom Doherty Associates book"
ISBN 0-312-86184-2 (hc)
ISBN 0-312-86312-8 (pbk)
1. Science fiction, American. 2. American fiction—
20th century. I. Nielsen Hayden, Patrick.
PS648.S3S656 1998
813'.0876208'0904—dc21

98-8266
CIP

First Hardcover Edition: November 1998
First Trade Paperback Edition: October 1999

Printed in the United States of America

10 9 8 7 6 5 4 3 2 1

Copyright Acknowledgments

CONTENTS

INTRODUCTION

WELCOME AGAIN TO *STARLIGHT*, AN ORIGINAL SF AND FANTASY anthology series. You'll note the phrase "and fantasy" in that sentence. Many readers and reviewers of *Starlight 1* commented on the prominent presence of fantasy in the book, although the jacket called it a "science fiction" anthology. In fact, these readers and reviewers were correct. Inside the industry, we tend to see the two genres as joined at the hip: they share the same shelves in bookstores because they share the same readers, and I have yet to hear a definition of science fiction or fantasy that cleanly separates them from one another. Much of what is published as "science fiction" is actually fantasy with hardware—nor is this a bad thing; meanwhile, it's difficult to reconcile an intricate, brilliantly demanding modern fantasy novel like Christopher Priest's *The Prestige* with the idea that fantasy is somehow intellectually "easier" than SF.

(In fact, a common joke within the field holds that the boundary between "science fiction" and "fantasy" is ultimately a matter of clothing and props. If a story features swords, it's fantasy, unless it features rockets as well, in which case it's SF. Telepathy, by itself, won't turn a story about Tolkienland into SF; but telepathy plus recognizable biotech just might. Telepathy in a present-day setting is definitely SF, unless the story also features intrusions of people wearing archaic clothes. In general, the presence of *technology recognizable as such* tends, in the minds of most readers, to pull a story over to the SF side. Once a story-in-progress has thoroughly established itself as SF, what single piece of set-dressing might transform it back into fantasy? Teresa Nielsen Hayden was once asked this question, and gave the best answer I've heard yet. "The Holy Grail," she said.)

There are, of course, those who work to hold up the banner of SF-as-distinct-from-fantasy, and for that matter fantasy-as-distinct-from-SF. The paired reprint annuals from St. Martin's Press, Gardner Dozois's *Year's Best Science Fiction* and Ellen Datlow and Terri Windling's *Year's Best Fantasy and Horror*, make a strong effort to separate the two genres, and David Hartwell's new reprint annual from HarperCollins, *Year's Best SF,* makes a programmatic point of declaring itself to be firmly about SF. "Other books," writes Hartwell in his introduction to the first of these, "have so blurred the boundaries between science fiction and everything else that it is possible to conclude that SF is dead or dying out." But if we are to take SF as an organic thing that might "die" or be "dying out," then we must reflect that organic things do not in fact flourish in isolation, but rather in a web of interdependencies with other organic things. Similarly, SF, fantasy, and other forms of the fantastic have always been healthiest, not hermetically sealed away from one another, but at play with one another, breathing one another's air. It's my intention, with *Starlight*, to encourage that kind of play, and that kind of inspiration.

Once again, this project owes thanks to a number of people. To John D. Berry, Charles N. Brown, Avedon Carol, Gardner Dozois, Mike Farren, Jim Frenkel, Neil Gaiman, David Hartwell, Virginia

Kidd, Tappan King, Beth Meacham, Lydia Nickerson, Maureen Kincaid Speller, Terri Windling, and Jane Yolen for invaluable support and encouragement. To Claire Eddy, *Starlight*'s in-house editor, for patience and troubleshooting. To art director Irene Gallo and managing editor Jeff Dreyfus for a superb package inside and out, and to Tom Doherty and Linda Quinton for running the kind of publishing company they do. To Scraps de Selby, short-SF database and good friend. To my indispensable assistant Jenna Felice. And, as ever, to my wife and colleague Teresa Nielsen Hayden, essential partner in everything.

I hope you find the stories herein entertaining, and I hope you'll rejoin us in the year 2000—*the year 2000!*— for *Starlight* 3.

—Patrick Nielsen Hayden

ROBERT CHARLES WILSON

DIVIDED BY INFINITY

I

In the year after Lorraine's death I contemplated suicide six times. Contemplated it seriously, I mean: six times sat with the fat bottle of Clonazepam within reaching distance, six times failed to reach for it, betrayed by some instinct for life or disgusted by my own weakness.

I can't say I wish I had succeeded, because in all likelihood I *did* succeed, on each and every occasion. Six deaths. No, not just six. An infinite number.

Times six.

There are greater and lesser infinities.

But I didn't know that then.

I was only sixty years old.

I had lived all my life in the city of Toronto. I worked thirty-five years as a senior accountant for a Great Lakes cargo brokerage called Steamships Forwarding, Ltd., and took an early retirement in 1997, not long before Lorraine was diagnosed with the pancreatic cancer that killed her the following year. Back then she worked part-time in a Harbord Street used-book shop called Finders, a short walk from the university district, in a part of the city we both loved.

I still loved it, even without Lorraine, though the gloss had dimmed considerably. I lived there still, in a utility apartment over an antique store, and I often walked the neighborhood—down Spadina into the candy-bright intricacies of Chinatown, or west to Kensington, foreign as a Bengali marketplace, where the smell of spices and ground coffee mingled with the stink of sun-ripened fish.

Usually I avoided Harbord Street. My grief was raw enough without the provocation of the bookstore and its awkward memories. Today, however, the sky was a radiant blue, and the smell of spring blossoms and cut grass made the city seem threatless. I walked east from Kensington with a mesh bag filled with onions and Havarti cheese, and soon enough found myself on Harbord Street, which had moved another notch upscale since the old days, more restaurants now, fewer macrobiotic shops, the palm readers and bead shops banished for good and all.

But Finders was still there. It was a tar-shingled Victorian house converted for retail, its hanging sign faded to illegibility. A three-legged cat slumbered on the cracked concrete stoop.

I went in impulsively, but also because the owner, an old man by the name of Oscar Ziegler, had put in an appearance at Lorraine's funeral the previous year, and I felt I owed him some acknowledgment. According to Lorraine, he lived upstairs and seldom left the building.

The bookstore hadn't changed on the inside, either, since the last time I had seen it. I didn't know it well (the store was Lorraine's turf and as a rule I had left her to it), but there was no obvious evidence that more than a year had passed since my last visit. It was the kind of shop with so much musty stock and so few customers that it could have survived only under the most generous circumstances—no doubt Ziegler owned the building and had found a way to finesse his property taxes. The store was not a labor of love, I suspected, so much as an excuse for Ziegler to indulge his pack-rat tendencies.

It was a full nest of books. The walls were pineboard shelves, floor to ceiling. Free-standing shelves divided the small interior into box canyons and dimly-lit hedgerows. The stock was old and, not that I'm any judge, largely trivial, forgotten jazz-age novels and *belles-lettres*, literary flotsam.

I stepped past cardboard boxes from which more books overflowed, to the rear of the store, where a cash desk had been wedged against the wall. This was where, for much of the last five years of her life, Lorraine had spent her weekday afternoons. I wondered whether book dust was carcinogenic. Maybe she had been poisoned by the turgid air, by the floating fragments of ivoried Frank Yerby novels, vagrant molecules of *Peyton Place* and *The Man in the Gray Flannel Suit*.

Someone else sat behind the desk now, a different woman, younger than Lorraine, though not what anyone would call young. A baby-boomer in denim overalls and a pair of eyeglasses that might have better suited the Hubble Space Telescope. Shoulder-length hair, gone gray, and an ingratiating smile, though there was something faintly haunted about the woman.

"Hi," she said amiably. "Anything I can help you find?"

"Is Oscar Ziegler around?"

Her eyes widened. "Uh, Mr. Ziegler? He's upstairs, but he doesn't usually like to be disturbed. Is he expecting you?"

She seemed astonished at the possibility that Ziegler would be expecting anyone, or that anyone would want to see Ziegler. Maybe it was a bad idea. "No," I said, "I just dropped by on the chance . . . you know, my wife used to work here."

"I see."

"Please don't bother him. I'll just browse for a while."

"Are you a book collector, or—?"

"Hardly. These days I read the newspaper. The only books I've kept are old paperbacks. Not the sort of thing Mr. Ziegler would stock."

"You'd be surprised. Mysteries? Chandler, Hammett, John Dickson Carr? Because we have some firsts over by the stairs. . . ."

"I used to read some mysteries. Mostly, though, it was science fiction I liked."

"Really? You look more like a mystery reader."

"There's a look?"

She laughed. "Tell you what. Science fiction? We got a box of paperbacks in last week. Right over there, under the ladder. Check it out, and I'll tell Mr. Ziegler you're here. Uh—"

"My name is Keller. Bill Keller. My wife was Lorraine."

She held out her hand. "I'm Deirdre. Just have a look; I'll be back in a jiff."

I wanted to stop her but didn't know how. She went through a bead curtain and up a dim flight of stairs while I pulled a leathery cardboard box onto a chair seat and prepared for some dutiful time-killing. Certainly I didn't expect to find anything I wanted, though I would probably have to buy something as the price of a courtesy call, especially if Ziegler was coaxed out of his lair to greet me. But what I had told Deirdre was true; though I had been an eager reader in my youth, I hadn't bought more than an occasional softcover since 1970. Fiction is a young man's pastime. I had ceased to be curious about other people's lives, much less other worlds.

Still, the box was full of forty-year-old softcover books, Ace and Ballantine paperbacks mainly, and it was nice to see the covers again, the Richard Powers abstracts, translucent bubbles on infinite plains, or Jack Gaughan sketches, angular and insectile. Titles rich with key words: *Time*, *Space*, *Worlds*, *Infinity*. Once I had loved this sort of thing.

And then, amongst these faded jewels, I found something I did *not* expect—

And another. And another.

The bead curtain parted and Ziegler entered the room.

He was a bulky man, but he moved with the exaggerated caution of the frail. A plastic tube emerged from his nose, was taped to his cheek with a dirty bandaid and connected to an oxygen canister slung from his shoulder. He hadn't shaved for a couple of days. He wore what looked like a velveteen frock coat draped over a t-shirt and a pair of pinstriped pajama-bottoms. His hair, what remained of it, was feathery and white. His skin was the color of thrift-shop Tupperware.

Despite his appearance, he gave me a wide grin.

"Mr. Ziegler," I said. "I'm Bill Keller. I don't know if you remember—"

He thrust his pudgy hand forward. "Of course! No need to explain. Terrible about Lorraine. I think of her often." He turned to Deirdre, who emerged from the curtain behind him. "Mr. Keller's wife . . ." He drew a labored breath. "Died last year."

"I'm sorry," Deirdre said.

"She was . . . a wonderful woman. Friendly by nature. A joy. Of course, death isn't final . . . we all *go on*, I believe, each in his own way. . . ."

There was more of this—enough that I regretted stopping by—but I couldn't doubt Ziegler's sincerity. Despite his intimidating appearance there was something almost willfully childlike about him, a kind of embalmed innocence, if that makes any sense.

He asked how I had been and what I had been doing. I answered as cheerfully as I could and refrained from asking after his own health. His cheeks reddened as he stood, and I wondered if he shouldn't be sitting down. But he seemed to be enjoying himself. He eyed the five slender books I'd brought to the cash desk.

"Science fiction!" he said. "I wouldn't have taken you for a science fiction reader, Mr. Keller."

(Deirdre glanced at me: *Told you so!*)

"I haven't been a steady reader for a long time," I said. "But I found some interesting items."

"The good old stuff," Ziegler gushed. "The pure quill. Does it strike you, Mr. Keller, that we live every day in the science fiction of our youth?"

"I hadn't noticed."

"There was a time when science seemed so *sterile*. It didn't yield up the wonders we had been led to expect. Only a bleak, lifeless solar system . . . a half-dozen desert worlds, baked or frozen, take your pick, and the gas giants . . . great roaring seas of methane and ammonia. . . ."

I nodded politely.

"But now!" Ziegler exclaimed. "Life on Mars! Oceans under Europa! Comets plunging into Jupiter—!"

"I see what you mean."

"And here on Earth—the human genome, cloned animals, mind-altering drugs! Computer networks! Computer *viruses*!" He slapped his thigh. "I have a *Teflon hip*, if you can imagine such a thing!"

"Pretty amazing," I agreed, though I hadn't thought much about any of this.

"Back when we read these books, Mr. Keller, when we read Heinlein or Simak or Edmond Hamilton, we longed to immerse ourselves in the strange . . . the *outré*. And now—well—here we are!" He smiled breathlessly and summed up his thesis. "*Immersed in the strange.* All it takes is time. Just . . . time. Shall I put these in a bag for you?"

He bagged the books without looking at them. When I fumbled out my wallet, he raised his hand.

"No charge. This is for Lorraine. And to thank you for stopping by."

I couldn't argue . . . and I admit I didn't want to draw his attention to the paperbacks, in the petty fear that he might notice how unusual they were and refuse to part with them. I took the paper bag from his parchment hand, feeling faintly guilty.

"Perhaps you'll come back," he said.

"I'd like to."

"Anytime," Ziegler said, inching toward his bead curtain and the musty stairway behind it, back into the cloying dark. "Anything you're looking for, I can help you find it."

Crossing College Street, freighted with groceries, I stepped into the path of a car, a yellow Hyundai racing a red light. The driver swerved around me, but it was a near thing. The wheel wells brushed my trouser legs. My heart stuttered a beat.

. . . and I died, perhaps, a small infinity of times.

Probabilities collapse. I become increasingly *unlikely*.

"Immersed in the strange," Ziegler had said.

But had I ever wanted that? *Really* wanted that?

"Be careful," Lorraine told me one evening in the long month before she died. Amazingly, she had seemed to think of it as my tragedy, not hers. "Don't despise life."

Difficult advice.

Did I "despise life"? I think I did not; that is, there were times when the world seemed a pleasant enough place, times when a cup of coffee and a morning in the sun seemed a good enough reason to continue to draw breath. I remained capable of smiling at babies. I was even able to look at an attractive young woman and feel a response more immediate than nostalgia.

But I missed Lorraine terribly, and we had never had children, neither of us had any close living relations or much in the way of friends; I was unemployed and unemployable, confined forevermore within the contracting walls of my pension and our modest savings . . . all the joy and much of the simple structure of my life had been leeched away, and the future looked like more of the same, a protracted fumble toward the grave.

If anything postponed the act of suicide it wasn't courage or principle but the daily trivia. I would kill myself (I decided more than once), but not until after the news . . . not until I paid the electric bill . . . not until I had taken my walk.

Not until I solved the mystery I'd brought home from Finders.

I won't describe the books in detail. They looked more or less like others of their kind. What was strange about them was that I didn't recognize them, although this was a genre (paperback science fiction of the 1950s and '60s) I had once known in intimate detail.

The shock was not just unfamiliarity, since I might have missed any number of minor works by minor writers; but these were major novels by well-known names, not re-titled works or variant editions. A single example: I sat down that night with a book called *The Stone Pillow*, by a writer whose identity any science fiction follower would instantly recognize. It was a Signet paperback circa 1957, with a cover by the artist Paul Lehr in the period style. According to the credit slug, the story had been serialized in *Astounding* in 1946. The pages were browned at the margins; the glued spine was brittle as bone china. I handled the book carefully, but I couldn't resist reading it, and in so far as I was able to judge it was a plausible example of the late author's well-known style and habits of thought. I enjoyed it a great deal and went to bed convinced of its authenticity. Either I had missed it, somehow—in the days when *not* missing such things meant a great deal to me—or it had slipped out of memory. No other explanation presented itself.

One such item wouldn't have worried me. But I had brought home four more volumes equally inexplicable.

Chalk it up to age, I thought. Or worse. Senility. Alzheimer's. Either way, a bad omen.

Sleep was elusive.

The next logical step might have been to see a doctor. Instead, the next morning I thumbed through the yellow pages for a used-book dealer who specialized in period science fiction. After a couple of calls I reached a young man named Niemand who offered to evaluate the books if I brought them to him that afternoon.

I told him I'd be there by one.

If nothing else, it was an excuse to prolong my life one more interminable day.

Niemand—his store was an overheated second-story loft over a noisy downtown street—gave the books a long, thoughtful examination.

"Fake," he said finally. "They're fake."

"Fake? You mean . . . counterfeit?"

"If you like, but that's stretching a point. Nobody counterfeits books, even valuable books. The idea is ludicrous. I mean, what do you do, set up a press and go through all the work of producing a bound volume, duplicate the type, flaws and all, and then flog it on the collector's market? You'd never recoup your expenses, not even if you came up with a convincing Gutenberg Bible. In the case of books like this the idea's doubly absurd. Maybe if they were one-off from an abandoned print run or something, but hell, people would *know* about that. Nope. Sorry, but these are just . . . fake."

"But—well, obviously, somebody *did* go to the trouble of faking them."

He nodded. "Obviously. It's flawless work, and it can't have been cheap. And the books are genuinely old. *Contemporary* fakes, maybe . . . maybe some obsessive fan with a big disposable income, rigging up books he *wanted* to exist. . . ."

"Are they valuable?"

"They're certainly odd. Valuable? Not to me. Tell you the truth, I kind of wish you hadn't brought them in."

"Why?"

"They're creepy. They're *too* good. Kind of *X-Files*." He gave me a sour grin. "Make up your own science fiction story."

"Or live in it," I said. *We live in the science fiction of our youth.*

He pushed the books across his cluttered desk. "Take 'em away, Mr. Keller. And if you find out where they came from—"

"Yes?"

"I really don't want to know."

Items I noticed in the newspaper that evening:

GENE THERAPY RENDERS HEART BYPASS OBSOLETE

BANK OF ZURICH FIRST WITH QUANTUM ENCRYPTION

SETI RESEARCHERS SPOT "POSSIBLE" ET RADIO SOURCE

I didn't want to go back to Ziegler, not immediately. It felt like admitting defeat—like looking up the answer to a magazine puzzle I couldn't solve.

But there was no obvious next step to take, so I put the whole thing out of my mind, or tried to; watched television, did laundry, shined my shoes.

None of this pathetic sleight-of-hand provided the slightest distraction.

I was not (just as I had told Deirdre) a mystery lover, and I didn't love this mystery, but it was a turbulence in the flow of the passing days, therefore interesting. When I had savored the strangeness of it to a satisfying degree I took myself in hand and carried the books back to Finders, meaning to demand an explanation.

Oscar Ziegler was expecting me.

The late-May weather was already too humid, a bright sun

bearing down from the ozone-depleted sky. Walking wasn't such a pleasure under the circumstances. I arrived at Finders plucking my shirt away from my body. Graceless. The woman Deirdre looked up from her niche at the rear of the store. "Mr. Keller, right?" She didn't seem especially pleased to see me.

I meant to ask if Ziegler was available, but she waved me off: "He said if you showed up you were to go on upstairs. That's, uh, really unusual."

"Shouldn't you let him know I'm here?"

"Really, he's expecting you." She waved at the bead curtain, almost a challenge: *Go on, if you must.*

The curtain made a sound like chattering teeth behind me. The stairway was dim. Dustballs quivered on the risers and clung to the threadbare coco-mat tread. At the top was a door silted under so many layers of ancient paint that the moulding had softened into gentle dunes.

Ziegler opened the door and waved me in.

His room was lined with books. He stepped back, settled himself into an immense overstuffed easy chair, and invited me to look at his collection. But the titles at eye level were disappointing. They were old cloth volumes of Gurdjieff and Ouspenski, Velikovsky and Crowley—the usual pseudo-gnostic spiritualist bullshit, pardon my language. Like the room itself, the books radiated dust and boredom. I felt obscurely disappointed. So this was Oscar Ziegler, one more pathetic old man with a penchant for magic and cabbalism.

Between the books, medical supplies: inhalers, oxygen tanks, pill bottles.

Ziegler might be old, but his eyesight was still keen. "Judging by the expression on your face, you find my den distasteful."

"Not at all."

"Oh, fess up, Mr. Keller. You're too old to be polite and I'm too old to pretend I don't notice."

I gestured at the books. "I was never much for the occult."

"That's understandable. It's claptrap, really. I keep those volumes for nostalgic reasons. To be honest, there was a time when I looked there for answers. That time is long past."

"I see."

"Now tell me why you came."

I showed him the softcover books, told him how I'd taken them to Niemand for a professional assessment. Confessed my own bafflement.

Ziegler took the books into his lap. He looked at them briefly and took a long drag from his oxygen mask. He didn't seem especially impressed. "I'm hardly responsible for every volume that comes into the store."

"Of course not. And I'm not complaining. I just wondered—"

"If I knew where they came from? If I could offer you a meaningful explanation?"

"Basically, yes."

"Well," Ziegler said. "Well. Yes and no. Yes and no."

"I'm sorry?"

"That is . . . no, I can't tell you precisely where they came from. Deirdre probably bought them from someone off the street. Cash or credit, and I don't keep detailed records. But it doesn't really matter."

"Doesn't it?"

He took another deep drag from the oxygen bottle. "Oh, it could have been anyone. Even if you tracked down the original vendor—which I guarantee you won't be able to do—you wouldn't learn anything useful."

"You don't seem especially surprised by this."

"Implying that I know more than I'm saying." He smiled ruefully. "I've never been in this position before, though you're right, it doesn't surprise me. Did you know, Mr. Keller, that I am immortal?"

Here we go, I thought. The pitch. Ziegler didn't care about the books. I had come for an explanation; he wanted to sell me a religion.

"And you, Mr. Keller. You're immortal, too."

What was I doing here, in this shabby place with this shabby old man? There was nothing to say.

"But I can't explain it," Ziegler went on; "that is, not in the depth it deserves. There's a volume here—I'll lend it to you—" He stood, precariously, and huffed across the room.

I looked at his books again while he rummaged for the volume in question. Below the precambrian deposits of the occult was a small sediment of literature. First editions, presumably valuable.

And not all familiar.

Had Ernest Hemingway written a book called *Pamplona*? (But here it was, its Scribners dust jacket protected in brittle mylar.) *Cromwell and Company,* by Charles Dickens? *Under the Absolute,* by Aldous Huxley?

"Ah, books." Ziegler, smiling, came up behind me. "They bob like corks on an ocean. Float between worlds, messages in bottles. This will tell you what you need to know."

The book he gave me was cheaply made, with a utilitarian olive-drab jacket. *You Will Never Die,* by one Carl G. Soziere.

"Come back when you've read it."

"I will," I lied.

"I had a feeling," Deirdre said, "you'd come downstairs with one of those."

The Soziere book. "You've heard of it?"

"Not until I took this job. Mr. Ziegler gave me a copy. But I speak from experience. Every once in a long while, somebody comes in with a question or a complaint. They go upstairs. And they come back down with *that*."

At which point I realized I had left the paperbacks in Ziegler's room. I suppose I could have gone back for them, but it seemed somehow churlish. But it was a loss. Not that I loved the books, particularly, but they were the only concrete evidence I had of the mystery—they *were* the mystery. Now Ziegler had them back in his possession. And I had *You Will Never Die*.

"It looks like a crank book."

"Oh, it is," Deirdre said. "Kind of a parallel-worlds argument, you know, J.W. Dunne and so on, with some quantum physics thrown in; actually, I'm surprised a major publisher didn't pick it up."

"You've read it?"

"I'm a sucker for that kind of thing, if you want the truth."

"Don't tell me. It changed your life." I was smiling.

She smiled back. "It didn't even change my mind."

But there was an odd note of worry in her voice.

Of course I read it.

Deirdre was right about *You Will Never Die*. It had been published by some private or vanity press, but the writing wasn't crude. It was slick, even witty in places.

And the argument was seductive. Shorn of the babble about Planck radii and Prigogine complexity and the Dancing Wu-Li Masters, it came down to this:

Consciousness, like matter, like energy, is preserved.

You are born, not an individual, but an *infinity* of individuals, in an infinity of identical worlds. "Consciousness," your individual awareness, is shared by this infinity of beings.

At birth (or at conception; Soziere wasn't explicit), this span of selves begins to divide, as alternate possibilities are indulged or rejected. The infant turns his head not to the left or to the right, but both. One infinity of worlds becomes two; then four; then eight, and so on, exponentially.

But the underlying *essence of consciousness* continues to connect all these disparate possibilities.

The upshot? Soziere says it all in his title.

You cannot die.

Consider. Suppose, tomorrow afternoon, you walk in front of a speeding eighteen-wheeler. The grillwork snaps your neck and what remains of you is sausaged under the chassis. Do you die? Well, yes; an infinity of you *does* die; but infinity is divisible by itself. Another infinity of you steps out of the path of the truck, or didn't leave the house that day, or recovers in hospital. The *youness* of you doesn't die; it simply continues to reside in those remnant selves.

An infinite set has been subtracted from infinity; but what remains, remains infinite.

The *subjective* experience is that the accident simply doesn't happen.

Consider that bottle of Clonazepam I keep beside the bed. Six times I reached for it, meaning to kill myself. Six times stopped myself.

In the great wilderness of worlds, I must have succeeded more often than I failed. My cold and vomit-stained corpse was carted off to whatever grave or urn awaits it, and a few acquaintances briefly mourned.

But that's not *me*. By definition, you can't experience your own death. Death is the end of consciousness. And consciousness persists. In the language of physics, consciousness is *conserved*.

I am the one who wakes up in the morning.

Always.

Every morning.

I don't die.

I just become increasingly *unlikely*.

I spent the next few days watching television, folding laundry, trimming my nails—spinning my wheels.

I tossed Soziere's little tome into a corner and left it there.

And when I was done kidding myself, I went to see Deirdre.

I didn't even know her last name. All I knew was that she had read Soziere's book and remained skeptical of it, and I was eager to have my own skepticism refreshed.

You think odd things, sometimes, when you're too often alone.

I caught Deirdre on her lunch break. Ziegler didn't come downstairs to man the desk; the store simply closed between noon and one every weekday. The May heat wave had broken; the sky was a soft, deep blue, the air balmy. We sat at a sidewalk table outside a lunch-and-coffee restaurant.

Her full name was Deirdre Frank. She was fifty and unmarried and had run her own retail business until some legal difficulty closed her down. She was working at Finders while she reorganized her life. And she understood why I had come to her.

"There's a couple of tests I apply," she said, "whenever I read this kind of book. First, is it likely to improve anyone's life? Which is a trickier question than it sounds. Any number of people will tell you they found happiness with the Scientologists or the Moonies or whatever, but what that usually means is they narrowed their focus—they can't see past the bars of their cage. Okay, *You Will Never Die* isn't a cult book, but I doubt it will make anybody a better person.

"Second, is there any way to test the author's claims? Soziere aced that one beautifully, I have to admit. His argument is that there's no *subjective* experience of death—your family might die, your friends, your grade-school teachers, the Princess of Wales, but never *you*. And in some other world, *you* die and other people go on living. How do you prove such a thing? Obviously, you can't. What Soziere tries to do is *infer* it, from quantum physics and lots of less respectable sources. It's a bubble theory—it floats over the landscape, touching nothing."

I was probably blushing by this time.

Deirdre said, "You took it seriously, didn't you? Or half seriously. . . ."

"Half at most. I'm not stupid. But it's an appealing idea."

Her eyes widened. *"Appealing?"*

"Well—there are people who've died. People I miss. I like to think of them going on somewhere, even if it isn't a place I can reach."

She was aghast. "God, no! Soziere's book isn't a fairy tale, Mr. Keller—it's a horror story!"

"Pardon me?"

"Think about it! At first it sounds like an invitation to suicide. You don't like where you are, put a pistol in your mouth and go somewhere else—somewhere better, maybe, even if it is inherently less *likely*. But take you for example. You're what, sixty years old? Or so? Well, great, you inhabit a universe where a healthy human being can obtain the age of sixty, fine, but what next? Maybe you wake up tomorrow morning and find out they cured cancer, say, or heart disease—excluding you from all the worlds where William Keller dies of a colon tumor or an aneurism. And then? You're a hundred years old, a hundred and twenty—do you turn into some kind of freak? So *unlikely*, in Soziere's sense, that you end up in a circus or a research ward? Do they clone you a fresh body? Do you end up as some kind of half-human robot, a brain in a bottle? And in the meantime the world changes around you, everything familiar is left behind, you see others die, maybe millions of others, maybe the human race dies out or evolves into something else, and you go on, and on, while the universe groans under the weight of your unlikeliness, and there's no escape, every death is just another rung up the ladder of weirdness and disorientation. . . ."

I hadn't thought of it that way.

Yes, the *reductio ad absurdum* of Soziere's theory was a kind of relativistic paradox: as the observer's life grows more unlikely, he perceives the world around him becoming proportionately more strange; and down those unexplored, narrow rivers of mortality might well lie a cannibal village.

Or the Temple of Gold.

What if Deirdre was too pessimistic? What if, among the all

the unlikely worlds, there was one in which Lorraine had survived her cancer?

Wouldn't that be worth waiting for?

Worth *looking* for, no matter how strange the consequences might be?

News items that night:

NEURAL IMPLANTS RESTORE VISION IN FIFTEEN PATIENTS

"TELOMERASE COCKTAIL" CREATES IMMORTAL LAB MICE

TWINNED NEUTRON STARS POSE POTENTIAL THREAT, NASA SAYS

My sin was longing.

Not grief. Grief isn't a sin, and is anyway unavoidable. Yes, I grieved for Lorraine, grieved long and hard, but I don't remember having a choice. I miss her still. Which is as it should be.

But I had given in too often to the vulgar yearnings. Mourned youth, mourned better days. Made an old man's map of roads not taken, from the stale perspective of a dead end.

Reached for the Clonazepam and turned my hand away, freighted every inch with deaths beyond counting.

I wonder if my captors understand this?

I went back to Ziegler—nodding at Deirdre, who was disappointed to see me, as I vanished behind the bead curtain.

"This doesn't explain it." I gave him back *You Will Never Die*.

"Explain," Ziegler said guilelessly, "what?"

"The paperbacks I bought from you."

"I don't recall."

"Or these—"

I turned to his bookshelf.

Copies of *In Our Time*, *Our Mutual Friend*, *Beyond the Mexique Bay*.

"I didn't realize they needed explaining."

I was the victim of a conjuror's trick, gulled and embarrassed. I closed my mouth.

"Anomalous experience," Ziegler said knowingly. "You're right, Soziere doesn't explain it. Personally I think there must be a kind of critical limit—a degree of accumulated unlikeliness so great that the illusion of normalcy can no longer be wholly sustained." He smiled, not pleasantly. "Things *leak*. I think especially books, books being little islands of mind. They trail their authors across phenomenological borders, like lost puppies. That's why I love them. But you're awfully young to experience such phenomena. You must have made yourself very unlikely indeed—more and more unlikely, day after day! What have you been *doing* to yourself, Mr. Keller?"

I left him sucking oxygen from a fogged plastic mask.

Reaching for the bottle of Clonazepam.

Drawing back my hand.

But how far must the charade proceed? Does the universe gauge intent? What if I touch the bottle? What if I open it and peer inside?

(These questions, of course, are answered now. I have only myself to blame.)

I had tumbled a handful of the small white tablets into my hand and was regarding them with the cool curiosity of an entomologist when the telephone rang.

Pills or telephone?

Both, presumably, in Soziere's multiverse.

I answered the phone.

It was Deirdre. "He's dead," she told me. "Ziegler. I thought you should know."

I said, "I'm sorry."

"I'm taking care of the arrangements. He was so alone . . . no family, no friends, just nothing."

"Will there be a service?"

"He wanted to be cremated. You're welcome to come. It might be nice if somebody besides me showed up."

"I will. What about the store?"

"That's the crazy part. According to the bank, he left it to me." Her voice was choked with emotion. "Can you imagine that? I never even called him by his first name! To be honest—oh, God, I didn't even *like* him! Now he leaves me this tumbledown business of his!"

I told her I'd see her at the mortuary.

I paid no attention to the news that night, save to register the lead stories, which were ominous and strange.

We live, Ziegler had said, in the science fiction of our youth.

The "ET signals" NASA scientists had discovered were, it turned out, a simple star map, at the center of which was—not the putative aliens' home world—but a previously undiscovered binary neutron star in the constellation Orion.

The message, one astronomer speculated, might be a warning. Binary neutron stars are unstable. When they eventually collide, drawn together by their enormous gravity, the collision produces a black hole—and in the process a burst of gamma rays and cosmic radiation, strong enough to scour the Earth of life if the event occurs within some two or three thousand light-years of us.

The freshly discovered neutron stars were well within that range. As for the collision, it might happen in ten years, a thousand, ten thousand—none of the quoted authorities would commit to a date, though estimates had been shrinking daily.

Nice of our neighbors to warn us, I thought.

But how long had that warning bell been ringing, and for how many centuries had we ignored it?

Deirdre's description of the Soziere book as a "bubble theory" haunted me.

No proof, no evidence could exist: that was ruled out by the theory itself—or at least, as Ziegler had implied, there would be no evidence one could share.

But there *had* been evidence, at least in my case: the paperback books, "anomalous" books imported, presumably, from some other timeline, a history I had since lost to cardiac arrest, a car accident, Clonazepam.

But the books were gone.

I had traded them, in effect, for *You Will Never Die*.

Which I had returned to Oscar Ziegler.

Cup your hands as you might. The water runs through your fingers.

There was only the most rudimentary service at the crematorium where Ziegler's body was burned. A few words from an Episcopal minister Deirdre had hired for the occasion, an earnest young man in clerical gear and neatly-pressed Levis who pronounced his consolations and hurried away as if late for another function. Deirdre said, afterward, "I don't know if I've been given a gift or an obligation. For a man who never left his room, Mr. Ziegler had a way of weaving people into his life." She shook her head sadly. "If any of it really matters. I mean, if we're not devoured by aliens or god knows what. You can't turn on the news these days. . . . Well, I guess he bailed out just in time."

Or moved on. Moved someplace where his emphysema was curable, his failing heart reparable, his aging cells regenerable. Shunting the train Oscar Ziegler along a more promising if less plausible track. . . .

"The evidence," I said suddenly.

"What?"

"The books I told you about."

"Oh. Right. Well, I'm sorry, but I didn't get a good look at them." She frowned. "Is *that* what you're thinking? Oh, shit, that fucking Soziere book of his! It's *bait*, Mr. Keller, don't you get it? Not to speak ill of the dead, but he loved to suck people into whatever cloistered little mental universe he inhabited, misery loves company, and that book was always the bait—"

"No," I said, excited despite my best intentions, as if Ziegler's cremation had been a message, his personal message to me, that the universe discarded bodies like used Kleenex but that consciousness was continuous, seamless, immortal. . . . "I mean about the evidence. You didn't see it—but *someone* did."

"Leave it alone. You don't understand about Ziegler. Oscar Ziegler was a sour, poisonous old man. Maybe older than he looked. That's what I thought of when I read Soziere's book: Oscar Ziegler, someone so ridiculously old that he wakes up every morning surprised he's still a human being." She stared fiercely at me. "What exactly are you contemplating here—*serial suicide?*"

"Nothing so drastic."

I thanked her and left.

The paradox of proof.

I went to Niemand's store as soon as I left Deirdre.

I had shown the books to Niemand, the book dealer. He was the impossible witness, the corroborative testimony. If Niemand had seen the books, then I was sane; if Niemand had seen the books they might well turn up among Ziegler's possessions, and I could establish their true provenance and put all this dangerous Soziere mythology behind me.

But Niemand's little second-story loft store had closed. The sign was gone. The door was locked and the space was for lease.

Neither the jeweller downstairs nor the coffee-shop girl next door remembered the store, its clientele, or Niemand himself.

There was no Niemand in the phone book. Nor could I find his commercial listing. Not even in my yellow pages at home, where I had first looked it up.

Or remembered looking it up.

Anomalous experience.

Which constituted proof, of a kind, though Ziegler was right; it was not transferable. I could convince no one, ultimately, save myself.

The television news was full of apocalypse that night. A rumor had swept the Internet that the great gamma-ray burst was imminent, only days away. No, it was not, scientists insisted, but they allowed themselves to be drawn by their CNN inquisitors into hypothetical questions. Would there be any safe place? A half-mile underground, say, or two, or three? (*Probably not,* they admitted; or, *We don't have the full story yet.*)

To a man, or woman, they looked unsettled and skittish.

I went to bed knowing she was out there, Lorraine, I mean, out among the plenitude of worlds and stars. Alone, perhaps, since I must have died to her—infinities apart, certainly, but enclosed within the same inconceivably vast multi-universe, as alike, in our way, as two snowflakes in an avalanche.

I slept with the pill bottle cradled in my hand.

The trick, I decided, was to abandon the charade, to *mean* the act.

In other words, to swallow twenty or thirty tablets—a more difficult act than you might imagine—and wash them down with a neat last shot of Glenlivet.

But Deirdre called.

Almost too late.

Not late enough.

I picked up the phone, confused, my hands butting the receiver like antagonistic parade balloons. I said, or meant to say, "Lorraine?"

But it was Deirdre, only Deirdre, and before long Deirdre was shouting in an annoying way. I let the phone drop.

I suppose she called 911.

II

I woke in a hospital bed.

I lay there passively for more than an hour, by the digital clock on the bedstand, cresting waves of sleep and wondering at the silence, until I was visited by Candice. Her name was written on her lapel tag. Candice was a nurse, with a throaty Jamaican accent and wide, sad eyes.

"You're awake," she said, barely glancing at me.

My head hurt. My mouth tasted of ashes and quicklime. I needed to pee, but there was a catheter in the way.

"I think I want to see a doctor," I managed.

"Prob'ly you do," Candice agreed. "And prob'ly you should. But our last resident went home yesterday. I can take the catheter out, if that's what you want."

"There are no *doctors*?"

"Home with their families like everybody else." She fluffed my pillow. "Only us pathetic lonelyhearts left, Mr. Keller. You been unconscious ten days."

Later she wheeled me down the corridor—though I insisted I could have walked—to a lounge with a tall plate glass window, where the ward's remaining patients had gathered to talk and weep and watch the fires that burned fitfully through the downtown core.

Soziere's curse. We become—or we make ourselves—less "likely." But it's not our own unlikeliness we perceive; instead, we see the world growing strange around us.

The lights are out all over the city. The hospital, fortunately, has its own generator. I tried to call Deirdre from a hospital phone, but there was no dial tone, just a crackling hiss, like the last groove in an LP record.

The previous week's newspapers, stacked by the door of the hospital lounge, were dwindling broadsheets containing nothing but stark outlines of the impending gamma-ray disaster.

The extraterrestrial warning had been timely. Timely, though we read it far too late. Apparently it not only identified the threatening binary neutron stars—which were spiralling at last into gaudy destruction, about to emit a burst of radiation brighter than a billion galaxies—but provided a calculable time scale.

A countdown, in other words, which had already closed in on its ultimate zero. Too close to home, a black hole was about to be born.

None of us would survive that last flash of annihilating fire.

Or, at least, if we did, we would all become *extremely* unlikely.

I remember a spot of blue luminescence roughly the size of a dinner plate at arm's length, suspended above the burning city: Cherenkov radiation. Gamma rays fractured molecules in the upper atmosphere, loading the air with nitric oxides the color of dried blood. The sky was frying like a bad picture tube.

The hard, ionizing radiation would arrive within hours. Cosmic rays striking the wounded atmosphere would trigger particle cascades, washing the crust of the Earth with what the papers called "high energy muons."

I was tired of the ward lounge, the incessant weeping and periodic shouting.

Candice took me aside. "I'll tell you," she said, "what I told the others. I been into the medicine cupboard. If you don't want to wait, there are pills you can take."

The air smelled suddenly of burning plastic. Static electricity drew bright blue sparks from metal shelves and gurney carts. Surely this would be the end: the irrevocable death, the utter annihilation, if there can ever be an end.

I told Candice a nightcap might be a good idea, and she smiled wanly and brought me the pills.

III

They want me to keep on with my memoirs.

They take the pages away from me, exchange them for greater rations of food.

The food is pale, chalky, with the clay-like texture of goat cheese. They excrete it from a sort of spinerette, white obscene lumps of it, like turds.

I prefer to think of them as advanced machines rather than biological entities—vending machines, say, not the eight-foot-long centipedes they appear to be.

They've mastered the English language. (I don't know how.) They say "please" and "thank you." Their voices are thin and reedy, a sound like tree branches creaking on a windy winter night.

They tell me I've been dead for ten thousand years.

Today they let me out of my bubble, let me walk outside, with a sort of mirrored umbrella to protect me from the undiluted sunlight.

The sunlight is intense, the air cold and thin. They have explained, in patient but barely intelligible whispers, that the gamma ray burst and subsequent bath of cosmic radiation stripped the earth of its ozone layer as well as much of the upper atmosphere. The oxygen that remains, they say, is "fossil" oxygen, no longer replenished. They soil is alive with radioactive nuclei: samarium 146, iodine 129, isotopes of lead, of plutonium.

There is no macroscopic life on Earth. Present company excepted.

Everything died. People, plants, plankton, everything but the bacteria inhabiting the rocks of the deep mantle or the scalding water around undersea volcanic vents. The surface of the planet—here, at least—has been scoured by wind and radiation into a rocky desert.

All this happened ten thousand years ago. The sun shines placidly on the lifeless soil, the distant blue-black mountains.

Everything I loved is dead.

I can't imagine the technology they used to resurrect me, to *recreate* me, as they insist, from desiccated fragments of biological tissue tweezed from rocks. It's not just my DNA they have recovered but (apparently, somehow) my memories, my self, my consciousness.

I suppose Carl Soziere wouldn't be surprised.

I ask about others, other survivors reclaimed from the waterless desert. My captors (or saviours) only spindle their sickeningly mobile bodies: a gesture of negation, I've come to understand, the equivalent of a shake of the head. There are no other survivors.

And yet I can't help wondering whether Lorraine waits to be salvaged from her grave—some holographic scrap of her, at least; information scattered by time, like the dust of an ancient book.

There is nothing in my transparent cell but bowls of water and food, a floor soft enough to serve as a mattress, and the blunted writing instruments and clothlike paper. (Are they afraid I might commit suicide?)

The memoirs run out. I want the extra food, and I enjoy the diversion of writing, but what remains to be said? And to whom?

I've learned to distinguish between my captors.

The "leader" (that is, the individual most likely to address me directly and see that others attend to my needs) is a duller shade of silver-white, his cartilaginous shell dusted with fine powder. He (or she) possesses many orifices, all visible when he sways back to speak. I have identified his speaking-orifice and his food-excreting orifice, but there are three others I haven't seen in use, including a tooth-lined maw that must be a kind of mouth.

"We are the ones who warned you," he tells me. "For half of a million years we warned you. If you had known, you might have protected yourself." His grammar is impeccable, to my ears anyway, although consonants in close proximity make him stumble and hiss. "You might have deconstructed your moon, created a shield, as we did. Numerous strategies might have succeeded in preserving your world."

The tocsin had sounded, in other words, for centuries. We had simply been too dull to interpret it, until the very end, when nothing could be done to counter the threat.

I try not interpret this as a rebuke.

"Now we have learned to transsect distance," the insectile creature explains. "Then, we could only signal."

I ask whether he could re-create the Earth, revive the dead.

"No," he says. Perhaps the angle of his body signifies regret. "One of you is puzzle enough."

They live apart from me, in an immense silver half-sphere embedded in the alkaline soil. Their spaceship?

For a day they haven't come. I sit alone in my own much smaller shelter, its bubble walls polarized to filter the light but transparent enough to show the horizon with vicious clarity. I feel abandoned, a fly on a vast pane of dusty glass. And hungry. And thirsty.

They return—apologetically—with water, with paper and writing implements, and with a generous supply of food, thoughtfully pre-excreted.

They are compiling, they tell me, a sort of interstellar database, combining the functions of library, archeological museum, and telephone exchange. They are most grateful for my writings, which have been enthusiastically received. "Your cosmology," by which they must mean Soziere's cosmology, "is quite distinctive."

I thank them but explain that there is nothing more to write—and no audience I can even begin to imagine.

The news perplexes them. The leader asks, "Do you need a human audience?"

Yes. Yes, that's what I need. A human audience. Lorraine, warning me away from despair, or even Deirdre, trying vainly to shield me from black magic.

They confer for another day.

I walk outside my bubble at sunset, alone, with my silver umbrella tilted toward the western horizon. When the stars appear, they are astonishingly bright and crisp. I can see the frosted breath of the Milky Way.

"We cannot create a human audience for you," the leader says, swaying in a chill noon breeze like a stately elm. "But there is perhaps a way."

I wait. I am infinitely patient.

"We have experimented with time," the creature announces. Or I think the word is "experimented." It might as easily have been the clacking buzz of a cricket or a cicada.

"Send me back," I demand at once.

"No, not you, not physical objects. It cannot be done. Thoughts, perhaps. Dreams. Speaking to minds long dead. Of course, it changes nothing."

I rather like the idea—when they explain it—of my memoirs

circulating through the Terrestrial past, appearing fragmented and unintelligible among the night terrors of Neanderthals, Cro-Magnons, Roman slaves, Chinese peasants, science fiction writers, drunken poets. And Deirdre Frank, and Oscar Ziegler. And Lorraine.

Even the faintest touch—belated, impossible—is better than none at all.

But still. I find it difficult to write.

"In that case," the leader says, "we would like to salvage you."

"Salvage me?"

They consult in their own woody, windy language, punctuated by long silences or sounds I cannot hear.

"Preserve you," they conclude. "Yourself. Your soul."

And how would they do that?

"I would take you into my body," the leader says.

Eat me, in other words. They have explained this more than once. Devour my body, *hoc est corpus*, and spit out my soul like a cherry pit into the great galactic telephone exchange.

"But this is how we must do it," the leader says apologetically.

I don't fear them.

I take a long last walk, at night, bundled against the cold in layers of flexible foil. The stars have not changed visibly in the ten thousand years of my absence, but there is nothing else familiar, no recognizable landmarks, I gather, anywhere on the surface of the planet. This might be an empty lakebed, this desert of mine, saline and ancient and, save for the distant mountains, flat as a chessboard.

I don't fear them. They might be lying, I know, although I doubt it; surely not even the most alien of creatures would travel hundreds of light years to a dead planet in search of a single exotic snack.

I do fear their teeth, however, sharp as shark's teeth, even if (as they claim) their bodies secrete an anaesthetic and euphoriant venom.

And death?

I don't fear death.

I dread the absence of it.

Maybe Soziere was wrong. Maybe there's a teleological escape clause, maybe all the frayed threads of time will be woven back together at the end of the world, assembled in the ultimate library, where all the books and all the dreams are preserved and ordered in their multiple infinities.

Or not.

I think, at last, of Lorraine: really think of her, I mean; imagine her next to me, whispering that I ought to have taken her advice, not lodged this grief so close to my heart; whispering that death is not a door through which I can follow her, no matter how hard or how often I try. . . .

"Will you accept me?" the leader asks, rearing up to show his needled mouth, his venom sacs oozing a pleasant narcotic.

"I've accepted worse," I tell him.

SUSANNA CLARKE

MRS MABB

IN THE LATE SPRING OF 18—— A LADY IN THE VILLAGE OF Kissingland in D——shire suffered a bitter disappointment.

Mrs Fanny Hawkins to Mrs Clara Johnson

". . . and I know, my dear Clara, that you will share my vexation when I tell you what has happened. Some months ago my sister, Miss Moore, had the good fortune to captivate an officer in the Regulars. Captain Fox shewed a decided preference for Venetia from the start and I was in great hopes of seeing her respectably settled when, by a stroke of ill fortune, she received a letter from an acquaintance, a lady in Manchester who had fallen sick and was in need of someone to nurse her. You may imagine how little I liked that she should leave Kissingland at such a time, but I found that, in spite of all I could say, she was determined to undertake the expense and inconvenience of the journey and go. But

> now I fear she is too well punished for her obstinacy, for in her absence the wretched Captain Fox has forgot her entirely and has begun to pay his respects to another lady, a neighbour of ours, Mrs Mabb. You may well believe that when she comes back I will always be quarrelling with her about it. . . ."

Fanny Hawkins' amiable intention of quarrelling with her sister proceeded, not merely from a general wish to correct faulty behaviour, but also from the realization that if Venetia did *not* marry Captain Fox then she must look to Fanny for a home. Fanny's husband was the curate of Kissingland, a person of no particular importance in the society of the place, who baptised, married, and buried all its inhabitants, who visited them in their sick-beds, comforted them in their griefs, and read their letters to them if they could not do it for themselves—for all of which he received the magnificent sum of £40 a year. Consequently any moments which Fanny could spare from domestic cares were spent in pondering the difficult question of how an income which had never been sufficient for *two* might now be made to support *three*.

Fanny waited for her sister's return and, with great steadiness of purpose, told Mr Hawkins several times a day how she intended to quarrel with her for letting Captain Fox slip his bonds. "To go off like that with the business entirely unsettled between them. What an odd creature she is! I cannot understand her."

But Fanny had a few oddities of her own, one of which was to delight in fancying herself disagreeable and cold-hearted, when in truth she was only ill-used and anxious. When at last Miss Moore returned to Kissingland and when Fanny saw how white and stricken the poor girl was to hear of her lover's defection, all of Fanny's much-vaunted quarrelsomeness dwindled into a shake of her head and, "Now you see, Venetia, what comes of being so obstinate and liking your own way above what other people advise"; and even this she immediately followed with, "There, my dear, I hope you will not distress yourself. Any man who can play you such a shabby trick as this is not worth thinking of. How is your friend in Manchester?"

"Dead." (This in a tearful whisper.)

"Oh! . . . Well, my dear, I am very sorry to hear it. And Mr Hawkins will say the same when I tell him of it. Poor girl!—you have a sad homecoming."

That evening at supper (a very small amount of fried beef to a great deal of boiled turnip) Fanny told Mr Hawkins, "She has gone to bed—she says she has a shocking headache. I dare say she was a great deal more attached to him than we believed. It was never very likely that she should have escaped whole-hearted from the attentions of such a man as Captain Fox. You may recall I said so at the time."

Mr Hawkins said nothing; the Hawkins' domestic affairs were arranged upon the principle that Fanny supplied the talk and he the silence.

"Well!" continued Fanny, "We must all live as cheaply as we can. I dare say there are more savings I can make." Fanny looked around the shabby parlour in search of any luxuries that had hitherto gone undiscovered. Not finding any, she merely remarked that things lasted a great deal longer than those people supposed who always like to have every thing new; indeed it had been a very long time since Fanny had had any thing new; the worn stone flags of her parlour floor were bare, the chairs were hard and inconvenient, and the wallpaper was so ancient and faded that it appeared to shew withered garlands of dead flowers tied up with dry brown ribbons.

The next morning Fanny's thoughts ran upon the subject of her grievances against Captain Fox and her anger against him was such that she found herself obliged to speak of it almost incessantly—while at the same time continually advising Venetia to think of Captain Fox no more. After half an hour Venetia said with a sigh that she thought she would walk in the fresh air for a while.

"Oh!" said Fanny, "Which way do you go?"

"I do not know."

"Well, if you were to go towards the village then there are several things I need."

So Venetia went along Church-lane to Kissingland and, though it would benefit the dignity of the Female Sex in general to report that she now despised and hated Captain Fox, Venetia was not so unnatural. Instead she indulged in many vain sighs and regrets, and tried to derive such consolation as she could from the reflection that it was better to be poor and forgotten in Kissingland, where there were green trees and sweet flowery meadows, than in Manchester where her friend, Mrs Whitsun, had died in a cold grey room at the top of a dismal lodging house.

Captain Fox was a tall Irishman of thirty-six or seven who bore the reputation of having red hair. Indeed in some weathers and lights it did appear to have a little red in it, but it was more his name, his long ironical grin and a certain Irish wildness that made people believe they saw red hair. He also had a reputation for quite unheard-of bravery, for he had once contradicted the Duke of Wellington when all around were most energetically agreeing with that illustrious person.

It had been a question of boots. The boots (ten thousand pairs of them) had been proceeding east from Portugal upon the backs of seventy mules to where the British army, with boots entirely worn out, anxiously awaited them. Without the new boots the army was entirely unable to begin its long march north to retake Spain from the French. The Duke of Wellington had been in a great passion about it, had talked a great deal about the nuisance of delay and what the British might lose by it, but in the end he had admitted that the soldiers could do nothing without new boots. Upon the contrary, Captain Fox had cried; it would be better by far for the boots to travel along a more northerly path to the city of S—— where they could meet the army on its way north—which would mean that for the first part of the march the men would be coming ever closer to their new boots—a cheerful thought that would doubtless encourage them to go faster. The Duke of Wellington had thought for a while; "I believe," he had said at last, "that Captain Fox is right."

Upon turning the corner at Blewitt's yard Venetia came in sight of a substantial stone house. This was the residence of Mr Grout, a well-to-do lawyer. So vigorous were the roses in Mr Grout's garden that one of the walls of his house seemed to be nothing but a trembling cliff of pale pink; but this delightful sight only served to remind Venetia that Captain Fox had been excessively fond of pale pink roses, and had twice told her with significant glances that, when he married and had a garden of his own, he did not think he would have any other sort.

She determined upon thinking of something else for a while but was immediately thwarted in that resolve when the first person she saw in the High-street was Captain Fox's servant, Lucas Barley.

"Lucas!" she cried, "What! Is the Captain here?" She looked about her hastily, and only when quite certain that the Captain was not in sight did she attend properly to Lucas. She saw with some surprize that he had undergone a strange transformation. Gone was his smart brown coat, gone his shining top boots, gone his swaggering air—the air of someone with a proper consciousness of the fact that his master had once given the Duke of Wellington a flat contradiction. In place of these he wore a dirty green apron several sizes too big for him and wooden pattens on his feet. He was carrying two enormous pewter tankards that slopped beer into the mud. "What are you doing with those jugs, Lucas? Have you left the Captain's service?"

"I do not know, Miss."

"You do not know! What do you mean?"

"I mean, Miss, that should I ever lay eyes on Captain Fox

again I shall certainly ask him for his opinion on that point; and if he should ask me for my opinion on that point I shall certainly say to him that I do not care about it one way or the other. You may well look surprized, Miss—I myself am in a state of perpetual astonishment. But I am not alone in that—the Captain is parting with all his old friends."

And, having no hands disengaged to point with, Lucas indicated by a sort of straining expression of his face that Venetia should look behind her, to where a most beautiful brown-black mare was being led into Mr Grout's mews.

"Good Lord!" cried Venetia, "Belle-dame!"

"A message has come from Mrs Mabb's house that she is to be sold to Mr Grout, Miss."

"But is the Captain quitting the regiment?"

"I do not know, Miss. But what will such a little, round man as Mr Grout do with such a horse as that? He had better take care that she does not mistake him for a turnip and eat him."

Indeed the mare seemed to have some thoughts of her own in that direction; the disdainful light in her wild brown eye shewed that she was aware of having come down in the world, and thought someone ought to suffer for it, and was at this moment turning over in her mind exactly whom that someone ought to be.

"It happened like this, Miss," said Lucas, "The morning after you left, Mrs Mabb sent a message to the Captain to ask him if he would make a fourth at cards; and I went with him—for someone once told me that Mrs Mabb has a great number of aunts and nieces and female relations living with her, every one of them more beautiful than the last—and I hoped to make myself acquainted with any as was not too proud to speak to me. But when we got to the house I was made to wait in a little stone antechamber as cold as a tomb and furnished with nothing but a few bones in the hearth. I waited and I waited and I waited and then I waited some more; and I could hear the sound of the Captain talking and the sound of female laughter, high and loud.

And after a while, Miss, I saw that my fingernails were getting longer and I felt that my chin was all bristles—which gave me quite a fright as you may suppose. So, the front door being open, I shot through it and ran all the way back to Kissingland, where I discovered that I had been standing in Mrs Mabb's little stone room for three days and three nights."

"Good Lord!" cried Venetia. She pondered this a moment. "Well," she said at last with a sigh, "If people discover they were mistaken in their affections or find that they like another person better . . . I suppose she is very beautiful?"

Lucas made a scornful sound as though he would like to say something very cutting about the beauty of Mrs Mabb and was only prevented by the fact of his never having seen her.

"I do not think that Mrs Mabb ought to be named with you in the same day, Miss. The Captain told me several times, Miss, that you and he would marry soon and that we would all go off to Exeter to live in a little white house with a garden and a trellis of pink roses; and I had made myself a solemn vow, one morning in church, to serve you very faithfully and honourably—for you were always very kind to me."

"Thank you, Lucas. . . ." said Venetia, but she found she could get no further. This picture of what would never come to pass affected her too strongly and her eyes filled with tears.

She would have liked to have given Lucas a little money but there was nothing in her purse but what would pay for the bread that she had come out to buy for Fanny.

"It is of no consequence, Miss," said Lucas, "We are all of us a great deal worse off on account of Mrs Mabb." He paused. "I am sorry I made you cry, Miss."

Which remark, said with a great deal of kindness, was enough to make her glad to hurry away to the bakery where melancholy fancies of Captain Fox gaily abandoning his career for the sake of Mrs Mabb, and Mrs Mabb laughing loudly to see him do it, so took off her attention from what she was doing that when she got home and opened up the packages she found to her surprize that she had bought three dozen French milk-rolls and an apricot-jam tart—none of which were the things that Fanny had wanted.

"What in the world were you thinking of?" cried Fanny in great perplexity when she saw what Venetia had done. Fanny was quite appalled by the waste of money and under the baneful influence of the milk-rolls and the jam tart became snappish and cross, a mood that threatened to last all day until Venetia remembered that, just before she died, her friend Mrs Whitsun had given her some curtains as a wedding-present. Now that there was to be no wedding it seemed both proper and kind for Venetia to fetch the curtains down from her bedroom and make a present of them to Fanny. The material was very pretty—primrose-yellow with a fine white stripe. Fanny's good humour was restored upon the instant and with Venetia's help she set about altering the curtains for the parlour window and when they were settled at their work, "Fanny," asked Venetia, "Who is Mrs Mabb?"

"A very wicked person, my dear," said Fanny happily brandishing her large black scissors.

"In what way is she wicked?"

But Fanny had no precise information to offer upon this point and all that Venetia could learn was that Mrs Mabb's wickedness chiefly consisted in being very rich and never doing any thing if she did not like it.

"What does she look like?" asked Venetia.

"Oh, Lord! I do not know. I never saw her."

"Then she is quite recently come into the neighbourhood?"

"Oh, yes! Quite recently. . . . But then again, I am not quite sure. Now that I come to think of it I believe she has been here a great long while. She was certainly here when Mr Hawkins came here fifteen years ago."

"Where does she live?"

"A great way off! Beyond Knightswood."

"Near to Dunchurch, then?"

"No, my dear, not near Dunchurch. Nearer to Piper than anywhere, but not particularly near there either. . . ." (These were all towns and villages in the neighbourhood of Kissingland.) ". . . If you leave the turnpike road just before Piper and go by an overgrown lane that descends very suddenly, you come to a lonely stretch of water full of reeds called Greypool, and above that—atop a little hill—there is a circle of ancient stones. Beyond the hill there is a little green valley and then an ancient wood. Mrs Mabb's house stands betwixt the stones and the wood, but nearer to the wood than the stones."

"Oh!" said Venetia.

The next day Fanny declined Venetia's offer to walk to the village again to buy bread and instead sent her off with a basket of vegetables and some soup to pay a charity visit to a destitute family in Piper. For, as Fanny said, mistakes in purchases came expensive, but if Venetia were so inattentive as to give the soup to the wrong paupers it would not much signify.

Venetia delivered the basket to the destitute family in Piper, but on the way back she passed an opening in a hedge where a narrow, twisting lane descended steeply from the turnpike road. Massive ancient trees grew upon each side and their branches overarched the path and made of it a confusing, shadowy place where the broken sunlight illuminated a clump of violets here, three stalks of grass there.

Now all of English landscape contained nothing that could hold Venetia's gaze quite as rapt as that green lane, for it was the very lane that Fanny had spoken of as leading to the house of Mrs Mabb, and all of Venetia's thoughts ran upon that house and its inhabitants. "Perhaps," she thought, "I will just walk a little way along the lane. And perhaps, if it is not too far, I will just go and take a peep at the house. I should like to know that *he* is happy."

How she proposed to discover whether or not the Captain was happy by looking at the outside of a strange house, she did not consider too exactly, but down the lane she went and she passed the lonely pool and climbed up to the ancient stones and on and on, until she came to a place where round green hills shut out the world.

It was a quiet and empty place. The grass which covered the hills and the valley was as unbroken as any sheet of water—and, almost as if it were water, the sunshiny breeze made little waves in it. On the opposite hill stood an ancient-looking house of grey stone. It was a very tall house, something indeed between a house and a tower, and it was surrounded by a high stone wall in which no opening or gate could be discerned, nor did any path go up to the house.

Yet despite its great height the house was overtopped by the bright sunlit forest wall behind it, and she could not rid herself of the idea that she was actually looking at a very small house—a house for a field mouse or a bee or a butterfly—a house which stood among tall grasses.

"It will not do to linger," she thought. "Suppose I should chance to meet the Captain and Mrs Mabb? Horrible thought!" She turned and walked away quickly, but had not gone far when she heard the drumming of hooves upon the turf behind her. "I shall not look behind me," she thought, "for, if it is Captain Fox, then I am sure that he will be kind and let me go away undisturbed."

But the sound of hooves came on and was joined by many more, till it seemed that a whole army must have risen up out of the silent hills. Greatly amazed, she turned to see what in the world it could be.

Venetia wore a queer old-fashioned gown of fine blue wool. The bodice was embroidered with buttercups and daisies and the waist was low. It was none too long in the skirt but this was amply compensated for by a great number of linen petticoats. She mused upon this for a moment or two. "It appears to be," she thought, "a costume for a milkmaid or a shepherdess or some such other rustic person. How odd! I cannot recall ever having been a milkmaid or a shepherdess. I suppose I must be going to act in some play or other—well, I fear that I shall do it very ill for I do not remember my speeches or any thing about it."

"She has got a little more colour," said Fanny's anxious voice, "Do not you think so, Mr Hawkins?"

Venetia found that she was in Fanny's parlour and Mr Hawkins was kneeling on the flagstones before her chair. There was a basin of steaming water on the floor with a pair of ancient green silk dancing slippers beside it. Mr Hawkins was washing her feet and ancles with a cloth. This was odd too—she had never known him do such a thing before. When he had finished he began to bathe her face with an air of great concentration.

"Be careful, Mr Hawkins!" cried his wife, "you will get the soap in her eyes! Oh, my dear! I was never so frightened in my life as when they brought you home! I thought I should faint from the shock and Mr Hawkins says the same."

That Fanny had been seriously alarmed was apparent from her face; she was commonly hollow-eyed and hollow-cheeked—fifteen years' worrying about money had done that—but now fright had deepened all the hollows, made her eyes grow round and haunted-looking, and sharpened up her nose until it resembled the tip of a scissor blade.

Venetia gazed at Fanny a while and wondered what could have so distressed her. Then she looked down at her own hands and was surprized to find that they were all scratched to pieces. She put her hand up to her face and discovered tender places there.

She jumped up. There was a little scrap of a looking-glass hung upon the opposite wall and there she saw herself, face all bruises and hair pulled this way and that. The shock was so great that she cried out loud.

As she remembered nothing of what had happened to her it was left to Fanny to tell her—with many digressions and exclamations—that she had been found earlier in the day wandering in a lane two or three miles from Piper by a young man, a farmer called Purvis. She had been in a state of the utmost confusion and had answered Mr Purvis's concerned enquiries with queer rambling monologues about silver harness bells and green banners shutting out the sky. For some time Mr Purvis had been unable to discover even so much as her name. Her clothes were torn and dirty and she was barefoot. Mr Purvis had put her on his horse and taken her to his house where his mother had given her tea to drink and the queer old-fashioned gown and the dancing slippers to wear.

"Oh! but, my dear," said Fanny, "do not you remember any thing at all of what happened?"

"No, nothing," said Venetia, "I took the soup to the Peasons—just as you told me—and then what did I do? I believe I went somewhere. But where? Oh! Why can I not remember?"

Mr Hawkins, still on his knees before her, put his finger to his lips as a sign that she should not be agitated and began gently to stroke her forehead.

"You tumbled into a ditch, my dear," said Fanny, "That is all. Which is a nasty, disagreeable thing to happen and so naturally you don't wish to dwell upon it." She started to cry. "You always were a forgetful girl, Venetia."

Mr Hawkins put his finger to his lips as a sign that Fanny should not be agitated and somehow contrived to continue stroking Venetia's forehead while patting Fanny's hand.

"Fanny," said Venetia, "Was there a procession today?"

"A procession?" said Fanny. She pushed Mr Hawkins' hand away and blew her nose loudly. "Whatever do you mean?"

"*That* is what I did today. I remember now. I watched the soldiers ride by."

"There was no procession today," said Fanny, "The soldiers are all in their lodgings, I suppose."

"Oh! Then what was it that I saw today? Hundreds of riders with the sunlight winking on their harness and the sound of silver bells as they rode by. . . ."

"Oh! Venetia," cried Fanny in great irritation of spirits, "do not talk so wildly or Mr Hawkins and I will be obliged to send for the physician—and then there will be his guinea fee and all sorts of medicines to buy no doubt. . . ." Fanny launched upon a long monologue upon the expensiveness of doctors and little by little talked herself up into such paroxysms of worry that she seemed in grave danger of making herself more ill than Venetia had ever been. Venetia hastened to assure her that a physician was quite unnecessary and promised not to talk of processions again. Then she went up to her room and made a more detailed examination of her own person. She found no injuries other than scrapes and bruises. "I suppose," she thought, "I must have fainted but it is very odd for I never did so before." And when the household sat down to supper, which was rather late that evening, Venetia's strange adventure was not mentioned again, other than a few complaints from Fanny to the effect that the Purvises had still got Venetia's gown.

The next morning Venetia was stiff and aching from head to toe. "I feel," she thought, "as if I had tumbled two or three times off a horse." It was a familiar sensation. Captain Fox had taught her to ride in the previous November. They had gone up to a high field that overlooked Kissingland and Captain Fox had lifted her up onto Belle-dame's back. Beneath them the village had been all a-glow with the ember colours of autumn trees and the candlelight in people's windows. Wisps of vivid blue smoke had drifted up from bonfires in Mr Grout's gardens.

"Oh! how happy we were! Except that Pen Harrington would always contrive to discover where we were going and insist on coming with us and she would always want the Captain to pay attention to her, which he—being all nobility—was obliged to do. She is a very tiresome girl. Oh! but now I am no better off than she is—or any of those other girls who liked the Captain and were scorned by him for the sake of Mrs Mabb. It would be far more natural in me to hate the Captain and to feel sisterly affection towards poor Pen. . . ."

She sat a while trying to arrange her feelings upon this model, but at the end of five minutes found she liked Pen no better and loved the Captain no less. "I suppose the truth is that one cannot feel much pity for a girl who wears a buttercup-yellow gown with lavender trimmings—buttercup-yellow and lavender look so extremely horrid together. But as for what happened yesterday the most likely explanation is that I fainted in the lane and Mr Purvis found me, picked me up and put me on his horse, but subsequently dropped me—which would account for the bruises and the holes in my clothes. And I suppose that he now is too embarrassed to tell anyone—which I can well understand. The Captain," she thought with a sigh, "would not have dropped me."

That morning as the sisters worked together in the kitchen (Venetia shelling peas, Fanny making pastry), they heard the unexpected sounds of a horse and carriage.

Fanny looked out of the window. "It is the Purvises," she said.

Mrs Purvis proved to be a fat, cheerful woman who, the moment she set eyes upon Venetia, gave a delighted cry and embraced her very heartily. She smelt of sweet milk, new bread and freshly turned earth, as if she had spent the morning in the dairy, the kitchen and the vegetable-garden—as indeed she had.

"I dare say, ma'am," said Mrs Purvis to Fanny, "you are surprized at my warmth but if you had seen Miss Moore when John first brought her in, all white and shaking, then I think you would excuse me. And I know that Miss Moore will excuse me for she and I got to be great friends when she was in my kitchen."

"Did we, though?" thought Venetia.

"And you see, my dear," continued Mrs Purvis, delving in a great canvas bag, "I have brought you my little china shepherdess that you liked so much. Oh! Do not thank me. I have half a dozen other such that I scarcely look at. And here, ma'am . . ." She addressed Fanny respectfully, ". . . are asparagus and strawberries and six beautiful goose eggs. I dare say you will agree with me that it is scarcely any wonder that our young ladies faint dead away when they let themselves get so thin."

Fanny always liked visitors and Mrs Purvis was precisely the sort to please her—full of harmless gossip, and deferring to Fanny as a farmer's widow should defer to a curate's wife. Indeed so pleased was Fanny that she was moved to give each of the Purvises a small biscuit. "I did have a bottle of very good madeira-wine," she told them, "but I fear it is all drunk." Which was true—Mr Hawkins had finished it at Christmas eight years before.

Of the queer, old-fashioned gown Mrs Purvis had this to say: "It was my sister's, Miss Moore. She died when she was about your age and she was almost as pretty as you are. You are welcome to keep it, but I expect you like to have everything of the new fashion like other young ladies."

The visit ended with Mrs Purvis nodding and making signs to her son that he should say something. He stammered out his great pleasure in seeing Miss Moore looking so much better and hoped that she and Mrs Hawkins would not object to his calling upon them again in a day or two. Poor man, his blushing countenance seemed to shew that Venetia had not been alone in sustaining some hurt from the previous day's adventures; her rescuer also appeared to have received a blow—in his case to the heart.

When they were gone Fanny said, "She seems a very worthy sort of woman. It is however extremely provoking that she has not brought back your clothes. I was several times upon the point of asking her about it, but each time I opened my mouth she began to talk of something else. I cannot understand what she means by keeping them so long. Perhaps she thinks of selling them. We have only her word for it that the clothes are spoiled."

Fanny had a great deal of useless speculation of this sort to get through but she had scarcely begun when she discovered that she had left her huswife in her bedroom and sent Venetia upstairs to fetch it.

In the lane beneath Fanny's bedroom window Mrs Purvis and her son were making ready to drive away. As Venetia watched John Purvis took a big wooden pail out of the back of the ancient gig and placed it upside-down on the ground as an extra step for his mother to mount up to the driver's seat.

Venetia heard Mrs Purvis say, "Well, my mind is much eased to see her looking so much better. It is a great blessing that she remembers nothing about it."

Here Purvis said something, but his face was still turned away and Venetia could not hear what it was.

"It was soldiers, John, I am sure of it. Those great slashes in her gown were made by swords and sabres. It would have frightened them both into fits—as much as it frightened me, I am sure—to see how cut about her clothes were when you found her. It is my belief that this Captain Fox—the same I told you of, John—must have set on some of his men to frighten her off. For all that he has treated her so cruel she may still love him. With such a sweet nature as she has got it is the likeliest thing in the world. . . ."

"Good God!" whispered Venetia in great astonishment.

At first the horror which she ought to have felt was quite overtaken by her indignation on the Captain's behalf; "I dare say she was very kind to take me in, but she is a very stupid woman to invent such lies about Captain Fox, who is every thing that is honourable and would never do harm to any one—always excepting, of course, in pursuit of his military duties." But then, as images of her poor, ill-treated gown rose up before her fancy, the disagreeable impression which Mrs Purvis's words had created grew until Venetia was thoroughly frightened. "What in the world can have happened to me?" she wondered.

But she had no satisfactory answer.

On the following day after dinner, Venetia felt in need of

fresh air and told Fanny that she thought she would walk out for a while. She went down Church-lane and turned the corner at Blewitt's yard; looking up she saw something behind the walls of Mr Grout's kitchen garden—Oh! the most terrible thing in all the world!—and the fright of it was so great that her legs gave way beneath her and she fell to the ground.

"Young lady! Young lady! What is the matter?" cried a voice. Mr Grout appeared with his housekeeper, Mrs Baines. They were very shocked to find Venetia crawling on the ground and she was scarcely less shocked to be found. "Young lady!" cried Mr Grout, "What in the world has happened to you?"

"I thought I saw a strange procession coming towards me," said Venetia, "but now I see that what I took for pale green banners fluttering in the breeze are only the tops of some birch trees."

Mr Grout looked as if he did not very well understand this.

Mrs Baines said, "Well, my dear, whatever it was, a glass of marsala-wine is sure to put it right."—and, though Venetia assured them that she was quite well and was certain to stop shaking in a moment, they helped her into the house where they made her sit down by the fire and gave her marsala-wine to drink.

Mr Grout was an attorney who had been settled many years in Kissingland, where he had lived quietly and inexpensively. He had always appeared friendly and was generally well thought of, until he had suddenly got very rich and bought two farms in Knightswood parish. This was all quite recent, yet long enough for Mr Grout to have acquired a reputation as a most unreasonable landlord who bullied the farmers who worked his land and who increased their rents just as it suited him.

"You will eat something, perhaps?" said Mr Grout to Venetia, "My excellent Mrs Baines has been baking this morning if I am not mistaken. I smell apple tarts!"

"I want nothing, sir. Thank you," said Venetia and then, because she could not think of any thing else to say, she added, "I do not think I was in your house, sir, since I was a little girl."

"Indeed?" said Mr Grout, "Then you will see a great many improvements! It is a curious thing, young lady, but wealth don't suit everybody. The mere notion of great quantities of money is enough to make some people uneasy. Happily I can bear the thought of any amount with equanimity. Money, my dear, does more than provide mere material comforts; it lifts the burden of cares from one's shoulders, it imparts vigour and decisiveness to all one's actions and a delicate clearness to the complexion. It puts one in good humour with oneself and all the world. When I was poor I was not fit to be seen."

Money did indeed seem to have worked some curious changes in Mr Grout: his lawyer's stoop had vanished overnight, taking with it all his wrinkles; his silver hair shone so much that, in certain lights, he appeared to be sanctified; and his eyes and skin had a queer sparkle to them, not entirely pleasant to behold. He was known to be more than a little vain of all these new graces and he smiled at Venetia as though inviting her to fall in love with him on the spot.

"Well, sir," she said "I am sure that no one could deserve good fortune more. You made some cunning investments no doubt?"

"No, indeed. All my good fortune has sprung from the same noble source, a great lady who has employed me as her man of business—for which I may say I have been very handsomely rewarded. *Mrs Mabb* is the lady's name."

"Oh!" said Venetia, "She is someone I have a great curiosity to see."

"I do not doubt it, young lady," said Mr Grout laughing pleasantly, "For she has got your sweetheart, the bold Captain Fox, has she not? Oh! there is no need to pretend that it is not so, for, as you see, I know all about it. There is no shame in being seen from the field by such a rival as Mrs Mabb. Mrs Mabb is a pearl beyond price and praise. The soul delights in the smallest motion of her hand. Her smile is like the sunshine—No! it is better than sunshine! One would gladly live in darkness all the days of one's life for the sake of Mrs Mabb's smile. Oh, young lady! The curve of Mrs Mabb's neck! Her eyebrow! Her smallest fingernail! Perfection every one!"

Venetia sighed. "Well," she said and then, not knowing very well how to continue, she sighed again.

"In her youth, I believe," continued Mr Grout, "she was most industrious in managing her estates and ordering the affairs of her relations and dependents—who are very numerous and who all live with her—but at length the follies of the world began to disgust her and for many years she has lived a very retired life. She stays at home where she is very busy with her needle. I myself have been privileged to examine yard upon yard of the most exquisite embroidery, all of Mrs Mabb's production. And all her spinster cousins and maiden aunts and other such inferior females as she condescends to keep about her embroider a great deal too, for Mrs Mabb will not tolerate idleness."

"She lives near Piper, does she not?" said Venetia.

"Piper!" cried Mr Grout. "Oh no! Whatever gave you that idea? Mrs Mabb's house is not half so far and in quite another direction. It is reached by the little path that crosses the churchyard and goes out by the ivy-covered arch. The path, which is somewhat overgrown with cow parsley and foxgloves, passes a little pool full of reeds and then climbs a smooth green hill. At the top of the hill the visitor must climb through a gap in a ruined wall of ancient stones—whereupon he finds himself in Mrs Mabb's garden."

"Oh!" said Venetia. "How strange! For I am sure that someone told me that she lived near Piper. But, sir, I promised my sister that I would not be gone long and she is sure to grow anxious if I do not return soon."

"Oh!" said Mr Grout, "But we are just beginning to get acquainted! My dear, I hope you are not one of those prim young misses who are afraid to be alone with an old friend. An old friend, after all, is what I am, for all I look so young."

In Church-lane Venetia climbed up and looked over the

churchyard-wall. “So that is the path that leads to Mrs Mabb’s house, and there is the ivy-covered arch!”

She could not remember ever having observed either of them before. “Well! I do not think it can do any harm to go up very quietly and privately to look at her house.”

And so, quite forgetting that she had told Mr Grout that Fanny would worry if she did not return home soon, she slipped into the churchyard and beneath the ivy-covered arch, and climbed the hill and passed the pool and came at last to the broken wall.

“I wonder that such a great lady should have no better entrance to her house than this inconvenient gap in an ancient wall!”

She passed through.

Majestic trees of great age and height stood about a great expanse of velvety green lawn. The trees had all been clipped into smooth rounded shapes, each one taller than Kissingland church tower, each one a separate mystery, and each one provided by the evening sun with a long shadow as mysterious as itself. Far, far above a tiny moon hung in the blue sky like its own insubstantial ghost.

“Oh! How quiet and empty it is! Now I am quite certain that I ought not to have come, for I was never in so private a place in my life. Any moment now I shall hear silver bells and hooves upon the turf, I know I shall! And as for the house I do not see one.”

Yet there was something; at the one end of the lawn stood a round tower built of ancient-looking, grey stones, with battlements at the top and three dark slits for windows very high up. It was quite a tall tower, but in spite of its height it was overtopped by a monstrous hedge of pale roses that stood behind it and she could not rid herself of the idea that the tower was actually very tiny—a tower for an ant or a bee or a bird.

“I suppose it is that monstrous hedge that confuses one. It must be a summerhouse. I wonder how you get inside—I do not see a door. Oh! Someone is playing a pipe! Yet there is no one here. And now a drum! How odd it is that I cannot see who is playing! I wonder if . . . Two steps forward, curtsey and turn. . . ."

The words came from nowhere into her head and the steps came from nowhere into her feet. She began to dance and was not at all surprized to find that, at the appropriate moment, someone took her outstretched hand.

Someone was crying very quietly and, just as before, Mr Hawkins knelt by Venetia's chair and washed her feet.

"And yet," she thought, "they will never be clean if he washes them in blood."

The water in the basin was bright red.

"Fanny," said Venetia.

The crying stopped and a small sound—something between a squeak and a sniff—seemed to shew that Fanny was nearby.

"Fanny, is it evening?"

"It is dawn," said Fanny.

"Oh!"

The curtains in Fanny's parlour were drawn back, but in the grey light of early dawn they had lost all their primrose colour. And everything outside the window—Fanny's vegetable-garden, Robin Tolliday's barn, John Harker's field, God's sky, England's clouds—all could be seen with perfect clarity but all had lost their colour as if all were made of grey water. Fanny began to cry again. "Perhaps she is in pain," thought Venetia, "For there is certainly a pain somewhere."

"Fanny?" she said.

"Yes, my love?"

"I am very tired, Fanny."

Then Fanny said something which Venetia did not hear and Venetia turned her head and when she opened her eyes she was in bed and Fanny was sitting in the wicker-chair, mending a hole in Mr Hawkins's shirt, and the curtains were drawn against the bright sunshine.

"Oh, Venetia!" said Fanny with a sigh and a despairing shake of her head, "Where in the world have you been? And what in the world have you been doing?"

It was not the sort of question that expected an answer but Venetia attempted one anyway; "I remember that I drank a glass of wine at Mr Grout's house, but I told him very plainly that I must come home, for I knew you were waiting for me. Did I not come home, Fanny?"

"No, Venetia," said Fanny, "you did not." And Fanny told Venetia how she and Mr Hawkins and their neighbours had searched through the night, and how, just before dawn, John Harker and George Buttery had looked into the churchyard and seen the pale shape of Venetia's gown billowing out in the darkness. She had been under the big yew tree, turning and turning and turning, with her arms spread wide. It had taken both of them holding tight on to her to make her stop.

"Two pairs of shoes," sighed Fanny, "One entirely gone and the other in tatters. Oh, Venetia! Whatever were you thinking of?"

Venetia must have fallen asleep again for when she woke it seemed to be late evening. She could hear the clatter of plates as Fanny got the supper ready downstairs; and as Fanny went back and forth between parlour and kitchen she talked to Mr Hawkins: ". . . and if it should come to that, she shall not be sent to the madhouse—I could not bear that she should go to one of those horrid places and be ill-treated. No, indeed! Take warning, Mr Hawkins, that I expressly forbid it. . . ."

"As if he would suggest such a thing!" thought Venetia, "So good as he is to me."

". . . I dare say that mad people are no more expensive to keep than sane ones—except perhaps in the articles of medicines and restraining chairs."

Early next morning Fanny, Venetia and Mr Hawkins were at breakfast in the parlour when there was a loud knocking at the door. Fanny went to the door and returned in a moment with Mr Grout, who wasted no time upon apologies or explanations but immediately addressed Venetia in accents of great displeasure.

"Young lady! I am expressly sent to you by Mrs Mabb who has bid me tell you that she will not have you creeping around and around her house!"

"Ha!" cried Venetia, so loudly that Fanny started.

"Mrs Mabb's relations and dependents," continued Mr Grout with a severe look at Venetia's exulting expression, "have all been frightened out of their wits by your odd behaviour. You have given her aged uncles bad dreams, made the children afraid to go asleep at night and caused the maids to drop the china upon the floor. Mrs Mabb says that there is not one complete dinner service left in the house! She says that the butter will not come in the churns because you have given her cows malicious looks—Miss Moore, will you stop tormenting this lady?"

"Let her give up Captain Fox to me," said Venetia, "and she shall never hear of me again."

"Oh, Venetia!" cried Fanny.

"But young lady!" cried Mr Grout, "It is Mrs Mabb that the Captain loves. As I think I have explained to you before, Mrs Mabb is as fair as the apple-blossom that hangs upon the bough. One glance of Mrs Mabb's eyes . . ."

"Yes, yes! I know!" cried Venetia impatiently, "You told me all that before! But it is just so much nonsense! It is *me* the Captain loves. Had it been otherwise he would have told me so himself—or at least sent me a letter—but I have neither seen nor heard any thing of him since I returned from Manchester. Oh! Do not tell me that Mrs Mabb forbade him to come or some such other foolishness—Captain Fox is not the man to be dissuaded from doing his duty by any body. No, depend upon it, this is another trick of Mrs Mabb's."

"Young lady!" cried Mr Grout, very much appalled, "It ill becomes a young person of no consequence, such as yourself, to go about slandering great people in all the dignity of their property!"

"Mr Grout!" cried Fanny, unable to keep silent a moment longer, "Do not speak to her so! Use milder language to her, sir, I beg you! Can you not see that she is ill? I am, of course, extremely sorry that Mrs Mabb should have been put to any inconvenience by Venetia's going to the house—though I must say you make a great piece of work of it—and merely remark, in justice to Venetia, that all these cows and uncles must be extraordinarily nervous creatures to have been put in such a pickle by a poor, sick girl looking at them! But I tell you what I shall do. To keep her from wandering abroad and causing further nuisance to our neighbours I shall hide the green slippers the Purvises gave her—which are the only shoes she has—where she cannot find them and then, you know," Fanny concluded triumphantly, "she must remain at home!"

Mr Grout looked at Venetia as though hopeful that she would admit defeat.

But Venetia only said sweetly, "You have my answer, sir, and I advise you to go and deliver it. I dare say Mrs Mabb does not tolerate procrastination."

For the next two days Venetia waited for an opportunity to go in search of Mrs Mabb but in all this time Fanny neither left her alone nor answered any of her inquiries about Mrs Mabb. But on the third day Fanny was called away after dinner to take some elderflower tea and peppermint cordial and other remedies to John Harker's maid who had a bad cold. As Fanny went up Church-lane to Harker's farm it seemed probable that among the things her basket contained were the green silk dancing slippers, for when Venetia came to look for them she could not find them anywhere.

So she wrapped her feet up in rags and went anyway.

In a golden light, by what the inhabitants of Kissingland were pleased to call a river and which other, less partial people would probably have called a stream, in a fresh green meadow, beneath blossoming May-trees, some children were playing. One boy with a tin whistle was the Duke of Wellington, another boy with a drum was the entire British army and four little girls in grass-stained gowns of blossom-coloured muslin gave a lively portrayal of the ferocity and indomitable spirit of Napoleon and his French generals.

By the time Venetia passed by in the lane in search of Mrs Mabb her feet were very sore. She thought she would stop and bathe them; but as she went down to the river the two boys began to play a melancholy air upon the whistle and the drum.

Upon the instant Venetia was seized by a terror so blind that she scarcely knew what she did. When she recovered herself she found that she was holding fast to the hand of a most surprized little girl of eight or nine years of age.

"Oh! I beg your pardon. It was only the music that frightened me," she said; and then, as the girl continued to stare at her in astonishment, she added, "I used to be so fond of music you see, but now I do not care for it at all. Whenever I hear a pipe and drum I am certain that I shall be compelled to dance forever and ever without stopping. Does not it strike you that way sometimes?"

The little girls looked very much amazed but did not answer her. Their names were Hebe, Marjory, Joan and Nan, but as to which was which Venetia had not the least idea in the world. She bathed her feet and lay down to rest—for she was still very weak—in the sweet green grass. She heard Hebe, Marjory, Joan or Nan observe to the others that Miss Moore had, as was well known, run mad for the love of handsome Captain Fox.

The little girls had got some daisies to pull apart and as they did so they made wishes. One wished for a sky-blue carriage spotted with silver, another to see a dolphin in Kissingland river, one to marry the Archbishop of Canterbury and wear a diamond-spangled mitre (which she insisted she would be entitled to do as an Archbishop's wife, though the others were more doubtful), and one that there would be bread and beef dripping for her supper.

"I wish to know where I may find Mrs Mabb's house," said Venetia.

There was a silence for a moment and then either Hebe, Marjory, Joan or Nan remarked contemptuously that every one knew that.

"Everyone, it seems, but me," said Venetia to the blue sky and the sailing clouds.

"Mrs Mabb lives at the bottom of Billy Little's garden," said another child.

"Behind a great heap of cabbage leaves," said a third.

"Then I doubt that we can mean the same person," said Venetia, "Mrs Mabb is a very fine lady as I understand."

"Indeed, she is," agreed the first, "The finest lady that ever there was. She has a coachman . . ."

". . . a footman . . ."

". . . a dancing master . . ."

". . . and a hundred ladies-in-waiting . . ."

". . . and one of the ladies-in-waiting has to eat the dull parts of Mrs Mabb's dinner so that Mrs Mabb only ever has to eat roast pork, plum-cake and strawberry jam . . ."

"I see," said Venetia.

". . . and they all live together at the bottom of Billy Little's garden."

"Do not they find that rather inconvenient?" asked Venetia, sitting up.

But Hebe, Marjory, Joan and Nan could not suppose that there would be any particular inconvenience attached to a residence at the bottom of Billy Little's garden. However, they were able to provide Venetia with the further information that Mrs Mabb drank her breakfast coffee out of an acorn-cup, that her chamberlain was a thrush and her coachman a blackbird, and that she herself was "about the size of a pepper-pot".

"Well," said Venetia, "what you tell me is very strange, but no stranger than many of the things that have happened to me recently. Indeed it seems to me to be all of a piece with them—and so perhaps you will have the goodness to shew me where I may find this curious house."

"Oh!" said one child, clapping her hand to her mouth in alarm.

"You had much better not," said another kindly.

"She could turn you into butter," said a third.

"Which might melt," observed the fourth.

"Or a pudding."

"Which might get eaten."

"Or a drawing of yourself on white paper."

"Which someone might set fire to, you know, without meaning to."

But Venetia insisted upon their taking her to Mrs Mabb's house straight away, which at length they agreed to do.

Billy Little was an ancient farm labourer of uncertain temper who lived in a tumbledown cottage in Shilling-lane. He was at war with all the children of Kissingland and all the children of Kissingland were at war with him. His garden was at the back of the cottage and Venetia and Hebe, Marjory, Joan and Nan were obliged to bend low to creep past his uncurtained window.

Someone was standing on the window-sill. She wore a brightly coloured gown, and had a cross expression upon her face.

"There you are, at last!" said Venetia. She straightened herself and addressed this lady in the following words: "Now, madam! If I might trouble you to answer one or two questions. . . ."

"What are you doing?" hissed Hebe, Marjory, Joan or Nan and took hold of Venetia by her gown and pulled her down again.

"Oh! Do you not see?" said Venetia. "Mrs Mabb is just above us, on the windowsill."

"*That* is not Mrs Mabb!" whispered Hebe, Marjory, Joan or Nan. "*That* is only Billy Little's Betsy-jug, with his Toby-jug beside it."

Venetia popped her head back up, and this time she observed the china lady's china husband. The couple were indeed jugs for they had large handles sticking out of their backs.

"Oh! very well," said Venetia, crossly.

"But," she thought to herself, "I have half a mind to push her off the window-sill anyway—for it is my opinion that, where Mrs Mabb is concerned, you never can tell."

Beyond the heap of cabbage leaves and other dark, decaying matter, the path led past a sad-looking pond and up a steep bank. At the top of the bank was a smooth expanse of bright green grass, at one end of which a dozen or so tall stones and slates were piled together. It was possible they were intended for a bee-hive, but it was equally possible that they were simply left over from some ancient wall. Tall flowers grew behind them—meadowsweet, cow parsley and buttercups—so that it was the easiest thing in the world to fancy one was looking at a tower or castle-keep on the edge of an ancient wood.

"Now this is odd," said Venetia, "for I have seen this place before. I know I have."

"There she is!" cried one of the children.

Venetia looked round and thought she saw a quivering in the air. "A moth," she thought. She approached and the shadow of her gown fell across the stones. A dark, damp chill hung about them, which the sunlight had no power to dissipate. She stretched out her hands to break apart Mrs Mabb's house, but upon the instant a pale-green something—or a pale-green someone—flew out of a gap in the stones and sprang up into the sunlight—and then another, and another—and more, and more, until the air seemed crowded with people, and there was a strange glitter all around, which Venetia associated with the sight of sunlight glinting on a thousand swords. So rapid was the manner in which they darted about that it was entirely impossible to hold any of them in one's gaze for more than a moment, but it seemed to Venetia that they rushed upon her like soldiers who had planned an ambush.

"Oh!" she cried, "Oh! You wicked creatures! You wicked, wicked creatures!"; and she snatched them out of the sparkling air and crushed them in her hands. Then it seemed to Venetia that they were dancing, and that the steps of their dance were the most complicated ever invented and had been devised on purpose to make her mad; so she took great pleasure in knocking them to the ground and treading upon their pale green clothes. But, though she was certain that some were killed and dozens of others were sent away injured, there never appeared to be any diminution in their number. Gradually the strength of her own passion began to exhaust her; she was sure she must sink to the ground. At that moment she looked up and saw, just beyond the battle's fray, the pale, heart-shaped face of a little girl and Venetia heard her say in a puzzled tone, "'Tis only butterflies, Miss Moore."

Butterflies? she thought.

"It was only butterflies, my love," said Fanny, smoothing Venetia's cheek.

She was in her own room, laid upon her own bed.

"A cloud of pale-green butterflies," said Fanny. "Hebe, Marjory, Joan and Nan said that you were crying out at them and beating them down with your fists and tearing them apart with your fingers until you fell down in a faint." Fanny sighed. "But I dare say you remember nothing about it."

"Oh! But I remember perfectly well!" said Venetia, "Hebe, Marjory, Joan and Nan took me to Mrs Mabb's house, which as you may know is at the bottom of Billy Little's garden, and Captain Fox was inside it—or at least so I suppose—and had Mrs Mabb not sent the butterflies to prevent me, I would have fetched him out, and—"

"Oh, Venetia!" cried Fanny in exasperation.

Venetia opened her hand and found several fragments of a pale-green colour, like torn paper yet not half the thickness of paper and of no weight whatsoever: the broken remains of two or three butterflies.

"Now I have you, Mrs Mabb," she whispered.

She took a scrap of paper and folded the broken butterflies up inside it. Upon the outside she wrote, 'For Mrs Mabb'.

It was not difficult for Venetia to prevail upon Mr Hawkins (who loved her dearly and who was particularly anxious about her at this period) to deliver the folded paper to Mr Grout.

Next morning Venetia waited hopefully for the return of Captain Fox. When he did not appear she determined to go in search of him again—which both Fanny and Mr Hawkins seemed to have expected, for Fanny had hidden Venetia's dancing slippers in an empty rabbit-hutch in the garden and Mr Hawkins had fetched them out again half an hour later. Mr Hawkins had placed them upon Venetia's bed, where Venetia found them at three o'clock, together with a page torn from Mr Hawkins's memorandum book upon which was drawn a map of Kissingland and the surrounding woods—and deep within those woods, the house of Mrs Mabb.

Downstairs in the kitchen Mr Hawkins was blacking Fanny's boots and—what was very strange—doing it very ill, so that Fanny was obliged to stand over him and scold him about it. She never heard Venetia slip out of the front door and run down the lane.

The map shewed Mrs Mabb's house to be much deeper in the woods than Venetia had ever gone before. She had walked for an hour or so—and was still some way off from Mrs Mabb's house—when she came to a wide glade surrounded by great oaks, beeches, elders and other sweet English trees. At the furthest end of this glade a cloud of insects rose up suddenly against the sunlit wood and a man appeared. But whether he had stepped out of the wood or out of the cloud of insects would have been impossible to say. His hair had the appearance of being a sort of reddish-brown, and he wore the blue coat and white britches of General ——'s regiment.

"Venetia!" he cried the moment he saw her, "But I thought you had gone to Manchester!"

"And so I did, my dear, dear Captain Fox," said she, running towards him in great delight, "and am now returned."

"That is impossible," said Captain Fox, "for we parted only yesterday and I gave you my watch-chain to wear as keepsake."

They argued about this for some time and Venetia said several times how almost four months had passed since last they met and Captain Fox said how it was nothing of the sort. "It is very odd," thought Venetia, "His virtues are all exactly as I remember them, but I had entirely forgot how very exasperating he is!"

"Well, my love," she said, "I dare say you are right—you always are—but perhaps you will explain to me how the trees in this wood got so heavy with leaves and blossoms and buds? I know they were bare when I went away. And where did all these roses come from? And all this sweet fresh grass?"

At which Captain Fox crossed his arms and looked about him and frowned very hard at the trees. "I cannot explain it," he said at last. "But, Venetia," he said more cheerfully, "you will never guess where I have been all this time—with Mrs Mabb! She sent me a message asking me to make a fourth at Casino but when I arrived I found that all she wanted was to talk love and all sorts of nonsense to me. I bore with it as long as I could, but I confess that she began to try my patience. I tell you, Venetia, she is a very odd woman. There was scarcely a stick of furniture in the place—just one chair for her to sit on and then everybody else must prop himself up against the wall. And the house is very queer. One goes through a door—thinking perhaps to fetch a cup from the kitchen or a book from the library—and suddenly one finds oneself in a little wood, or upon some blasted heath, or being drenched by the waves of some melancholy ocean. Oh! And someone—I have not the least idea who—came several times to the house. Which put all the family and servants in a great uproar, for it was a person whom Mrs Mabb most emphatically did not wish to see. So they were at great pains to get rid of this unwelcome visitor. And what a piece of work they made of it! The third time several of them were killed outright. Two bloody corpses were brought home not more than an hour ago—wrapped in paper—which was a little odd, I thought—with 'For Mrs Mabb' written on the top. I observed that Mrs Mabb grew pale at the sight of them and declared that the game was not worth the candle and that, much as she detested yielding to any body, she could not allow any more noble spirits to be destroyed in this cause. I was glad to hear her say so, for I fancy she can be obstinate at times. A little while afterwards she asked me if I should like to go home."

"And what did you do, my love, while Mrs Mabb's servants were removing this troublesome person?" asked Venetia sweetly.

"Oh! I dozed quietly in the back-parlour and let them all rampage about me if that was what they wished. A soldier—as I think I have told you before, Venetia—must be able to sleep any where. But you see how it is: if the head of a household is governed by passion instead of by reason—as is the case here—then confusion and lack of discipline are quickly communicated to the lower orders. It is the sort of thing one sees very often in the army. . . ." And as Captain Fox expounded upon the different generals he had known and their various merits and defects, Venetia took his arm and led him back to Kissingland.

They walked for some time and had a great deal to say to each other and when twilight fell it brought with it a sweet-smelling rain; and birds sang on every side. There were two lights ahead—at the sight of which Venetia was at first inclined to feel some alarm—but they were immediately discovered to be lanterns—only lanterns, the most commonplace articles in the world; and almost as quickly one of the lanterns swung up to reveal Fanny's thin face and; "Oh, Mr Hawkins!" came her glad cry, "Here she is! I have found her!"

M. SHAYNE BELL

LOCK DOWN

As soon as the last member of Night Team A hauls his tired ass up the ladder, you lead your team down it, into the time bubble. The bubble smells like sweat, and Megan hits on the fan first thing, like always, though you all know it won't chase out the smell: you don't give the fan time to make the bubble smell decent.

You don't have the time to give it.

"Secure hatch," you call back to Megan, your Operations Expert, and you know she's already started, you can hear the bolts slamming into place. You don't even bother to order Paulo to replace the battery and check the cabling in the time stabilizer because you've heard him snap open the case and tear into it, and while you check that the time stabilizer is synchronized with Mission Control/Greenwich/Tokyo you think: this is a good team. These people know their jobs, and you know yours, and you can do your jobs. The three of you are Deep Night Team B, and you want to be promoted to Deep Night Team A before the break in time is locked down, which means you've got to break some records—which means you'll work to maybe lock down a whole day on this shift.

"Hatch sealed," Megan calls out.

You flip switches that start the pressurization, and the constant hiss you hear behind all your work starts up again.

"Batteries replaced, full charge, ready to go," Paulo calls out. You'll work till the batteries are within 4 or 5 percent of 10. You won't come back sooner no matter how much actual time you've worked. "Cables check out 100 percent."

"Hatch double check, Paulo," you tell him. "Megan, battery and cable double check."

You double, then triple check everybody's work because you don't ever want to be in fractured time with a bad seal or bad batteries. You don't know exactly what happens to teams lost, for a time, like that—it's classified info—but the rumors aren't good, and you don't want to find out which are true and which are stupid stories like the ones older guys told you when you started training for this job. Besides, you know without being told the two choices a lost team has: suffocate, or depressurize to take on air—and expose yourselves to a timeline on which maybe nothing adds up to you and you are sundered from existence. You check the backup batteries yourself. You check the seals on the hatch and the main batteries yourself after Megan and Paulo have checked them. You all check the time stabilizer, its cables, its synchoronization, the air tanks, and the virtual tether that hooks you back to real time and snakes out silver behind your bubble through the fractured mess you're heading into.

A green light flashes on above the main computer: Mission Control's info dump is finished. You've got the data hundreds of research teams brought back since the last shift went out, true time data on everything and everyone surrounding the point in time you're going to. You strap yourselves in. Out of all the chronometers in front of you, you look first at the one in the upper left-hand corner of your console, the one that records the total amount of time the last team managed to lock down: 2 hours, 13 minutes, 17.56.24 seconds—what were they doing? You think: a whole shift for only two hours and thirteen minutes.

"Move us out," you radio to Mission Control.

And they move you out into fractured time.

The radio is instantly dead. You know you're there. You follow back the break, which occurred between 12:11:32:46:22 P.M. on July 14, 1864, and a time you remember, not too far back, that you don't like to think about. Teams are working from both ends of the break, and yours is working up from the bottom: you're at March 19, 1948, following Marian Anderson, the opera singer, because the break centers on one life and the events in it, and for now it's centered on Marian Anderson—and from each breath she takes, from each turn of her head so that she sees something new, from each word she speaks to another person uncountable futures shatter off, and all the possible actions of all the people she meets or passes or speaks to become possible again, all the evil in their hearts and all the good, and it's your job to lock down what actually happened, no matter what that is, no matter what you watch, because no one knows if the world can persist if you don't get it right.

And no one knows how much time you've got to get time right.

"Night Team locked down at 6:45:10:59:36 P.M., March 19, 1948," Paulo calls out behind you, to your left. "That's where we start."

"Hold us there, Megan," you say, while you check the probability calculations on record at the end of Night Team A's shift. Computer checks them out at 100 percent. Hand calcs say the same. "Move us forward," you say.

And time starts running.

You watch Marian Anderson try to hold the train of her burgundy satin concert gown out of wet snow as Franz Rupp, her accompanist, helps her climb out the window of her room in Hotel Utah and start down the fire escape. Franz follows her out. Bessie George, Marian's servant and friend, closes and latches the window behind them, then takes the stairs down and exits through the hotel's main doors.

You'd already followed them as they'd boarded the Great Northern in Vancouver for Salt Lake City the day after Marian's concert on March 15, and you'd locked that down, and you'd been the team that locked down their arrival in Salt Lake on March 18, at 9:45 A.M. on the dot—trains had prided themselves on being on time like that back then, utterly dependable—and you'd followed her in the taxi through heavy snow and almost impassable streets to Hotel Utah, where the doorman had stopped Marian from entering through the main doors under the canopy that sheltered them from the blizzard. When Franz had protested, the manager had come out to stop Marian from entering, and finally Franz had gone in to check them all into the hotel. They hadn't known where else to go in a blizzard or if anywhere in Salt Lake would treat them any better. Marian had stood outside on the sidewalk with Bessie and all their luggage. After a time, Franz had walked out with keys to their rooms. He'd looked embarrassed, but Marian hadn't seemed at all embarrassed or surprised when he'd led her around to the servants' entrance to the kitchens and an icy fire escape above the first two floors. Bessie had taken the keys, helped a bellboy collect all the luggage, went through the main doors and up to their rooms on the sixth floor to open the windows to Franz and Marian.

"Marian's better than all those people who don't want her in their hotel," Megan had said.

It disgusts you to see the meanness thrown at Marian in places like New York, Los Angeles, Chicago, Philadelphia, and now this place. It disgusts you to have to lock it down—to realize that no place in America treated her better.

"She sings Brahms and makes people weep," Paulo had said.

And Marian was black. In America in 1948, that meant you couldn't go through the front doors of a hotel.

You'd already locked that into true time on your last shift, and on this shift it is now time for Marian's concert in the Mormon Tabernacle on Temple Square. You watch her climb down the icy fire escape, trying to hold her concert gown out of the slush, and walk the half block to the Tabernacle to warm up—"literally," Megan says—for her concert. Franz goes to work immediately to make sure the piano is tuned—oh, the Tabernacle staff assures him it is, but he checks anyway, and he plunks away at a key he can't get right, tightening, then loosening the string, then tightening it again, while Marian runs through scales in the space under the choir seats—the Tabernacle equivalent of backstage—and Bessie makes Marian a lukewarm tea and squeezes a lemon into it. The Tabernacle fills to less than half capacity—exactly 2,347 people—though in that small audience the Democratic governor of Utah, Herbert Brown Maw, and his wife Florence take good seats near the front.

You're watching the calcs, and they aren't good. "Probability's slipping," you say. The total measures out at only 75.467 percent now.

"What's gone wrong?" Megan says, and it's your jobs to find out.

"Weather: heavy snow—the blizzard out there—99.876 percent of all possible true time has that," Paulo calls out. "Storm holds true."

You start checking the probability of each person waiting for the concert to begin having actually attended the concert, even during a blizzard, and they all check out at over 90 percent, including the governor. Franz keeps plunking at the key in front of the small audience, and now the Tabernacle tuner on staff is out helping him get it right. You hear that key plunk and plunk—always just a little flat—while you frantically run the calcs.

"*Mãe de deus*— what key is that?" Paulo asks.

"C sharp over middle C," Megan says. "I'm checking that:

comp's going over recordings of past tunings of this piano in the Tabernacle—that key might be our problem. It rates only 48.575 of possible true time."

"That's still high," you say. "Let it run." Sometimes the only way to find where time took a wrong turn is to let it play out to some completely illogical end and backtrack from that.

Franz and the staff tuner get the key in tune, the plunking stops, and Franz hurries down the steps and through curtains to the space under the choir seats to enter behind Marian when the time comes. A young girl stands poised to pull back the curtains. While Franz and Marian stand there waiting to go on, the girl looks up at Marian. "Are you frightened?" she asks.

Marian smiles. "A little," she says. "But when I start to sing I always forget my surroundings and, as you forget your surroundings, you also forget to be afraid."

Marian nods, and the girl pulls back the curtains. Marian and Franz walk out. Suddenly there is applause, though not much since the Tabernacle isn't full. The concert begins. Marian sings one selection from Handel, "Serse, Recitative and Aria": "To win ones' true treasure one must be cunning," the words go. "Vivacious laugh, a quick glance can make one fall in love. Sometimes it is necessary to trick and fool—ah, I can do all these things!"

Marian's voice is clear, the register deep and low at first. She sings with such confidence the notes seem effortless. The audience applauds, louder this time, and Marian sings Brahms.

"The probability of this order of music is only 33.678 percent," you say.

"No other concert on the tour had this order so far," Megan confirms. "It's usually Handel, then a couple other Baroques, then Schubert."

But the Brahms is lovely, and you still can't put your finger on exactly where time took its wrong turn. "Let it keep playing," you say. After intermission Marian turns from Brahms to Tchaikovsky's "None but the Lonely Heart," and the applause is louder now, and the governor stands to applaud Marian. She sings more Tchaikovsky, then spirituals—to a standing ovation. Florence Maw is crying—trying to clap, then wipe her eyes, then clap some more—and the governor calls out "Ave Maria!" and the applause gets louder and louder. Marian sings five more spirituals as encores, and the small audience keeps calling her back. She sings an aria from Massenet's opera *Le Cid*, and the governor shouts "Ave Maria!" again. When Marian comes out for the seventh time, she sings it. She knows which Ave Maria the governor is asking for: the Gounod, based on the Bach prelude. At the end of that song not only Florence is weeping. Florence and the governor go backstage to find Marian, Franz, and Bessie bundling up to face the blizzard.

"You walked over!" the governor says to Marian, incredulous. "You'll ride back with us."

And they do. Franz and Bessie and Marian all look at each other when the limousine stops in front of the hotel's main doors, under the canopy, out of the storm. The governor and Florence sweep them out of the limousine and partway up the steps. "Let's get you something hot to drink," Florence says, and she starts inside through the revolving doors. The governor motions for Marian and the rest to follow. Marian hesitates, then suddenly pulls up the skirts of her gown and does follow.

The doorman stops her.

"What's this?" the governor demands.

"She can't come through here, sir," the doorman says.

Florence stands on the inside now. She looks back, confused.

"What do you mean she can't come through here?" the governor says. "Isn't she a guest at this hotel?"

"I am," Marian says.

"Well, then." The governor takes Marian's arm and leads her toward the door—but the doorman actually puts out his hand and holds Marian back.

"*You* can enter here," the doorman tells the governor. "But her kind enters around back."

"They're making Marian climb the fire escape to her room," Franz calls out from the bottom steps.

Florence pushes her way back out through the revolving doors, and the hotel's night manager follows her. When he sees who is standing with Marian Anderson—the governor of the state of Utah and the first lady—he looks troubled.

"Your doorman tells me," the governor says, "that some of your guests may not enter this hotel through the main doors—including this woman, who happens to be the greatest singer of our nation, perhaps of the entire world."

"She is a Negro," the night manager says, nothing more.

"She is to be my guest for hot chocolate in your coffee shop. Florence and I are walking there with her. So how do we go? By way of a fire escape around back?"

"Governor, you and the first lady may of course enter through these front doors. I'll escort Mrs. Anderson to the coffee shop myself. We won't be long."

"Through what entrance will you escort Mrs. Anderson?"

The night manager says nothing.

Florence steps forward then and takes Marian's arm. "Are your rooms here adequate?" she asks.

Marian nods.

"What floor have they put you on?"

"The sixth."

"And you climb fire escapes up and down to get to your room?"

"Part of the way is inside through the servant's entrance to the kitchens," Marian says.

"Would you be a guest in my home instead?" Florence asks. "We'll take you through the front door of this state's governor's mansion and put all of you in our guest rooms, then make ourselves hot chocolate in the kitchen."

"We'd be honored," the governor says.

Marian accepts. Franz and Bessie hurriedly pack their and

Marian's things, and they all drive with the governor and his wife to Utah's governor's mansion where Marian stays as an honored guest.

"Fast forward, Megan," you say. "Prepare for backtrack." And while you and your team prepare to take the bubble back to find out where time went wrong, you watch events on this timeline rush by. The story of Marian and the governor and his wife is in all the Utah papers the next day, and the day after that in all the papers in America and after that, abroad. Utah is shamed by what happened: but more than that, the governor introduces legislation outlawing discrimination based on race in all public institutions in Utah, and—after months of hard lobbying, behind the scenes deals, and arm twisting—it passes. Utah becomes a bastion of civil rights in 1948. It shows America the way forward.

"Hold us there, Megan," you call out. You know this didn't happen. You wish you could lock it down, but you know this didn't happen.

"It could have happened like that," Megan says. "It was in their hearts."

But it didn't happen like that. You go back to 6:45:10:59:36 P.M., March 19, 1948, and you inch forward, checking every probability. You follow a different timeline. As you watch it, you think this must be what had happened. You see Marian climb out the window in her gold silk concert gown, the one with real pearls sewn on the cuffs and around the neck, and both Bessie and Franz go down the fire escape with her to help her keep the gown out of the slush. "Good probability on that gown," Megan says. "Marian hasn't worn it since San Francisco." You realize Megan isn't checking probability calcs to say that; she's just watching and using common sense. Marian had worn the burgundy in Vancouver just days before. She would likely wear a different gown now.

"It's the C above middle C—not C sharp—they can't tune," Paulo says while you all listen to Franz plunk the C above middle C over and over.

"That C rates 86.277 of possible true time," Megan says.

"Close," you say, in the middle of figuring the probability of filling the Tabernacle on the night of a blizzard—5,667 people to be exact, which is how many attend on this timeline. But close isn't good enough. Something's wrong, again.

Marian begins with the same Handel, then turns to Schubert's "Suleika":

> I envy you your humid wings, oh western wind
> For you can tell him how long I suffer, now we are
> parted! . . .
> Yet do not grieve him, but hide my sorrow.
> Tell him modestly, that his love is my life,
> That if I am with him, two will rejoice.

Then Marian sings Brahms; after intermission, Tchaikovsky and the spirituals, as before. Marian receives a standing ovation again. Florence is crying—trying to clap, then wipe her eyes, then clap some more—and the governor calls out "Ave Maria!" and the applause gets louder and louder. There are cheers this time from the audience. The concert ends after five encores—the last the Bach/Gounod Ave Maria—and the governor and Florence drive Marian, Bessie, and Franz to Hotel Utah and sweep them out of the limousine and partway up the steps. "Let's get you something hot to drink," Florence says. She starts inside through the revolving doors. The governor motions for Marian and the rest to follow. Marian hesitates, then suddenly pulls up the skirts of her gown and does follow.

The doorman stops her.

"What's wrong?" the governor demands.

"She can't come through here, sir," the doorman says.

Florence stands on the inside now. She looks back, confused.

"What do you mean?" the governor says. "Isn't she a guest at this hotel?"

"I am," Marian says.

"Then you are mistaken," Governor Maw tells the doorman. The governor takes Marian's arm and leads her toward the door—but the doorman actually puts out his hand and holds Marian back.

"*You* can enter here," the doorman tells the governor. "But her kind enters around back."

"They're making Marian climb the fire escape to her room," Franz calls out from the bottom steps.

Florence pushes her way back out through the revolving doors, and the hotel's night manager follows her. When he sees who is standing with Marian, he looks troubled.

"Your doorman tells me," the governor says, "that some of your guests may not enter through the main doors—including this woman, who happens to be the greatest singer of our nation, perhaps of the entire world."

"She is a Negro," the night manager says, nothing more, as if that explained everything.

"She's to be my guest for hot chocolate in your coffee shop. Florence and I are walking there with her. So how do we go? By way of a fire escape around back?"

The night manager hesitates. "Of course not, sir," he says, finally. "Please, will all of you follow me." And to the astonishment of the doorman, the night manager leads everyone—including Marian Anderson—inside, through the main doors. Guests sitting in the lobby stare, but say nothing.

The calcs aren't good. "We're losing it," you say.

"I get only a 13.227 percent probability that the night manager would do what he just did," Megan says.

"But it was in his heart," Paulo says.

"Only 13.227 percent of it," Megan says.

"He just didn't act on that 13.227 percent," Paulo says.

But you know that what was in the night manager's heart doesn't matter. What matters is what he actually did. "Fast forward, Megan," you say. "Prepare for backtrack." And while you and Megan and Paulo prepare to take the bubble back, you let time run forward. The papers do not mention the governor's intercession on Marian's behalf the next day. He himself is quiet about it. He's running for reelection that year and is not sure how his intercession would play with the voters. But he knows the general manager of Hotel Utah, and he suggests to him privately that he ought to change the hotel's ridiculous policy of not allowing someone like Marian Anderson to walk in through the front doors. "I'll change the policy at once," the general manager says, and he does write a new policy that same day, but he sets it aside to think about it overnight. The next day he looks at it on his desktop, then wads it up and throws it in the trash can under his desk.

"Take us back, Megan," you say.

And you are back at 6:45:10:59:36 P.M., March 19, 1948, and you inch forward, checking every probability. You watch Marian try to hold the train of her green satin concert gown out of the wet snow as Franz helps her climb out the window of her room in Hotel Utah and start down the fire escape. Franz follows her out. Bessie closes and latches the window behind them, then takes the stairs down and exits through the hotel's main doors. "99.678 percent probability on that gown," Megan says. She's talking from computer *and* hand calcs this time, not just common sense. Marian hasn't worn that gown since Philadelphia.

"Its the *B* above middle C they can't tune!" Paulo exclaims. "Nearly 100 percent on that, too."

"Lock it down," you say. Paulo hits the timelock switch, and the time bubble shudders, then stills. You look at the chronometer in the upper left-hand corner of your console and see that you've added 1 hour, 13 minutes, and 29.52.17 seconds to true time.

This is not going to be a record shift.

But everything on this timeline checks out at nearly 100 percent for hours after that. The Tabernacle fills with 6,104 people—it's standing room only: the box office sells 138 standing-room tickets for $1.20, half price—and the fire marshal won't let anyone else in. The girl at the curtains does not speak to Marian on this timeline. Marian begins with a different Handel, "Floridante":

> Dear night, bring back my love.
> At times I fancy my beloved standing in the doorway
> but alas, 'tis only a dream—how long must I wait in vain?

After that she sings another Handel, then Frescobaldi, Legranzi, four Schubert lieder and the Massenet aria—all before intermission.

"No Brahms," Megan says. "We're at 98.662 percent on that."

After the intermission, Marian sings "None but the Lonely Heart," four other early twentieth-century pieces, then the spirituals. Florence does not cry, though some in the audience do. Marian sings three encores: "Coming through the Rye," "Will 'o the Wisp," and the Bach/Gounod Ave Maria, then she, Franz, and Bessie bundle up and walk back to Hotel Utah. Marian and Franz enter through the servant's entrance and climb up the fire escape to their rooms where Bessie has opened the windows.

All your calcs check out at 98 plus percent. "This is it, isn't it?" you say. You look back at Megan and Paulo. Their calcs match yours. You've got time right. You've seen what really happened the night of Marian Anderson's only concert in Salt Lake City. "We have to lock this down," you say, but after seeing what might have been you hesitate.

"Come on guys," Megan says, finally. "We've got a job to do."

And you know she's right. You don't like it, but you know

she's right. You wish you had a choice, but you don't. "Lock it down," you say.

Paulo does, and the time bubble shudders.

You look at the chronometer: 4 hours, 17 minutes, 22.36.08 seconds locked down. "We beat Night Team A," you announce. You look back at Megan and Paulo. Megan looks up from her calcs and grins, but that's it. It doesn't feel like the times when you've had a good shift, beat Night Team A, maybe locked down a day without indignities in Marian's life.

"Batteries at 48 percent," Megan says. "Air tanks at 60."

You can stay out a little longer. You let time run through the true-time night, checking the probabilities, locking down blocks of time as you go. At 7:30 A.M., Franz checks out for his party; Bessie and a bellboy load the luggage in a taxi; and Marian hurries down the fire escape and out the servant's entrance to meet the train to Denver. You've locked down 12 hours, 9 minutes, 46.22.54 seconds—not your team's best, but a good shift's work.

"Batteries at 14 percent now," Megan announces, which is as close to the 10 percent edge as you come. "Air tanks, 33."

"Prepare for return," you say.

While the three of you make the necessary adjustments and check each other's work, you let time run. You are still stationed above Hotel Utah. At 7:46 A.M.—you notice the time because you're setting comp's main chronometer for the return just then—two maids hurry out the back of the hotel with blankets, sheets, pillowcases, towels, and a bedspread in their arms. "Those were in Marian's room," Megan says. "She had the cream bedspread." And for a short time, while you strap yourselves into your seats, you all watch to see what these women are doing with the bedding and towels from Marian's room. They hurry through the slush and cold to the incinerator where refuse from the kitchen's breakfast is burning, and they throw everything on the flames and stand there to watch it burn.

"Take us home, Megan," you say.

And she does. You follow the silver virtual tether across all the fractured time left between 1948 and your own time. You leave Marian in 1948, with its unacted good locked in people's hearts where it never mattered. The radio comes to life. You turn Mission Control over to Paulo while Megan depressurizes the bubble. You download your reports. Then you follow your team up the ladder.

RAPHAEL CARTER

CONGENITAL AGENESIS OF GENDER IDEATION

BY K. N. SIRSI AND SANDRA BOTKIN

"WHAT WE CALL LEARNING IS REALLY REMEMBERING," Socrates says in the *Phaedo*; for our ideas, in their abstract perfection, could not be formed by observation of this sloppy and imperfect world. For Descartes, too, such immutable ideas as "God," "mind," "body," and "triangle" could not be derived from the swirl of sense-impressions reaching our eyeballs and fingertips, but must be already present at our births. Locke, on the other hand, believed that ideas were derived from experience: "the natural and regular production of Things without us, really operating upon us."

The days are past when questions such as this were argued using reason and introspection; now we solve them by magnetic resonance imaging and DNA sequencing. The study of brain-damage patients and people with learning disabilities has been especially useful in wresting the great questions from philosophy. The two of us and our colleagues have now unlocked the answers Plato sought, and resoundingly confirmed Descartes's view of the mind.

The Parable of the Television

To see what brain damage can teach us about the mind, imagine that you are trying to learn how television works by examining several broken television sets. Even without opening the sets, you could learn something about their workings by studying what happens when they break. Suppose, for example, that some sets work perfectly in all respects *except* that the faces are distorted and unrecognizable. You might guess that these sets have a problem with displaying flesh tones, or with shapes that are roughly oval. But if the sets displayed hands and eggs correctly while garbling even the green faces of midnight-movie aliens, you could deduce that faces are processed differently from other images. There must be some special function of the television just for faces—some face-generation circuitry.

No such disorder of televisions exists, or can exist. Faces on a TV screen are produced by arranging the same pixels as hands, or furniture, or any other object. But minds work differently. Lesions to certain parts of the brain produce an inability to recognize people by their faces, but do not affect any other brain function. This disorder, called prosopagnosia, leaves its victims perfectly able to read, to name objects they see, and to recognize voices; but present them with a photograph of a close friend, and they are at a loss. The real brain, like the imaginary television, must contain a special module for faces—a face-recognition organ.

Disorders like prosopagnosia help us decide between two basic views of the brain. In one, the brain is a universal computer with an all-purpose ability to perceive and reason; this ability is often called "general cognition." In the other, the brain is a toolbox full of instruments specialized for different tasks.

The existence of prosopagnosia shows that face recognition, at least, is a specialized tool. But this does not mean that general cognition does not exist. Most scientists believe that the brain has some specialized tools for common tasks, such as face recognition and grammar, but falls back on general cognition for everything else. In fact, most prosopagnosics use general cognition to partially overcome their disability: one patient identifies people by noting the length of their hair (but is confused anew every time a friend visits the beauty salon!).

A Family in Rajasthan

Our work on ideas began as a study of language. One of us (Sirsi), a neurologist, became interested in the work of the Canadian linguist Myrna Gopnik. Gopnik's research indicated that a single dominant gene could lead to an inability to apply basic grammatical rules that the rest of us take for granted ("Impairments of Tense in a Familial Language Disorder," *Journal of Neurolinguistics,* No. 8, 1994, pp. 109–133.) Children with the gene could learn a present-tense verb such as "pray," but could not readily inflect it to get the past tense "prayed." Yet these children had no serious auditory impairment and seemed intellectually normal in other respects.

Follow-up studies (such as Ricci and Serafini, 1999; Leman and Lander, 2000; Acacia and Myrmidon, 2002) continued to show that other functions of the brain were unaffected by the disorder. In fact, many people with grammatical impairments were able to use general cognition to partially compensate for their disability: rather than conjugating verbs instinctively, they mentally recited a memorized rule, much as people do when learning a second language in adulthood. This strongly suggested that normal grammatical competence is produced by an inborn "grammar instinct."

But how, Sirsi wondered, does the language organ work? Is it a generalized instrument for recognizing patterns in sounds? Or is it specifically attuned to such basic features of language as verb tenses and grammatical gender?

To find out, Sirsi undertook that rarest of activities for a neurologist, fieldwork. While on an extended vacation in Jaipur, India, he visited schools to distribute small photocopied coloring books that he had designed with the help of a teacher of Hindi. Each page was divided into two panels. One panel illustrated a nonsense word, using it in a sentence. The other contained an incomplete sentence requiring the child to fill in an inflected form of the word. Some of the nonsense words were in Roman characters and sounded like English ("to wuzzle"), while others, in Devanagari script, had Hindi or Marwari endings. Sirsi offered a small packet of M&Ms for the return of completed coloring books. This plan nearly ended in disaster when more coloring books were returned than had been handed out—some teachers had traced them onto ditto masters and produced their own copies—and he ran out of candy. Luckily, the disgruntled parents that appeared at Sirsi's doorstep were pacified with tea, *churma*, and curd by a quick-witted servant, and analysis of the coloring books could begin.

Sirsi had hoped to find children who had trouble with the same grammatical rules in all three languages. At first he thought he had found many such cases, but it turned out that these coloring books had been filled out by children younger than the eight-year-olds Sirsi had targeted. Other anomalies were due to children who spoke no English or no Marwari, or whose dialects of English simply lacked the features being tested. This left only one anomalous result: two children who apparently spoke no Marwari had incorrectly formed the feminine of adjectives in Hindi—a task that has no analogue in English. The children were evidently siblings; they had the same surname and lived at the same address. A dispirited Sirsi visited their home, assuming he would find a family fluent only in English and some other Indian language—perhaps Bengali, which lacks morphological gender distinctions. When he arrived at the door, however, he found himself unable to explain his purpose to the children's parents because both spoke fluent Hindi but no English!

Returning the next day with a servant (she of the *churma* and curd) as an interpreter, Sirsi showed the coloring books to various members of the children's extended family. Eight out of the seventeen family members that Sirsi tested had difficulty with the gender of adjectives. When such problems were presented, their answers were correct no more than half the time. Yet they correctly answered all the remaining questions in Sirsi's repertoire. Sirsi found no other indication of neurological impairment; school records showed I.Q. scores of 104 and 108 for the two children, along with a history of good grades. The oldest family member with the disorder was the children's maternal grandfather, who had passed it on to all of his daughters but none of his sons—a pattern that suggested dominant inheritance on the X chromosome.

Sirsi next obtained MRI images of the brains of six family members as they answered a second series of grammatical fill-in-the-blanks. As a control, he ran the same tests on two family members whose grammar was unimpaired.

As expected, the MRIs showed differences in brain activity between the affected and normal patients when they tried to inflect gendered adjectives. But the differences were nowhere near the areas of the brain usually associated with grammar. Instead they were in regions of the frontal lobe associated with higher cognition and memory. Despite this anomaly, Sirsi wrote up the results in the *Journal of Neurolinguistics* (No. 16, 2004, pp. 189–195.) Partly on the strength of this publication, he was offered a non-tenure-track teaching position at the University of Toronto, and reluctantly set his plans for further fieldwork aside.

A few months after his article appeared, Sirsi received a letter from Dr. Sandra Botkin. Botkin, an occupational therapist, recalled working with a patient who had been admitted after an

8 mm. hole was bored diagonally through his brain during an archery competition. This patient had consistently referred to the male nurses on staff as "she." After hearing staff members grouse about the patient's sexism on three separate occasions, Botkin had begun to suspect that he really could not help himself. When she presented him with photographs cut from *People* magazine and Polaroid snapshots of obstetrics personnel, she found that he consistently identified short-haired women as men, and men in nurse's uniforms as women. She presented this finding to the patient's neurologist, who identified it as a limited form of prosopagnosia: the patient was unable to identify gender cues in faces. But Botkin, who had logged far more hours with the patient than the neurologist had, felt that the disorder went deeper than mere facial recognition.

Botkin's letter then called attention to one of the drawings that Sirsi had used to elicit gendered adjectives from his subjects. (A page from the coloring book had been reproduced with the article.) The first panel showed a very tall building and used the feminine form of a nonsense adjective. The second panel showed a very tall man and required the respondent to fill in the masculine form of the adjective. Did all the questions Sirsi had asked rely on pictures of men and women to elicit gendered adjectives, Botkin queried? If so, might his subjects—like her patient—simply have been unable to identify the drawing as a man rather than a woman? This would explain why they answered such questions incorrectly about half the time. It would also explain why the differences in brain activity were not in the expected regions. Perhaps her patient and Sirsi's subject shared the same disorder—one neither perceptual nor linguistic, but cognitive. Perhaps the misfired gene and the misfired arrow had abolished the power to distinguish the sexes of humankind.

"I know it sounds strange," she concluded, "but it's really no weirder than hemi-neglect or blind-sight." Blind-sight, a condition resulting from lesions to certain areas of the brain, results in apparently total blindness. Yet when asked to humor the researcher and guess where a light has been placed, the patient with blind-sight can point to it almost infallibly—all the while insisting that he cannot see a thing. Hemi-neglect is a loss of awareness of one half of the body; some victims wash only the right half of their bodies, and ardently deny ownership of their own left arms.

Finding the Gene

Sirsi was sufficiently intrigued by Botkin's hypothesis to contact his former servant in Rajasthan. After a frustrating and expensive series of international phone calls, he tried to ask her to talk to the family he had studied and report any curiosities in their use of pronouns. But no sooner had he made this request than the servant said that yes, of course, several members of that strange family had acted as if she were a man. She had not mentioned it because it didn't matter; hadn't the study been about language? Since he had been deliberately vague about his study's topic in order to keep her from accidentally influencing the results, Sirsi had to swallow his frustration.

Sirsi and Botkin could not immediately go to Rajasthan, so they used samples Sirsi had previously taken in an effort to identify the gene for agenesis of gender ideation, hoping to find it in families closer to home. A preliminary analysis found six candidate genes on the X chromosome that were present in all the affected family members but none of the others. Two of these genes had well-known functions and could be discarded, but Sirsi and Botkin had to find and interview people with each of the other four. Ten years ago this would have been an impossible task; the availability of genetic databases made it feasible, though not precisely easy (people are understandably alarmed when asked to come in for tests based on a cell sample taken five years ago).

Eventually Sirsi and Botkin did find an individual who sorted photographs of men and women with little better than chance accuracy. Though everyone in the family denied that anything was odd about their views of gender, three women and one man proved to have the condition (by this time dubbed *genagnosia*). The genagnosics seemed to compensate for their disability by not using gendered pronouns to refer to a person until they had managed to overhear some hint of his or her gender. This works fairly well in a language like English, in which only pronouns are gendered; it would be useless in Hindi.

To avoid unconscious bias in the selection of photographs, Sirsi and Botkin used DVD movies for their first experiment. A computer displayed random frames from the disks in a DVD-ROM carousel, and, using speech synthesis, asked a question from a randomized list. The genagnosics in this study were able to correctly answer "Where is the actress?" with "She is behind the plant," and "Where is the actor?" with "He is on the wing of the plane"—demonstrating that they could use pronouns correctly as long as they had a hint about the gender of the person referred to. However, when chance produced a reversal of pronouns—e.g., when a question asked for a description of "the actress" and the only person on screen was John Travolta—the subjects carried over the incorrect gender rather than substitute a correct pronoun. On questions that provided no clue to the actor's gender, at least forty percent of the time they referred to Arnold Schwarzenegger as "she" and Meryl Streep as "he." A control group achieved one hundred percent accuracy in this task.

In another experiment, Sirsi and Botkin asked genagnosics to choose photographs that showed potential mates. The objects of desire they chose were male and female at a ratio of almost exactly 1:1. It is a puzzle how three successive generations of genagnosics in this family managed to legally marry; perhaps they responded to encouragement or discouragement from unaffected friends and relatives, or perhaps they were guided by preferences for particular sex acts that even a genagnosic could not confuse. Sirsi tried to sound out one of the older family members on this subject, but determined that the topic was too sensitive to broach. He did, however, manage to determine by experiment that one young genagnosic who frequently expressed disdain for homosexuals was in fact unable to tell a same-sex couple from an opposite-sex one.

"I Don't Think It's Me"

Sometimes an experiment reveals more about the experimenters than the subjects. Initially, rather than having a computerized voice ask questions, Sirsi and Botkin used graduate students who had not been told what they were trying to prove. But these assistants had to be replaced, one after another, for arguing with the subjects about their answers. "There's something about this disease," Sirsi says. "When a prosopagnosic is trying to identify the picture, you watch in a kind of mute horror. When a genagnosic says Glenn Close is a man, your instincts tell you he's just being difficult."

Transcripts of these arguments were preserved, and they are in some ways more compelling than the experiments' official results. One first-time assistant, astonished that a subject had called Danny DeVito "the actress," kept asking the same question over and over in hope of getting a different answer. The subject repeated the same answer three times, growing more and more frustrated each time, and finally snapped "One of us is wrong here, and I don't think it's me."

Sirsi and Botkin eventually realized that the exact scope of their subjects' impairment would have to be teased out by interview, producing the following remarkable exchange:

Sirsi: "Do some people have breasts?"

X: ". . . Yes."

Sirsi: "Which people?"

X: "All people."

Sirsi [regrouping]: "Breasts larger than a teacup?"

X: "Some of them."

Sirsi: "And can some people bear children, out of their own bodies?"

X: "Some of them."

Sirsi [triumphantly]: "Now, those two kinds of people we just talked about, are they the same people?"

X thought about this for nearly fifteen seconds before answering, "Sometimes." When Sirsi repeated the question a few minutes later, X repeated his answer, annoyed; but when he asked it again during the next weekly session, X again had to think a long time before answering. X could not remember the association between breasts and childbirth from session to session. And no amount of badgering could convince him to combine individual observations about men and women into a unified concept of gender.

THE NUCLEATION MODEL

This result led Sirsi to the theory of innate ideas he presented in his famous paper, "Congenital Agenesis of Gender Ideation in a Midwestern Family" (*Journal of Neurolinguistics* No. 20, 2006, pp. 35–44). "X could understand correlations between the various traits that make up manhood or womanhood," Sirsi wrote, "but he could not retain the information—as if he had no mental file drawer to put it in."

Sirsi likens the mind to a fluid in which all the raw data of perception are dissolved. An innate concept, like a seed crystal, can cause ideas to solidify around it. Some perceptions will crystallize while others remain dissolved; a different seed could produce different ideas. But a seed will not produce crystal unless the right kind of perceptions are in solution—which helps keep innate concepts from producing mental models that are radically at odds with our experience.

Sirsi contrasts his nucleation model with the "mandation model" that the discovery of innate ideas might tempt us to adopt. We might suppose that the ideas we are born with directly control our understanding; but if that were true, we would not be able to change our minds or to learn anything. On the nucleation model, innate ideas merely help our perceptions to structure themselves. So transient and local information about the sexes, such as differences in clothing and hairstyle, can become part of our ideas of gender—like an impurity in the crystal—even though they are too variable to be directly programmed by our genes. Also, useful perceptions may languish in unconsciousness because there is no seed for them; but above a certain concentration, ideas may precipitate without seed. True, the idea of gender did not crystallize in X's mind even when Sirsi attempted to seed it with an elementary association. But other ideas, Sirsi hopes, may prove more plastic.

Minnesota Twins

Botkin, still working as an occupational therapist at St. Eleggua Hospital in Minneapolis, received a phone call one day from a graduate student working in an ongoing identical-twin study. The researchers had found "her gene" in a pair of identical twins; the twins, however, displayed no obvious impairment of gender ideation. Would she be interested in interviewing them?

Botkin was. Again she applied the technique of asking the subjects to identify photographs, but this time she used only photos of doctors in surgical garb—reasoning that this epicene apparel would reveal even a well-hidden cognitive defect. The twins, however, effortlessly identified all the pictures as male or female—except one. That photograph—of Dr. Lisa D'Aout, a pediatric urologist—they refused to classify. When pressed, each twin independently produced the same word of a private language the two had shared as children, and declined to explain further.

Puzzled by this result, Botkin mused aloud in the hospital cafeteria as to just what trait of D'Aout's might have produced the twins' anomalous response. At last an R.N. with whom

Botkin was dining explained what, seemingly, everyone on staff but Botkin knew. D'Aout was a female pseudohermaphrodite. She had been the plaintiff in a landmark 2001 case against the hospital, applying the Minnesota Human Rights Act's provisions for transgendered people to intersexuals.

Botkin explained her results to D'Aout, who responded with skepticism. But after being introduced to the twins, D'Aout agreed to put out a request for photographs in the newsletter of a national intersex organization. Not only did the twins correctly sort these photographs from the male and female controls, they distinguished accurately between such different intersexual conditions as true hermaphroditism, gonadal agenesis, and male and female pseudohermaphroditism. The most impressive result involved women with complete Androgen Insensitivity Syndrome, who have XY chromosomes. The twins distinguished these women from those with XX chromosomes with one hundred percent accuracy on the basis of head and shoulders photographs—a feat that no endocrinologist on staff could duplicate!

Although the twins had not been told what the study was trying to prove, by this point they clearly knew what was going on, so Botkin asked them if they could provide any further information about the control photographs. After some hesitation—which Botkin attributes, not to the difficulty of the task, but to a crisis of trust—they picked up the pile of control photographs and sorted them into a total of 22 categories, each one corresponding to a word in their private language. Botkin numbered these categories and began to investigate what they might mean. Categories 9 and 21 proved to identify women born with clitoromegaly and men born with hypospadias, respectively, even though these are minor cosmetic conditions of the genitals with no known effect on clothed appearance. Category 6 comprised people with high scores on the Bem test of psychological androgyny. Again, it is not clear how this could be distinguished from a photograph, but the twins' identifications have proved to be repeatable. Number 18, whose exact biological meaning is unclear, includes a disproportionate number of people with a family history of osteoporosis; two women and one man in the category have since been diagnosed with bone loss themselves. Perhaps most strikingly, categories 4 and 9 identified men and women who took artificial sex hormones rather than producing them naturally, even when this was the result of hysterectomy or accidental castration rather than of a genetic difference.

Of the nine categories that still elude analysis, Botkin says: "I'm convinced that these identify real things too. There's a kind of a family resemblance among the people in each category. I've found myself meeting a person and thinking, 'I know he's an eight. He's got to be an eight.' I can *see* it. But I can't define it."

"The last straw," as Botkin puts it, came when she visited the twins after being told by her physician that she was entering an early menopause. Upon hearing this, the twins exchanged what Botkin calls "significant glances" and said: "Don't worry. Your sex won't be changing for another few years yet." It didn't.

These results led Botkin to propose a new model for the influence of genes on gender ideation. She suggests that patients with genagnosia are not impoverished by a lack of information, but bewildered by an overplus; the concepts "male"and "female" identify too great a range of variation to be understood. What the gene knocks out, then, is a filtering capacity that tells us what information to ignore. The twins Botkin studied were able to overcome this handicap—aided by their high intelligence and, perhaps, by their ability to compare notes.

Confirming this model of innate concepts will require more evidence than a single pair of twins, however. One of us (Sirsi) still prefers the nucleation model, which most of our colleagues have found more plausible. The twins' ability to tell men from women could be explained by variable penetration of the genagnosia gene. Their feats of identification might be duplicated by others with sufficient practice. Only further study will tell for sure.

The Voice of the Whirlwind

As we observed at the beginning of this essay, philosophers have been talking about innate ideas at least since Plato. Most have supposed that innate ideas were given by God, and therefore must be true. If we find instead that our innate ideas were formed by evolution, then they need not be correct at all, as long as they lead to the reproduction of the genes that produce them. Even modern thinkers that embrace the concept of innate ideas, such as Noam Chomsky, have often failed to come to grips with this possibility. As Geoffrey Sampson points out in his 1980 volume *Making Sense*: "Chomsky does not suggest that we might have innate predispositions to analyse the world in terms of inappropriate concepts or to hold false beliefs, although logically this should be equally compatible with the notion of innately limited minds" (p. 6).

Our findings provide no defense against this troubling suggestion. We may indeed cling to mistaken ideas because our mental organization requires them. We may reject plain facts because our minds cannot grasp them. Even science, for all its self-correcting mechanisms, may be permanently unable to arrive at certain truths. Dr. Anne Marlowe-Shilling, a noted critic of sex-differences research, pointed out to us that while many thousands of studies have been done to tease out sex-linked capabilities and personality traits, none, until our chance discovery, had been done to determine whether some people might be genetically predisposed to believe in "brain sex." Indeed, preliminary research indicates that the propensity to do brain sex studies is at least as strongly influenced by genetics as any of the traits such studies have analyzed. One of our graduate students is now trying to find a gene that determines whether the brain-sex researcher will find a positive result.

How, then, can we know whether we know anything? The very discovery that has raised this question may eventually provide an answer to it. Perhaps one day we will transcend the limits of human knowledge by consulting such people as Botkin's twins and the family in Rajasthan. Sirsi has now begun a series of studies designed to find out whether genagnosics' perceptions might not be *more* accurate in some respects than other humans'. For example, when genagnosics are asked to sort photographs of people into "short," "average," and "tall" without reference to sex, their choices correlate well with statistical norms. Most control subjects cannot discard gender from their considerations, even when they are admonished to do so.

Sirsi points out that other humans can match the genagnosics' accuracy at height-sorting if they are told the average height and shown photographs of people standing in front of a height scale, as in a police lineup. So perhaps general cognition can overcome the predispositions foisted on us by innate ideas. Sirsi cites a study in which a chimpanzee was allowed to choose between two stacks of candy, then was given the stack he did *not* choose (Boysen & Bernston, 1995). Although he clearly understood the rules of the game, he chose the larger stack every time—only to immediately cover his eyes in self-reproach, realizing he had once again been trapped by instinct. When the experimenters taught the chimpanzee Arabic numerals, however, he could readily choose the smaller number to get the larger treat. Using numbers rather than real candy seemed to help the chimp overcome an instinctive response and use general cognition instead. Sirsi suggests that humans may prove "as smart as chimps"—we, too, may be able to use general cognition to overcome our innate ideas, if we cling fast to symbolic manipulation and quantification and try to ignore common sense.

Botkin, however, suspects that the problem may go even deeper. Rather than applying general cognition to a problem ordinarily handled by its own cognitive organ, Botkin sees the twins as using one specialized function to substitute for another. "Most people think that general cognition is a sort of fluid that sloshes in to fill any gaps between the innate ideas," she says. "I think the brain is more like a box full of specialized tools—but if your toolbox is missing a hammer, you can always pound nails with a screwdriver."

In particular, she suspects the twins have converted a brain function ordinarily used to recognize species of animal. Unlike the gender ideation organ, this faculty does not require a division into only two classes, so it does not filter out as much information. It filters enough, however, to keep the twins from having to avoid pronouns. "The twins are saying, 'suppose the sexes are like species.' They're not compensating with general cognition, they're compensating by metaphor."

"People want to believe in general cognition," she adds. "We want to believe that the brain is some sort of universal computing engine that can do anything—learn any possible fact, entertain any possible idea. So when we find something like a separate module for gender ideation, they just say that, well, that isn't a part of general cognition, but everything else still is. Maybe so. But what if we just keep carving away at general cognition until there's nothing left?"

If Botkin is right, then we can never be completely free of our innate ideas. By applying several metaphors successively we may be able to limit their effects, but even if we overcame all of them, we could never be sure that we had. Our knowledge of the world, although not totally illusory, is filtered through an unreliable narrator whose biases deny us direct access to the truth.

"It's easy to act as if nothing has changed," Botkin muses. "Most days I don't even think about the implications of what we've found. And then I'll meet someone, and I'll start thinking, 'He's a twelve. I know he's a twelve. How do I know he's a man?' "

MARTHA SOUKUP

THE HOUSE OF EXPECTATIONS

"Are you having an affair?" Miranda asked him. Tom watched her as she sat on the edge of the bed rubbing her feet, pinched and red after a night of performing in spike heels.

"No," he said.

She gave him a considering look over the foot propped up on her knee. She had taken off the long red plastic fingernails, but her toenails were still painted bright and strange on her shoe-deformed toes. Tom wondered why women did that.

"That's too bad," she said. "Might do you some good."

She was fresh out of her four A.M. shower, wrapped in a huge towel with the name of the casino and hotel they both worked for woven into the pile. The false eyelashes were in a heap on the bathroom counter with the plastic fingernails and all the various hairpins; the blue and black and red and peach-colored powders and creams had swirled down the shower drain. The red toenails were the only color left that wasn't her. Dark tangles of hair clung wetly to her neck and forehead. Her breasts swung under the towel as she rubbed her foot. Tom thought she was a hundred times more beautiful than the feathered and corseted figurine the tourists had watched in a line of identical figurines hours ago: that he was a hundred times more lucky to be looking at her now.

He pushed down an impulse to shake the cool certainty off her face.

"I don't," he said carefully, "want anyone else."

"Oh bullshit," Miranda said. "You're a man."

"That's not fair and you know it."

"When's the last time we had sex?" she said, reaching for the bottle of lotion.

It was not a conversation he wanted to be having. It was not a fight he wanted to have again. There were never any words to just make things be the way they should be, simple and straightforward. What he wanted to say was, Stop it. Stop making things complicated. We'll make love now, or if we don't we won't make it worse by going *on* about it.

He'd said that. He'd said it enough times that it had distilled into the short version: Jesus Christ just shut up, would you?

That didn't work either. Rather spectacularly it didn't.

So he said, "That doesn't matter," which wasn't exactly true or false, but was better than following Miranda into the whole morass of complications made, as far as he could tell, of words alone.

"Bullshit," she said again. "I get home after three, you go to work at eight, we have sex once a month and at least one of us is exhausted. This doesn't bother you? Look me in the eye and say that."

"Do you want me to find a night job?"

"Jesus," she said. "I'm not trying to tell you how to run your life. I'm just asking you to be honest."

"You're telling me to go have an affair!"

Miranda shrugged. "Stress management."

"You don't mean it."

"Sex is sex, Tom," Miranda said. "That's not the problem in our relationship."

"But— What's the problem in our relationship?" he asked her, baffled and frustrated. "Is there a problem?"

"If you want there to be."

He had set the alarm to be awake when she got home, and even had thought it might be one of those nights when, groggy though he was on first waking and tired though she was after a night's work, they would put everything aside and he would prove through her body with his how much he did love her, leaving words and jobs and schedules behind for a sweet, strenuous hour of certain goals and clarity. Or half an hour. A lecture about looking for orgasms elsewhere was not what he'd expected.

He lay on the bed staring at the wall away from Miranda, listening to her long shallow breaths. A fight couldn't keep her awake when she was as tired as dancing with forty-pound headpieces on made a person.

Stupid damn job.

He kept his foot and leg and arm from touching her in any place and itched for the feel of flesh on flesh.

Or anything he understood.

What the hell did she want from him?

"You don't try to understand them," Phil said. He was selling Tom a shipment of laundry soap, at an introductory industrial price fifteen percent cheaper than the detergent the hotel had been using. They'd both known they were going to agree to the deal two minutes after Phil walked in, so they were killing time bullshitting over coffee. Tom needed it. "Look, I'm married seven years, right? I figured out six years ago you don't try to understand them."

"So how do you stay married seven years?" Tom asked. He

couldn't imagine asking Miranda to marry him. What kind of look would she give him? He had no idea.

"Shit, there's no trick. You just stay married."

"How do you keep things the way they were?"

"Jesus, man, nothing stays the way it was," said Phil. He refilled his cup from Tom's office coffeemaker and put his feet up on the couch. "You look around and see kids and mortgages and bullshit and it's not exactly like the day you first wondered if you'd be getting her bra off, sweet days of youth, you know the story. She stops looking at you like you're the man, but hell, you're looking at her tit with a kid on it, it's not the sexiest thing in the world, so, fair enough."

"But you stay."

"Pretty expensive not to," Phil said. He grinned. "Anyway, the kids are corkers, you want to know, and the old lady and I get along okay no complaints if I don't try to understand her, which I'm giving you some advice here I'm guessing is a problem you've got. You don't expect it to be like it was when you were a kid and this is the person made you the horniest. You bring home flowers every couple of months, that covers the ground, don't ask me."

"Flowers," Tom said.

"And to keep the juice flowing, you go somewheres sometimes. If you don't keep the little guy awake he's never going to notice your woman after a while either, that's my theory, so it's to her benefit."

"My girlfriend says I should have an affair," Tom said.

"Well, shit! You got it covered. Smart woman at home and whatever you want away. Must be about a hundred million men in the country would envy the hell out of you." Phil laughed.

"She doesn't mean it," Tom said. He laughed too, matching Phil.

"Hey, whatever she meant she said it, you've got the out. You do what you want, man, but if your woman is going to say things like that you'd be stupid not to go with it."

"Guess so."

"She shouldn't say things she couldn't handle. You want to play this thing safe, though, keep it businesslike. You're in the great state of Nevada, man, you're in the one part of the country everyone's sensible about this stuff. A clean transaction, nothing sloppy or lingering like some woman suing you for palimony or phoning you up all the time. That's the way to do it."

Tom laughed again and reached for the detergent contract, signed it and sent Phil to his next appointment. He told his secretary to hold his calls for ten minutes. Supply negotiations held no attraction. His chest was tight. He was never going to do it.

A manila envelope came the next day printed with the return address of Phil's supply company. Tom opened it and looked at the handful of brochures inside. One of them had a Post-It on it: "Been there, done that, thumbs up!" He thought about running into Phil at a brothel out of town and slid the brochure in the trashcan. The others he put in his briefcase.

He showed them to Miranda as she was preparing for work. "Cathouses, sure," she said. She took up the top brochure. "Management is a bitch at this one. Sandy worked there for a couple of months before she got in the show. You should hear the stories she tells."

She riffled through the others.

"This one's okay. I've never heard anything bad about these guys. They've got a great benefits package. This one's new, I don't know about them."

Tom stared at her. The roses, white and pink, were in a vase she'd put on the dresser. She tossed the brochures next to them.

"Stay away from the Love Ranch if you don't want to collaborate in oppressing the worker—of course, you're management yourself, maybe you get off on workers being oppressed—other than that I don't think you're likely to go wrong." She threw the rest of her makeup and underwear into her duffle. "Gotta go. Kiss."

Feeling surrealistic, like he was in a dream or a sitcom, he kissed her goodbye.

The last digit on the clock changed from 3 to 4 to 5 through 0 and back to 3. And again. The roses didn't smell like anything in particular. Eventually he picked up the brochure for the place too new for Miranda to have an opinion about and got out the car keys to go call her bluff of calling his bluff.

If she insisted on bluffing him. If she was going to make him do it.

The House of Expectations was twenty minutes drive outside of town. Tom expected a ring on his pocket phone, Miranda calling to tell him how foolish he was falling for her joke.

The phone was silent in his pocket as he walked through the tasteful oak doors of the house.

He'd lived in Reno for ten years but had never been to one of these places. They were for the tourists. Certainly not for a man who could get a real woman.

Whatever he'd expected in the House of Expectations, it wasn't a reception desk. The woman at it was secretarial, efficient, smiling, and wearing a blouse open just wide and low enough to show a bit of the lace edging her bra and of the golden flesh lifting the lace. "May I help you?" she asked Tom, in a voice like warm caramel.

He had no plans for what to say. She seemed nice enough: under normal circumstances, if she were a receptionist with her blouse buttoned up and he were a single guy, he might have worked his way around to asking her out.

Double doors on the other side of the reception room opened. "Thanks, hon," said the big man who came through them to the receptionist. Truck driver, Tom thought. The man gave the woman a wink and she smiled back.

"See you Thursday, Pete," she said.

"Thursday, Annie," the man said. There was a current of warm air through the room as he left.

"I'm sorry," the woman, Annie, said to Tom. "You were saying?"

He was trying to think of a graceful way out. What kind of pathetic loser must he look? Buying it. At a place with regulars.

If he said, "Sorry, changed my mind," at least no one knew his name.

His pocket phone tingled.

She was calling to take it back *now*, when he was already facing down the Gorgon's receptionist? A little damn late, honey, he thought. The blood already flushing his cheeks seemed to run hot down his spine. You can just deal with what you've started.

The phone kept tingling against his hip as he told Annie, "Yes. You can help me."

It looked like a hotel on the other side of the double doors, after all: a building of some internal contradiction. Annie had pulled from her desk a drawer that contained a rack of keys, old-fashioned hotel keys, very old-fashioned, a flag of teeth appending to a long brass rod with an oval head. A small red pasteboard banner was wired to the head, the number 118 written on it in black fountain pen. Annie explained there was a microchip concealed in the antique-looking pasteboard set to chime when his time was up: key and timer, both.

In complete contrast to the efficient, modern office, the hotel walls were covered in velvet-flocked wallpaper, softly lit by electric lanterns esconced every half-dozen paces on the walls. He had to think "electric," because he might as well otherwise have stepped back more than a hundred years in time.

There was, though, an elevator, which he passed on his way to room 118. In the office, he had filled out a short form asking him what he looked for in an assignation, selecting keywords that suggested practicality and a minimum of fuss. When he handed it to Annie the receptionist, she had slotted it into her desktop, remarking that his preferences would be saved, but that he could change them when he came back to the House of Expectations.

When he came back. Unlikely, once Miranda had a chance to reflect. To his other concern, Annie assured him that everything in the House's system was coded and double-coded. "Our patrons' privacy is paramount," she'd assured him, in the rounded tones of a motto.

The elevator opened. Out came an unremarkable, short, balding man. Who glowed. There was no other way to describe him. Where Pete the presumed truck driver had left with the matter-of-fact satisfaction of a man who'd just had a decent steak dinner, this man—accountant?—casino money changer?—had the beatific air of a priest who had just communed with a secret god and all the universe. Tom looked away, embarrassed to have troubled this man with his scrutiny, though the other showed no sign of having noticed him.

He quickened his step, passing doors 112, 113, 114. His blood sounded in his ears. He was a simple, monogamous man, who would prove that to his woman. His pulse beat his waking cock against the increasing snugness of his briefs.

At door 118 he took a deep breath, and put the long brass key rattlingly into the keyhole.

Tom had as many images of prostitutes as he'd seen in movies and sniggered over in junior-high gym class. He expected someone who made herself up as Miranda did when she was working: false, painted; maybe giggling.

Instead Cynthianne, true to what he had checked on the palm-pad form, was straightforward, casual, and pleasant. She reminded him more than a little of Miranda, the first time he had met her, scrubbed and casual on her way to work at their mutual employer the casino.

Cynthianne chatted with him about the weather and poured him a drink from the room's wet bar. She was someone Tom would ask out. But he had employed her, and the next hour's script was set in its principles if not in its particulars. He nearly thought he should apologize, but Cynthianne herself seemed too at ease for there to be sense in that.

She was very pretty, in a long, sleeveless cotton dress and sandals, a little lightly dressed for the air conditioning, her dark hair hanging loosely round her shoulders. In the draft, her nipples stood against the thin material of the dress. His erection became uncomfortable in its confinement, as he tried to figure out what to say.

"Don't worry," Cynthianne said, smiling a practiced smile, "I'm the professional here."

And half an hour later she sighed and hitched her scooped-out bra back on.

"I'm sorry," Tom said. "I guess this won't look good on your record, but it's not your fault, I promise it isn't."

"Don't worry. These things happen. I'm a salaried professional, I don't get my buck by the bang."

"You're really beautiful and everything—"

"Really, my ego isn't tied up in this," she said. "I know I'm good at what I do. My record's quite good. Probably I just wasn't your type."

She was exactly his type, trim, curvy, confident, smart and straightforward. It was mortifying to have his body betray him, his insistent erection think better of things and duck out the back without him.

"You're very beautiful," was all he could think of to say, stupidly, again.

"Don't sweat it. Sex is sex," Cynthianne said. She pulled the sundress down over sleek shoulders, perfect breasts, tender barely-rounded belly and rounder sweet lips, lovely, perfect, sensible, distant. Tom felt even more uselessly naked. He scrambled for his briefs and hastened into them.

"Look, it really is okay," she said as he fished under the bed for his socks, not meeting her eyes. "You're a nice guy. And I get paid anyway. It happens, you'd be amazed how often it happens."

"It never happens to me" would be a weak cliche. Had she been a date instead of—a hire—Tom would have offered to do something to make sure she was happy. He'd been told he was good with his tongue. He'd even suggested it, but she'd smiled gently and told him that wasn't what she was there for, though she was willing if it was what he really wanted, for a slight extra charge.

Which had rather deflated him the rest of the way.

Cynthianne slid her sandals onto her bare feet, running a finger along the back straps to adjust them, and opened the drawer in the bedside table. "If you need any proof that it happens, look where we keep the forms. Ready at a moment's notice." She held out a piece of paper; he zipped his fly and took it. "The House has a guarantee of satisfaction. Annie at the desk told you, right? Right. You just fill this out and give it to her. Wait a sec, give it back." She initialed a spot in the lower corner.

"I'm not looking for a freebie," Tom said.

"Don't think of it as a freebie. You haven't got what you paid for. We're new on the block, we mean to be the best. That's what they tell us and you should believe it."

"You're—just fine, I don't want anyone thinking you—"

"Really. It won't reflect on me. I'm not what you came here looking for. They'll have you fill out more questionnaires and find out what you really want. No harm done." She smiled again, kindly. "Whichever woman it is won't have any complaints. You're a very good-looking man."

Tom left the form on the bed and hurried out, down the halls, through the front door, past Annie the receptionist, who waved.

The place needed a back door.

When Miranda washed off her show face and came to bed he was startled that her naked face was so different from Cynthianne's. The woman (he couldn't think "prostitute") had, obscurely but bothersomely, reminded him of when he was first dating Miranda, when he had been able to convince himself their needs coincided.

He watched her through his eyelashes, pretending sleep, until she turned out the light and rolled over away from him, as content not to be touched as the woman at the House of Expectations: not unhappy when he was running his hands over her breasts and licking the scallops of her ears, not unhappy when he gave up, content in herself either way. To fail such a perfectly reasonable woman was. Was. Not what he had expected.

When Miranda's breathing slowed, he relaxed somewhat. She had not wakened him to ask about his sex date with a hooker: he hadn't had to say anything about it, or about why she would call him only after he had time to get to the brothel. But when the alarm went off at seven—Miranda grunted once and rolled over—he had not slept.

In the morning, in his office, he checked the messages on his pocket phone. The call the evening before had been from his mother in North Carolina.

He had put his work number on the preference form instead of his home number; he should have put a fake. "Mr. Aaron? It's Annie from the House of Expectations. Cynthianne tells us things didn't work out for you."

"She was fine," Tom said. "Excellent. She deserves a raise. Really I'm quite satisfied, thanks very much, goodbye."

The phone rang again. "We don't want you to walk away unsatisfied, Mr. Aaron," Annie's warm voice said. "Many of our clients take a time or two to find what they're looking for. Some of them are a little embarrassed: that's normal and nothing to worry about, but please allow us to make it up to you. Satisfaction is our specialty. We want you to be fully satisfied."

"I'm not looking for anything," Tom said.

"That's fine, Mr. Aaron. Your account is on file. It we can be of help to you in future, do remember that it's on us until you are happy with the service."

He thanked her and hung up again.

Miranda never asked. A week later he brought home flowers, tiger lilies this time. It was one of her days off, which didn't coincide with his, but he was ready for her, and she was relaxed and cheerful. He made dinner, put on music, and had her clothes off by ten P.M., though it was still morning for her and she rarely aroused so early.

She did.

He didn't.

But she told him it wasn't important.

"Mr. Aaron, it's good to see you again," said Annie. Her business suit's blouse was buttoned demurely to her neck, but she sat far enough back from the desk for him to see the high slit in her woolen skirt, and the barest edge of a garter. If he worked in brothel supply instead of hotel supply, he'd know the garter vendor. He wanted to ask.

Instead he filled out another electronic form on the palmtop. This one asked a lot of unrelated questions: what flavor ice cream he liked and what he liked on it, the last two gubernatorial candidates he'd voted for, what color a dog should be, the best method of disciplining recalcitrant children, what name he'd take if he woke the next morning as a woman. Ridiculous questions.

A middle-aged woman was leaving as he finished, an embarrassed, pleased flush on her face. The House of Expectations, its brochure pointed out, served both sexes and all tastes.

"Mmmmm," Annie said, when she'd slotted in his data and looked at her readouts. "I tell you what. We'll give this a try, but remember if it's not to your liking, you can come right back and let me know about it."

Room 206 was dark. He didn't see Kira at first when he edged open the door.

"Here," she said from the shadows. "Now."

"Um," Tom said.

The bed was a four-poster. Leather straps at its four corners; something unidentifiable hanging from the ceiling. Once he and Miranda had had some pot and some wine and he'd tied her to the bed's legs with some of her old stockings. It had been okay, but they never bothered with it again.

"I'm Kira," she said. "Strip."

He tried. He did. His erection was disconcertingly fierce; his cock strained as though for escape.

But when she lightly slapped his testicles he yelped. He felt like someone sneering during a movement of Beethoven. When she told him to lick her instep until she told him he'd got it right, it was like the hated dance unit in seventh-grade gym: is this the right movement, that, what does it look like from where the teacher is standing? Kira clipped something to the tender skin over his balls and he yelped again, feeling in equal parts the shock of pain and a detached bemusement at the soberness of her performance. She sent a low buzz of electricity through him, and it simply was a feeling he had no referent for, alien and unsexual.

He didn't have a script. The erection surprised him with persistence, but in his self-consciousness it came to no more than that, until his arousal itself became another alienated source of discomfort he could do nothing about.

"I'm really sorry," he said finally. "Could you unbuckle me?"

Kira swung her leg back from across his neck to the bed and loosed his bonds. "You usually don't do this, right?"

"You could say that," Tom said. She tossed him his briefs and he put them on gratefully. "This, uh, guys go for it?"

"Guys, women," she said. "It's a people thing. Control issues, power issues, everything's tied up with sex. You should excuse me saying. I usually get the newbies. This room's for tame. Guys find out what they really like and graduate to specialists."

"I guess I flunked," Tom said.

"No grief," said Kira. "I get my nut in any case."

Tom smiled and winced and rubbed his crotch gingerly.

"You should excuse me saying. Don't sweat it, anyway. It's just sex." Outside the perplexing script, she wasn't that much different than Cynthianne: matter-of-fact. Or Miranda. Actually now that he was feeling more comfortable with her, the pressure in his balls and cock was subsiding. It was something of a relief.

Kira initialed a form for him and waved an offhanded good-bye from the shadows of her room.

"You must be having an affair," Miranda said slantwise from her pillow. "Or the cathouse thing. Is it helping?"

"I don't want to," Tom said.

"Fuck?"

That too, he thought. "Fight again."

"Who said it's fighting? You say that," she said.

He put in earplugs and rolled over.

Annie was wearing a demure dark business dress. When she turned to answer the phone, Tom saw the back was scooped down far enough to show she couldn't be wearing panties. "Midnight will be fine, Mr. P.," she said. "Kate will look forward to it." She typed a few things into her desk system and looked up. "Mr. Aaron, what a pleasure."

"I know it's been a while," he said.

"Five weeks is nothing between friends and business associates," she said pleasantly. Her hair was up in a loose bun, fastened with a small silver spear, one lock trailing down her neck, down her bare back. She was utterly untouchable. As many horny clients as passed through her door, Tom was sure, none of them would ever attempt to lay a finger on her.

"You know, that Kira you sent me to last time," he said. "She was a nice girl. Woman."

"Thank you. We're very pleased with her. She gets excellent notices."

"But not, well, my type."

"Alas, apparently."

"You guarantee satisfaction."

"If you need satisfaction, Mr. Aaron, we will find it for you. Whatever it may take," said Annie in her golden voice.

He was taken to a white and steel room. He was given a score more tests. White-coated technicians drew blood. His brain was scanned while music played and lists of words were read into headphones.

"You understand, Mr. Aaron," Annie said, "that your satisfaction is guaranteed for your initial payment. There is no fee for any of this work, and no payment for the happy fulfillment of your deepest expectations. If what you require is expensive: well, one might say, the first taste is free. You must decide from there on. We believe in satisfaction and in honesty."

"Thanks," said Tom. Some obscure stubbornness drove him to take up the House of Expectations on their pledge and Miranda at her word. He guessed he'd had a thousand free orgasms in his life, two thousand, if you didn't count things like dinner bills, and he wasn't about to start budgeting for them now. He could still have an orgasm in the privacy of his office bathroom, for god's sake. Absolutely free, and no itchy condom. Big deal, this that everyone paid so much money for.

The House owed him exactly one good orgasm. More than one, for his troubles, but he was a reasonable man.

They finished their tests and Annie came to him, in a business suit with no slits or plunges or openings at all that made him wish she were touchable. She told him they had one person who might suit. He would have to sign a nondisclosure agreement. A nondisclosure agreement. He imagined unsavory things—underage Mormon teenagers kidnapped from Utah. Women kept in cages twenty-four hours a day. Animals. What did they think they saw in their ridiculous tests? He was a simple man looking for nothing complicated, nothing kinky or convoluted, just the smallest accommodation.

"There is nothing illegal in this House, Mr. Aaron," Annie said. "Nothing our employees have agreed to has come to the disapproving attention of lawmakers. There is no reason to change that, when we are fulfilling our vocation to provide satisfaction on all sides."

"You can't legally bind me to agree to cover up a crime," Tom said, testing; "That's quite right, Mr. Aaron," she agreed, serenely.

He signed the agreement and was sent home. His room, Annie said, would be ready the next evening.

The key was labeled 323. It was on the top floor of the House of Expectations. Tom walked slowly up the stairs. The nondisclosure agreement had not been long: he was accustomed to signing long contracts. It was short, to the point, and without loopholes. He wasn't to tell anyone what he encountered in room 323, as long as it involved nothing illegal.

He was in no hurry to find what was on the other side of the door. It could be the most beautiful woman in Nevada, and he didn't know that he'd respond in this mood.

All down the hall he found no room numbered 323. When he was about to give up, he noticed a door wholly unlabeled.

He hesitated, then tried the key in the lock.

The room was simple. A bed, a desk, a dresser, a chair. In the chair sat a woman, reading.

She was blond, small. Her hair was straight and her clothes simple. She was probably a few years younger than he was, twenty-six, twenty-seven. She was nice-looking enough, not someone he'd look at twice in the grocery. She seemed nothing like a working girl.

Maybe a customer, he thought. Kira had women clients.

"Excuse me," he said. "These old-fashioned locks, I always thought you could open one with any key if it jostled right— Um. Is this room 323?"

She put down her book and smiled at him. "Yes. Hi."

"Do. Um. Do you work here?"

"I live here," she said.

"You live here?" She nodded. The hotel he worked for had a few permanent residents. Tom could have had a suite there himself if he hadn't been more comfortable elsewhere. "Are you related to the owners?"

She smiled again, delightedly. "It's family, yes," she said. "What's your name?"

Her name was Elspeth, which was the last thing he found out about her for a long time, because somehow he was telling her everything about himself instead. How he had come to Reno as a twenty-year-old college graduate to make his fortune; how tedious being a successful executive had turned out to be; how he missed going to Braves games, still, after ten years; how he'd met Miranda in the hotel coffeeshop, in her jeans and a t-shirt and no makeup, and saw her later in the casino's showroom and kept his proud secret, the real woman, his, under the make-believe for-tourists glitter.

Elspeth had taken his hand. He told her how Miranda had become harder and harder to be with, how inexplicably difficult everything had become.

"It's not fair," she told him. "You're a wonderful man, you would make anyone happy."

"Not her," he said. "She doesn't act like I'm anything wonderful."

"I think you're wonderful," she said.

And he told her what he could never imagine telling Miranda about, the abortive attempts with Cynthianne and Kira. That they'd made him nervous somehow. It wasn't embarrassing to tell Elspeth. "I don't know anything about the people who work here," she said.

"That's it," Tom said. "They're working. It shouldn't matter, should it?"

"Of course," she said, "of course it matters. You deserve so much more than that, Thomas. Not like you were some—"

"John."

"I can't even say that word. What do poor men named John think of it? You deserve someone who sees how wonderful you are."

When she said it he believed it. He took her other hand and squeezed it. She wasn't ordinary-looking at all, really she was beautiful with her eyes lit up like that. He looked into her eyes and he kissed her, and she kissed back.

The key chimed. The microchip in the pasteboard: he hadn't got so far on the two appointments he'd had, with Cynthianne and Kira. He didn't want Annie sending anyone to look for him, and finding him here.

"I'll see you again," he said to Elspeth.

"Thomas," she said, and her breath caught and she smiled like the sun rising over the desert.

Annie didn't say anything when he laid the key on her desk and left. She smiled, cool and professional.

He wanted to phone her but he didn't know how to ask for her. He could reach her through the central switchboard, probably, but then Annie would answer. No.

If he just went back.

He did.

"Mr. Aaron, how are you? Satisfied?"

"Sure. Fine. I'd like the same again, please."

Annie raised a perfect eyebrow. "That's expensive, Mr. Aaron, you understand."

He nodded and let her run his credit card again and took the stairs by twos. The key still opened the door. He thought to knock before pushing the door open.

"Come in?"

When she saw it was him, Elspeth put down the book she was reading, her face alight. "Thomas!" Then she was in his arms, kissing him.

"Oh, I'm sorry!" she said, pulling back a moment. "I shouldn't assume—I was just so happy to—"

"Elspeth," he said. "Elspeth."

She wouldn't leave her room: two small rooms, it turned out, with a connecting door, a tiny suite. They would lie together holding hands like teenagers on her little bed, as he tried to talk her into moving in with him. "It's not a good place to live," he argued. "Not that I'd say anything about the way anyone makes an honest living—"

"My friends are all here," she said.

"Do you love me?" he asked.

"Oh Thomas." She curled her fingers in his hair and sighed and smiled. "I love you."

"Won't you do it for me? It's so hard to see you here."

"Anything for you, Thomas, anything," she said, honest, adoring, perfect. "But I can't leave my friends. I can't leave my home. They visit me here." From anyone else he would argue. But he would do nothing to make her unhappy.

That month, Miranda moved out. He felt sadder telling Elspeth and hearing her gentle sympathy than he had when he came home and found the note: a sweet sadness Elspeth comforted.

The bill on his credit card ran up.

But he knew. Had expected it, perhaps, though he hadn't thought he had.

"Mr. Aaron, if you can wait an hour," Annie said, "for your usual seven o'clock." A keyhole cut in her white blouse displayed subtle formations of rounded flesh.

"I know it's six," Tom said. He had spent the day caressing Elspeth's shoulders, breasts, thighs, in his mind, talking to her, impatient with everyone else's vapid conversation. "I'll just let myself in."

"Mr. Aaron, if you'll—"

He was through the double doors and up the steps in double strides. He didn't have the key but she would let him in if the door was locked.

The door wasn't locked.

Somewhere in the middle of it he recognized the man in his Elspeth's bed. The bald accountant-type he had seen months before, the man distinguishable by nothing other than his glow.

"Edward," Elspeth was murmuring over and over: "Edward, Edward! Oh." He recognized the light in her eyes, and in the accountants'. The lover's adoration she turned on him. The communion only lovers had.

The accountant was smaller and older than he and unprepared. Tom hauled him out of bed by the underarm and a thin thigh. The evidence of the other man's ardor slapped his forearm and Tom's gorge rose. He threw his naked, sweating, shocked rival into the hall.

"Edward!" Elspeth cried. She ran to the door, but he pulled her away and slammed it shut. He hardly recognized her own naked body, sticky and pale. He grabbed her shoulders and shook her. Confusion fluttered through her eyes. "Thomas?"

"Sorry I'm not your boyfriend," he said, furious. "You might have told me. How many?"

"Thomas, what's wrong?"

"How many!"

"I don't know what—"

"You said you didn't work here," he said. But part of him thought: she had said she didn't know anyone who worked there, just that. "Damn whore, I told you I loved you!"

"Thomas, what has upset you? Talk to me—"

"Who was that man? Your damn john?"

She frowned in concentration. ". . . My friend."

"But you swore you loved me—"

"I love you, Thomas," she said. "That was a friend. You are my love, I love you, more than the world, more than the sky—"

And she kept saying it, when turned away, when he ran into the bathroom and threw up, her voice behind him: "Thomas, Thomas, are you all right? I love you—"

The security men came in and took him away. The little accountant type was with them, bleating, "Elspeth, are you all right, Elspeth, I love you, tell me you're all right—"

The guards holding Tom's arms kept him from covering his ears. He heard "I love you too, Edward," in the same voice she had said. "I love you, Thomas," the first time, and a thousand times later, each time so pure and true, even to moments before when he was retching his guts out, her pure true voice rising clearly over the sound.

"Mr. Aaron, you have thoroughly broken the terms of the basic House contract," Annie said. "We are legally entitled to ask for reparations. Our lawyers have advised me to say this to you."

He didn't understand. But she wouldn't stop explaining, however much he wished.

Elspeth loved him. She loved the little accountant. She loved the guard who pulled Tom away, a man she had never seen before.

"Not real," he moaned.

"Mr. Aaron," Annie said, "not to put too fine a point on it, you have come to a brothel. You have paid for services. The ones which you did not find satisfactory, we did not charge you for. You rejected willing bodies and willing minds. We are the only house in Nevada which can supply what you came here for. Mr. Aaron, do you think love is easy to supply?"

"She isn't real."

"Of course she is," Annie said.

Elspeth's mind, body, personality were those she had always had. The only thing added was a minute microprocessor hard by her brain's septal region, experimental treatment for depression and anhedonia. She had gone to a clinic in Finland seeking medical happiness; she had returned the most helplessly loving human being a slip of medical science had ever created.

Wholly loving. If she had been a lesbian, the doctors presumed she would have felt the way toward every woman she now felt for every man.

"Not illegal," Annie said. But not something to draw attention to. "Where would she be put? A locked medical ward? We know how to take care of her, Mr. Aaron."

"It isn't real. . . ."

"She is happy. Look to your own unhappiness, Mr. Aaron. You are in no position to judge what will satisfy our employee and our ward."

He signed half a dozen more forms and waivers and the House agreed not to sue him. He didn't think they'd want the exposure of a lawsuit, but he signed anyway. They wouldn't let him see her again. He didn't want to. A hole had been kicked in his heart.

"We have failed to satisfy you, after all, Mr. Aaron," Annie said to him on the phone one day. He was in his office, his secretary holding his calls. Annie had called his personal phone.

"It doesn't matter," he said. But it did.

"What will it take to satisfy you, Mr. Aaron?

"What is your heart's desire? What do you want?"

They both knew the answer.

A key rattled in the door, and, with a tentative swing, it opened. Tom put down his book, a novel full of wonderful people, to see who it was. A woman, fiftyish, fidgety, expectant. Her makeup was awkwardly applied and she clutched at her purse.

His heart filled. She was beautiful. She needed him.

He stood, hopeful, to see if she would only just come in.

DAVID LANGFORD

A GAME OF CONSEQUENCES

THERE WERE TWO OF THEM IN THE HOT ROOM, ON THE DAY that went bad but could have been so much worse. The Mathematical Institute's air-conditioning was failing as usual to cope with heat from the angry bar of sunlight that slanted across Ceri's desktop and made the papers there too blindingly white to read. Through the window she could see an utterly cloudless sky: each last wisp of vapour had been scorched away.

Across the room where the light was kinder, Ranjit had perched on the stool and hunched himself over his beloved keyboard, rattling off initialization sequences. "Breakthrough day today!" he said cheerily.

"You say that every bloody day," said Ceri, moving to look over his shoulder.

"Yes, but this week we're getting something. I've been starting to feel a sort of, sort of . . . resonance. That's what you want, right?"

It was what she wanted. She really shouldn't feel resentful

that her frail and beautiful tracery of theory needed a computer nerd to pit it against stubborn fact. A nerd and a quantum-logic supercomputer like the Cray 7000-Q, the faculty's latest toy.

Not that Ranjit was precisely a classic nerd or geek. The man was presentable enough, not conspicuously overweight or bizarrely hair-styled, thirtysomething like Ceri herself. She might yet end up sleeping with him. Among campus women there was some mild speculation that he was gay, but Ceri put that down to his one addiction, the one he was indulging now. Sinking through the now blossoming display into a world of electronic metaphor. The rapture of the deep. She found herself worrying at a line from Nietzsche: if you struggle over-much with algorithms, you yourself become an algorithm. Gaze too long into virtual spaces, and virtual spaces will gaze into you.

False colours began to bloom in the oversized display screen as the model of Nothing shuffled itself into multi-dimensioned shape. "I like *this* color palette," he murmured. "Reminds me of being in church." It reminded Ceri of a smashed kaleidoscope.

Her virtual-space analogy—maybe some day to be expounded in a triumphalist paper by Ceri Evans Ph.D. and, oh damn, Ranjit Narayan M.Sc.—hovered on the shady side of respectable physics. Down in the spaces underneath space, so certain lines of mathematics implied, the observer and the observed melted together like Dali's soft watches. There seemed to be an entangledness, a complicity between any sufficiently detailed model and the actual dance of subatomic interaction. Then (it was her own insight, still lovingly fondled in the mind) suppose one tuned the computer model for mathematical "sweetness", for structures whose elegant symmetry had the ring of inevitable truth: a resonance with reality, a kind of chord. And then . . . what then? Maybe a digital telescope that could spy on the substrate below quantum complexity. Maybe just a vast amount of wasted computer time.

"Hey, how about a cup of coffee, Ceri?"

This, of course, was what mathematical physicists were good

for once they'd churned out a testable hypothesis. Making the coffee. She stalked through the cruel slash of sunlight to the hiding-place of her illicitly imported kettle.

There had been four of them in the hot garden, more than twenty years before: Sammy and Ceri and Dai and the English boy whose name she'd forgotten. Somewhere beyond the sheltering trees was a strong clear sun, its light flickering and strobing through leaves stirred by a breeze from up the valley. Ceri remembered pointing out how momentary apertures in the foliage acted like pinhole cameras, projecting perfect little sun-discs on to flat ground. This was of some small interest, but could not compete with the afternoon's major attraction. Sammy had an air rifle.

They made paper targets and sellotaped them to the brick wall at the garden's far end. Why was it so hard to draw a freehand circle, let alone properly concentric ones? Despite that changing dapple of light, the worn old .177-inch rifle was surprisingly accurate if you held it properly, and conventional targets soon grew boring. The English boy drew a hilarious—well, once Ceri knew who it was meant to be—caricature of Mr. Porter at the High School. When Porter had been well peppered and had only empty holes for eyes, other teachers got the same treatment.

"Moving targets, that's what!" said Sammy when a trace of tedium had again set in. But woodlice could not be persuaded to crawl sportingly along the back wall. It was populated with hundreds of the tiny, tireless mites they called red spiders, but these became invisible at any decent range.

"Oh, of course. The twigs are all moving in the breeze," Ceri suggested, and obscurely wished she hadn't. There were cries of "Bloody *hell*!" as the four came to grips with the difficulty of holding the airgun steady while firing upward at slender, swaying pencils of wood. Eventually Dai brought down a fragment of twig—"Gre-e-at! I'm the champ!"—and Ceri, mostly by luck, snipped free a broad sycamore leaf that sideslipped and jinked as it drifted reluctantly groundward.

Sammy took the rifle and reloaded. "I'll give *him* a fright," he announced, pointing to a greenfinch eyeing them from a middling-high branch.

"No," said Ceri.

"Just going for the branch, *stupid.*"

Fly away, fly away now, she thought urgently, but the bird only cocked its head to look down with the other eye. The flat *clack* of the airgun seemed especially loud, and there was a dreadful inevitability in the fall of the little green-brown bundle of feathers.

Afterwards, besides the private heartache and the recriminations concerning .177" holes that had appeared in the windows of quite surprisingly distant houses, the thing that rankled was that Sammy had been too fastidious to touch the bloodied finch. "There's things crawling on it," he said. Worse, its eye had failed to close in the proper decorum of death, and stared emptily. The English boy scraped a hole and Ceri dropped the bird into it. It was still warm.

The steady glare through the window had changed its angle now, and a third cup of coffee was going lukewarm beside the mousemat. Why did one sweat so much more than in those hot remembered days of childhood? Perhaps it was the square-cube law: more body mass, more internal heat to shed, proportionally less skin area to sweat through? Two hours of translating her mathematical intuitions into appropriate quasi-shapes and pseudo-angles for Ranjit's algorithmic probes had left Ceri with a slight headache and a tendency to stray off into such mental byways.

Ranjit stirred slightly. "I think . . . I think we might be there. In the sort of space you specified."

The flickering multicoloured gridwork on the screen looked

no different; or was it firmer, somehow more confident? "How do you know?" she asked.

"It feels right somehow. Locked-in. As though the simulation has picked up a kind of inertia." A kaleidoscope whose images were hardening from randomness to a compelling pattern, to something "real".

"Which might mean it's resonating with real—superstring phenomena, say. Sub-particles."

"I'm bloody glad you said 'might'. We could just be looking into a mirror, seeing stuff we put there ourselves. Your neatest idea today was when you said it felt like a cellular-automata gameboard. From that angle, a lot of things clicked for me. Now that thing—" he indicated a complex node false-colored in shifting shades of blue near the top of the monitor "—*could* be a sort of stable oscillator, like you used to see in the old Life-game programs."

Ceri nodded in mild approval. "Which feels about right, because if particles aren't stable oscillations in the quantum field, then what are they? We're seeing the right kind of map—although, as the man said, 'the map is not the territory.' But if we can ever develop this thing to the point of pulling out information that isn't in the physics books, and if the information is good . . ."

"Yes, I had begun to gather that. Over the weeks of you telling me it."

"The shaky part of this entanglement theory is that the mapping ought to be two-way. Heisenberg's principle: you can't observe without affecting the thing observed. But the mechanism . . . the scaling factors . . ." She frowned and gnawed her lip. "All right, all right, you need more coffee."

Ranjit said slowly, "Wait a minute. I'm going to try something." His brown fingers rippled over the keys.

There had been three of them in the chem lab, Sammy and Ceri and the girl with the harsh Cardiff accent, whose name she had long forgotten. It was another sweltering day, and the rest of the school had emptied itself into the open air at the first clang of the lunch bell. Here the reek of old reagents and spillages bit acridly at your throat, and the smell of the new stuff they were carefully filtering through big paper-lined funnels led to occasional coughs which no one could stifle.

"This is the biggest batch ever," Sammy chortled. "Going for the world record!" As usual, although it was Ceri who first found and read that worn Victorian volume of *Amusing and Edifying Scientific Parlour Tricks*, the project had become all Sammy's.

The black paste of precipitate had many uses. Once dried, it was amazingly touchy stuff. Smeared on chalkboards and left for an hour, it produced amusing crackles and bangs when Mr. Whitcutt scrawled his illegible algebra workings; underfoot, it made whole classrooms (and on one glorious morning, the school assembly hall) a riot of minor explosions and puffs of purple smoke; packed into a lock, it could blast the inserted key right back into its holder's hand, often with painful force.

Then the door to the back room opened. Ceri winced. They'd counted on Mr. Davies, the elderly lab technician, either going out for lunch or staying placidly put and brewing his tea as usual. White-haired Mr. Davies had seen everything that could happen in labs; his experience went back to days before ordinary benzene was declared a carcinogen, days when the pupils routinely used it to sluice organics from their hands.

"Terrible smell of ammonia in here," he said mildly. "Someone ought open a window."

The Cardiff girl—Rhiannon, could it have been?—silently obeyed.

Mr. Davies, looking at no one in particular, added: "People ought to know not to make nitrogen tri-iodide in kilogram lots. That much of the stuff's unstable even if you do keep it wet. And it doesn't help anyone's career if they're short of a few fingers." He retreated through his private door.

"That was a hint," said Ceri.

"We've made it now," Sammy said crossly.

"Come *on*. If anything goes bang anywhere this week, they're going to know who it was."

Mumbling to himself, Sammy scraped together the precious black sludge, dumped it in the sink built into the teacher's demonstration bench, and gave it a quick flush from the tap. In another sink, Ceri carefully rinsed the soiled filter papers before binning them; the Cardiff girl splashed water over the glassware. But Sammy had a look on his face that Ceri had seen before. "I'm just going to try something," he muttered, and tilted a huge reagent bottle over the demo-bench sink. There was a powerful whiff of hospital-like fumes. To Ceri's silent relief, nothing happened.

When the chemistry lesson came around that afternoon, Mr. Porter held up a large Erlenmeyer flask and announced, to general apathy, that he was about to perform a simple demonstration. What it was going to be remained a mystery, since when he put the glass cone in the sink to fill it there followed a sharp explosion, a dramatic cloud of purple smoke, and an upward spray of glass fragments that slashed his hands and face in a dozen places. In the echoing pause while Mr. Porter stared in fascination at tattered, part-flayed fingers, Ceri realized what Sammy had poured down there: a measure of ether that had washed away the water in the sink trap and swiftly evaporated, leaving the tri-iodide bone-dry and potent. She thought for an instant of a bright globule of blood on the downy breast of a small, greenish bird.

With one awful eye—blood was streaming into the other—the chemistry master surveyed his class. He pointed unerringly at Sammy and cried *"Jones!"* Old Davies had presumably identified the explosive ringleader, but anyway one would need to be blind not to notice the outraged innocence of Sammy's expression—

the body language that conveyed, "I couldn't have known it would do *that*."

The harsh sunlight brightened sharply; a tiny corner of Ceri's mind longed for the return of some healing cloud. Cloud? What was obscurely odd today about sun and cloud? Her critical attention, though, was focused on the computer display's fractal gridlines, and the strange pulse of activity in the node which Ranjit had indicated some minutes earlier. Now the false-color mapping showed the shape breaking into new colours on either side of blue: a speckle of green, larger irregular blocks of indigo and violet.

"It's gone interactive," Ranjit said. "What you said about Heisenberg: probing it digitally is *changing* stuff in there. Like sending pulses into a neural-net grid."

"We're . . . changing a particle's state by measuring it?"

"Isn't that exactly what your pal Herr Heisenberg said? Isn't it what *you* said? Tickling it in just the right rhythm is keeping it—well—doing whatever it's doing now. Higher energy level? Spinning faster? Or something with one of the weird quantum numbers like strangeness. Hell, I don't know, but it's fun. Like keeping a yo-yo moving."

It was too hot to think straight. *Damn* that lousy, feeble air conditioning. A plastic folder on the glaring desktop had curled and shrivelled as never before. Ceri had always—or at any rate since she'd been a schoolgirl—felt brilliantly sunlit days to be fraught with a sense of obscure, gathering disaster. She felt it now.

"I'm just going to try something," said Ranjit again. "I think I can nudge it a step further—"

It was some echo in his words, rather than the actual tone or content, that made her snap: *"No."*

"Don't be silly. I'm recording everything. We can reboot the simulation whenever—What the fuck!"

Ceri had yanked the power lead from his computer workstation, and the stained-glass complexities died from the screen.

There had been just the two of them, Sammy and Ceri, on a blinding-hot day at the Gaer. The place was a broad hillock of grassy, bracken-infested wasteland, named for an old Roman camp whose trenches and ditches had left their scars around the summit. More attractive was the rumor, never verified, of adders somewhere in the Gaer's gorse and bracken.

A branch railway line curled around one side of this common land, separating it from a more orderly park and golf course. Feeble attempts at fencing off the railway had, it seemed, been long abandoned. Here the wire links were neatly snipped through, there they were undermined, and in several places the whole fence had sagged to the ground under the weight of many climbers. It was the perfect spot for what Ceri, in a phrase from history lessons, called debasing the coinage. Old, brassy threepenny bits were the best, if you could find them. Place one on the nearer rail, wait five or ten or twenty minutes for the long rumble of a goods train, and a marvellously flattened, doily-edged medallion would be flung aside by the thunderous succession of iron wheels.

When coins began to pall, though, it was hard to think of interesting variations. Glass marbles (secured with a blob of chewing gum) simply burst into powder, and small stones to grit. Ceri had managed to talk Sammy out of his "biological experiment" featuring a white mouse in a cardboard box.

Today he produced something new from his shoulder-bag: a short length of copper pipe, capped at both ends. It was quite hard to balance this on a rail, but—while Ceri kept watch for approaching trains—Sammy used angular stone fragments from the railside to wedge the thing against rolling off.

"Should be good. Better than thruppences!" he confided as they crouched in their usual hidey-hole amid yellow-flowering gorse clumps close by the line.

"What is it, Sammy? Nothing *alive*?"

"No no no. I just thought I'd try something. Weedkiller and stuff. I can't get the compression at home."

Ceri had a sense of distant alarms ringing. "Weedkiller and *sugar*? Maybe we should—"

Her hesitant voice was lost in the approaching train's roar, and the bulk of the engine (so much huger from down here than from a station platform) blotted out the angry sun. A not very emphatic crack or bang was succeeded by the usual long rattle and squeak of two dozen or so hopper wagons. Ceri had felt Sammy jerk and cry out, as though wasp-stung or bitten by the dread adder. He slumped forward. She shook and turned him slightly. A stone fragment, they told her later, had flown like shrapnel from the explosion. The sight of the gory ruin that had been Sammy's left eye remained too vivid a memory for too long a time, and it was no comfort to be assured again and again that for him it was instantaneous.

There were still, after all, two of them in Ceri's office, where quite easily there might by now have been none.

"What are you *waiting* for?" he said again.

"Ssh." She kept her eyes on her watch. The light striking through the window lessened in its intensity, as though a thin cloud had drifted in front of the sun.

"Iesu Grist," Ceri whispered.

"What?"

"Oh . . . Welsh. Jesus Christ. I counted eight minutes and twenty seconds, which is about right. Jesus. I'd actually said it out loud, too, I said we didn't know the scaling factors."

"How about an explanation in words of one syllable for the mere technical staff?"

"How about if you make the coffee this time, Ranjit, just for a change?" Had her soft pad of scribbling paper really turned pale brown in the hot glare? "I knew there was something wrong but

I didn't know I knew it. I just had this feeling of someone walking on my grave. But that's how science officially operates, isn't it? You get an intuition and then you think back and work out why it came. You see, the sun got brighter."

"Too bloody right it did," said Ranjit, spooning out coffee granules. "You're still not, um, making any actual sense."

"Ranjit, there's not a cloud in the sky. There hasn't been all day. Clear blue everywhere, and it's way past noon. But a few minutes after you'd started interfering with that pattern in the Cray simulation, the sun *suddenly* got brighter."

"Oh, come on. What a vivid imagination some people have."

"Look. Just about eight minutes and twenty seconds from the time I pulled the plug, the sunlight dropped to normal again. That's the time the light takes to reach us across 149 million kilometers. You saw it. And there's still no cloud up there."

A pause. "Fuck," he said uncertainly. "I was just going to tweak it harder, see what the limits were. . . . I couldn't have known it would do *that*!" Ranjit pushed his lips in and out a few times, calculating, as though playing for time or pushing some bad thought away from him. "Shouldn't the lag have been nearer seventeen minutes, sort of eight and a half each way?"

"What can I say? I could talk about quantum nonlocality, but I'd only be gibbering. I'll have to think it through. The first guess is that this thing doesn't play by the Einstein rules."

Ranjit filled and raised a coffee cup. "So here's to the Nobel?" The tone of voice dismayed her. It conveyed that enormity was already receding into a game, a silly hypothesis they'd entertained for a silly moment, a physicists' in-joke like that hoary "proof" that heaven is hotter then hell. Easy with a little Bible-juggling, she remembered. According to Revelations, hell contains an eternal lake of brimstone which must simmer below 444.6° Centigrade, the boiling point of sulphur. According to one reading of Isaiah, the light of heaven is that of the sun multiplied fiftyfold, leading by simple radiation physics to a local temperature of 525°C. Again . . . *Iesu Grist.*

Ceri stared out of the window, thinking of a world full of eager Sammies who would be itching to take her small experiment one step further. How could anyone ever predict what might come boiling out of an innocuous-seeming theoretical bottle? There were wisps of smoke beyond the campus buildings now—flash fires, perhaps, or cars that had veered too abruptly in the sudden dazzle—and no doubt people out there with damaged retinas from looking the wrong way when things changed. For some reason she found herself picturing a small bird with bloody feathers, eyes darkened by too much light, on a long slow fall into the sun.

CARTER SCHOLZ

THE AMOUNT TO CARRY

Et la Splendide-Hôtel fut bâti dans le chaos de glaces et de nuit du pôle.

—RIMBAUD

THE LEGAL SECRETARY OF THE WORKMAN'S ACCIDENT Insurance Institute for the Kingdom of Bohemia in Prague enters the atrium of the hotel. Slender, sickly, his tall frame seems bowed under the weight of his title. But dark darting eyes, in a boyish face pale as milk, take in the hotel excitedly.

What a fantastic place! The dream of a visionary American, the hotel has been under construction since the end of the War. A brochure lists its many firsts: an observatory, a radio station, a resident orchestra (Arnold Schönberg conducting), an indoor health spa, bank kiosks open day and night for currency exchange. An escalator carries guests to the mezzanine, where a strange aeroplane is suspended, naked as a bicycle, like something designed by Da Vinci or a Cro-Magnon, nothing like the machines he saw at the Brescia air show, years ago.

The secretary likes hotels. He loses himself in their depths, in the many corridors, the buzz of conversation, the chiming of lifts, the jangle of telephones, the thump of pneumatic tubes.

The freedom of anonymity, with roast duck and dumplings on the side.

A placard near the reception desk proclaims in four languages, "Conference of International Insurance Executives, Registration." Europe has gone mad for conferences. Other placards welcome professional and amateur groups diverse as rocketeers, philosophers, alpinists, and the Catholic Total Abstinence Union. So many conferences are underway that the crowd seems formed of smaller crowds, intersecting, breaking apart, and reforming on their ways to meetings, meals, or diversions, jostling like bemused ducks.

The absolute falsity of public places. Their implacable reality.

Hotels he likes, but not conferences. His first was eight years ago. Terrified beyond stage fright, he spoke on accident prevention in the workplace. He felt sure that the men listening would fall on him and tear him apart when they understood what he was saying. But he was wrong. They recognized that with safer conditions fewer claims would be filed. With a lawyer's cunning he had put altruism before them as self-interest. He felt such relief as he left the stage that he was unable to stay for the other talks. Uncontrollable laughter welled up in him as he bolted for the door.

That was 1913, the year his first book was published. Now, at thirty-eight, he is becoming known for his writing, but finds himself miserably unable to write. Summoned to the castle but kept at the gate. And his time grows short. Last month at Matliary he underwent another hopeless treatment. It rained the whole time. At the end of his stay the weather cleared, and he hiked in the mountains. On his return, Prague seemed more oppressive than the sanatorium. Some dybbuk of the perverse made him volunteer for the conference.

The secretary pauses at a display of models. Marvels of America, of engineering. New York City! Finely carved ships are afloat in a harbor of blue sand. Pasteboard cliffs rise from the sand, buildings and spires. On an island stands a green figure, female, tall as a building, holding aloft a sword.

Beyond a glass terrace is the hotel's deer park, an immense enclosed courtyard. On its grass walk peacocks, tails dragging. One turns to face him. The iridescent blue of its chest. The pitiless black stones of its eyes.

The sideboard in his suite holds fresh flowers, a bottle of champagne, a bowl of oranges, a telephone. From his window he sees a lake and thinks of Palestine.

The gentleman from Hartford pauses at the cigar stand. A wooden Indian shades its eyes against the sun of an imaginary prairie. The gentleman purchases a panatela. Bold type on a magazine arrests his eye: *de stijl.* Opening it he reads, *The object of this magazine will be to contribute to the development of a new consciousness of beauty.* On the facing page, a photo of this very hotel. Beauty. Is that what surrounds him? He looks from a photograph of the lobby into the lobby. He adds the magazine and a Paris *Herald* to his purchase, receiving in change a bright 1920 American dime. His wife Elsie regards him sidelong from its face.

Morning crowds rush to their first appointment. Mr Stevens is free until lunch. In truth, his presence here is unnecessary to his agency's business, but he has developed a knack of absences from home and from his wife.

His attention is taken by a scale model of the hotel itself, accurate even to the construction scaffolding over the entrance. Through a tiny window of the tiny penthouse he sees two figures bent over blueprints unfurled between them.

In *de stijl,* Stevens reads: Like the young century itself, the hotel is a vortex of energies and styles. It thrusts upward, sprawls sideways, even sends an arm into the lake, where a glassed walkway slopes into aqua depths occupied by a houseboat colony designed by Frank Lloyd Wright, fresh from his triumphant Imperial Hotel in Tokyo. Many architects have been engaged, Gropius and Le Corbusier, de Klerk and Mendelsohn; they draw up plans, begin work, are dismissed or quit; so the hotel itself remains more an idea than a thing, a series of sketches of itself, a diffracted view not unlike M. Duchamp's notorious *Nude* in the New York Armory Show of some years ago. The hotel is a sort of manifesto-in-progress. To a multiple futurism, as though the very idea of the modern is too energetic and protean to find a single unified expression.

It occurs to Stevens that the hotel is unreal. Reality is an exercise of the most august imagination. This place is a hodgepodge. It gives him a sense of his own unreality. Then again, the real world seen by an imaginative man may very well seem like an imaginative construction.

He shuts the magazine and looks for a place to smoke in peace.

The senior partner of Ives & Myrick awakes right early.

The morning light is wrong. Where is Harmony, his wife? Outside, birds sing their dawn chorus, hitting all the notes between the notes. He remembers the two pianos side by side in the Sunday school room of Central Presbyterian. One piano by chance had fallen a quartertone out of tune from the other. He tried out chords on the two of them, right hand on one piano, left hand on the other. There are notes between notes—an infinity of notes! Again and again he struck those splendid new chords. Out of tune—what an idea! Can nature be out of tune?

He remembers where he is. The conference. It should be Mike here. He's better at this hail-fellow-well-met stuff. But Mike said he should go. Do you a world of good, Charlie. Write some music on the boat. Give Harmony some time off from you.

Ives was laid up for three months after his second heart

attack. It wore Harmony out, caring for him. Mike's right, she deserves a vacation from him. That's right, she went with Edie to the Adirondacks.

These memory lapses worry him. His job, his future, how long can he keep it up? Forty-seven years old, calling in sick, not pulling his weight. Shy Charlie, who's never sold a policy in his life, has come to the conference to prove the point—to himself, he supposes—that he's still an asset to the agency, and no loafer.

Out of bed, then. On the desk is the latest draft of his essay, "The Amount To Carry," condensed for his luncheon talk. Just the key points. It is at once a mathematical formula for estate planning and a practical guide to making the sale. Sell to the masses! Get into the lives of the people! I can answer scientifically the one essential question. Do you know what that is?

Ives & Myrick have taken in two hundred million dollars in the past twelve years. Two millions of that has gone to Ives. By any measure he's a rich man, but still he dreads retirement. The end of his usefulness, his strength. Much of his income now comes from renewal commissions. Normally the selling agent gets a nice piece of change every time a policy is renewed, but that takes years, and the younger men are impatient, so they've been selling their commissions to him at a discount. A little irregular, but they're happy to get the money!

He has to provide for his family. They adopted Edie five years ago, and her parents are still asking for money. It amounts to buying the child. But isn't Edie better off with them? When Harmony lost their baby, Charlie and she wept nightlong. For a month she lay in hospital. Sick with despair and worry, Charlie set to music a Keats poem:

> The spirit is too weak;
> Mortality weighs heavily upon me
> Like unwilling sleep,
> And each imagined pinnacle and steep

Tells me I must die,
Like a sick eagle looking towards the sky.

From that day he knew that they must carry one another. It scared him, then, for two people to so depend.

The money's for his music too. It cost him $2,000 last year to print the "Concord" Sonata. And it will cost a sight more to bring out the songs. But the only way the lily boys and the Rollos will ever hear this music is if he prints it himself. He mailed seven hundred copies of the "Concord" to names culled from *Who's Who* and the *Musical Courier's* subscription list. Gave offense to several musical pussies. All those nice Mus Docks and ladybirds falling over in a faint at the sight of his manly dissonances.

In open rehearsal last spring, Paul Eisler, holding a nice baton, led the New Symphony through Ives's "Decoration Day". Musicians dropped out one by one, till by the last measure one violinist in the back row was the sole survivor. *There is a limit to musicianship,* said Eisler coldly, handing the score back to him.

A limit to someone's, anyway.

But this fuss with revisions and printers is hollow. The truth is he hasn't begun anything new since his illness—since the War, really. If music is through with him, he guesses he can take it, he's written enough. But how do you get it heard? Isn't it enough to write it? Do you have to carry it on your back into the town square?

Wilson dead and the League of Nations with him. That weak sister Harding in the White House.

He's getting into one of his black moods that Harmony so hates, and he'd better not, not with the talk ahead of him. He remembers seeing a piano in a parlor off the main lobby. Playing it might put him right.

When K was hired in 1908, the Institute was a scandal, not unlike the life insurance companies in New York a few years before, though it was a scandal of Bohemian incompetence rather than American greed. For twenty years the institute had run at a loss. K's hiring coincided with a sweeping reform; he was made to put a cash value on various injuries: lost limbs, fingers, hands, toes, eyes, and other maimings. He adjusted premiums, which had been constant, to correspond to levels of risk in specific occupations. In the course of travel to verify claims, he found himself examining production methods and machinery. Once he redesigned a mechanical planer.

"Even the most cautious worker is drawn into the cutting space when the cutter slips or the lumber is thrown back, which happens often, when he presses the piece he is planing against the cutter spindle. It is impossible to foresee or to prevent the wood from rising and sliding back, since this can occur when the wood is knotty, when the blade isn't moving fast enough, or shifts position, or when the hand presses on the wood unevenly. Accidents usually take off several finger joints or whole fingers."

How modest these people are. Instead of storming the institute and smashing the place to bits, they come and plead.

Stevens locates an armchair. At one end of the bronze-trimmed parlor stands a potted palm, in which a mechanical bird twitters silently. The dime is still in his hand. The master carving by Adolph Weinman, twelve inches across, rests on their mantelpiece in Hartford. Certainly she is beautiful: Elsie in a Phrygian cap, the Roman symbol of a freed slave. Does he oppress her? Does Weinman think so, is the cap a message? Its wings tempt confusion with Mercury, Hermes, messenger, god of merchants and thieves, patron of eloquence and fraud. Holder of the caduceus, whose touch makes gold. On the reverse, a bundle of sticks, Roman fasces. He tucks the coin into a vest pocket, feeling his ample flesh yield beneath the cloth. That monster, the body.

He unfolds the *Herald*. Victor Emmanuel III is losing power to blackshirted anarchists called *fascisti*. The Paris Peace Conference demands 132 billion gold marks in reparations from Germany, prompting a violent protest from the new chairman of the National Socialist German Workers' Party: some berber with a Chaplin-Hardy mustache. European politics is *opera buffa*, when not *bruta*. Stevens turns to the arts section. New Beethoven biography by Thayer. Music festival in Donaueschingen. Caruso still being mourned. Play by Karel Capek, *R.U.R.*, opens in Prague. Review of a Carl Van Vechten book.

At the Arensbergs' once, Elsie said, *I like Mr Stevens's writing when it is not affected. But it is so often affected.* What she liked was being the focus of it. When the poems went out to a larger audience she resented it. Lately Van Vechten suggested Stevens assemble a book, and promised to give it to Alfred Knopf. Surely it's time for his first book, whatever friction it causes with Elsie. Stevens is forty-two.

He unrings the panatela, rolling it between his fingers as he turns titles in his mind. Supreme Fiction. The Grand Poem: Preliminary Minutiae. How little it would take to turn poets into the only true comedians.

As he's about to light up, a obersided balding type sidles over to the piano. New York suit, Yankee set to his jaw. After a moment he starts to play plain chords, sounding as from a harmonium in a country church. Stevens thinks he knows the hymn, from his Lutheran childhood, but then there are wrong notes and false harmonies, played not with the hesitations and corrections of an amateur, but with steady confidence. A pianist himself, Stevens listens closely. At an anacrucis, the trebel disjoints from the bass and goes its own way, in another key and another time. His listening mind is both enchanted and repelled. Music then is feeling, not sound.

A tall thin Jew with jug ears and a piercing gaze, *echt mitteleuropisch,* has paused in the doorway to hear the Yankee's fantasia.

—*Doch, dass kenn' ich,* he says, when the Yankee stops.

The Yankee starts, but says nothing.

—That, that music you play. *In München war's, seit zehn Jahren. Max Brod hab' ich am Konzert begleiten. Mahler dirigiert. Diese Melodien, genau so.*

—Huh? says the Yankee.

—Something about a concert, Stevens interjects from his chair, startling Ives again. He says he's heard that song before. At a concert in Munich ten years ago. Conducted by Mahler.

—Gustav Mahler?

—*Ja ja, Gustav Mahler. Erinnere mich ganz klar, ganz am Schluss kommen die Glocken, gegen etwas vollkommen anders in die Streicher. Unheimlich war's.*

—He says a bell part, against strings at the end, in, apparently, two different keys?

—Yes! Glocken and Streicher! The Yankee's German is atrocious.

—*Glocken,* agrees the Jew. *Ganz unheimlich.*

—An uncanny effect, says Stevens.

—That's my *Third Symphony*! It's never been performed. How could he have heard it? Tams, my copyist, he once told me that Mahler stopped by his office looking for American scores. This was in 'ten, when Mahler was conducting the New York Phil. Tams said he took my Third. I never believed it, I thought Tams lost it and made up a tale. By God, it's true!

The Yankee, now excited and voluble, rises from the piano bench, extending a hand.

—Charles Ives, Ives & Myrick agency, New York. Life insurance.

—Frank Kafka. Of Workman's Accident Insurance Institute in Praha. I am very pleased to meet you.

—Cough . . . ?

—Kafka.

Stevens, having unwisely involved himself, cannot now politely withdraw to the solitary pleasure of his cigar.

—Stevens, Hartford Casualty. Surety bonds.

—Hartford? says Ives. We used to have an office in Hartford. Are you a Yale man?

—Harvard '01.
—Yale '98, says Ives, defensively.
—Do you live in New York, Mr Ives?
—New York and Redding.
—Reading! Pennsylvania?
—Redding Connecticut.
—Oh, Redding. I'm from Reading Pennsylvania.
—I thought you said Hartford.
—I was born in Reading. As was my wife.
—My wife Harmony's a Hartford girl. Her father, the Reverend Joe Twitchell, he's the man that married and buried Mark Twain.
—I've heard of Twain, says Stevens drily.
—A great American writer, says Kafka.
—Are you married, Mr. Kavka? asks Ives.
—Married . . . no. An elderly . . . bachelor? With a habit of, ah, *Verlobungen?* You say, engagements?

Ives appears shocked by loose European mores. Stevens hastens to change the subject.

—Mr. Ives, do you happen to know Edgard Varèse?
—Who?
—A composer. He moved to Greenwich Village from Paris. He founded the New Symphony a few years ago.

Ives narrows his eyes.

—Never heard of him. Some Bohemian city slicker, I guess.
—Bohemian? asks Kafka.
—An expression meaning an artistic type, says Stevens. Are you artistic, Herr Kafka?

The faint smile on Kafka's face vanishes. Dismay fills his serious dark eyes.

—Oh no, not in the least.

Ives strides briskly to the luncheon. He's keyed up. He took to the hotel at once, its brash mix of styles, chrome steel and ormolu together, like a clamor of Beethoven, church hymns, and camp marches. He passes the scale model of Manhattan, so finely made he can almost pick out the Ives & Myrick office on Liberty Street. But what is this? South and east of Central Park are two unfamiliar needletopped skyscrapers, even taller than the Woolworth Building. The downtown building is where the Waldorf-Astoria should be. Surely that's not right, yet something about them projects a natural authority. As he puzzles, he hears a shout.

—Fire!

People turn. Ives smells smoke. A clerk steps forward.

—Please! No cause for concern! There is always a fire somewhere in the hotel. We have the most modern sprinkler and containment systems. Everything is under control.

And indeed, the smoke has already dispersed. Alarm gives way to sheepishness as guests return to their occupations.

At luncheon, Stevens is seated across from Kafka. Kafka slides his *veau cordon bleu*, fatted calf, to one side of the plate and diligently chews some *haricots verts*. Stevens looks on with, he realizes as Kafka's penetrating gaze meets his, the jaundiced eye that Oliver Hardy turns on Stan Laurel. Stevens fingers his ginger mustache.

—Life Insurance is doing its part in the progress of the greater life values, Ives is saying.

Stevens, on his third glass of Haut-Medoc, cocks an eyebrow at the podium. Can Ives believe this hogwash? Has he forgotten the Armstrong Act? Just fifteen years ago, the life insurance business was so corrupt that even the New York legislature couldn't ignore it. Sales commissions were fifty, eighty, one hundred percent of the premiums. Executive parties were bacchanals. Mutual president Richard McCurdy, before his indictment, called life insurance "a great benevolent missionary institution". His benevolence, before he was indicted, had enriched his family by fifteen millions. The state shut down half the agencies and sent any number of executives into forced retirement. Come to think of it, that's probably how young Ives got his start, stepping into that vacuum.

As a surety claims attorney, Stevens is inclined to finical doubt. Defaults, breaches, and frauds are his profession. He is a rabbi of the ways and means by which people fail their commitments, and how they excuse themselves. He feels that the attempt to secure our interests against chance and fate is noble but vain. Insurance is a communal project but a capitalist enterprise, a compassionate ideal ruled by the equations of actuaries. In the risk pool, it appears that the fortunate succor the misfortunate, but that is a salesman's fiction; the pool is more precisely like a mass of gas molecules in Herr Boltzmann's kinetic theory. The position of the individual is unimportant. We are dust in the wind. What can we insure?

Cemeteries have been found by a number of offices to be a very definite market for the Hartford's All Risk Securities Policy.

Kafka is still chewing.

But insurance is only the prelude to Ives's fugue: now he is off onto nationwide town meetings, referenda, the will of the people, the majority! Quotations from Shakespeare, Lamb, Emerson, Thoreau. He's lost his audience.

—Deny a claim for a year, Stevens hears from a tablemate, and most people give up.

Stevens feels a fleeting pang for Ives's pure, unreal belief. The poet chides himself: Have it your way. The world is ugly, and the people are sad.

The final belief is to believe in a fiction which you know to be a fiction, because there is nothing else.

Hotel of the future. Once a grand hotel in the Continental style, it has been made completely new. Even the location has changed. With over a thousand rooms and more added every day, twenty ballrooms, a retail arcade, an underground parking garage, automatic elevators, and a mooring mast for aircraft, it is the hotel of the future.

Tradition. Yet tradition is not forgotten. Arthur, the original owner, now in his late sixties, has been kept on as concierge. Take him aside, offer him a bowl of haschisch, and he may tell you tales of old Java, of gunrunning in Ethiopia. His ravaged face, wooden leg, and clinking moneybelt are reminders of a more colorful, dangerous, and perhaps more actual world.

Cellars. Some say, if you pass muster with Arthur, he may press a key into your palm, and whisper directions to the labyrinthine cellars. There your every whim can be indulged.

Apparatus. Others swear that the cellars are not like that at all, but are filled with machinery, row upon row of brass rods and cogwheels, brightly lit by hanging electric globes, churning with a peculiar clacking noise and a smell of oiled metal. A small rack of needles, like a harrow, pivots to hold for a moment a punched card, until a hiss of compressed air shoots it down a runnel and another card is grasped. The apparatus is said to control all the hotel's workings, from the warmth of the hothouses to the accounting of bills.

Life itself. It is a remarkable piece of apparatus, not so different from the Hollerith tabulating machines that have lately made themselves essential to the insurance industry. The apparatus is based on designs by the late Charles Babbage of England, William Seward Burroughs, Herr Odhmer of Sweden, and the Americans Thomas Watson and Vannevar Bush. But no one fully understands it, for it is self-modifying. Some say that elements of reason and intelligence, of life itself, have accrued to it.

Work in progress. As with the apparatus, it is hard to know what in the hotel is finished and what is in progress. The raw concrete walls of the natatorium may be a bold statement of modernity, or may await a marble cladding. The genius of the hotel may be precisely this ambiguity, this unwillingness to declare itself.

Transnational. The owner calls the hotel a machine for living away from home. The master plan calls for groundbreakings in six continents, every hotel different, yet supplying the same level of service and accommodation. Even Antarctica, that chaos of ice and polar night, will one day fly the hotel's flag. Home, the owner believes, is an obsolete fiction.

After his talk, Ives feels depressed and uncertain. His exhilarations are often followed by a crash. He doubts that he put over any of it, apart from the business formulas. Yet surely, after the War, after the Spanish influenza that swept the globe, all men must see that their common good is one.

The fabric of existence weaves itself whole. His music and his business are not separate: his talk was as pure an expression of his belief and will as any of his music. He's given it his best, and now he has no interest for the rest of the proceedings. He's ready to go home.

The hotel, which at first delighted him, has begun to oppress him. It seems endless. He leaves behind the meeting rooms overfull with conventioneers, passes vacant ballrooms with distant ceilings, he walks down deserted corridors where the repeating patterns of carpet, the drift of dust in afternoon sun, are desolate with melancholy, ennui, loss. Once he hears a distant music, possibly Busoni's transcription of Bach's "Chaconne," but the instrument is some strange ethereal organ. It begins to frighten him, this vast, unfathomable place. He is overcome with a sense of futility. He thinks of his father's band playing gavottes at the battle of Chancellorsville.

Turning a corner, he spots the one-legged concierge, limping and clanking down the hall. The old rogue comes up to Ives.

—I carry about in my belt 16,000 francs in gold. It weighs over eight kilos and gives me dysentery.

—Why do you carry it? asks Ives.

—For my art! To insure my liberty. Soon I will have enough.

—I see. Can you tell me which way to the main lobby?

Scornfully the ancient laughs and points.

—You see nothing. That way.

The elevator lurches, halting between floors.

There are numbers between numbers, thinks Stevens. Between the integers are fractions, and between those the irrationals, and so on to the dust of never-quite-continuity. If numerical continuity is an illusion, perhaps temporal continuity is as well. Perhaps there are dark moments between our flickers of consciousness, as between the frames of a movie. The *Nude* of Duchamp descends her staircase in discrete steps. Where is she between steps? Perhaps here at the hotel. At this moment, stuck between floors, where am I?

Stevens presses the button for ROOF. The elevator begins to move sideways.

Past its glass doors windows slide by, offering views of the city, shrunk to insignificance by height. The car seems to be traveling along the circumference of a tower. After a quarter circuit, the outer windows cease, and shortly the car halts again, then resumes ascent.

Its doors open to verdancy. The rooftop garden is a maze, a forest, an artificial world. A hothouse opens onto a short arcade that corners into an arbor. Thyme grows between the cobbles and he crushes fragrance from it as he walks. In his more virile youth, he often hiked thirty miles in a day up the Hudson from New York, or ferried to New Jersey to ramble through the open country near Hackensack, Englewood, Hohokus. Slowly he finds a geography in the paths, steps, and terraces. It is indeed a world. Small signs, like lexical weeds, mark frontiers. From SOUTH AFRICA and its spiked succulents with their starburst flowers of yellow and pink and blue he enters MEXICO. On the path is a fallen tomato verde. The enclosing lantern, which the fruit has not quite grown to fill, is purple at the stem and papery, but at the tip has decayed to a tough, brittle lace of veins, like an autumn leaf. Inside the small green fruit is split. His fingers come away gummy.

Abruptly, past espaliered pears, there is the roofedge, cantilevered into air. Light scatters through the atoms of the air: blue. Not even sky is continuous.

Distant snowcapped peaks shelve off into sky. He remembers with sharp yearning his camping and hunting trip in British Columbia with Peckham and their rough guides. Twenty years ago. Another lost paradise.

His elate melancholy follows the ups and down of the range: however long he lives, how much and well he writes, no poetry can compass this world, the actual.

K decides to walk abroad in the city, but the hotel baffles his efforts to leave it. Curving corridors lead past ballrooms and parlors, but never reach the atrium. After ten minutes, K stops at a desk in an arcade.

—*Bitte, wie geht man hinaus?*

—And why do you want to go out?

Though the clerk has clearly understood K's question, he answers in English, and with another question. K is annoyed, but perseveres in German.

—*Ich will spazieren.*

—But you can walk in the hotel. Try the lake ramp, the deer park, the rooftop gardens. Here is a map.

—*Danke nein.*

K turns through several corridors at random. At the end of one he sees sunlight, and although the exit door is marked CLOSED UNDER CONSTRUCTION it is unlocked. He transgresses and finds himself in a small grotto, perhaps a corner of the deer park. The hotel walls rise sixteen floors to a cantilevered roof.

He is in a graveyard of worn stones. His fingers move right to left over the nearest stone, reading. Beautiful eldest, rest in peace, Anshel Mor Henach. 5694 Sivan 3.

The gentleman from Hartford has dined alone. Susceptible with wine he follows the chance of shifting crowds through the lobby.
—*Faites vôtres jeux, mesdames, messieurs.*

The casino's entrance columns remind Stevens of the Hartford office. A temple to probability, and the profit to be had from it.

Dice chatter, balls racket round their polished course, cards slap and sigh on baize. In his good ear rings the bright syrinx of hazard. In his bad, the dull hoo-hoo of drums. Chance and fate, high flute and groaning bass.
—*Un coup de dés jamais n'abolira le hasard.*

Stevens bets. The wheel rumbles, the ball rattles.

In the spa, K glimpses himself in a full length mirror. Hollow cheeks, sunken stomach, spindly legs, ribs like a charcoal sketch of famine. Other nude bodies, ghostly in steam, pass in a line. In modesty he turns away, but he sees then uniformed men, like guards in some *Strafkolonie*, herding the others through doors. The flesh of their bodies is as haggard as their faces. The men are all circumcised. Then come the women. Faces downcast, but some turn to him. His sisters.
—Ottla! Elli! Valli!

The line goes on forever. Is there no end to it? Another woman turns her imploring face to him.
—Milena!

The doors close, and he is alone but for two guards murmuring in German, the angelic tongue of Goethe and Kleist. K is invisible to them. Their gleaming leather boots, their gray uniforms, the stark black and white device on their red armbands show none of the Prussian love of pomp. This is something new. Yet it is the old story.

Enough! Let it be done! Let every child of Israel be run through the Harrow and tattooed with the name of his crime: *Jude.* All but K the invisible, the impervious. Instead of him they take Milena, not even a Jew, for the crime of having loved him.

The vision passes. K dresses, slowly apprehending that the hotel is not style, but a force as implacable as history. He has lived through one world war and will not see another. But unlike Ives with his one-world utopianism, unlike Stevens in the protected precincts of his being, K knows that another war is coming.

Style is optional, history is not.

In his room that night, Ives tries to compose.

Six years past, in the Adirondacks, he had a vision of earth, mountains, and sky as musical planes. In the predawn it seemed that he was high above the earth, Keene Valley stretched below him, mist lying in its sinuous watercourse and the lights of the town burning within it like coals in smoke. The last stars were fading, and the horizon held bands of rose, orange, and indigo. The greening forests took on color and depth, the fallow fields, the curdling mist.

He imagined several orchestras, and huge conclaves of singing men and women, placed in valleys, on hillsides, on mountain tops. The "universe in tones" or a Universe Symphony.

The plan still terrifies him. He's made notes and sketches, but the real work hasn't begun. He doubts he can do it. The vision is remote now, a fading memory, impalpable as his childhood. He sits, he sketches, he notes. Even at this hour from some far part of the hotel the sound of construction is unceasing. Danbury and Redding seem another world. He no longer knows how things go together.

Pulmonary edema due to arteriosclerotic and hypertensive heart disease with probable myocardial infarction.

He sees an old man outside the house in Redding. An airplane buzzes overhead, and the old man shakes his cane at it. The hillsides and valleys roll away into the haze of distance. It's all there, the old man thinks. If only I could have done it.

Sleepless, K sits writing to Max, to Klopstock, to his sisters Elli and Ottla. He starts and tears up another letter to Milena. What more is there to say?

His windows are black as peacock eyes. Memory is a pyre that burns forever. Felice, Grete, Milena, how shamefully he has treated them.

The life one lives and the stories one tells oneself and others about it are never the same. There are tales within tales. Every moment has a secret narrative, so intertwined with those of other moments that finding the truth about anything becomes a labor of Zeno. An endless maze of connecting tunnels, branching and intersecting without end.

He sips at a glass of water, swallows with difficulty.

Laryngologische Klinik
Pat.-Nr. 135
Name: Dr Kafka Franz
Diagnose: Tbc. laryngis
Pat. ist völlig appetitlos u. fühlt sich sehr schwach.
Pupillen normal, reagieren prompt.
Pat. ist leicht heiser.
Hinterwand infiltriert.
Taschenbänder gerötet.
Haemsputum.

What is it, to write? I want rather to live.

He will give Milena all his diaries. Let her see what he is, let her take him entire. Is this contrition? Or a sly way of freeing himself from his burden? Or is it, at last, the only marriage he can make?

A curious small voice addresses the secretary. *It was late in the evening when K arrived. The village was deep in snow.* He holds the pen unmoving.

A faint squeaking comes from the floor. Near the head of the bed is a mousehole, from which a small gray head peers.

—*Guten Abend, Fräulein Maus.* What a pretty voice, what a singer you are! Would you like to come in?

The small pink nose winks at him from the hole.

—Come, here is a nice warm slipper for you to sleep in.

He edges his foot forward, slipper on his toe. Whiskers twitch and the mouse is gone, running in the tiny corridor behind the baseboard, through all the secret passages of the hotel, unwatched, unsuspected, secure.

It is late. The model Manhattan is a cordillera of skyscrapers. At the island's southmost tip rise a pair of silver towers, blunt as commerce. Stevens feels old, past meridian. His own assumed worldliness reproves him. He understands nothing of the cold wind and polar night in which he moves. But he knows that he will live through awful silences to old age.

There is no insurance. There is no liberty. Elsie is his wife, despite his yes her no. He must be better to her.

The airplane has come and gone. The Redding air is still. He listens to the silence: his blood thrums, a jackdaw cries, wind rustles an oak. Universe symphony. And Edith calls, running towards him:

—Daddy! Carry me!

He catches her up and lifts her to his shoulders. Her thin legs dangle down.

—Carry me! she commands again, and he starts towards the house, where Harmony has stepped onto the porch. She sees them, and the moment is so full he misses his step; he stumbles and recovers, as she calls in concern:

—Charlie! Your heart!

In the morning, from uneasy dreams the secretary awakens transformed. A coverlet recedes before him like the Alps. He holds out his hands, seeing spindly shanks, thin gray fur, grasping claws. There comes a heavy knock at the door. He scampers across the bed, his claws digging into the fabric as he goes down the side and under the bed. Cowering there, nose twitching, chest heaving, tail wrapped round his shivering flanks, he sees the enormous legs of the maid moving about the room. She is sweeping with a broom as big as a house. Crumbs fly past him like stones; in a storm of dust he sneezes and trembles.

Near the head of the bed he spies the dark hole in the baseboard, and without a moment's thought he dashes for it. The maid exclaims, the shadow of the broom descends, he is squeaking in terror, running, and then he is in his burrow, in the darkness, in the walls of the hotel, carrying nothing, but wearing, as it were, the whole world.

ELLEN KUSHNER

THE DEATH OF THE DUKE

THE DUKE WAS AN OLD MAN, AND HIS YOUNG WIFE HAD never known him when his hair grew dark and heavy, and lay across the breasts of his many lovers like a mantle.

She was a foreigner, and so she did not understand, when he'd come home to his city to die, and the nursing of him through his final illness began to tax her strength, why his relations were so concerned to help her in the choosing of a manservant to attend him.

"Let him be pretty," said gentle Anne with a blush.

"But not *too* pretty." Sharp Katherine flashed her a look.

"By all means," the young wife said, "why not let him be as pretty as may be, if it will please my husband, so long as he is strong and careful?"

And since neither one would answer her, nor even look at her nor at each other, she chose a lovely young man whose name was Anselm. She did not know how badly he had wanted the job.

Anselm had a steady hand and clear eyes. He could fold linen and pour medicine, slip a shirt on and off with a minimum of fuss, and wield a razor quickly and efficiently. The Duke insisted on being presentable at all times, although he was no longer able to go anywhere. In his youth, the Duke's cuffs had foamed with lace, breaking like waves over the backs of his hands. His hands had been thin then, but they were thinner now.

Now the old Duke lay in the bed he had not lain in for twenty years, in the house he had built, furnished and decorated and then abandoned. In a time when today's young lovers were not yet born, the Duke had left his city and his rights and his duties to follow his lover, the first and oldest and best, to a far island where they might live at last for love, although the word was never spoken.

Sitting by him on the bed, his young wife said to the Duke, "There was an old woman outside, waiting for me in the doorway of your house. She took me by the wrist; quite strong, her fingers. 'Is he in there?' she asked me. 'Is he? They say he's come back home. They say that he is in there dying.' "

The Duke's smile had always been thin as a whip. "I hope you told her they were right."

His wife pressed his hand. She loved him helplessly and entirely. She was to be the last of his loves. Knowing it comforted her only a little; sometimes, not at all.

"Go and dress," he told her. "It will take you longer than you think to dress for the sort of party you are going to tonight."

She hated to leave him. "My maid can lace me up in no time."

"There's still your hair, and the jewels and the shoes. . . . You'll be surprised."

"I want to stay with you." She snuggled into the bony hollow of his shoulder. "Suppose you're hungry, or the pain starts up again?"

"Anselm will bring me what I need." The Duke twined his

fingers in her hair, stroking her scalp. "Besides, I want to see if they fitted it properly."

"I don't care. I'm sure it's a beautiful gown; you chose it."

The stroking stilled. "You *must* care. They must learn to know you, and to respect you."

She said, "At home, no one could respect a wife who left her husband to go to a party when he was—when he was ill."

"Well, things are different here. I told you they would be."

It was true. But she would come with him. Five years ago, she had married a stranger, a man wandering her island half-crazed with the loss of his lover, the oldest and the best. In her village, she was past the age of being wed. But it was only that she had been waiting for him: a man who saw her when he looked at her. He surprised her with her own desires, and how they could be satisfied.

That he had once been a duke in a foreign country was a surprise he'd saved for the end. The rings on his hands, which he'd never removed, not even in his grief, he wanted to return to his family himself. She had begged to come with him on this final journey, although they both knew that it would end with him leaving her there alone. She wanted to see his people, to visit the places he had known; to hear him remember them there. She wanted his child to be born in the house of his fathers.

The last jewel was set in place on his wife's gown, the last curl pinned, the last flower arranged to suit the Duke's discerning eye. Exotic and stylish, livid and bright, the Duke's foreign wife went off in the carriage in a clatter of hooves and outriders, a blazon of flambeaux.

Candles were lit by the Duke's bed. Anselm sat quietly in a shadowed corner of the room.

"My wife," the Duke said, his eyes shut, white face against white pillow, "was the daughter of a great physician. He taught her all he knew, passed on to her his philtres and potions. She was justly proud, and healed a king with them. She loved a boy, a nobleman, but he was haughty, and did not return her love, nor could she make him. There are no philtres for that, whatever anyone may tell you." His own laugh made him catch his breath in pain. "Nor for this. It vexes her. And me."

Anselm said, "I wish it could be otherwise."

The Duke said dryly, "You're very kind. So do I. I suppose, being old, I should be graceful about it, and pretend not to mind much. But I have never lived to gratify others."

"No," said the lovely servant, whose loveliness went unnoticed. The Duke's eyelids were thin, almost blue, stretched over his eyes. His mouth was stiff with pain. "You caused some trouble in your time."

The taut face softened for a moment. "I did."

Anselm approached him with a drink poured into a silver cup. The cup was engraved with the Duke's family crest, a swan. There was no telling how old it was.

The Duke was tall, long-boned. There was not much flesh left on him and his skin was dry and parchment-thin. Anselm held him while he took the drink. It was like holding the mirror of a shadow: light instead of dark, edged instead of flat.

"Thank you," said the Duke. "That ought to help, for awhile. I will sleep, I think. When she comes home, I want to hear what happened at the party. Something is bound to have, her first time out."

"You want to cause some trouble now, do you?" his servant gently teased.

The thin lips smiled. "Maybe." Then, "No. Not now. What would be the use?"

"What was the use then?"

"I wanted . . . to be amused."

Closer now, the planes of his own face gilded by candlelight, Anselm said, "Men died for you."

"Not for me. For him."

"He killed them for you."

"Yesss . . ." A long breath of satisfaction.

Anselm leaned closer. "And you remember. I know you do. You were there. You saw it all. How they were good, but he was the best." His strong hand was dark against the linen sheet. "There is no swordsman like him now."

"But there never was." The Duke's voice was stretched so thin that Anselm, bending close, must hold his breath to hear. "There never was anyone like him."

"And will not be again, I think." Anselm said as softly, and as much to himself.

"Never."

The Duke lay back, his color gone, and the pillow engulfed him, welcoming him back to his new world, the world of brief strengths and long weaknesses.

Still glittering with finery, and the kiss of wine and rich company, the Duke's wife returned to him, to find out whether he slept, or whether he waited for her in the darkness.

From the huge bed his thin, dry voice said, "You smell of revelry."

She struck a light, revealing herself in splendor. The flowers were only a little withered at her breast. Despite the scratch of lace and the weight of gold, she settled herself beside him on the bed. "Ah! That's good, now I no longer need to be held up." She sighed as he slowly unlaced her stays. "I pretended—" She stopped, then went on, shyly, determined not to be afraid of him, "I told myself they are your hands, keeping my back straight before them all."

He chuckled. "And were people so hard on you?"

"They *stare* so! It is not polite. And they say things I do not understand. About each other, about you . . ."

"What about me?"

"I don't know. I don't understand it. Empty, pointless things that are supposed to mean more than they say. How you must find the city changed, and old friends gone."

"All true. I hope you were not too bored."

She pinched his shoulder. "Now you sound like them! No, I was not bored. I even got a compliment. An old man with diamonds and bad teeth said I was a great improvement on your first wife. He had very poor color—liver, I should think," she added hurriedly, having spoken of something she had intended not to.

"Yes," her husband said, impervious. "They can forgive me a foreigner better than they can an actress. Or maybe I finally merit pity, not censure, because I am sicker than any of them would like to be. Maybe that's all it is." His ruminations gave way to a story, more disjointed than he intended, a tale of past insult, of revenge. A lover spurned, the Duke's first wife publicly hissed; a young man's anger and the answer of money and steel. Blood and no healing, only scars closing over a dirty wound.

These were not stories that she had heard before, on the sunny island where they had been wed among the bees' hum and the thyme. They did not even describe a man she knew.

Lying undressed in the dark, next to his thin and burning body, she wondered for the first time if they had been right to come here to this place of his past.

His hand moved, half-aware, to her shoulder blade, cupping it like a breast. Her whole body flushed with memory. She desired him suddenly, wanted her strong lover back. But she knew the disease, she knew its course, and clenched her heart around the knowledge that that would not happen. All that had passed between their bodies was done, now, and was growing in her belly. In the future it would comfort her, but not now.

"People do not forget," he said. She'd thought he was asleep, his breathing was so quiet.

"You," she said tenderly. "They do not forget you."

"Not me. Themselves. I was important only for what I made them feel. Remember that." His fingers tightened on her, urgent and unalluring. "And do not trust anyone from my past. They have no cause to love me."

"I love you."

A little later, he sighed in his sleep, and spoke the name of his first wife, while he held her. She felt her heart twist and turn over, close to the child she carried, so that there was room for little inside her but pain and love.

Physicians hoping to make their fame and fortunes came to bleed him.

"There isn't enough left of me as is," said the Duke. He sent his wife down to chase them all away, knowing it would give her satisfaction to have someone else to be angry with.

Anselm was shaving him, gently and carefully. "In the old days," Anselm said, "you would have had them skewered."

The Duke did not even smile. "No. He did not kill unarmed men. There was no challenge in it."

"How did you find challenges for him? Did you have a good eye?"

Now the old lips quirked. "You know—I must have. I never thought of it. But there was a certain kind of bully I delighted in provoking: the swaggering cocksure idiot who pushed everyone out of the way, and beat up on the girl who worked to keep him in funds. That sort generally carried a sword."

"And would you know now?" Anselm busied himself with cleaning the brushes. "Would you know a decent swordsman if you saw one—by the swagger, say, or by the stance?"

"Only," said the Duke, "if he were being particularly annoying. May I see that?"

When Anselm offered the brush for inspection, close, so the weak eyes could focus on it, the Duke closed his fingers around the young man's wrist. His touch was paper-dry. Anselm kept his arm steady, although his eyelids trembled, a fringe of dark lashes surrounding blue eyes so dark as to be almost violet.

"You have a good wrist," the Duke observed. "When do you practice?"

"In my room." Anselm swallowed. His skin was burning where the bony fingers barely touched it.

"Have you killed anyone?"

"No—not yet."

"They don't kill much, nowadays, I hear. Demonstration bouts, a little blood on the sleeve."

The Duke's wife came in at the door without knocking, full of her achievement. But the Duke held his servant's wrist for one moment more, and looked at his face, and saw that he was beautiful.

Visitors sometimes were allowed, although not the ones who promised a miracle cure. The pain came and went; the Duke took to asking his wife two and three times a day whether there were enough poppy juice in the house laid by. The medicine made his mind wander, so that he talked with ghosts, and she learned more of his past than sometimes she wanted to hear. When visitors came, people who were still alive, she often sat quietly in a corner of the room, willing herself invisible, to learn more. Other old men, more robust than her husband, she still found not half as beautiful. She wondered how he ever could have touched them, and tried to imagine them young and blooming.

Lord Sansome came to gloat, her husband said, or maybe to apologize; either way, it would be amusing to see what time had done with him. She thought admitting such a man unwise, but he made a nice change from the ghosts.

Sansome had bad teeth and a poor color, but he took the glass of wine that Anselm offered. The nobleman approved the young servant up and down. He settled by the bed with his gold-headed stick upright between his knees.

The Duke watched his visitor through half-lidded eyes; he was tired, but wanted no drugs until he'd gone.

Sansome uttered no commonplaces, nor was he offered any. And so there was silence until the Duke said, "Whatever you are thinking is probably true. Thank you for coming. It is prodigious kind."

His foreign wife didn't know what *prodigious* meant. It sounded like an insult; she readied herself for action. But Lord Sansome continued to sit.

The Duke closed his eyes but kept on talking: "I do not think that I am going to die while you sit there. Though I know it would please you greatly."

Across the room, Anselm made a noise that in a less well-bred servant would have been a snort. He busied himself with the brushes, so that all they could hear was their *hush-hush-hush* as he cleaned.

At last, Sansome spoke. "I thought you gone years ago. No one knew where you were. I thought you'd died of a broken heart."

"It mended."

"You told me you didn't have one."

"Wishful thinking. I see that yours beats on."

"Oh, yes." Sansome's thick-veined hands opened and closed on the gold ball of his stick. "Mine does. Though we never know what's around the corner, do we?"

"I believe I do."

"Perhaps something may yet surprise you." Unexpectedly, Lord Sansome smiled warmly at the Duke's manservant. Anselm looked annoyed.

"He's good with a blade," Sansome observed.

"You've had the pleasure?"

"Once or twice. A nice, close shave."

"Oh." The old Duke laughed, and kept on laughing at a joke no one else could see, until his breath drew in pain, and wife and servant shut him off from view while they held and gave him drink to ease him.

When Lord Sansome was gone, "People do not forget," the Duke said dreamily. "I think this pleases me. Or why would I have come back?"

"My references came from somewhere." Anselm was curt with the Duke, who had been goading him with revelations. They were alone together. "I never would have gotten in to you without them. Your family checked; and I do know how to valet. Now tell me again. Tell me about how he held his hands."

"They were never empty. He was always doing something: gripping bars to strengthen his wrists, squeezing balls, tossing a knife . . . and other things." The Duke smiled most annoyingly to himself. Anselm was coming to know that smile, and knew that there was no coaxing out of the Duke whatever memories it hid.

The old man's face clouded, and he began to swear, inelegantly, with pain. Anselm wiped his sweating face with a cold cloth, and kept on this way until the Duke could speak again: "As an adventure, this is beginning to pall. Life grows dull when all I have to wonder about is how long my shirt will stay dry, and whether I am going to swallow soup or vomit it up. I would say, let's have it over and done with, but my wife will not like that. Of course," he bared his teeth in a painful grin, "she doesn't like me in this condition, either. There really is no pleasing some people."

"You must take comfort in the child that is to come."

"Not really. That was only to please my wife. I do not want posterity. I was a great disappointment to my parents."

Anselm shrugged. "Aren't we all?"

"But when I am dead, it will keep her from doing something stupid. That is important."

Anselm was good at catching hints. "Shall I fetch your lady?"

"No." The Duke's hand was cold on his. "Let us talk."

"I'm not like you," Anselm said hopelessly. "Words are not

my tools. All I can do is ask questions. You are the one who knows things, sir, not I. What I want to know, even you cannot show me."

"Annoying for you," the sick man said; "since sometimes I do see him, yet—in the corners of the room. But it's only the drugs, since he never answers when I speak."

"He was the greatest swordsman who ever lived. If taking drugs would let me see him, I'd do it." Anselm paced the room, his measured valet's demeanor given way to an athlete's ardent stride. "I wonder, sometimes, if there is any point even in trying. He took his secrets with him. If only I could have watched how he did what he did!" The sick man made no reply. "You were there. You saw. What did you see? Can't you tell me? What did you see?"

The Duke slowly smiled, his vision turned inward. "It was beautiful; not like this. He killed them quickly, with one blow, straight to the heart."

"How?" Anselm demanded, fists clenched. "No one offers his heart to the sword."

With every one of his fighter's senses, he felt the Duke's regard full upon him, unclouded by dream or pain. It drew him back to the bed, as though to close with an opponent, or a partner.

"No one?" the Duke whispered. Anselm knelt to hear him. "Not no one, boy."

The Duke's hand drifted down into his dark and springy hair.

Anselm said, "You are a terrible man." He seized the fingers, tangled in his hair with his own, and pulled them through his curls down to his mouth.

Lying by him in the dark, the Duke's wife said, "I have seen so many women through childbirth, I should be more afraid. But I am not. I know this will be a good child. I hope that you will see him."

His hand was on her gently rounded belly. "I hope he will not be too unhappy."

"As you were?" she answered sadly. "No, my darling. This one will know that he is loved, I promise you!" She gripped his fragile hand; fading, like the rest of him, even in the dark. "And he will know all about his father, that I promise, too."

"No," the man said; "not if it makes him unhappy."

"He will be happy."

"You promise that, do you?" She heard his smile. "Will you take him back to the island, then, to run with the goats?"

"Certainly not!" Sometimes the things he assumed amazed her. "He will stay here, with his family. He must be raised in your city, among people who know you."

"I think he would be more happy on the island." The Duke sighed. "I wish I could go back there, after, and rest on a hill above the sea. But I suppose it is impossible."

In a small voice she said, "I suppose it is. Where will you go, then?"

"I shall lie in the Stone City: ranks and ranks of tombs like houses, with all my ancestors, my family—that should please your sense of decorum. They are not the company I would have chosen, but I suppose I will not care then."

"I will bring him there. To visit you."

He pulled his hand away. "By no means. I forbid it."

"But I want him to know you."

"If you insist on telling the child stories about me, do it somewhere nice, with a fire, and bread and milk. . . ." She had given him poppy syrup; soon he would sleep. "I hope he will be beautiful. Not like me. Beautiful as you are. As *he* was."

Some of the time, he spoke of people she did not know. But she knew this one well, this loved ghost from his past, the beautiful, the rare, first love and best. She willed her breath to evenness, her arms to softness. A memory, nothing, against a living child.

"I wanted him to kill me. Years ago. But he never got round to it."

"Hush, love, hush."

"No, but he promised! And so I hold him to it. In the end he failed me, he left me. But he will come for me. Long ago he promised to come for me. He is my death."

She held him tightly to her, hoping he was too far gone to notice her sobbing breath, and the tears that fell on both their skins.

Lord Sansome did not come again, though he sent the Duke's bodyservant, Anselm, a gift of money.

"What will you spend it on?" the Duke inquired; "swords or sweethearts?"

His servant frowned. "I feel I should return it. It isn't right for me to take what I do not intend to earn."

"Oh, re-eally?" Weariness drew out the old man's drawl. "But surely my old friend can be nothing but pleased that you care for me so thoroughly? It is his right to tip you if he wishes."

Anselm drew back. "Do you want to be shaved or don't you?"

"Is anyone expected?"

"No one but Her Ladyship, and that not until noon."

"She will not mind. The way I look, I mean. Put that thing down, Anselm. It is the wrong blade for you. Lord Sansome doesn't know it, but I do. I do."

The hours when he knew her grew farther apart. At last, she was uncovering every thing that he had kept from her—promises to his first wife, quarrels with his lovers, games with his sister—she heard a young man's voice, disputing with a tutor, and murmuring provocation so sweet it could only be to his old lover, the first and best. Did she give him more poppy than she should, to keep the voices coming, and to shield him from the pain? She tried, but in the end she had to fail, as even love could not appease the author of the play that he was in. He did not eat, he barely spoke. The old tart who had known him young came back to the door. His lady would not let her in to see him now, but, seeking her own comfort, went down to sit a moment with this relic of his past.

In the shadowed room, the Duke's patient servant waited.

The old Duke opened his eyes wide and looked at him.

"Oh," he said. "I didn't think it would be now."

"When else?" said the swordsman. "I promised, didn't I?"

"You did. I thought you had forgotten."

"No. Not this."

"I always wanted you to."

"Of course you did. But that wasn't the time."

"How bright it is! Do it quickly. I'm afraid of pain."

The other end of the bright blade laughed. "You can't breathe properly. You can't even feel your feet. This will be quick. Open your arms, now."

"Oh," said the old Duke again; "I knew you'd come."

Tucson, Arizona, Dec. 24, 1996

For Delia Sherman, with thanks for her part of the dialogue

IN MEMORIAM: *Dallas B. Sherman*

Feb. 22, 1908–Dec. 24, 1995

ESTHER M. FRIESNER

BROWN DUST

"SANTOS, WHAT DO YOU SEE?"

"The white Christ." The boy shrugs his shoulders, dusky and thin as twigs with just a little afterthought of meat wrapped around them. "What else can you see from everywhere in Rio?"

The other boy is bigger, stronger, older. His fists are just the size of Santos' face. His skin is lighter too. He leans forward, rises on the balls of his bare feet, and the growl wells up from inside him. He is proud, sensitive to any show of insolence. He is ready to fight.

"Adao, no." Teo, the older boy's second-in-command, lays a staying hand on his master's arm. "The stories I told you about this one . . . they're true."

"True?" Adao casts a skeptic's eye over Santos. Can those flimsy ribs cage anything as fugitive as truth? There is nothing extraordinary about the brown boy. Scabby, knappy skull, easily smashed in with a loose cobblestone or scored open with the board-and-nail mace that Adao carries as his sign of mastery.

Rags. Stink. He's not even pretty enough to attract the attention of the men who are willing to pay for such things. That is the truth of Santos, as Adao sees it.

Still Teo insists: "Piri didn't listen to him."

Piri is dead.

Adao knows that death limits every argument here. This life he and his friends live is a scanty, dry-sucked thing, life on the rind, but death—! Even the wisdom of rats flees it, and rats are maybe all that lives worse than he and his gang, little accidents of humanity. Adao knows how death excels at hide-and-seek up streets and down dark alleys, in the cold shadow of the shining buildings, under the very feet of the white Christ. Death plays tag using the bullets of grown men who hunt them like rats because they are poor and small and who will miss them?

The game is to slip away from that last, cold meeting for as long as possible, gain meat, grow, until there is a chance that you can run the streets on your own, or convince a girl to walk them for you. Adao is almost there. He did not come this far, live this long, by being a fool.

"What do you see for me tonight, Santos?" he repeats, and his fists are only filthy hands now.

The brown boy's smile is gray and green. "What are you paying me to see?"

The music from the true streets dances into the alley, drapes the children with invisible roses. It is Carnaval. Goodbye to meat. The days of abstention are upon us, if we are pious and of the One True Faith. The children of Rio are very pious all the year around.

"You remember Marta?" Adao's throat is tight.

"Your sister?" Santos studies his nails. They are encrusted with grime and broken, but he once read this gesture—casual, elegant—in the mind of a tourist, long ago, and he has taken it for his own. The tourist looked right at him and never saw him there. Santos looked right at the tourist, and took the glowing image of a man, pulsing black and white and shades of gray, lounging against a tall white pillar in the moonlight, contemplating the shining perfection of his own nails. He would have taken more from the tourist, but he was only four then, and new to the life. He did not yet know all he could do.

"Marta has work," Adao says. "In the hotel, the one with the red sign, the one two streets over from where Joao was run over."

"I know the place. That's where she takes her men?"

Adao's fists remain simply hands. It is no insult to hear a puny nothing of a brown boy like Santos intimate that your sister is a whore—your sister, who is even whiter than you! Your mother was a whore, but not a very good one, or you would still be with her, she would still be alive. Your sister sold her body when she was ten to a man who was so white he made her look brown beside him. Adao saw it all, remembers it all, though he was only three. The man paid extra to have Adao watch him with Marta, and patted the boy on the head and gave him candy. But Marta was too plain and skinny to sell herself with much success after her virginity was gone.

"Marta doesn't have any men to take anywhere," Adao tells Santos. "She's a chambermaid."

Santos lets out a long, low whistle of admiration. "No shit! Where does she live, then?" *And why do you still live on the streets?* his eyes add with a knife.

Adao lets the question pass. His silence puts out thorns that are black at the tips with venom or dried blood. "There's a man," he begins.

Santos makes kissing sounds and wastes languishing looks on Adao. He gets no reaction, so he adds to this his reedy voice raised in a song of unrequited lovers dying of their pain.

And he blinks and gulps and thrashes in Adao's grip at his throat like an iguana pinned by the sudden downthrust of a forked stick. The older boy brings his face close to Santos', stink to stink, and lets the words out only through the thin line of shadow between his teeth.

"Did you see *that* coming, cocksucker?" he hisses. "Can you see what's coming to you now?"

Santos gulps again. He is dangling on tiptoe, his cracked black and yellow toenails just barely scraping against the street, but he still drags on a dog's grin.

"You only have a broken razor left, the blade keeps slipping loose from its handle," he says, every word an air-starved whisper. "That and a board with a nail. Your good knife is gone, you think it's lost, but it's in the bottom of your sister's scrub-bucket. She thinks that if you have no knife, it will keep you out of big fights. She took it from you while you slept out in back of the hotel, with the rest of the garbage, and you didn't notice it was gone until you stole that jackfruit from Mama Conceicao's stand. Her man chased you, he almost caught you by the blue house near Ogun's sacred ground, and when you reached for your knife to cut him away from you, that was when you discovered it was gone." The Santos-dog has found an offering of dead things in the sidewalk to roll in and to eat; he grins wider. "You had to run very fast then, my brother."

Adao lets Santos drop. The older boy's face is tight, screwed up into more creases than a monkey's asshole. He is afraid, and because he is almost a man he makes it sound like anger. "How do you *do* it, you headless mule? How do you see, how do you *know*?"

The other children look from Adao's anger to Santos' graceful indifference. The boy shrugs again, but he never shrugs the same way twice. He has borrowed a thousand ways to pretend that nothing in life is of any consequence, a nosegay of idle poses plucked from the pampered daughters of the old cacao families, the sons of the coffee kings who wear the university ring of medicine or law. He has watched them from the shadows, laid hands on them inside and out because he could, but as to the *how* of it all—

"I don't know." A new way to shrug, this one a *fado* singer's creation, the last gesture those honey-colored shoulders made as she cast aside her rich protector for the poor black truck driver she loved. Santos took it from her dying mind just as the old man's knife opened her throat to let out blood instead of music. "I just *see*. Not everything, not any more—" The shudder that blows over his bones in dreadful recollection of those lunatic times is no one's but his alone. "I didn't choose to see you make that grab for me, but if I had— Ah, the hell with it. You want to pay me for talk or work?"

An empty question. "There's a man," Adao says once more, back to business, just as if time could fold back on itself like an old flour sack. "He's taken a room in Marta's hotel. She says he's rich, she's seen the rings he wears, and once he left his wallet on the table by his bed. She never *saw* so much money."

The other children murmur and roll their eyes. Marta works in the hotel where the tourists come, Marta sees money every day, many kinds—dollars, milreis, cruzeiros, francs, yen, deutschmarks. For *her* to say such a thing . . . Probably enough money for her to take some and the loss to go unnoticed. They can scarcely get their minds around the idea of so much, such plenty. The murmurs sink down into awed silence like rain into arid earth.

"And what?" Santos asks. "You want to rob him? Your sister hasn't got the guts to lift his roll herself, scared she'll lose her shitass job, that it? You want me to see where he'll go some night, a lonely place, a devil's hour? Sure, that's not so—"

"I want you to see what he'll do to me when we're alone," Adao says.

Santos tilts his head, letting the words slide in at one ear, letting his scurf-flecked brows meet in a frown of perplexity. "But you don't want to *do* it," he protests. "You're wrapped so tight against the thought of it that he'll need a wedge to—"

Teo siezes Santos by the back of his neck and shakes him twice, hard. Little bones go crick-crick-crack under the skin. "Adao's not paying you to ask questions."

Santos is the aristocratic Englishman who turned away in

cold disgust from the little nigger who dared to occupy the same sidewalk as his tailormade linen self. Santos let Teo know without a word that he is a spreading stain on the earth and the sooner gone, the better. Teo feels Santos' borrowed scorn pour over his skin like icy oil. He lets Santos go.

"All right," he says to Adao, blowing Teo away like sea mist. "You want to know that much, that little from me, fine. You want to know what happens when you're with the man, but which man? You better tell me that. You plan to do this now, maybe for the same reason you'll do it again, again, again. I can't see how your first fuck's going to be different from your fifteenth, your fiftieth. You want me to see, you have to let me know."

The air hums and keens around Adao's slender body. The shouts and cries of distant Carnaval blow into this alley on a wind that plays a different tune over lives pulled taut and thin as harpstrings. "What do you need to know?"

"What he looks like."

"I don't know that yet. Marta says he's white, tall, curly brown hair, brown eyes that look a little green sometimes, strong." He tastes his own lips, tastes sand, salt, dread. "Very strong."

"No picture of him in your mind, nothing there to help me." Santos is cross. "Not unless he's the only man in the whole hotel who looks like that. Any scars? Any limp when he walks? Anything, anything?"

"I told you what Marta told me." Adao meets Santos' crossness with a sullen look of his own. "That he's tall, that he's white—"

"White! Lord of Bomfim, Adao, even *you* look white!"

"Hey, the man won't be the only one there for this, stupid. Can't you tell what'll happen between us by looking at *me*?"

Santos is silent. He has walked this thread before, and it scores the soles of his feet like a burning wire. Even the *thought* of doing what Adao asks squeezes his guts dry. To read Adao's path holds too many possibilities, opens too many doors. If he ventures inside the older boy's skull the future will splinter into a million chances, the lottery of the dead. Paths will close and open as he watches, like the mouths of baby birds, steel blades will sweep across the scope of his vision, bullets will make their sharp, unanswerable arguments, disease will settle in comfortably under Adao's smutty skin to drink the marrow and gnaw the bone, and for what? For a last vision of brown dust blown away on the wind of rich men's speeches and tourists' laughter?

When Santos was just a little past his fourth year, soon after he first knew what he could do, he threw himself into the embrace of his visions, wrapped himself up in their warmth the way the other children of the streets flung their bodies into flimsy newspaper coccoons against the rain. His gift was very strong; he was too young to suspect the danger. Because he *could* know, he *would* know. The city at the white Christ's feet teemed with lives and dreams and futures. Hunger and cold and curses that snapped in his face like the flick of a whip's supple tongue all taught him that any life was better than his own, even if he only borrowed it. Famished, belly and heart, the child Santos made the lives and dreams and futures his, all his, all of them, all at once, because he could.

They found him thrashing in his madness, the women in their brightly flounced and tiered skirts, the good steeds of the *orixás* Xango and Exú and Oxumare. They had carried these gods of their ancestors within their bodies often enough to think they recognized what had happened to this child. They brought him to the sacred ground where they danced and gave his flailing body to their *paesanto*. Santos woke in the godspeaker's arms to the beating of the drums, the smell of the offerings, the chanting of the people, the prophecies and commands that the *orixás* spoke out of the mouths of their human steeds. His vision was only in his eyes.

What the *paesanto* told him was a simple truth: He was too young to bear the weight of so much seeing, even if he owned the power to summon it. He taught the child to make himself door and doorkeeper and gave him into the protection of Exú Tiriri, made him the devil's own, for only the devil has the strength enough to shield a child from demons.

Yet for all this, he could still hear the *paesanto*'s last warning: *Do not seek to look down all the paths, child, for every path that awaits us is guarded by a demon's gate, and not even Exú Tiriri can destroy so many demons.*

Santos remembers good advice and bad dreams. He tells Adao a lie: "It doesn't work that way. Your head's too full of garbage for me to see where this will lead you. I can only do this through the man. Go back, ask your sister more about him, try—"

"Forget it." Adao turns away, impatient, tired of courting a skinny kid he could break in two with a single blow. "I'll look after myself. Teo, my razor's broken, crap, can you lend me yours?"

Teo is about to give his master what he asks, his razor, his soul, his love. Teo is thinking that Santos tells the truth when he says he can't see everything, when he claims Adao's set against doing this thing with the rich man. How set against it can Adao be when Teo knows that the beautiful boy and he have already—But then it was Adao who was the top dog, Adao who said how and how many times, when to begin, when to stop, Adao who never spoke of it after and beat his loyal Teo's head against the plastered wall of a house the one time the other boy was the one to offer the first inquiring touch. Teo reaches for his razor and finds Santos standing in the way before the blade sees light.

"And if he's got the way to take it from you?" Santos shouts into Adao's face. "Already you're afraid of him, fear loosens your fingers along with your bowels. It won't be hard for him to break your grip on that shitty razor. Then what? You're dead in the backstreet next morning, a slash across the throat instead of a bullet in the head, but still just as dead as Piri. Better let your big white sweetheart do anything he wants with you, even what hurts, even if you die from being hurt so bad. This death, that, that man's hand with Teo's blade in it or one of the death squads' men with a gun shoved through your teeth, who cares? The stupid ones always die."

Rage bloodies Adao's eyes, but this time when he makes a grab for the little brown boy, Santos steps aside. He moves only as fast and as far as it takes for Adao's hands to close on air, and then he laughs and closes his eyes. He doesn't even need to look at Adao to see which way he'll strike next. Santos *sees*. He bobs and dodges and bows in a mocking minuet that any *capoeira* master might envy. He does this even when Teo bulls his way unasked into this farce of a fight. He does it until the other children are laughing with him, while Teo and Adao stand frustrated, foiled, shackled immobile in every muscle but the tongues that pour foulness over Santos and his kin.

Santos tells them, "My mother's dead, if she ever lived at all. Let her be a whore, if you want it that way. All of our dead mothers are whores, in *their* eyes." He nods to where bright lights flicker just beyond the alley's dark mouth, where pretty women worry if it will take all vacation to find a bartender in this wild and foreign place who knows how to make a *decent* martini. "You can die and be dust under their feet now, or you can use what I can share."

Adao lowers his head. This horse feels the bridle. "What else do you need before you can see for me? I don't know anything much. Marta didn't even tell me his room number, just what he looked like and that he was really rich and that he wanted a boy."

"A white boy," Santos corrects him.

"I never said—"

"You didn't have to." Santos smiles, and Adao claps his hands over his ears as if to stop his thoughts leaking out like an infection. This only makes Santos laugh. He tells Adao what they must do if the older boy wants his answer.

Marta is not pleased to see her brother, less pleased to see he's brought a friend. Ascanio who wrangles the hotel's big trashcans is always the one who lets Adao in. He does this because he adores Marta and because Marta fears him enough to let him fuck her any time he likes, old as he is, touched as he is by the signs of the sickness that will eat him up alive. Once he was a pretty boy too. When Marta sees her brother with this scabby little nigger she knows she'll have the usual price to pay Ascanio for it later. Her mouth grows small with distaste, already prepared to spit seed.

"Who is this?" she demands, glowering at Adao's companion. "Adao, are you crazy? I told you, never bring anyone here! My job—"

"Give him back his knife, you stupid bitch," Santos says, showing his gravemold smile. "Go fish it out of the bottom of your bucket, dry it off, rub out the five little rust spots near the hinge. You want him to stay alive, you think *not* having a knife will save him from fights? Better you start thinking with what stinks between your legs than with what's missing between your ears."

Marta gasps and makes the sign of the cross, then clutches the little talisman of the *orixá* Yansen that hangs from her neck. "Adao . . ." With trembling voice she gropes for her brother's support against this monster.

"Santos sees things," Adao replies calmly. "Do what he tells you about the knife later. Listen to me now."

Marta listens. Marta tells Santos all she can about the man in Room 903. He is indeed very rich. He hasn't even noticed that he's lost money and one of his rings this week to her dancing fingers. He seems to like her. After all, hasn't he spoken to her with respect, called her *Dona* Marta, asked her if maybe she knows of a boy, clean, white? Not just one of the usual whores, no, but one who'll be doing this for the first time, a virgin, one he can keep with him for the rest of the time he'll be staying in Rio. He's a fine man, educated, speaking Portuguese with no trace of foreign accent, though his passport makes him American, and he's named a fine price for the boy, a finder's fee for Marta.

"A *virgin*?" Santos sputters with glee.

"With the men," Marta says, stiff with dignity. She looks at her brother and repeats, "A virgin with the men."

"Oh, well he's *that.*" Santos speaks for Adao. "One way, at least, the way this one wants, I bet. If it were any tighter, it'd be sewed shut."

"Well?" Marta asks. "Now can you tell us? The man who wants Adao, is he safe? If my brother goes with him—" She doesn't ask the rest. Even a child without Santos' gift could know that rest of her question: *If my brother goes with him, will I have a brother left alive after?*

Santos only says, "Get the knife."

Later the rich man in Room 903 opens his door to Marta and Santos. The chambermaid has an ingratiating smile, a pleading look in her eyes that mirrors the whip constantly upraised against her, invisible to all but she. "Sir, here he is," she says.

As expected, the man frowns to see the little brown thing she has in tow. He shakes his head briskly, barks a few words: *White. Clean. Stupid girl.* Marta begs his pardon while Santos wanders leisurely through his skull, reading big cars and big meals and good liquor. There are many shadows there too, but none of them seems to hold blood. Santos lingers among the shining visions until Marta grabs him by his tattered sleeve and drags him away, vowing to the rich man that this time she will get it right.

"It's safe," Santos tells Adao, and so Marta sneaks her brother into a bathtub, gets him cleaned up, presentable, and takes him to his man. She is grateful to Santos for his reassurance—a pity if her doubts had put the rich man's money in some common pimp's pocket!—and she sneaks him down to the hotel kitchen where he feasts on the room service leavings until his belly sticks out like a cannonball. Fullness lulls him. He goes out back to where the garbage cans are kept and in Adao's familiar place of refuge he sleeps.

The shadow finds him there, where the roaches scurry and the rats wink red eyes. The shadow is a brighter red than the rats' eyes, a red that smells of steel and copper, keen, its color heightened by a scream that only sounds inside a boy's head. Santos bolts awake, Adao's face before him, shiny silver tape across his mouth, shiny silver tape strapping wrists to ankles, his old knife flickering just out of reach in the last light before his eyes.

"No," Santos breathes into the darkness. He leaps to his feet, but his legs shake and fold beneath him. The sight of Adao's bound body melts into the outline of a glossy red sports car, a plate of crisply roasted duckling, a man who smiles.

He is there, tall and white, brown hair, brown eyes that sometimes look green, strong. Strong enough to step out of mere words into reality, to be outside of Santos' skull as well as within. His body fills the gap that leads from the alley to the street. Dawn is staining the air behind him gray. He stands with hands on hips, and through the open triangles his arms describe Santos glimpses a drunk who staggers past on the far side of the street. A woman fledged in yellow plumes and pink sequins slouches by in the other direction, dead-eyed. Neither one of them cares about what's happening in the alley, though the woman is briefly curious. Santos feels her idle inquiry brush his mind, even though he has not chosen to read her, a dancing particle of dust that slips through the slats of a tightly-drawn blind. He is losing his control because he is so afraid.

The man says only, "You'll come with me."

His grip on Santos' arm is powerful. The brown boy doesn't waste his effort struggling against it. The man escorts him in through the kitchen, up the service elevator, into the room where Adao's corpse lies bleeding on the bed. The man must be very, very rich; he hasn't even bothered to use the bathtub for his sport. Adao's left eye is a silver coin, his right a gaping hole in the universe through which Santos sees fading galaxies of pain. The man gives the brown boy a clear view, then says, "This can be you."

Then he makes him sit on a chair and gives him a sandwich to eat, ham on bread so white and soft that the boy's fingers dig dirty brown craters in it right down to the pink slice of boiled ham. Santos stares but doesn't eat, doesn't move, thinks he has forgotten how to breathe. When all the world has traded its cold reliabilities for wildfire madness, best to keep very still and wait for salvation or death.

The man seems troubled by Santos' inattention to the food. "Aren't you hungry? You look like you ought to be hungry. When I was your age, I was hungry all the time, and the streets weren't any kinder then than now." He takes a heavy-sided water glass from a table beside the bed, beside Adao's corpse, and fills it with Coca-Cola. "Drink."

Santos follows orders. There are no lights on in this room, but he reads the path the man's hand takes in the dark just as he read the shape and shadings of Adao's body, the way an ordinary person might see a drift of sand draped in the shape of a flower and know that a rose lies buried beneath the windblown grains. Santos reaches out his own hand to take the glass, but he is shaking so badly that he drops it.

Cold liquid splashes up, runs in sticky trails through the filth between his toes. The man curses. Santos believes that now he's going to die. There is no sense left in holding onto reality, in holding off all the things that he can see, not with the edge of a knife pacing off the boundary of his breath. Better to die too crazy to know that you are dying. Santos lets his mind open and welcomes all the clamoring images that desire to come in.

Nothing. Nothing, nothing, nothing but darkness beyond black, darkness the color of space without stars. Santos gasps and the man laughs. "I've put my walls around you," he says. "It's as if I'd dropped you into the bottom of a deep glass jar. Then I paint the inner surface with what I want you to see. This is how I did it, how I blocked your visions. That was easy. Changing them to fictions of my own, that was hard, but they don't pay me for doing what's easy."

And only now Santos feels a corner of the darkness peel

away, senses his mind regaining its special sight. There is a boy—not Santos, not Adao, none of the bird-boned children of invisibility and forgetfulness, no one Santos knows. This boy too walks under the shadow of the white Christ, he prowls the glare of the white sand beaches, he filches what he can from anywhere, anyone, and he feels a belly that never knows the meaning of *enough*. He isn't very pretty, but he looks almost white: Long-limbed, brown hair, brown eyes that are sometimes flecked with green, weak. He has filled his eyes with things unseen by others: Cobbled streets where children lie dead or sleeping, Carnaval revelers whose bones are as ready to snap as to dance, little girls who sell the bloody breaking of their maidenhoods for bread, mothers who call on God and die at the devil's hands.

He has seen enough.

Lights go on in the hotel room. The man takes something out of his jacket pocket and shows it to Santos. "Do you know what this is?" Santos can't read, but he knows.

"Law," is all he can say.

The man smiles. "Very good." He folds away the signs of his honorable profession, the insignia of one who has dedicated his life to keeping the great city of Rio clean of the vermin that breed crime. "They found me on the street when I was a couple of years older than you. They were going to kill me; they'd already killed my friend Nico. But before they could put a bullet in my brain, I started screaming things at them, things I knew about each one just by being near him, things that they had never brought into the light. They might've taken me for a lunatic except for the truth of every dirty thing that broke from my mouth. I screamed and screamed their secrets in their faces until one of them ran away, one crumpled like a paper cup, but the third—"

The man shakes his head and chuckles fondly, as if he is remembering a birthday party, the sweet taste of yellow cake, rich with eggs and butter, the festival sight of ribbon-wrapped presents. "The third man, he *saw*. He saw without being able to see the way you and I can. He looked past the shame of his own hidden sins—the secrets I was screaming out of hiding—and understood what I was and what I could be. He put his arm around me and took me home." The man's smile still lies across his lips, but Santos sees a drowned face float up out of the depths beneath it, a boy's face emptied of everything but fear.

The man is speaking again, but Santos doesn't hear. The man's words fill him with images and icons, pour themselves into the cistern of his brain until Santos imagines that the words will never stop, that they will keep on flowing until they come bursting out in twin floods from his eyes.

What is this man telling him, what is he saying? Promises, offers, rewards, life. A life of clean rooms, new clothes, food brought to his plate instead of scrounged from a gutter, education, favors, praise, a single path that soars straight and wide and soft all the way to heaven. This, all this for Santos when the man names him his son.

"They'll whisper about it, of course," the man is saying. "A kid? Me? Me and some woman? I got tired of women long ago, before any of the men I work with really got to know me. They think I've never wanted a woman. Well, not any more. Nothing there to see with women, just them wanting plain things—love, care, cash, babies. With men at least you get them hating it, the ones I pick. I don't go after the butterflies—too much like women—only the ones who do it for the money, because it's what they've got to do to eat even if they hate it. Hate that can never break out, lift a hand against you, not even *breathe* on you because you've got too much power, because *you* can break *them* any time you like and the poor bastards know it." He smiles. "Delicious."

Santos says nothing. Santos is still mesmerized by the deathmask of the time-drowned boy that drifts across the leering face of the man.

The man is still speaking. He needs no one to listen for his words to be real. He is his own reality. "They know how I am, they *think* they know, at the station, but no one says a word. With all I can give them, no one's got the balls to cross me, not even when I let them know I only want the young ones now. Oh, if I asked for the captain's son, I suppose he'd find a way to buy me off, but if I insisted—" A shrug. This is one that Santos will let go by, unborrowed.

"I'm good. No hound can trace things like I can. One man I met at the gaming table, an American, he caught on to me. An educated man, a scientist, I think. He was fascinated, and he was young. It gets better when they're young." His eyes slew towards the bed.

Leaves tumble over the brown boy's eyes. Suddenly he is himself a hound running through woods he has never known, trees that are cold and gray, crowned with red and umber and gold. He hears an unfamiliar voice like a wind rushing through the treetops, a voice that puts a hard American edge to the soft caress of Portuguese. It is telling the man that such highly developed powers of mind might be genetic, a mutation become a heritage, a wonderful gift to be cultivated like the heavy pods of the finest cacao trees. The power dwells in every part of him, cell and seed, each thought an entity, electric, holding an independent world, imperceptible to the eye yet still there. The voice tells of the particles that teem through the bolts of ungoverned lightning that scatter themselves across the skies, speaks lovingly of those same grains of fire and light after men have read their secrets, guided them into the civilized paths of circuits and wires.

Then the voice is asking the man to come away with him to the land where these strange trees grow, to give himself to the brick-walled university, to open doors. *Let us learn what you are. Let us in.*

Santos claps his hands over his eyes. Now the voice is screaming, screaming, pain and fear and betrayal all combined, twisted into a tight braid of shrill sound that runs red with the young American's blood and Piri's and Adao's and others, others, others. . . .

". . . Disney World," the man is saying. "I'll take you there too, or you can wait until you're old enough to go with a group of your school friends. Mickey Mouse? You know Mickey Mouse? Would you like to see him? Would you like to hear him laugh?" A hand touches Santos, warm and damp. "Now I know how that American felt when he found me. The pleasure of discovering a wonderful thing, a beautiful monster! You're a grubby little piece of shit right now, but I'll make you beautiful. I knew as soon as I saw you, the instant you first tried to look inside me."

"I . . . couldn't." Santos swallows bile between the words.

"Stupid, of course not!" Even now the man's mind gives up nothing, not even a name. "If what I am, what *we* are, comes through the blood, who knows how many other fields my father ploughed, how many others like me slid out between some whore's thighs? Never thought of that, did you, little blackbird?" He cuffs the side of Santos' head with a ghastly tenderness. His fond look fills Santos' mind with the image of a serpent's fang, a honey-colored drop of poison trembling pendant from the tip. "My second life is sweet, precious, protected. I've met others—not as good as I, but with their own touch of our talent. They like to play fortune-telling games, pouncing on stray scraps of their victims' thoughts, using the grain of truth they scavenge to become the foundation for a mountain of lies, bleeding the fools white—"

He stops himself, throws back his shoulders, enjoying a memory that brings only more self-satisfaction. "My first case, one of those charlatans. He was conning the wife of a cabinet minister, can you imagine the nerve of that black bastard? Oh, the look in his eyes when he realized what I was, when he knew he'd stuck his hand down a rabbit hole and pulled out a tiger—!"

The man laughs, but his laughter breaks off abruptly. The brown eyes that are sometimes flecked with green hide for a moment beneath heavy lids. "But he almost touched me. His mind crept too close to mine, I could feel it, and that was when I knew it must never happen again. I kept him alive in the jail cell long enough to practice setting up my shields. He helped me learn how keep my thoughts safe."

"Walls." The word slips from Santos' lips. A black wind blows it from his mind and the boy finds that the thick-walled jar into which he has been dropped is flawed. There are tiny cracks no thicker than a single blonde hair that shiver over the glass sides.

The man nods. To him it is only a word the boy has chosen to say. "Not around me," he says. "Why make myself a prisoner? Walls that run in an endless curve around *them*, yes; let *theirs* be the minds locked away! But never let them know it until *I* choose. I paint the glass with false images, counterfeits, so the snoops believe they're seeing my thoughts when all they touch is the soapbubble skin of a lie."

Santos doesn't ask what became of the unlucky fortune-teller after he'd outlived his value as this man's teacher. Some answers come without the need to ask the question, some thoughts come without the need to summon them as visions. Let the dead bury their dead.

The boy's silence and disinterest displease the man. A scowl grooves the smoothly shaven face, its pallor tinted ever so slightly with the blood that made his mother's skin brown. "Well?" the man demands. "What do you say? I've made you a good offer. Will you take it or do you miss your friend there?" He jerks his head to where Adao lies.

Santos touches the little coin in his pocket, all that Adao and the others could afford to pay him for his vision, a fortune. What Adao would have earned for letting this man invade his body was going to be split among all the children in the pack. Already Teo was dreaming of meat, the little sinner. "He wasn't my friend," Santos says from a parched throat. "Just another fool."

This answer makes the man happy again. "Then I can guess your answer. Good. We'll make a fine team, when you're grown and I've got you properly trained, you and your sons after you. I'd breed my own if I could, but—" He blushes and there is a brief flash in Santos' skull of a doctor's office, words, a verdict, denial, proof, rage. The man speaks on rapidly, using words to scoop the escaped images back into his own private thoughts.

His hand drops heavily onto Santos' shoulder. "And when you're big enough, you'll help me in my task, my son; our finest mission. You and I, we'll track them down together. There won't be a single one of those hairless rats we won't be able to find. We'll make this city beautiful, clean, free of them. I do well enough now, but the captain keeps taking me away from my pleasures. Abductions, murders, all the cases I must handle dutifully while the city rots away under our feet." He spits in disgust, cleaning his mouth of the foul taste of street children.

Inside his keeping jar, Santos is treated to a fine show. Images flicker and fly around the curved sides, driven in through the glass by the force of the man's mind. The glass itself is made of small, separate grains, the images are made of smaller ones still; they find the countless cracks and penetrate. Santos can not stop them.

He sees bold men stalk the streets, heroes whose quest is a cleansing. The children run, hide in all the darkened crannies where the dust of the street has always hidden, but this time the heroes come prepared. The hound races ahead, over the stones, and roots out a harvest of frightened faces. The hound smiles as the men see to the dirty business that will in time make the city clean.

Santos sees the last pleas for mercy in small eyes. Santos sees the knife and the gun and sometimes just the truncheon that breaks the side of a skull. He sees the bodies on the streets and in the alleyways and in the places of deep water. He can't turn away or close his own eyes against this gift of vision that the man urges upon him. The glass walls are not a prison to keep him in but a heavy shell to keep out all thoughts but those that the man decides are good for him to see.

They rasp against him, all these visions. They have a million tiny teeth that nibble at the core of Santos' mind. He feels it crumbling away, becoming motes of thought and will and desire blowing round and round inside his head. He lets it crumble, lets himself become those countless particles of dust that the wind whips against the glass walls. Dust alone escapes the prison, dust alone goes unnoticed underfoot. He feels himself break through, scattered, and the last thought left echoing behind inside the empty jar is: *Now I am free.*

One flying mote lodges itself behind a pair of small black eyes that haunt the baseboard of the room. The mouse peers out to witness the man's surprise when his comradely touch sends the thin body in the chair toppling over onto the rug. The mouse doesn't know why it is so important to observe this—there is a discarded ham sandwich also lying on the floor, a thing that ought to be of much greater moment to the little beast—yet still she keeps this vigil.

Now surprise is shock, shock is fury. The man picks up the slack, skinny body and makes it rattle down to the bones. When there is no response, he tosses it aside, swears. He yanks the telephone from its cradle, makes a call—"I've had some fun, Sargeant. Have the boys come look after the leavings. There's a chambermaid here you might need to deal with too. I'm heading home, I've had a shitty night, I'm tired."—and stalks out.

In the streets the dust blows across the face of the sun, into the face of the white Christ on His mountaintop. It sweeps down streets and alleyways. The sparks fall down, wild grains of freed knowledge and memory seeking new lodging, as the spirits of the *orixás* seek the bodies of their faithful steeds when the drums of the sacred ground throb the summons. The woman chosen to be Yemanjá's steed becomes the Lady of the Waters, the man who bears Exú Tiriri's spirit is the devil himself.

Teo huddles in the shadow of the cathedral. A breeze passes over his crusted eyelids, a single grain of Santos' scattered self steals into his mind. In dreams he learns the faces of his hunters, sees a hundred visions open, a hundred doors through which he can escape them if that is all he wants to do.

Teo stirs and snuffles in his sleep. He sees the face of the hound, and the trim, clean house where one man lives alone. The windows are never locked. The man sleeps on a white bed, dreaming that he is the only one capable of learning how to paint illusions on the curved glass walls he sets around his enemies. In dreams, Teo sees the brown boy's smiling face as Santos teaches him the lesson of the glass jar. He is Santos' steed, he carries all that Santos is or was or ever knew, and all that Santos tells him still needs to be done.

The window will be open, the man will be asleep. Teo will have a knife, and a glass jar painted with false images to drop over the sleeper's mind, and the image of Adao's ruined face to guide his hand.

In other corners of the city, other children stir. The sparks fall down, the seeds spread through their blood, and through the blood of all the children they will bring into the light. They will know their hunters. They will have the power to become the ones who hunt. The white Christ stretches out the shadow of His hands and a few scattered grains of Santos' self dance there, swirling on the wind.

The tourists feel the wind, and wipe away the grains of sand that sting their eyes to tears, and cough, calling for someone to do something to put an end to all this troublesome dust.

JONATHAN LETHEM

ACCESS FANTASY

THERE WAS A START-UP ABOUT A HALF-MILE AHEAD THE DAY before, a fever of distant engines and horns honking as others signalled their excitement—a chance to move!—and so he'd spent the day jammed behind the wheel, living in his Apartment On Tape, waiting for that chance, listening under the drone of distant helicopters to hear the start-up make its way downtown. But the wave of revving engines stalled before reaching his street. He never even saw a car move, just heard them. In fact he couldn't remember seeing a car move recently. Perhaps the start-up was only a panic begun by someone warming their motor, reviving their battery. That night he'd dreamed another start-up, or perhaps it was real, a far-off flare that died before he'd even ground the sleep out of his eyes, though in the rustle of his waking thoughts it was a perfect thing, coordinated, a dance of cars shifting through the free-flowing streets. Dream or not, either way, didn't matter. He fell back asleep. What woke him in the morning was the family in the Pacer up ahead cooking breakfast. They had a stove on the roof of their car and the dad was grilling something they'd bought from the flatbed shepherd two blocks away, a sheepsteak or something. It smelled good. Everything about the family in the Pacer made him too conscious of his wants. The family's daughter—she was beautiful—had been working as Advertising, pushing up against and through the One-Way Permeable Barrier on behalf of some vast faceless corporation. That being the only way through the One-Way Permeable Barrier, of course. So the family, her Ma and Pa, were flush, had dough, and vendors knew to seek them out, hawking groceries. Whereas checking his pockets he didn't have more than a couple of dollars. There was a coffee-and-donuts man threading his way through the traffic even now but coffee was beyond his means. He needed money. Rumors had it Welfare Helicopters had been sighted south of East One Thousand, One Hundred and Ninety-Fourth Street, and a lot of people had left their cars, drifted down that way, looking for easy cash. Which was one reason the start-up died, it occurred to him—too many empty cars. Along with the cars that wouldn't start anymore, like the old lady in the Impala beside him, the dodderer. She'd given up, spent most days dozing in the back seat. Her nephew from a few blocks away came over and tinkered with her engine now and again but it wasn't helping. It just meant the nephew wasn't at his wheel for the start-up, another dead spot, another reason not to bother waiting to move. Probably he thought now he should have walked downtown himself in search of welfare money drifting down from the sky. The state helicopters weren't coming around this neighborhood much lately. Alas. The air was crowded with commercial hovercraft instead, recruiters, Advertising robots rounding up the girl from the Pacer and others like her, off to the world on the other side of the One-Way Permeable Barrier, however briefly. The world of Apartments, real ones. Though it was morning he went back to his latest Apartment On Tape, which was a four bedroom two bath co-op on East One Thousand, Two Hundred and Fifteenth

Street, just a few blocks away but another world of course, remote from his life on the street, sealed off from it by the One-Way Permeable Barrier. He preferred the early part of the tape, before any of the furnishings arrived, so he rewound to that part and put the tape on slow and lived in the rooms as hard as he could, ignoring the glare of sun through his windshield that dulled his view of the dashboard television, ignoring the activities of the family in the Pacer up ahead as they clambered in and out of the hatchback, ignoring the clamor of his own pangs. The realtor's voice was annoying, it was a squawking, parroty voice so he kept the volume down as always and lived in the rooms silently, letting his mind sweep in and haunt the empty spaces, the rooms unfolding in slow motion for the realtor's camera. While the camera lingered in the bathroom he felt under his seat for his bottle and unzipped and peed, timed so it matched to the close-up of the automatic flushing of the toilet on his television. Then the camera and his attention wandered out into the hall. That's when he noticed it, the shadow. Just for a moment. He rewound to see it again. On the far wall of the hallway, framed perfectly for an instant in the lens the silhouette of a struggle, a man with his hands on the neck of another, smaller. A woman. Shaking her by the neck for that instant, before the image vanished. Like a pantomime of murder, a Punch-and-Judy show hidden in the Apartment On Tape. But real, it had to be real. Why hadn't he noticed before? He'd watched this tape dozens of times. He rewound again. Just barely, but still. Unmistakable, however brief. The savagery of it was awful. If only he could watch it frame by frame—slow motion was disastrously fast now. Who was the killer? The landlord? The realtor? Why? Was the victim the previous tenant? Questions, he had questions. He felt himself begin to buzz with them, come alive. Slow motion didn't seem particularly slow precisely because his attention had quickened. Yes, a job of detection was just what he needed to roust himself out of the current slump, burn off the torpor of too many days locked in the jam at the same damn intersection—why hadn't he gone Downtown at that last turnoff, months ago? Well, anyway. He watched it again, memorized the shadow, the silhouette, imagined blurred features in the slurry of video fuzz, memorized the features, what the hell. Like a police sketch, work from his own prescient hallucinations. Again. It grew sharper every time. He'd scrape a hole in this patch of tape, he knew, if he rewound too many times. Better to have the tape, the evidence, all there was at this point. He popped the video, threw it in a satchel with notebook, eyeglasses. Extra socks. Outside, locked the car, tipped an imaginary hat at the old lady, headed east by foot on West One Thousand, Two Hundred and Eighth Street. He had to duck uptown two blocks to avoid a flotilla of Sanitation hovertrucks spraying foamy water to wash cars sealed up tight against this artificial rain but also soaking poor jerks asleep, drenching interiors, the rotted upholstery and split spongy dashboards, extinguishing rooftop bonfires, destroying box gardens, soap bubbles poisoning the feeble sprouts. Children screamed and giggled, the streets ran with water, sluicing shit here and there into drains, more often along under the tires to the unfortunate neighboring blocks, everyone moaning and lifting their feet clear. Just moving it around, that's all. Around the next corner he ran into a crowd gathered staring at a couple of young teenage girls from inside, from the apartments, the other side of the Barrier. They'd come out of the apartment building on rollerblades to sightsee, to slum on the streets. Sealed in a murky bubble of One-Way Permeable Barrier they were like apparitions, dim ghosts, though you could hear them giggle as they skated through the hushed, reverent crowd. Like a sighting of gods, these teenage girls from inside. No one bothered to spare-change them or bother them in any way because of the Barrier. The girls of course were oblivious behind their twilight veil, like night things come into the day, though for them probably it was the people in cars and around the cars that appeared dim, unreachable. He shouldered his way through the dumbstruck crowd and once past this obstacle he found his man, locked into traffic like all the rest, right where he'd last seen him. The Apartments On Tape dealer, his connection, sunbathing in a deck chair on the roof of his Sentra, eating a sandwich. The backseat was stacked with realtor's tapes, apartment porn, and on the passenger seat two video decks for dubbing. His car in a sliver of morning sun that shone across the middle of the block, benefit of a chink in the canyon of towers that surrounded them. The dealer's neighbors were on their car roofs as well, stretching in the sun, drying clothes. "Hello there, remember me? That looks good what you're eating, anyway, I want to talk to you about this tape." "No refunds," said the dealer, not even looking down. "No, that's not it, I saw something, can we watch it together?" "No need since there's no refunds and I'm hardly interested—" "Listen, this is a police matter, I think—" "You're police then, is that what you're saying?" still not looking down. "No no, I fancy myself a private detective, though not to say I work outside the law, more adjacent, then turn it over to them if serves justice, there's so often corruption—" "So turn it over," the dealer said. "Well if you could just have a look I'd value your opinion. Sort of pick your brain," thinking flattery or threats, should have chosen one approach with this guy, stuck with it. The dealer said, "Sorry, day off," still not turning his head, chewing off another corner of sandwich. Something from inside the sandwich fell, a chunk of something, fish maybe, onto the roof of the car. "The thing is I think I saw a murder, on the tape, in the apartment." "That's highly unlikely." "I know, but that's what I saw." "Murder, huh?" The dealer didn't sound at all impressed. "Bloody body parts, that sort of thing?" "No, don't be absurd, just a shadow, just a trace." "Hmmm." "You never would have noticed in passing. Hey, come to think of it, you don't have an extra sandwich do you?" "No, I don't. So would you describe this shadow as sort of a flicker then, like a malfunction?" "No, absolutely not. It's part of the tape." "Not your monitor on the fritz?" "No," he was getting angry now, "a person, a shadow strangling another shadow." The chunk of sandwich filling on the car roof was sizzling slightly, changing color already in the sun. The dealer said, "Shadows, hmmm. Probably a gimmick, subliminal special effects or something." "What? What reason would a realtor have for adding special effects for God's sake to an apartment tape?" "Maybe they think it adds some kind of allure, some thrill of menace that makes their apartments stand out from the crowd." "I doubt very much—" "Maybe they've become aware of the black market in tapes lately, that's the word on the street in fact, and so they're trying to send a little message. They don't like us ogling their apartments, even vicariously." "You can't ogle vicariously, I think. Sounds wrong. Anyway, that's the most ridiculous thing I've ever—" "Or maybe I'm in on it, maybe I'm the killer, have you considered that?" "Now you're making fun of me." "Why? If you can solve crimes on the other side of the Barrier why can't I commit them?" The dealer laughed, hyenalike. "Now seriously," he continued, "if you want to exchange for one without a murder I'll give you a credit towards the next, half what you paid—" "No thanks. I'll hold onto it." Discouraged, hungry, but he couldn't really bother being angry. What help did he expect from the dealer anyway? This was a larger matter, above the head of a mere middleman. "Good luck, Sherlock," the dealer was saying. "Spread word freely, by the way, don't hold back. Can't hurt my sales any. People like murder, only it might be good if there was skin instead of only shadow, a tit say." "Yes, very good then, appreciate your help. Carry on." The dealer saluted. He saluted back, started off through the traffic, stomach growling, ignoring it, intent. A killer was at large. Weaving past kids terrorizing an entire block of cars with an elaborate tag game, cornering around the newly washed neighborhood now wringing itself out, muddy streams between the cars and crying babies ignoring vendors with items he couldn't afford and a flatbed farmer offering live kittens for pets or food and a pathetic miniature start-up, three cars idiotically nosing rocking jerking back and forth trying to rearrange themselves pointlessly, one of them now sideways wheels on the curb and nobody else even taking the bait he made his way back to his car and key in the lock noticed the girl from the Pacer standing in her red dress on the hood of the car gazing skyward, waiting for the Advertising people to take her away. Looking just incidentally like a million bucks. Her kid brother was away, maybe part of the gang playing tag, and her parents were inside the car doing housework dad scraping the grill out the window mom airing clothes repacking bundles so he went over, suddenly inspired. "Margaret, isn't it?" She nodded, smiled. "Yes, good, well you remember me from next door, I'm looking for a day or two's work and do you think they'll take me along?" She said, "You never know, they just take you or they don't." Smiling graciously even if a little confused, so long neighbors and they'd never spoken. "But you always—" he began pointing out. She said, "Oh once they've started taking you then—" Awkwardly, they were both awkward for a moment not saying what they both knew or at least he did, that she was an attractive young girl and likely that made a huge difference in whether they wanted you. "Well you wouldn't mind if I tried?" he said and she said "No, no," relieved almost, then added "I can point you out, I can suggest to them—" Now he was embarrassed and said hurriedly, "That's so good of you, thanks, and where should I wait, not here with you at your folks' car, I guess—" "Why not, climb up." Dad looked out the door up at them and she waved him off, "It's okay, you know him from next door he's going to work, we're going to try to get him a job Advertising." "Okay, sweetheart just checking on you." Then she grabbed his arm, said, "Look." The Advertising hovercraft she'd been watching for landed on the curb a half-block ahead, near the giant hideous sculpture at an office building main entrance, lately sealed. Dad said, "Get going you guys, and good luck," and she said, "C'mon." Such neighborliness was a surprise since he'd always felt shut out by the family in the Pacer but obviously it was in his head. And Margaret, a cloud of good feeling seemed to cover her. No wonder they wanted her for Advertising. "Hurry," she said and took his hand

and they hopped down and pushed their way around the cars and through the chaos of children and barking dogs and vendors trying to work the crowd of wannabees these landings always provoked, to join the confused throng at the entrance. He held onto his satchel with the video and his socks making sure it didn't get picked in this crowd. She bounced there trying to make herself visible until the one of the two robots at the door noticed her and pointed. They stepped up. "Inside," said the robot. They were ugly little robots with their braincases undisguised and terrible attitudes. He disliked them instantly. "I brought someone new," she said, pulling him by the hand, thrusting him into view. "Yes, sir, I'd like to enlist—" he started, grinning madly, wanting to make a good impression. The robot looked him over and made its rapid-fire assessment, nodded. "Get inside," it said. "Lucky," she whispered, and they stepped into the hovercraft. Four others were there, two men, two women, all young. And another woman stumbled in behind them, and the door sealed, and they were off. Nasty little robots scurrying into the cockpit, making things ready. "Now what?" he said and she put her finger to her lips and shushed him, but sweetly, leaning into him as if to say they were in this together. He wanted to tell her what he was after but the robots might hear. Would they care? Yes, no, he couldn't know. Such ugly, fascistic little robots. Nazi robots, that's what they were. He hated placing himself in their hands. But once he was Advertising he would be through the barrier, he'd be able to investigate. Probably he should keep his assignment to himself, though. He didn't want to get her into trouble. The hovercraft shuddered, groaned, then lifted and through the window he could see the cars growing smaller, his neighborhood, his life, the way the traffic was so bad for hundreds of miles of street and why did he think a start-up would change anything? Was there a place where cars really drove anymore? Well, anyway. The robots were coming around with the Advertising Patches and everyone leaned their heads forward obediently, no first-timers like himself apparently. He did the same. A robot fastened a patch behind his right ear, a moment of stinging skin, nothing more. Hard to believe the patch was enough to interfere with the function of the One-Way Permeable Barrier, that he would now be vivid and tangible and effective to those on the other side. "I don't feel any different," he whispered. "You won't," she said. "Not until there's people. Then you'll be compelled to Advertise. You won't be able to help it." "For what, though?" "You never know, coffee, diamonds, condoms, vacations, you just never know." "Where—" "They'll drop us off at the Undermall, then we're on our own." "Will we be able to stick together?" The question was out before he could wonder if it was presuming too much, but she said, "Sure, as long as our products aren't too incompatible, but we'll know soon. Anyway, just follow me." She really had a warmth, a glow. Incompatible products? Well, he'd find out what that meant. The hovercraft bumped down on the roof of a building, and with grim efficiency the ugly Nazi robots had the door open and were marching the conscripts out to a rooftop elevator. He wanted to reach out and smack their little exposed-braincase heads together. But he had to keep his cool, stay undercover. He trotted across the roof towards the elevator after her, between the rows of officious gesticulating robots, like they were going to a concentration camp. The last robot at the door of the elevator handed them each an envelope before they stepped in. He took his and moved into the corner with Margaret, they were really packing them in but he couldn't complain actually being jostled with her and she didn't seem to be trying to avoid it. He poked into the envelope. It was full of bills, singles mostly. The money was tattered and filthy, bills that had been taken out of circulation on the other side of the Barrier. Garbage money, that's what it was. The others had already pocketed theirs, business as usual apparently. "Why do they pay us now?" he whispered. She said "We just find our way out at the end, when the patch runs out, so this way they don't have to deal with us again," and he said "What if we just took off with the money?" "You could I guess, but I've never seen anyone do it since you'd never get to come back and anyway the patch makes you really want to Advertise, you'll see." Her voice was reassuring, like she really wanted him not to worry and he felt rotten not telling her about his investigation, his agenda. He put the envelope into his satchel with tape and socks. The elevator sealed and whooshed them down through the building, into the Undermall, then the doors opened and they unpacked from the elevator, spewed out into a gigantic lobby, all glass and polished steel with music playing softly and escalators going down and up in every direction, escalators with steps of burnished wood that looked good enough to eat, looked like roast chicken. He was still so hungry. Margaret took his hand again. "Let's go," she said. As the others dispersed she led him towards one of the escalators and they descended. The corridor below branched to shops with recessed entrances, windows dark and smoky, quiet pulsing music fading from each door, also food smells here and there causing his saliva to flow, and holographic signs angling into view as they passed: FERN SLAW, ROETHKE AND SONS, HOLLOW APPEAL, BROKEN SMUDGED ALPHABET, BURGER KING, PLASTIC DEVILS, OSTRICH LAKE, SMARTINGALE'S, RED HARVEST, CATCH OF THE DAY, MUTUAL OF FOMALHAUT, THNEEDS, et cetera. She led him on, confidently, obviously at home. Why not, this was what she did with her days. Then without warning, a couple appeared from around a corner, and he felt himself begin to Advertise. "How do you do today?" he said, sidling up to the gentleman of the couple, even as he saw Margaret begin to do the same thing to the lady. The gentleman nodded at him, walked on. But met his eye. He was tangible, he could be heard. It was a shock. "Thirsty?" he heard himself say. "How long's it been since you had a nice refreshing beer?" "Don't like beer," said the gentleman. "Can't say why, just never have." "Then you've obviously never tried a Very Old Money Lager," he heard himself say, still astonished. The Barrier was pierced and he was conversing, he was perceptible. He'd be able to conduct interrogations, be able to search out clues. Meanwhile he heard Margaret saying "Don't demean your signature with a second-rate writing implement. Once you've tried the Eiger fountain pen you'll never want to go back to those hen-like scratchings and scrawlings," and the woman seemed interested and so Margaret went on "our Empyrean Sterling Silver Collection features one-of-a-kind hand-etched casings—" In fact the man seemed captivated too he turned ignoring the beer pitch and gave Margaret his attention. "Our brewers hand-pick the hops and malt," he was unable to stop though he'd obviously lost his mark, "and every single batch of fire-brewed Very Old Money Lager is individually tasted—" Following the couple through the corridor they bumped into another Advertising woman who'd been on the hovercraft, and she began singing, "Vis-it the *moon*, it's nev-er too *soon*," dancing sinuously and batting her eyes, distracting them all from fountain pens and beer for the moment and then the five of them swept into the larger space of the Undermall and suddenly there were dozens of people who needed to be told about the beer, "Thirsty? Hello, hi there, thirsty? Excuse me, thirsty? Yes? Craving satisfaction, sparkle, bite? No? Yes? Have you tried Very Old Money? What makes it different, you ask—oh, hello, thirsty?" and also dozens of people working as Advertising, a gabble of pitches—stern, admonitory: "Have you considered the perils of being without success insurance?" flippant, arbitrary: "You never know you're out with the Black Underwear Crowd, not until you get one of them home!" jingly, singsong: "We've got children, we've all got children, you can have children too—" and as they scattered and darted along the endless marble floors of the Undermall he was afraid he'd lose her, but there was Margaret, earnestly discussing pens with a thoughtful older couple and he struggled over towards her, hawking beer—"Thirsty? Oof, sorry, uh, thirsty?" The crowd thinned as customers ducked into shops and stole away down corridors back to their apartments, bullied by the slew of Advertising except for the few like this older couple who seemed gratified by the attention, he actually had to wait as they listened and took down some information from her about the Eiger fountain pen while he stood far enough away that to keep from barking at them about the beer. Then once the older couple wandered off he took Margaret's hand this time, why not, she'd done it, and drew her down a corridor away from the crowds, hoping to keep from engaging with any more customers, and also in the right direction if he had his bearings. He thought he did. He led her into the shadow of a doorway, a shop called FINGERTOES that wasn't doing much business. "Listen, I've got to tell you something, I haven't been completely truthful, I mean, I haven't lied, but there's something—" She looked at him, hopeful, confused, but generous in her interpretation, he could tell, what a pure and sweet disposition, maybe her dad wasn't such a bad guy after all if he'd raised a plum like this. "I'm a detective, I mean, what does that mean, really, but the thing is there's been a murder and I'm trying to look into it—" and then he plunged in and told all, the Apartment On Tape, pulling it out of his satchel to show her, the shadow, the strangling, his conversation with the dealer and then his brainstorm to slip inside the citadel, slip past the One-Way Permeable Barrier that would of course have kept his questions or accusations from even being audible to those on this side, and so he'd manipulated her generosity to get aboard the hovercraft. "Forgive me," he said. Her eyes widened, her voice grew hushed, reverent. "Of course, but what do you want to do? Find the police?" "You're not angry at me?" "No, no. It's a brave thing you're doing." "Thank you." They drew closer. He could almost kiss her, just in happiness, solidarity, no further meaning or if there was it was just on top of the powerful solidarity feeling, just an extra, a windfall. "But what do you think is best, the police?" she whispered. "No, I have in mind a visit to the apartment, we're only a couple of blocks away, in this direction I believe, but do you think we can get upstairs?" They fell silent then because a man swerved out of FINGERTOES with a little paper tray of greasy fried things, looked like fingers or toes in fact and smelled terrific, he couldn't believe how hungry he was. "Thirsty?" he said hopelessly and the man popping one into his mouth said, "You called it brother, I'm dying for a beer." "Why just any beer when you could enjoy a Very Old Money—" and he had to go on about it, being driven nuts by the smell, while Margaret waited. The moment the grease-eater realized they were Advertising and broke free, towards the open spaces of the Undermall he and Margaret broke in the other direction, down the corridor. "This way," said Margaret, turning them towards the elevator, "the next level down you can go for blocks, it's the way out eventually too." "Yes, but can we get back upstairs?" "The elevators work for us until the patches run out, I think," and so they went down below the Undermall to the underground corridors, long echoey halls of tile, not so glamorous as upstairs, not nice at all really, the lengths apartment people went to never to have to step out onto the street and see car people being really appalling sometimes. The tunnels were marked with street signs, names of other Undermalls, here and there an exit. They had to Advertise only once before reaching East One Thousand, Two Hundred and Fifteenth Street, to a group of teenage boys smoking a joint in the corridor who laughed and asked Margaret questions she couldn't answer like are they mightier or less mighty than the sword and do they work for pigs. They ran into another person Advertising, a man moving furtively who when he recognized Margaret was plainly relieved. "He's got a girlfriend," she explained, somewhat enigmatically. So those Advertising could, did—what? Interact. But caught up in the chase now, he didn't ask more, just counted the blocks, feeling the thrill of approaching his Apartment On Tape's real address. They went up in the elevator, which was lavish again, wood panelled and perfumed and mirrored and musical. An expensive building. Apartment 16D so he pressed the button for the sixteenth floor, holding his breath, hardly believing it when they rose above the public floors. But they did. He gripped her hand. The elevator stopped on the sixth floor and a robot got on. Another of the creepily efficient braincase-showing kind. At first the robot ignored them but then on the fifteenth floor a woman got on and Margaret said, "The most personal thing about you is your signature, don't you think?" and he said, "Thirsty?" and the robot turned and stared up at them. The doors closed and they rode up to the sixteenth floor, and the three of them got out, he and Margaret and the robot, leaving the woman behind. The hallway was splendid with plush carpeting and brass light fixtures, empty apart from the three of them. "What are you doing up here?" said the robot. "And what's in that bag?" Clutching his satchel he said, "Nothing, just my stuff." "Why is it any of your business?" said Margaret, surprisingly defiant. "We've been asked to give an extended presentation at a customer's private home," he said, wanting quickly to cover Margaret's outburst, give the robot something else to focus on. "Then I'll escort you," said the robot. "You really don't have to do that," he said, and Margaret said, "Don't come along and screw up our pitch, we'll sue you," said Margaret bizarrely. Learning of the investigation had an odd effect on her, always a risk working with amateurs he supposed. But also it was these robots, the way they were designed with rotten personalities or no personalities they really aroused revulsion in people, it was an instinctual thing and not just him, he noted with satisfaction. He squeezed her hand and said, "Our sponsors would be displeased, it's true." "This matter requires clearance," said the robot, trying to get in front of them as they walked, and they had to skip to stay ahead of it. "Please stand to one side and wait for clearance," but they kept going down the carpeted hallway, his fingers crossed that it was the right direction for 16D. "Halt," said the robot, a flashing red light on its forehead beginning to blink neurotically and then they were at the door, and he rapped with his knuckles, thinking, hardly going incognito here, but better learn what we can. "Stand to one side," said the robot again. "Shut up," said Margaret. As the robot clamped a steely hand on each of their arms, jerking them back away from the door, its treads grinding on the carpet for traction, probably leaving ugly marks too, the door swung open. "Hello?" The man in the doorway was unshaven and slack-haired wearing a robe and blinking at them as though he'd only turned on his light to answer the door. "They claim to have an appointment with you sir," said the robot. The man only stood and stared. "It's very important, we have to talk to you urgently," he said, trying to pull free of the robot's chilly grip, then added, regretfully, "about beer." He felt a swoon at looking through the doorway, realizing he was seeing into his Apartment On Tape, the rooms etched into his dreamy brain now before him. He tried to see more but the light was gloomy. "—and fountain pens," said Margaret, obviously trying to hold herself back but compelled to chip something. "I apologize sir I tried to detain them to obtain clearance—" said the robot. *Detain, obtain,* what rotten syntax, he thought, the people who program these robots certainly aren't poets. The man just stood and blinked and looked them over, the three of them struggling subtly, he and Margaret trying to pull free of the robot, which was still blinking red and grinding at the carpet. "Cooperate," squawked the robot. The man in the robe squinted at them, finally smiled. "Please," said Margaret. "Fountain pens, eh?" the man in the robe said at last. "Yes," said Margaret desperately, and he heard himself add "And beer—" "Yes, of course," mumbled the man in the robe. "How silly of me. Come in." "Sir, for your safety—" "They're fine," said the man to the robot. "I'm expecting them. Let them in." The robot released its grip. The man in the robe turned and shuffled inside. They followed him, all three of them, into poorly-lit rooms disastrously heaped with newspapers, clothes, soiled dishes, empty and half-empty takeout packages, but still unmistakably the rooms from his tape, every turn of his head recalling some camera movement and there sure enough was the wall that had held the shadow, the momentary stain of murder. The man in the robe turned and said to the robot, "Please wait outside." "But surely I should chaperone, sir—" "No, that's fine, just outside the door, I'll call you in if I need you. Close it on your way out, thanks." Watching the robot slink back out he couldn't help but feel a little thrill of vindication. The man in the robe continued into the kitchen, and gesturing at the table said, "Please, sit, sorry for the mess. Did you say you'd like a beer?" "Well, uh, no, that wasn't exactly—if you drink beer you ought to make it a Very Old Money Lager for full satisfaction—but I've got something else to discuss while you enjoy your delicious, oh, damn it—" "Relax, have a seat. Can I get you something else?" "Food," he blurted. "Which always goes best with a Very Old Money," and meanwhile Margaret released his hand and took a seat and started in talking about pens. The man opened his refrigerator, which was as overloaded as the apartment, another image from the tape now corrupted by squalor. "You poor people, stuck with those awful patches and yet I suppose I wouldn't have the benefit of your company today without them! Ah, well. Here, I wasn't expecting visitors but would you like some cheese? Can I fix you a glass of water?" The man set out a crumbled hunk of cheddar with a butterknife, crumbs on the dish and so long uncovered the edges were dried a deep, translucent orange. "So, you were just Advertising and you thought you'd pay a house call? How am I so lucky?" "Well, that's not it exactly—" Margaret took the knife and began paring away the edges of the cheese, carving out a chunk that looked more or less edible and when she handed it to him he couldn't resist, but tried talking through the mouthful anyway, desperately trying to negotiate the three priorities of hunger, Advertising, and his investigation: "Would you consider, mmmpphh, excuse me, consider opening a nice tall bottle of Very Old Money and settling in to watch this videotape I brought with me because there's something I'd like you to see, a question I've got about it—" The man in the robe nodded absently, half-listening, staring oddly at Margaret and then said, "By all means let me see your tape—is it about beer? I'd be delighted but no hurry, please relax and enjoy yourselves, I'll be right out," and stepped into the living room, began rummaging among his possessions of which there certainly were plenty. It was a little depressing how full the once glorious apartment had gotten. He envisioned himself living in it and cleaning it out, restoring it to the condition on the realtor's tape. Margaret cut him another piece of cheese and whispered, "Do you think he knows something?" "I can't know he seems so nice, well if not nice then harmless, hapless, but I'll judge his reaction to the video, watch him closely when the time comes—" grabbing more cheese quickly while he could and then the man in the robe was back. "Hello, friends, enjoying yourselves?" His robe had fallen open and they both stared but maybe it was just an example of his sloppiness. Certainly there was no polite way to mention it. There was something confusing about this man, who now went to the table and took the knife out of Margaret's hands and held her hand there for a moment and then snapped something, was it a bracelet? around her wrist. Not a bracelet. Handcuffs. "Hey, wait a minute, that's no way to enjoy a nice glass of lager!" he heard himself say idiotically cheese falling out of his mouth jumping up as the man clicked Margaret's other wrist into the cuffs and he had her linked to the back of her chair. He stood to intervene and the man in the robe swept his feet out from under him with a kick and pushed him in the chest and he fell, feet sliding on papers, hand skidding in lumps of cheese, to the floor. "Thirsty!" he shouted, the more excited the more fervent the Advertising, apparently. "No! Beer!" as he struggled to get up. And Margaret was saying something desperate about Eiger Fountain Pens "*—self-refilling cartridge—*" The man in the robe moved quickly, not lazy and sloppy at all now and kicked away his satchel with the tape inside and bent over him and reached behind his ear and to tear the patch away, another momentary sting. He could only shout "Beer!" once more before the twilight world of the One-Way Permeable Barrier surrounded him, it was everywhere here, even Margaret was on the other side as long as she wore the patch, and he felt his voice sucked away to a scream audible inside the space of his own head but not elsewhere, he knew, not until he was back outside, on the street where he belonged and why couldn't he have stayed there? What was he thinking? Anyway it wouldn't be long now because through the gauze he saw the man in the robe who you'd have to call the man half out of his robe now open the door to let the robot in, then as the naked man grinned at him steel pinchers clamped onto his arm and he was dragged out of the room, screaming inaudibly, thrashing to no purpose, leaving Margaret behind. And his tape besides.

ANGÉLICA GORODISCHER

THE END OF A DYNASTY

OR THE NATURAL HISTORY OF FERRETS

Translated from the Spanish by Ursula K. Le Guin

THE STORY-TELLER SAID: HE WAS A SORROWFUL PRINCE, young Livna'lams, seven years old and full of sorrow. It wasn't just that he had sad moments, the way any kid does, prince or commoner, or in the middle of a phrase or something going on his mind would wander off, or he'd wake up with a heaviness in his chest, or break into tears for no apparent reason. All that happens to everybody, whatever their age or condition of life. No, now listen to what I'm telling you, and don't get distracted and then say I didn't explain it well enough. If anybody here isn't interested in what I'm saying, they can leave. Go. Just try not to bother the others. This tent's open to the south and north, and the roads are broad and lead to green lands and black lands and there's plenty to do in the world—sift flour, hammer iron, beat rugs, plow furrows, gossip about the neighbors, cast fishing nets—but what there is to do here is listen. You can shut your eyes and cross your hands on your belly if you like, but shut your mouth and open your ears to what I'm telling you: this young prince was sorrowful all the time, the way people are when they're old and alone and death won't come to them. His days, however full they might have been, were all dreary, grey, and empty.

Yet they were full, for these were the years of the Hehvrontes Dynasty, those proud, rigid rulers, tall and handsome, with white skin and very black eyes and hair, who walked without swinging their shoulders or hips, head high, gaze fixed somewhere beyond the horizon, not looking aside even to see their own mother in her death-agony, not looking down even if the path was rough and rocky, falling into a well if it was in the way and standing erect down inside the well, maintaining the dignity of the lords of the world. That's what they were like, I'm telling you, I who've read old histories till my poor eyes are nearly blind. That's what they were like.

Livna'lams' grandfather was the eighth emperor of the Hehvrontes Dynasty; and his father, well, we'll be talking about his father presently. That is, *I'll* be talking, because you ignorant boors know nothing of the secret history of the Empire, occupied as you are in the despicable business of accumulating money, decorating your houses out of vanity not love of beauty, eating and drinking and wallowing your way to apoplexy and death. I'll talk about him when the time comes. For now, suffice it to say that the pride of the Hehvrontes had elaborated a stupid, showy, formal protocol unequalled at any other period of the Empire except that of the Noörams, who were equally stupid but less showy and more sinister. Luckily, luckily for people like you, the Noörams killed each other off, and nobody believes the story that a servant saved from the bloodbath a newborn son of the Empress Tennitraä, called the She-Snake and The Unjust, though nobody can disprove the story either. . . .

The Protocol of the Hehvrontes involved everything. It filled the court and the palace and filtered down into public charities, the army, schools, hospitals, whore-houses—high class whore-houses, you understand, since anything that fell short of a considerable fortune or a sonorous title lacked importance and so escaped the Protocol. But in the palace, oh, in the palace! There the black-eyed, black-bearded lords had woven a real nightmare in which a sneeze was a crime and the tilt of a hatbrim a disgrace and the thoughtless twitch of a finger a tragedy.

Livna'lams escaped none of it. How could he, the crown prince, the tenth and, I'll tell you now, the last of the Hehvrontes, only son of the widowed Empress, on whom were fixed the eyes of the court, the palace, the capital, the Empire, the world! That's why he was sorrowful, you say? Come, come, my good people, ignorance has one chance at good sense: keeping its mouth shut. Or so say the wise. But I say that if you're utterly, hopelessly ignorant there isn't room in your skull for even that much sense. Come on, now, why would the Protocol make him sad? Why, when nine Hehvrontes before him had been perfectly happy, well maybe not nine but definitely eight—had been so happy that, attributing their beatific state to that very Protocol, they devoted themselves to augmenting and enriching the hundred thousand minute formalities that distinguished them from everybody else? No, he too might well have been happy and satisfied, being a prince, made like any other prince for the frivolous and terrible uses of power. But he wasn't. Maybe because the men in his family line had changed, since his grandfather took as his Empress a Southern woman reputed to be not entirely human. Or maybe because of the ceremony which his mother, the Empress Hallovâh, had added to the Protocol of the Palace. Or because of both those things.

So, now, let me tell you that the Empress Hallovâh was very beautiful, but I mean *very* beautiful, and still young. The young heart is the most open to life and love, say the wise, and then they smile and look into the eyes of the child eager to learn, and add: and to sickness and hatred. The empress always dressed in white, long white tunics of silk or gauze with no ornament, nothing but a fine, heavy chain of unpolished iron links round her neck, from which a plain locket hung on her breast. She was always barefoot, her hair loose. In expiation, she said. Her hair was the color of ripe wheat. Remember that she was a Hehvrontes by marriage only. By birth she was from the Ja'lah-dalva family, who had been moving upward rapidly for the last three generations. She had grey eyes, a fine mouth, a slim waist. She never smiled.

Precisely one hour after sunrise, seven servants, each dressed in one of the colors of the rainbow, entered Prince Livna'lams' room and woke him by repeating meaningless words about fortune, happiness, obligation, benevolence, in fixed phrases hundreds of years old. If I were to try to explain these words to you and tell how each man dressed in a different color each day so that the one who came in wearing blue today tomorrow would wear purple and yesterday wore red, if I tried to describe their gestures, the other words they said and the clothing they dressed the boy in and the tub they bathed him in and the perfumes assigned to each day, we'd have to stay here till the Short Harvest Feast, spending what's left of summer and the whole autumn and sitting through snow and frost to see false spring and then the ground white again and the sky all thick with clouds until the day when the shoots must be gathered before the sun burns them or the hail destroys them, and even then we'd have trouble getting through the ceremony of the Bath and the Combing of the Hair, and not just because of the torpid sluggishness of the tiny intellects inside your skulls.

The prince opened his eyes, black Hehvrontes eyes, and knew he had twenty seconds to sit up in bed and another twenty to get out of bed. The servants bowed, asserted their fidelity and respect in the formula proper for that day of the year, undressed him, and surrounding him closely escorted him to the bath, where other servants of inferior rank kept the tub ready, full of scented water, and the towels and sandals and oils and perfumes. After the bath they dressed him, never in clothes that he had worn before, and again surrounding him in a certain order, they escorted him to the door of the apartment, where another servant unlocked the lock and another opened both leaves of the door so that the boy might cross the threshold into the anteroom. There the lords of the nobility, clothed in the colors of the Imperial house, received him with more bows and more formulas of adulation, and informed him of the state of the weather and the health of the Empress Hallovâh, which was always splendid, and recited to him the list of activities he was to perform today in the palace, and asked him what he wished to have for breakfast. The prince always gave the same answer:

"Nothing."

This, too, by way of expiation, said the empress, except that it was a farce like all the rest, since nobody expected the child to die of hunger. Yet it wasn't a farce, because Livna'lams was never hungry. The nobles pleaded with him to eat so that he'd grow strong, brave, just, handsome, and good, as an emperor should be. The little boy assented, and they all went on to a dining room where a table was spread and eleven servants looked after the plates, the silver, the goblets, the platters, the napkins, the decorations, the water the crown prince drank and what little food he ate, while the noblemen looked on and approved, standing behind the chair of ancient, fragrant wood covered with cushions and tapestries. Every dish, every mouthful, every sip, every movement was meticulously planned and controlled by the Protocol of the Palace. And when all that was done, another servant opened the door of the room, and other noblemen escorted the emperor-to-be, and now came the moment, the only moment in the day, when the son and the mother met.

Even misfortune has its advantages, say the wise. Of course the wise say stupid things, because even wisdom has its foolishness, say I. But there's no question but that being down has its up side. If Livna'lams hadn't been such a sorrowful prince, in that moment he might have been frightened, or angry, or in despair. But sorrow filled him till he couldn't feel anything. Nothing mattered to him, not even the Empress Hallovâh, his mother.

She would be sitting dressed in white on a great chair upholstered in white velvet, surrounded by her seventy-seven maids of honor, who all wore bright colors and were loaded with gold and jewels, crowned with diadems, shod with embroidered satin slippers, their hands and wrists beringed and braceleted. As the prince came in all the ladies bowed deeply and the empress stood up, for though she was his mother, he would be emperor. She greeted him: "May the day be propitious for you, Prince."

He replied, "May the day be propitious for you, Mother."

Even you ignorant louts who don't know beans about anything let alone palaces and courts can see how differently they behaved towards each other. But then, while all the ladies in waiting stayed bowed down to the ground in submission, the Empress Hallovâh acted as if she felt tenderness towards the child: kissed him, stroked his face, asked him how he'd slept, if he'd had good dreams, if he loved her, if he'd like to go walking in the gardens with her. The prince would take one of the woman's hands in his and would reply: "I slept very well and my dreams were happy and serene, Mother. I love you very much, Mother. Nothing would please me more than to walk in the gardens, Mother."

When this section of the protocol was completed, the prince and the empress walked side by side holding hands to the great glass doors that opened on the gardens. As they reached them, the woman would stop and look at her son: "Though we are happy," she would say, "we cannot enjoy our good fortune until we have completed our duties, painful as they may be."

"I was about to suggest to you, Mother," said the prince, "that as leaders and protectors of our beloved people, we owe our happiness to them, and our principal task is to see that justice is done to the living and the dead."

"The dead can wait, prince."

At this point in the dialogue the ladies, still all doubled over, felt some relief at the thought that soon they'd be able to straighten up their shoulders and necks.

"That is so, Mother; but not the people, who await our judgment on which of the dead were great men and which were traitors."

The ladies straightened up. The prince and the empress were already in the gardens. Sun or snow or rain or wind or hail, lightning, thunder, whatever the weather, the two of them, the little boy and the woman in white, walked every morning to the central fountain, where eight marble swans opened their wings to the water falling from a basin of alabaster. South of the fountain, paths ran through a grove, and following one of them deep into the shadows—green in the sunlight, dark in storm—they came to what once had been a statue. Had been, I say. There wasn't much of it left. The pedestal was intact, but the pink-grained marble had been scratched all over with a chisel to erase the inscription, the names and dates. Above that nothing remained but a shapeless lump of white marble, whether pink-grained or not you couldn't tell, it was so battered and filthy. It might have been the figure of a man; looking carefully you could make out the stump of an arm, a ruined leg, a truncated, headless neck, something like a torso. In front of it the prince and the empress stood and waited. The noblemen arrived, then the ladies, then the officers of the palace guard and the army, magistrates, lawyers, and functionaries. And behind them came the servants, trying to peer over the heads of the gentry to see what happened.

What happened was, day after day, the same, always exactly the same. Some moments of silence, till everything within the palace walls seemed to have fallen still. And then suddenly, at the same instant, the joined voices of the mother and son: "We curse you!" they said. "May you be cursed, may you be damned, hated, loathed, despised forever! May your memory waken only rancor towards you, your face, your deeds. We curse you!"

Another silence, and the empress spoke: "Treason degrades and corrupts all that it touches," she said. "I vow to heaven and earth and all the peoples therein to expiate for the rest of my life the guilt of having been your wife, of having shared your throne, your table, and your bed."

Again everyone was silent. The boy prince took a whip which one of the noblemen offered him, a pearl-handled whip, seventeen strands, tipped with steel hooks. With it he struck at the statue, what was left of it: twenty blows that echoed through the grove. Sometimes a bird got the notion to start singing just at that moment, and this was considered a lamentable occurrence to be discussed in low voices during all the rest of the day throughout the palace, from the throne room to the kitchens. But we know that the birds and beasts, the plants, the waters all have their own protocol, and evidently have no intention of changing it for a human one.

And what happened next, you ask? Oh, good people, everything had been arranged, as you can imagine. Or can't imagine, since if you could imagine anything you wouldn't have come here to listen to stories and whine like silly old women if the story-teller leaves out one single detail. So, next another nobleman received the whip from the hands of the prince, who then approached his mother. The empress stooped, because her son was still very short, and held up the polished locket that hung from her neck on the chain of black iron links. She opened it. The boy spat into it, onto a face and name cut in the white stone and half scratched out with a sharp tool, the face and name of the dead man, his father, the emperor.

No, I'm sorry, but I can't tell you the name of the ninth emperor of the Hehvrontes dynasty, because I don't know it. Nobody does. It's something that is not remembered. His guilt and treason, it was said, had been so horrible that his name was never to be pronounced again. Moreover, that name was erased from the annals, the laws, the decrees, from history books, official registries, monuments, coins, escutcheons, maps, poems. Poems, because the emperor had written songs and poems ever since he was a boy. Unfortunately he'd been a good poet, good enough that the people got hold of his verses and sang them, in those happy days when he reigned in peace. And to tell you the truth, many of his poems survived despite everything, and it's said that Livna'lams heard them sung in distant provinces when he himself was Emperor. But memory's weak, and that's a blessing, so say the wise. And I know, because I know a lot of things, that it was a wise man who said or wrote that time's mirror loses all it reflects. Memory's weak, and people had forgotten where those songs came from. What mattered was that the name be forgotten; and it was.

So the empress left the despicable locket open on her breast, turned her back on the broken statue, and started back to the palace with her son. Then came the procession. The most important persons first, the others following, finally the servants, everyone passed the statue, and everyone did their utmost to express hatred and contempt. Some spat on it, some kicked it, some struck it with sticks or chains or their belts, some smeared it with mud or muck, and some, hoping that their exploit would reach the ears of the empress, went so far as to bring a little bag full of yesterday's turds and empty them out on the marble.

On their return to the galleries of the palace, the prince and the empress saluted each other and parted. She would spend the rest of the morning in meetings with her ministers; in the afternoon she was occupied with affairs of justice and official proceedings. The little boy met with his teachers and studied history, geography, mathematics, music, strategy, politics, dance, falconry, and all the things an emperor has to know so that later on he can do everything that makes him feel that doing it makes him the emperor.

I said he was a sorrowful prince, young Livna'lams; he was a bright one too, alert, intelligent. There's another of the advantages of sorrow: it doesn't dull the intellect as depression and rancor do. His teachers had soon discovered that the boy learned in ten minutes what might take most boys an hour, not to mention totally moronic princes incapable of learning anything. And as he was seven, an important age, and as the noblemen were always present during his studies to supervise the process, they had arrived at a tacit agreement to depart, secretly, from the Protocol: The teachers taught what they had to teach, Livna'lams learned what he had to learn, and then everybody could go do what they pleased—the schoolmasters could burrow into their books, or write boring treatises on themes they believed to be original and important, or get drunk, or play dice, or plot crimes against their colleagues, and the prince could seek a little solitude.

Sometimes he found it in the music rooms, sometimes in the stables or the libraries. But he always found it in the far corners of the palace gardens. Only if he was extremely lucky could he touch an instrument, talk to the horses and the mares with young foals, or read a book, without a music teacher appearing, or a riding master, or a librarian, bowing and scraping and asking to be of service or just standing around waiting for orders. But almost never, or in truth never, was there anyone under the garden walls, among the dense thickets, the hidden benches, the bricked-up doors, the dry fountains, the pergolas. I don't know what the prince did there. I think he just let time pass. I think he saw and heard things that had not been included in the Protocol. I think that, sorrowfully as ever, he tried to love something—beetles with hard, iridescent wingcases, sprouting weeds, the dirt, stones fallen from the walls.

Now listen carefully, because one day something happened. The day was grey and muggy, and what happened was this: the prince heard voices. I don't mean he went mad or was divinely inspired. He heard somebody talking, and it alarmed him.

Weren't the librarians and the riding masters enough? Was he going to have to start hiding even from the gardeners? He looked around, thinking that was it: some idiot had discovered these forgotten corners of the garden and decided to acquire merit by getting the paths sanded, the trees pruned, the benches restored, and worst of all, the thickets cut down.

"I think you're as crazy as I am," said a mild, slow voice.

A burst of laughter, and a second voice said, "Friend, I can't say you're wrong." This voice was deeper, richer, stronger.

Those aren't gardeners, Livna'lams said to himself. Gardeners don't talk like that, or laugh like that. And he was right. Do any of you have the honor of being acquainted with a gardener? They are admirable people, believe me, but they don't go around making comments on their own or other people's mental condition. They stay close to the ground, and know many names and languages, and nothing in this world impresses them much, since they see life in the right way, as it should be seen, from below looking up, and in concentric circles. But what do you know about all that and how could it interest you? All you want to know is what happened in the palace garden that day when the prince heard voices.

All right, all right, I'll tell you what happened, just as truly as if I'd been there myself. Those aren't gardeners, the little boy said to himself, and so nobody's going to come and clear out the thickets; and that pleased him. And since he was pleased, he got up from the steps he'd been sitting on and walked, trying not to make noise, towards the place where the men were talking. Now he wasn't used to walking silently in an overgrown garden; he might manage to be noiseless in the palace corridors, but not here. He trod on a dry stick, a pebble rolled under his foot, he brushed up against a bush, and there facing him was a huge man, the tallest, broadest man he'd ever seen, very dark, with coal-black beard and hair and eyes. The man took hold of the prince's arm with a gigantic, powerful hand. The prince squeaked out, "How dare you, you insolent fellow!"

The giant laughed. It was the deep, tremendous laugh Livna'lams had heard a minute earlier. But he didn't let go. "Ah ha ha ha!" he went, and then, "Come see what we've got here!"

He wasn't talking to the prince but to the owner of the other voice, who was standing behind the big man. This one was shorter and slighter, lanky, also very tanned, cleanshaven, with tangled black hair, bright black eyes that looked amused, a wide mouth and a long, delicate neck.

"I think it might be best to let him go," he said in a lazy, quiet voice.

"Why?" said the giant. "Why should I? No telling how long he's been listening. Better not let him go. Better give him a good beating to teach him not to spy, so he forgets that he even came around here this morning."

"No beatings," said the other man. "Unless you want us shorter by a head."

The big fellow considered this possibility, and you can bet your puny little life savings that he didn't like it; he opened his fist and let the boy go. The prince brushed off his silken sleeve and looked at the two men. He wasn't afraid. They say princes are never afraid but don't believe it, it's a lie. They're afraid not only when they ought to be but sometimes when there's nothing to fear, and there have even been some who have lived in fear and died of fear. But Livna'lams wasn't afraid. He looked at them and saw they wore coarse clothing like fieldworkers or bricklayers, ordinary sandals, a worn pouch hanging from the belt. He also saw that they weren't afraid of him, which didn't surprise him—what was there to fear?—and that they didn't seem disposed to bow or do homage or await his orders in silence. That did surprise him.

"Who are you?" he asked them.

"Oh, you'd like to know that, wouldn't you now!" said the great big fellow.

This totally non-protocolish reply, this rude and blustering reply, didn't offend the prince at all. He liked it.

"Yes, I'd like to know," he said, crossing his arms.

"But I'm not going to tell you, snotnose."

"Hey, hey, Renka," said the other man.

"And I'd like to know what you're doing here, too," said the young prince.

"We'd just finished our work, prince," said the shorter man, "and we were taking a break."

"How did you know who I am?" said the prince, at the same time as the big fellow said, "This tadpole is a prince?"

The man answered Renka first: "Yes, which is why I told you that if you gave him a lick they'd have our heads," and then, to Livna'lams: "By your clothes."

"What does a bricklayer know about what a prince wears?" the boy asked.

"Listen, tadpole," said Renka. "Listen up, because I don't care if you're a prince. We aren't bricklayers. We're adventurers, and therefore philosophers, and therefore although we aren't going to beat you up, being fond of having our heads attached at the neck, neither are we going to play monkey tricks and bob up and down in reverence to your majesty."

At this the boy did something really wonderful, really magnificent. He uncrossed his arms, threw his head back, and laughed with all his heart.

"We aren't clowns, either," said Renka, deeply insulted.

But the other man, who was called Loo'Loö, which isn't a name or if it's a name it's a very unusual one, threw his head back too and holding his sides he laughed right along with the prince. Big Renka looked at them, very serious, and scratched his head, and when Livna'lams and Loo'Loö quit laughing and wiped their eyes, he said, "If you want my opinion, you're both crazy. I'm not surprised. Philosophers and princes have a definite tendency to go crazy. Though I never heard of a tadpole with sense enough to go crazy."

The boy laughed again and then all three sat down on the ground and talked.

They talked about a lot of things that day, but when the sun was high in the sky the prince stood up and said he had to go, they'd be expecting him in the palace for lunch.

"Too bad," said Renka. "We've got cheese," and he gave a loving pat to the pouch that hung from his wide belt, "and we're going to buy wine and fruit."

The prince took this as an invitation. "But I can't," he said.

"How come?" said Renka.

Young Livna'lams turned away and set off. After a couple of steps, he stopped and looked back at the two men. Loo'Loö was still sitting on the ground, chewing a grass-blade. "I don't know," he said. "Tomorrow, when your work's done, will you come here again?"

"I say no," said Renka. "I say we've sweated enough in this damned part of this hellish city, but he insists on staying, and since I'm kind and generous and have a heart as tender as a dove in love and can't watch a friend suffer, I let him have his way." He sighed.

"Until tomorrow, then," said the prince.

The two waved goodbye.

"What'll you get to eat, tadpole?" Renka shouted after him.

"Fish!" the prince called back, running towards the palace.

He had never run before. You realize that he was seven years old and this was the first time he'd ever run? But within sight of the palace he slowed down, and walking as the princes of the Hehvrontes walked, he entered the diningroom where the nobles, the knights, the servants were waiting for him, the whole jigsaw puzzle all ready to be put together. The prince sat down, looked at his empty plate, and said, "I want fish."

It was like an earthquake. The Protocol in no way prevented an hereditary prince from ordering whatever he wanted for lunch, but nobody had ever heard this hereditary prince open his mouth to express any wish, and certainly not a wish for some particular food, since he'd never had any appetite. It cannot be determined whether a cook actually had a nervous breakdown and two footmen fainted, but the story is, and it seems to be true, that when informed, the Empress raised an eyebrow—some say it was the left eyebrow, others say the right—and lost the thread of what she'd been saying to one of her ladies of honor. The young prince ate two servings of fish.

Next day—no. I'm not going to tell you everything that happened next day, since it was just the same as the day before. Except for one of those things the Hehvrontes couldn't prescribe in the Imperial Protocol: It was sunny. How do I know that? Ah, my little man, that's my privilege, you know. And I have a further privilege, which is that you don't know what I know nor how I know it. So it was sunny, and the lanky fellow was lying in the grass, half hidden by some shrubbery, and big Renka was standing watching the overgrown path that led from the palace. It led to the palace, too, but Renka was watching for somebody coming.

"Think he'll come?" he asked.

Loo'Loö was watching a lazy lizard, maybe, or the weeds over his head. "I'd like to tell you that he will," he said.

Now even you people, with all the sensitivity of paving-stones, have figured out that the two adventurers, we'll call them that for now although only one of them really was one, had been drawn toward the young prince by more than mere chance. We may ask ourselves—ask yourselves, because I've done it already and come up with the answer—whether chance rules humankind or if all our acts are foreseen, as if by the demented Protocol of the Hehvrontes. And we can't ask this curious question of the wise, because while some of them insist that everything is chance, others say it plays no part, and maybe all of them are right, since they all suspect, behind chance or non-chance, the workings of a secret code. The lizard scarcely moved, enjoying the sunlight, elegant and silvery as a new coin.

"He'll come," said the lanky man. I don't know—this I don't know—whether he believed in chance.

"He'll come," he said again, and put his hand on the old leather bag that hung from his belt.

And he came. He said, "Hello!" and stood there.

He just stood there because he didn't know what else to say to them. To escape from the Protocol was thrilling, and he'd had a wonderful time the day before, but today our young prince realized that it might be dangerous, too. Yes, dangerous: think a little, if you're capable of thought, and you'll see that it's safer to obey a law however stupid it may be than to act freely; because to act freely, unless you're as wicked as certain emperors, is to seek a just law; and if you make a mistake, you've taken the first step towards power, which is what destroys men.

And so that you can understand me once for all I'll tell you that the little boy said nothing but hello because the Protocol didn't tell him how to behave towards these two men who were humble laborers, and adventurers and philosophers, according to Renka, but who were also something else, something indefinable, mysterious, great, attractive, and frightening.

"Hello, kid," said Renka.

The other man said nothing.

"I'll tell you something," said the big man. "I didn't call you tadpole because I've decided that maybe you aren't a tadpole." He smiled. "Maybe you're a ferret. Do you like ferrets?"

"I don't know," the prince said. "I've never seen a ferret."

He sat down near Loo'Loö, and Renka sat down too.

"I've got a present for you, prince," said the lanky man.

"Silence!" Renka thundered. "I'm about to give a lecture on ferrets!"

In that moment, Livna'lams thought that he didn't like being a prince, and that instead of commanding and deciding and giving orders he'd rather obey Renka, even if that meant he had to wait for his present.

"Ferrets," said the black-eyed giant, "are small, tawny animals with four paws and a snout. They use their front paws to dig their underground cities, to hunt rats, and to hold food and baby ferrets. They use their hind paws to stand up, to mount females, and to jump. They use all four paws to run, walk, and dance.

They use their snout for sniffing and to grow whiskers on, for eating, and to show their kind and benevolent feelings. They also have a furry tail, which is a source of pride to them. Justified pride, moreover, for what would become of a ferret who wasn't proud of being a ferret? Their congenital trait is prudence, but with time they acquire wisdom as well. For them, everything in the world is red, because their eyes are red, that being the appropriate eye-color for ferrets. They are deeply interested in engineering and music. They have certain gifts of prescience, and would like to be able to fly, but so far have not done so, prevented by their prudence. They are loyal and brave. And they generally carry out their intentions."

Renka looked at his companion and the little boy, smoothed his beard and mustache, and said: "I have done. We may apply ourselves to other tasks."

Livna'lams clapped his hands. "Good, Renka, very good! I like ferrets! I agree to being a ferret! And now, can I see the present Loo brought me?"

"Why not?" said Renka.

The lanky man opened his pouch and took out a folded, yellowish piece of paper. The prince put out his hand for it.

"Not yet," said Loo'Loö.

"You're a very young ferret," Renka said, "proud, prudent, but not yet wise enough."

The prince was taken aback, perhaps embarrassed, certainly confused. But you know what? He wasn't sorrowful. Of course since Renka was right and he was a very young ferret, he didn't know he wasn't sad any more, just as he hadn't known that the grain hidden deep in his Imperial body had been a grain of sorrow. Loo'Loö unfolded the yellow paper once, twice, three, seven times, and when it was entirely unfolded it was circular. From the center dangled a long, fine, strong thread. Loo'Loö unwound it. Then he pulled on it, and the circle became a sphere of yellow paper, delicate, translucent, captive.

Livna'lams held his breath. "Now what?"

"Now you blow into it," said Loo'Loö.

"Where?"

"Here, where the string goes in."

The prince blew. The yellow sphere bounced up. Loo'Loö put the end of the string into the little ferret's paw, and the balloon rose up into the air.

You have memories, you people listening to me—try to remember and spare me the labor of describing what the prince felt when he saw the yellow sphere rise up so high, and ferret-pride filled his heart. Do you feel anything, can you recapture some faint memory of those days? The prince returned to the palace with a stiff neck, and with a little folded yellow paper hidden in his fist. And with an appetite.

No, nobody knew anything, not yet. The days went by all alike, all settled beforehand, perfect, dry, and hard, as they had been since the first of the Hehvrontes. The ceremony of contempt took place every day at the ruined statue in the wood among the trees in which sometimes a bird sang; but it didn't matter to the prince. He no longer hated his nameless father, if ever he had hated him as they had told him he should do, because he loved Renka and Loo. Every misfortune has its lucky side, say the wise. And I'd add that every good thing has its disadvantages, and the disadvantage of love is precisely that it leaves room for nothing else, not even the prudence of ferrets.

On the day after the day of the yellow balloon, Renka taught the ferret-prince a poem which told about the night wind, forgetfulness, and a man who was sitting at the door of his house, waiting. Next day they told fortunes. Next day they got down on all fours on the dirt and crawled around looking for ferrets, but couldn't find any.

"Too bad," said Renka. "I've wanted for a long time to go down into their subterranean cities."

Another day Renka and Loo'Loö taught Livna'lams how to braid leather thongs, and he wanted to teach them how to play the rebec, but they laughed at him and told him they already knew how. Then he told them how he passed his days in the palace and they listened gravely. Another day it started raining while the three of them were discussing the several ways of rowing upstream in rough water, and the two men built a shelter with branches and covered the ferret-prince with their heavy smocks and the three of them sang at the top of their voices and completely out of tune with the ceaseless song of the rain. Another day the adventurers described the hunting and trapping of tigers, and Renka displayed a scar on his shoulder which he declared was from the claws of a tiger which he had strangled with his bare hands, and Loo'Loö laughed a lot but told Livna'lams that it was true: "Whereas, I, prince, have never hunted tigers. What for?" said he.

That night before he went to sleep the little boy thought about hunting tigers. He thought that some day he'd challenge tigers, all the tigers in the world, and Renka and Loo would be there, backing him up.

Another day they played sintu and Loo'Loö won every round.

These days the prince got through the tasks his teachers set him so quickly that he often had to wait a long time for the two men in the deserted corner of the gardens, and when they came he'd say, "Why did you take so long?" or, "I thought you weren't going to come," or "How come I can always get here before you do?"

Renka and Loo'Loö explained that they had to finish their work and it took a long time because there were a lot of latrines to clean in the servants' quarters of the palace. It occurred to the ferret-prince, of course, that two men as unusual as Renka and Loo shouldn't be cleaning latrines, but doing important things while wearing clothes of silk and velvet. But they told him he was mistaken; because, in the first place, jobs considered despicable by the powerful are those which favor philosophical discussion; in the second place, keeping servants' latrines clean is more important than it seems, since servants notice that somebody's paying attention to them and their well-being, which puts them in a good humor, and so they wait diligently on their masters, who in turn are satisfied and so incline towards benevolence and justice; and finally, because coarse linen is much more comfortable than embroidered velvet, being warm in winter and cool in summer, while rich fabrics are chilly in winter and suffocating in summer. The ferret prince said that was true. And it is. It is, of course it is, and it's why the wise say that gold is sweet in the purse but bitter in the blood. But who takes any notice of the wise, these days, except story-tellers or poets?

Renka and Loo'Loö agreed with what the wise say, being wise themselves, even if they didn't know it. What happened in those days proves it. In those days that were all alike, yet different from the earlier days that had been all alike, there occurred two notable events. Notable is scarcely the right word, but I use it because I can't find a word to signify total change in all respects, external, internal, political, cosmic. The first notable event was provided for in the Protocol and occurred annually; the second was not, and occurred once only. Now listen to me while I tell you the first event.

One morning the ferret-prince arrived later than usual at the abandoned corner of the garden, and this time it was the brown men in linen and leather who asked him why he'd taken so long. The little boy told them that he hadn't had lessons that day because it was the anniversary of the death of his uncle, the younger brother of his mother the Empress Hallovâh, the Lord of the Shining Glance—for such was the name he had merited in death for what he had been in life, scion of the now very powerful Ja'lahdalva family—the sixth anniversary, and so the prince had had to attend the ceremony of remembrance and homage.

Renka spat on the dirt. "Bah," he said. "All that wasted on unscrupulous scum."

"Don't talk that way, Renka," said Livna'lams.

"Why shouldn't I, little ferret?"

"My uncle was a great man."

Renka spat again. "You're sure about that?"

The ferret-prince thought hard about his uncle whom he hadn't known, and about the memorial observance. He thought about the noblemen and lords and magistrates all dressed in black, the veiled ladies, his mother in white. He remembered that his mother the empress wept only this one time in the year, and remembered the words of the elegy which it was his duty to speak. He remembered the gold urn that held his uncle's ashes, and the portraits of a fair man with eyes so clear they were almost transparent, wearing not linen, but brocade. He said, "No."

"Ha!" said Renka.

"What was the ceremony like, prince?" asked Loo'Loö.

The prince told him, but don't expect me to describe it all to you, because it isn't worth it: it was nothing but the reverse of the ceremony of contempt for the nameless Emperor, and it was a farce. As was the other one, as you'll soon see by what I have to tell you.

The second notable event of those days that were all alike happened to the two adventurers and the ferret prince one morning when a storm made its presence felt by thundering on the other side of the river, though it didn't break till the afternoon, which got dark all at once as if the world were a kettle and somebody had decided to beat on it after throwing cold water onto hot grease. But all morning the storm just crouched, waiting, and the three of them were crouching too, silently watching a busy scarab beetle rolling tiny balls of mud.

"Why's it doing that?" asked Livna'lams.

"Making a nest," said Loo'Loö.

"What's happening," said Renka, "is that the Lord of the Scarabs is provident, and when he knows that the moment has come, when his hard wings tremble and his jaws clack, he hurries to gather little balls of mud."

"But what for?"

"Don't rush it, because he doesn't rush it. He's ready, but he doesn't let himself be rushed," Renka went on. "When he's got a lot of little balls of mud, I don't know exactly how many because I've never been a scarab, but enough, he goes scuttling off to where a Lady Scarab is, and he finds her, infallibly. If there's another male beetle around, he opens his jaws wide and bites off its head. Then he brings the Lady of the Scarabs to where the little mudballs are, and they do together what they have to do, and she lays eggs and he covers them with the mudballs and hatches them, and she goes off, airhead that she is, hoping to meet another Scarab Lord. It's even possible she may say nasty things to him about the first one."

The ferret-prince put out a finger towards the beetle.

"Don't bother him," said Loo'Loö. "He'll feel very bad if you interrupt him."

"Great Ladies do things like that," Renka said, "and I don't like Great Ladies, not that I've known many."

"Come on, Renka," said Loo'Loö, "let's not start that again."

"I'm going to tell you a secret, little ferret," Renka went on as if nobody had said anything, or as if somebody might have said something but he hadn't heard it—"Your mother, the Lady Hallovâh, is a Great Lady, and your uncle Lord Hohviolol, scion of the ambitious Ja'lahdalvas, was a shameless, feeble, greedy, vicious turkeycock who instead of dying in a soft bed of a fever like an honest man should have been stoned to death in the public square. And your father was not a traitor."

Now, you good people listening to me, know this: the ferret-prince was not surprised. Know it as surely as I do, as if he himself had come from death across the years to tell us. Know that, instead of surprise, he felt the grain of sorrow in him was gone, and in its place was a grain of anger. And he was aware that it wasn't Renka who had done it in that moment, but that he'd been doing it himself, slowly, for a long time, with infinite patience and secrecy, but not alone. No, not alone. Strange as it seems, his mother the Empress Hallovâh had helped him in his great task, and so had the Protocol of the Hehvrontes.

"That's enough, Renka," said Loo'Loö.

And now the ferret prince *was* surprised. What surprised him was hearing the familiar voice speak in an unfamiliar tone, as if the strings of a lady's lute were to play a march to battle. And what surprised him was the look on the face of the lanky, gentle man who was or wasn't named Loo'Loö as he looked at him, at the prince, while he spoke to Renka. He heard and saw a tone and an expression that seemed familiar, though he didn't know why.

"Renka, will you tell me everything?" said Livna'lams the Ferret.

"Sure I will, little ferret," said big Renka.

"You will not," said Loo'Loö.

The two men faced each other, and the ferret-prince remembered the tigers. Not that Renka was a tiger—he was a mad elephant about to charge. The prince had seen an elephant gone wild, seen it sweep men and arms and wagons aside, trampling on whatever got in its way, heard its furious trumpeting while it killed and while it died, defeated at last. The other man, Loo'Loö, was the tiger, a splendid, supple tiger, serene and dangerous, defending his territory against everyone and everything. The ferret-prince thought for a moment that the tiger was going to spring and sink his claws in some vulnerable part of the elephant's hide. But they both held still, watching each other.

"I don't want that," said Loo'Loö.

"You don't, eh? Why did we come, then? Why are we here?"

"For other reasons."

"Ha!" Renka said again. "They're terrific, your reasons, it's a real treat the way you can string reasons together, pal."

"There are some things it's better not to meddle with," Loo'Loö said quietly. "I thought we agreed about that."

"We did," said Renka. "A long time ago. So long ago I don't

remember. But now we know him, and we've raised him to the rank of Ferret, right? He'll be emperor some day, right?"

"Yes," said Loo'Loö, smiling, and his smile filled the world of the ferret prince the way Renka's laughs and bellows filled it, but with light, not thunder.

"So," the big man said, "he needs information, he needs to know something more than music and politics and which foot to put first when he enters the council hall and which color of pen to write with on the third day of the week. I'm going to tell you something, pal: he needs to know everything, he needs to hear and see and touch and smell and taste and suffer everything so he can find out some day what kind of emperor he's going to be—right? At whatever cost."

"I agree," said Loo'Loö. "But I don't want that."

"You're lying!" Renka roared. "You're lying, there's nothing you want more!"

Again the ferret-prince thought the tiger and the elephant were on the point of destroying each other. But again Loo'Loö smiled.

"I don't want it," he said. "He's very young and shouldn't be troubled. He should be let alone, like the beetles. And the ferrets."

"He's no beetle, he's only a boy. But a prince, worse luck for him," said Renka. "Beetles know a lot more than he does. Not to mention ferrets."

And that, strangely enough, seemed to settle the question. Loo'Loö turned the fierce, steady stare of his dark eyes away from Renka and sat down on the ground and listened. And Renka told all, as he had said he would. And now I'll tell it to you people, who will never be emperors. I'm not telling it in the hope that you'll understand me, or understand the ferret-prince, but only because the wise say that words, being daughters of the flesh, spoil if they're kept locked up.

"Your father was a good man, little ferret," Renka began, "I can tell you that, since I was his friend for many years, and his only friend for many more years."

Yes, Livna'lams said to himself, yes, that's how it must have been, that's how it was. And he listened. Renka told him about a handsome man, black-eyed, black-haired, a tranquil, moderate, just man, an Emperor who protected his people and composed songs and built cities and enriched farmlands. A man who won the love of everyone who knew him, except his wife, who loved another man.

"An idiot," said Renka. "Which doesn't reflect much credit on your mother. An idiot, shameless, vicious, boastful, cowardly, greedy, and ambitious, which reflects even less credit on her. I'm sorry, but it's better that I tell you, so you don't find it out little by little, and keep telling yourself no, no, no, and filling yourself up with so much pain that finally the only way out is to say, yes, yes, yes."

"Let's stop there," said Loo'Loö. "You can go on about his father, since the only way to stop you would be to cut out your tongue, and I don't know that I want to. I don't think I do. But don't talk about his mother."

Renka laughed his usual laugh, just as when he told about his adventures or made fun of himself because he'd lost at sintu. "I always said you were crazy, partner," he said.

But believe me, the conversation didn't end there. Renka said nothing more about the Empress Hallovâh, but he told the ferret-prince how, when war came, when the enemy approached the borders of the empire, his father the emperor called the generals together and the army marched away. Flowers rained down, said Renka, armfuls of flowers, on the soldiers, and the emperor, who wasn't an ambitious coward like the other man, who was hiding in the palace pretending to be sick, and was sick, with fear—the emperor marched at the head of his troops. They fought on the border, Renka said, and they were all brave, but the bravest was the Ninth Emperor of the House of the Hehvrontes. But the other man had stayed behind in the palace, very pale, very blond, very scared, being looked after by his sister the Empress Hallovâh. And both of them expected and hoped that the emperor would die in battle.

"Not that it would have done them any good," said Renka, "since although she didn't know it, she already had you in her belly, little ferret."

And he went on with the story: Not only did the emperor stay alive, he defeated the enemy. Then, when news came that the invaders were retreating, when victory was certain, the two in the palace had to find another way: treason, since death had failed them.

"But the traitor wasn't your father," Renka said. "It wasn't him!"

And he told how somebody had made sure that the ministers found supposed proof of the emperor's treason.

"I said it was somebody," he insisted. "I didn't say it was her."

"It doesn't matter," said Loo'Loö. And, to the prince, "It really doesn't matter who it was, prince. What matters, since Renka wants it so, and maybe I do too, is that you know that *he* didn't betray you. Even though he didn't know either that you were going to be born."

"The proof," said Renka without looking at either of them, "was a letter, a secret copy of the secret letters kept in a very well-hidden drawer which now, inexplicably, wasn't well hidden. In this letter the emperor offered unconditional surrender and permanent submission to the enemy in exchange for gold, enough gold to fill his chests, enough to buy luxury, folly, vice."

The ferret prince sat up and looked, not at Renka, but at Loo'Loö. "Didn't he come back to say it wasn't true?"

It was Renka who answered: "A good question. Yes, little ferret, sure, he came back. But he came back in hiding, as if he really had been a traitor, because it's a very short step from the ministers to the generals, from the generals to the troops, and from the troops to the people. Good sense is inversely proportional to the number of brains, so say the wise. If you don't understand that, it means that the more people there are to think a thought, the uglier and more crippled and deformed the poor thing gets. So, if the ministers believed it, why not the generals and the troops and the people, eh? And why not, if the Emperor's personal seal was on the letter, eh? Of course somebody had access to his seal, who knows who, pal. Who knows. . . ."

The three were silent for a long time, listening to the rumbling of the black, indecisive storm on the other side of the river.

"And then?" Livna'lams whispered.

"I don't know anything more," said the giant.

"It's true," said Loo'Loö. "It's true, we don't know anything more. Nobody does."

"He died?" asked the little ferret.

"Maybe so, maybe not," said Renka. "Nobody knows. People say different things."

"What things?"

"They say somebody surprised him trying to enter the palace and killed him, nobody knows who, just somebody. They say nobody killed him. They say somebody else, I don't say who, some friend of his, warned him in time and so he got away. They say he killed himself. They say he didn't kill himself and went wandering over the fields, into the mountains. A lot of people say they've seen him disguised as a shepherd or a beggar or a monk, and in more than one city they've stoned and killed some poor fool who never dreamed of being emperor and had nothing to do with the Hehvrontes. They say that when your mother learned she was pregnant with you she wept and screamed and beat her belly to try to force you out. But you were very small and very well protected and all she could do was put on white clothes and go barefoot with her hair down and no jewellery. They say that the other man beat her when he found out, because she'd promised him to have nothing to do with her husband and to keep herself for him, and because your birth meant that it wouldn't be their blood, pure Ja'lahdalva blood, but your father's Hehvrontes blood that would rule the Empire. There was, evidently, one solution."

"You're just guessing," Loo'Loö said.

Renka burst out with a "Ha!" and the storm echoed him. "The solution was to wait it out, then say you'd been born dead and show your poor little corpse around for public mourning. What saved you, prince Ferret, was a prostitute. The other man caught a deadly fever from her. For over two years he lay in bed, really sick this time, burning up. And in that condition no man could engender sons, as everybody knows. Doctors and treatments and drugs that made him howl and writhe did no good. He died."

The storm shouted something very loudly in the distance but the ferret prince didn't know the language of storms the way gardeners do, and didn't understand it. Maybe he didn't hear it. Imagine, if you can: his world had changed utterly.

The wise say everything has its season, and each stage in a man's life has its sign, and it must be so, since the wise know what they're talking about and if sometimes we don't understand them it's not their fault but ours. What I say, and this is something I thought myself and never read or heard, is that in the ferret-prince's life the years of sorrow had ended and the years of anger had begun. The worst thing about sorrow is that it's blind, and the worst thing about anger is that it sees too much. But the prince's anger wasn't the kind that flares up and dies down in a few minutes, not like the stupid raging of a drunk or the fury of a jealous husband. It was growing unseen, unknown, hidden, in him, as he had grown in the Empress Hallovâh's womb. Now and then it made a little movement that showed it was there, as when Renka spoke for the first time of the nameless emperor. But then it would quiet down till it seemed not to exist. And since the anger wasn't fully formed yet and the sorrow was gone, all that was left was indifference, which is a heavy burden for a child of seven.

So it was that the little ferret went back to the palace that morning and performed all the acts expected of him and said everything that he was supposed to say and knew he was going to say. So it was that he went on playing his role in the life of the palace and in the ceremony of contempt, too, day after day, beside his mother in her white dress. So it was that he went on studying and taking part in official duties, escaping late in the morning to meet Renka and Loo'Loö and play and laugh and explore the ruined garden with them and sometimes ask them about his father. They always answered his questions, especially big Renka.

And all this time the anger never ceased; he felt it burning inside him, and his mother guessed it. The empress didn't know exactly what was going on, but every day she felt more uncomfortable with her son, and when she didn't see him, when he wasn't there, still she seemed to hear and see him through the walls and rooms of the palace. Occasionally he looked directly into her eyes, and that was the worst of all. Or he turned his head away so as not to look at her, and that was worse than the worst of all. She increased what she called her expiation, spending the nights on the bare marble floor of her rooms instead of in bed. When that did no good, she ordered the richest food for her table, but lived on bread and water for forty days. That did no good either. She kept on coughing and shaking with fever, shivering in her white clothes. The forty days of fasting and penitence were just ending when one morning in the ceremony of contempt the ferret prince looked up at his mother and, instead of spitting on her medallion, spat in her face.

Perhaps the lords and ladies and magistrates didn't notice, perhaps they did. Nobody said anything, nobody looked surprised, nobody moved, including the Empress Hallovâh. She decided, however, to kill her son. And so, on the pretext of her illness, she had a doctor come to her room, and asked him for a drug that would cure insomnia and help her sleep soundly at night, and the stupid ass gave it to her with a lot of advice about the dosage. The Empress kept the drug in a sealed glass flask and waited for the moment to use it.

She didn't use it, obviously, since you've all heard of Emperor Ferret, his life, his works, his madness, and his magnificent death. Fooling herself, telling herself she had to know when it would be safe to give Livna'lams the poison, she had him watched by one of her servants. And so she was informed of the existence of Renka and Loo'Loö.

If you've ever lived with somebody in trouble, or if you've ever been in bad trouble for a long time, you know the relief unhappy people feel when they find something or somebody to blame their trouble on. That's exactly what the empress felt. They say she even smiled. I'm not certain I believe it, but I know they say she smiled. And I know she sent for the captain of her bodyguards and ordered him to wait for her in her chambers with ten armed men and the executioner. Then she went barefoot, dressed in white, splendid, her eyes bright and her hair loose and her cheeks burning red, to perform the ritual farce at the broken statue among the trees.

Late that morning, the ferret prince and the two adventurers were playing a game of skill in which the one who was quickest and most skillful at making a fifteen-foot rope ladder would win the right to make three wishes, which the other two had to grant. Renka and Loo'Loö had brought the ropes all carefully measured and cut, and the big man handed them round, making sure that all three had the same number of pieces in the same condition. And it looked as if Loo'Loö was going to win.

"Captain, these two trespassers are to be taken and executed at once," said the empress appearing between the leafless bushes, her feet bruised by loose stones, her face very white, her hands very shaky, her cheeks very red.

Renka looked up and smiled. Loo'Loö stood up. Anger filled the young prince, forever.

The captain took a step forward. The weapons were raised and aimed. The empress cried out aloud.

It was a desolate, furious cry that had struggled to get loose for years, a cry far deeper and stronger than she was, a noise too big to come from that weak throat, those lips cracked with fever.

"Wait!" she said, defeated, when she could speak.

Nobody moved, nobody spoke, and a long while, a very long while passed in that unmoving silence.

"Who are you," said the pale empress.

"Two humble workmen in the service of your majesty's palace," said the enormous brown man. "I'm called Renka and my pal's called Loo'Loö, a very unusual name. So unusual that I've often thought it isn't really his name. But I've never been able to find out, because he knows how to keep a secret."

And then Renka smiled still more broadly, pleased with his speech, perfectly happy and cheerful, as if he weren't in danger, as if there weren't ten men pointing their weapons at him and Loo.

The captain of the guard, on the other hand, was disconcerted; he didn't yet know why he was there and whether he ought to kill these two fellows, or go silently away, or await further orders from his lady. A captain of the guard is invariably a brainless brute, but some, not always the least brutish, acquire a certain training, which in the best cases may lead to subtlety, making them act as appropriately as if they were capable of thought or reason. This captain knew, knew in his guts, that he was out of place in whatever was going on here. And so he signaled his men to lower their arms and step back, and he himself stepped back a few paces, and they waited behind the empress in case she needed them.

"You must die," she said, but she didn't sound as if she believed it.

"We all have to die, my lady," Renka said, still smiling. "In our case it's a pity, because there's a lot of foreign countries we haven't seen yet, a lot of rivers to cross, a lot of wine we haven't tasted, a lot of sweet women to cheer us up and for us to cheer up, nights. In your case, who knows."

That was an insult, in case you didn't notice, and yet the captain didn't stir from where he stood. It was the ferret-prince who spoke: "I pray you, Mother, take care," he said. "It is not my wish that these men die."

That wasn't an insult, it was an order. Remember what I told you at the start, remember that Livna'lams was heir to the throne, and when he was a little older or when his mother died, he'd be emperor. The empress kept her gaze fixed on one of the two men; she didn't look at her son, and paid no heed to the captain and his men or the executioner.

"But, thanks to the generosity of the prince," she went on as if nothing had been said, "your lives will be spared, on the condition that you leave the palace and the capital at once and never set foot again in the eastern provinces."

Renka got up; he made a heap of the unfinished rope ladder and shook the bits of hemp off his hands. "What do you think of the deal?" he asked.

"The lady is generous," said Loo'Loö.

"Oh really?" the big man sneered. "She's so generous, maybe you should ask her for another favor."

"It's all right, Renka. Let's go," said Loo'Loö, still looking at the empress.

"No," said Prince Ferret. "I don't want you to go. Renka, Loo, stay here."

"I hate to let a ferret down, but this time there's no help for it. We're going, young 'un."

"It is an order," said Livna'lams.

"Aha, ha, ahaha!" Renka boomed. "I don't like saying this any better, but there it is. Nobody gives us orders."

Loo'Loö turned to Prince Ferret. "Renka's always joking, prince," he said. "But we can't stay here. Not now. It wouldn't be a good thing."

The future Tenth Emperor of the Hehvrontes Dynasty understood. "Where will you go?" he asked.

"Oh, my little ferret," said Renka, "who knows, since we don't know? All the provinces aren't in the east, you'll find that out when you're emperor. In the western provinces there are mountains, in the northern ones there's snow, in the southern ones are marshes where barbarians live who'll kill you at a word and give their life for a friend. So long, prince, be a good emperor, and don't ever forget the things you've seen and heard."

Renka put his immense, dark hands on the prince's shoulders and looked down at him smiling, and then drew away from him and turned to go without a glance, even of mockery, at the empress. Loo'Loö, instead, bent down and hugged the little boy, and Livna'lams rested his head for a moment against the man's chest.

"Goodbye," Loo'Loö said, and looked at the pale woman, and went.

The two men disappeared among the branches. When the sound of their steps could no longer be heard, Prince Ferret called to the captain of the guard.

"Highness!" said the brute, squaring his shoulders and clicking his boot-heels.

"You will answer to me with your life for the lives of those two men," said Livna'lams in his high little boyish voice, in which you could already hear the tone of an emperor giving orders. "You will follow them without their seeing you. Others will be following you without your seeing them. You'll look out for them without their knowing it, and you'll be watched without your knowing it. And you will not come back to the palace till they're safely across the border of the eastern provinces."

The captain saluted again and marched off with his soldiers and his executioner. Prince Ferret looked at his mother with a certain icy curiosity, and she endured his gaze until she was doubled over by a spasm of coughing. Then they walked back to the palace, he leading, she following with bruised, bare feet.

You've all read something somewhere or heard something about Emperor Ferret's reign. Whatever you've read or heard, I tell you that he was a just man. He was crazy, but he ruled well.

Maybe you have to be a bit touched to be a ruler, good or bad. For, as the wise say, a sensible man looks after his garden, and a coward looks after his money; a just man cares about his city and a crazy man cares about government; and a wise man studies the thickness of fern-fronds.

He was the last emperor of the Hehvrontes Dynasty. During his reign the protocol so laboriously constructed by his ancestors began to deteriorate, and unforeseen phrases and unrehearsed gestures entered palace life. Very soon after the two adventurers left, while he was still a child, he stopped attending the ceremony of contempt for the nameless emperor, his father. Some say that the day before he stopped going, he had a long conversation with his mother, or rather that he talked for a long time and she listened, but this isn't written down anywhere and frankly I don't believe it. What is recorded in the history books is that the Empress Hallovâh never went back to the wood either, and so the ritual ceased. She locked herself up in her rooms, where she slowly consumed herself, seen by no one but her maids, giving her orders through an opaque screen. Young Livna'lams succeeded to the throne when he was ten, upon the death of his mother, whom he did not go to see when she was dying. He had her buried with all due honor, but he was not present at the funeral.

He married when he reached marrying age. He had a principal wife who was crowned Empress, and six secondary wives. But he never slept with any of them, or as far as I know with any woman, or man, or animal—nobody, nothing. He ordered all the noble families with children to leave the court and the palace; they could keep their goods and privileges, on condition that they never return as long as he lived. And more: any servant, soldier, magistrate, official, who had children or whose wife got pregnant, had to leave the court. And at the same time as he gave such orders, he was dealing out justice wisely, distributing land, founding schools and hospitals, beautifying the capital, the cities, and the towns, making food and water and medical help available to everybody, peacefully consolidating the borders, protecting the arts, and helping anybody who needed help.

Unfortunately, one of his untouched secondary wives got pregnant. She was very beautiful, stupid, and soft-hearted, and had a lovely voice.

He didn't punish her, as everybody thought he would. He let her go, free, rich, and healthy, with her lover, an assistant fencing-master in the officer training program, who was also beautiful, stupid, and probably soft-hearted, though quite unable to sing. Three days after that, Emperor Ferret signed the insane decree according to which every man who wished to stay at court must be castrated. He was mad, no doubt of it; but the men who preferred mutilation to leaving the court were madder. And there were plenty of them, since it was from among them that Obonendas I, the Eunuch, arose. He wasn't a bad emperor, though many would disagree.

Emperor Ferret never lost his anger, though in fact it didn't keep him from being sensible, just, insane, and possibly wise. And he was never a coward, for our songs still tell the glory of his death, even after so many years, lifting their triumphant rhythms in taverns and town squares, quarries and sawmills and battlefields. But that—as they say another story-teller used to say—is another story.

From *Kalpa Imperial*, two volumes of histories of an Empire so great it cannot be contained by time or geography.

GEOFFREY A. LANDIS

SNOW

THE SNOW WAS COMING DOWN HARDER NOW, NOT A GENTLE snow like memories of childhood Christmases that had never been, but wet gobbets plummeting out of the heavens like saliva, puddling half-frozen on the pavement. The temperature was continuing to drop. Before midnight, Sarah calculated, it would start freezing. The night would be a deadly one for anybody who didn't have shelter.

For a moment Sarah let herself slip into her other world, her private world that had no rain, no weather, no rummaging through dumpsters or begging for quarters. The crystalline beauty started to build itself around her. It was so tempting . . . she shook herself, hard, and stomped her feet. If she let herself go there now, she would die. It was that simple.

Stamping her feet had made Christie start to cry. Sarah pressed the baby closer to her and made soothing noises, but, once awake, Christie was not so easily satisfied. She really needed warmth, shelter. Sarah quickly ran through her options. Steam vents around Public Square . . . but lately the police had been rousting anybody who lingered too long. A mayoral election was coming. The shelter . . . but after what had happened the last time, she would never go back there. Even if they let her. That left various doorways and alleys that she knew. But it was going to be awfully cold for that.

Christie started crying again, this time wailing with all her energy, and Sarah gave up on trying to shush her. Let her cry; she had a right. The world was mightily unfair, and she had every right to complain about it.

Once Sarah's voices might have come to her aid with their unworldly advice, but for the last few months the voices had deserted her. That was something to think about, the fact that voices had, for now, gone away from her. Was it a good thing or a bad one? The voices had rarely offered practical advice, but they often told her how important she was, how the National Security Agency wanted to steal her brain; they had warned her about agents plotting against her, pretending to be social workers or psychologists or stray dogs. (But stray dogs don't have radios implanted in their heads; she had seen that, she had!) Had the voices left her for good? Was that even possible? The psychologist had said that the voices wouldn't go away unless she took the special medicines, but then, the psychologist was an agent. The voices had told her so.

But the voices sometimes lied, too.

In any case, she had no choice. Tonight she would need a room.

Shifting Christie to her left arm so she could examine her pockets with her right, she came up with a crumpled bill and fifty-eight cents in change found on the sidewalks. She uncrumpled the bill eagerly, hoping it might be a twenty, or even a fifty—it was possible, it was—but it was only a single. A dollar and a half. She'd need twenty for the cheapest room.

Two blocks down Superior she found Old Mother Rags huddled in her doorway. She was wearing what must be the remains of at least five different dresses, and was surrounded by more, a veritable department store of tattered plaids and patterns and corduroy. Sarah plumped Christie down among them. "Take the kid for me, okay?"

Mother Rags smiled, showing yellow and uneven teeth. "Ten dollars."

Sarah shook her head. "Two."

"Five," said the old woman slyly. "Five, and not dollar less."

"Okay, three," Sarah said. She pulled out her bait and held the crumpled bill out, dangling from her fingers. "I'll give you one now."

Mother Rags' smile grew wider. "Give," she said.

"Take the kid. Three dollars."

"Deal!" said Mother Rags, smiling greedily. "Now, give!"

Sarah dropped the bill into her lap, and Mother Rags scooped it up, the bill and the child together.

Christie would be warm and safe, for a while at least, and Sarah would be free to do what she had to. Besides, let Mother Rags deal with the kid for a while. Do them both some good.

The air was even colder, snow coming down like bullets through the yellow glow from the streetlights, and Prospect Street was as empty as an alien planet. Sarah huddled in a doorway, waiting. As she waited, she allowed her other world to creep into the edge of her mind. In her pocket she had four envelopes scavenged from trash cans, business-reply envelopes from some advertising promotion, one side beautifully blank. The cold made the other world clear, and she let it play in her mind, but refused to let herself go, despite the temptation of those beautifully pristine envelopes.

A car. She heard it before she could see it, tires ripping the wet asphalt, like tearing an envelope in two. She stepped out into the circle of light cast by the streetlight. A big Lincoln Towncar, tinted windows, power everything. It slowed slightly as it cruised past, but didn't stop. It turned at the corner. She waited, miserable. Half a minute later it came around again, slowed to a stop by the streetlight. Motionless, the car looked less pristine; the bumper slightly skew, the rear door-panel dented with patches of rust showing. A window purred down.

She leaned in. "Hey there, mister," she said, trying not to let her teeth chatter, trying to look pretty, not the least bit soaked and bedraggled. The car's heater caressed her face. "You looking for a party?"

She clutched the three crumpled ten-dollar bills. The guy had given her an extra five; a big tipper. She wondered if she'd ever met him before. Maybe he knew her, maybe that was why he gave her the extra five. Or maybe he just didn't have any fives. Either way, she had been almost sorry to leave the warm car.

On her way back to Superior she detoured to a gas station to change the ten. The kid in the armored booth didn't want to change it unless she bought something, which she wasn't about to do, but he didn't want her lingering in his station, either, so he did it, peeling out the singles slowly and methodically, never letting his eyes off her. Maybe he was an agent, assigned to watch her. Could they have guessed she'd visit that gas station? Maybe. Or maybe he was just worried that she'd pocket a handful of Lifesavers.

Christie was sleeping, almost buried under the mountain of rags. Old Mother Rags was dozing as well, but snapped out a palm as soon as Sarah touched the pile. "Give," she said.

It was worth the price. Sarah dropped two singles into the outstretched palm, and Mother Rags deposited them into some hidden cache under her fortress of cloth.

"Thanks," said Sarah.

She'd been in the hotel before, and the room clerk didn't even look up when she dropped the two tens on the scarred mahogany counter, just slid a key across the desk. He didn't ask her to sign the book, and she didn't offer; there was little chance that her twenty would ever show up on an accounting ledger.

The room was clean, if a bit threadbare. Long ago, it had been elegant. There was soap in the bathroom, and even, to her surprise, hot water. Sarah put Christie into the bed, tucked her in, and went back to the bathroom. She thought about washing her clothes in the sink, but reluctantly decided against it. The radiator was putting up a valiant, and quite noisy, effort, but she couldn't take the risk that it might not dry her clothes by checkout time.

But she could take a bath. A bath!

Later, her skin as wrinkled as the face of old Mother Rags, but with the cold of the streets steamed out of her bones, Sarah sat at the tiny desk. Christie was fast asleep, oblivious to the banging radiator. No stationery in the drawer. She had hardly expected that she would be so lucky, but when she pulled the drawer all the way out, and inspected behind it, she found two paperclips and a pencil. A pencil! The tip was broken, but she could deal with that.

She gnawed at the point, humming with contentment. A warm room, Christie asleep, and she still had eight whole dollars, and almost the whole night left. She had never needed very much sleep, only an hour or two, and when she had the pencil tip gnawed to a needle-like point, she had four envelopes to work with. A night's worth, at least; maybe more if she wrote very very small.

She took out the first envelope, and carefully spread it open. Her other world was very close, the world that she created out of herself. She knew that somewhere, somewhere out in the world there were other people who knew how to enter that other world. Sometimes she wondered if she had ever met any of them. But, she decided, that really didn't matter. What mattered was that other world.

She checked once more that Christie was sleeping soundly, and then, writing in almost invisibly tiny script, she started.

"Theorem 431. Consider the set of non-singular connections mapping an 8-dimensional vector space onto a differentiable Hausdorff manifold. . . ."

She paused for a moment, picturing the simple beauty of the eight dimensional complex mapping, and wondering for a second if there might be a straightforward extension of the theorem to arbitrary dimensionality. She smiled. Might that be Theorem 432?

The snow fell outside the window, mapping a divergenceless vector field in three-dimensional space.

It was a perfect day.

TED CHIANG

STORY OF YOUR LIFE

YOUR FATHER IS ABOUT TO ASK ME THE QUESTION. THIS IS the most important moment in our lives, and I want to pay attention, note every detail. Your dad and I have just come back from an evening out, dinner and a show; it's after midnight. We came out onto the patio to look at the full moon; then I told your dad I wanted to dance, so he humors me and now we're slow-dancing, a pair of thirtysomethings swaying back and forth in the moonlight like kids. I don't feel the night chill at all. And then your dad says, "Do you want to make a baby?"

Right now your dad and I have been married for about two years, living on Ellis Avenue; when we move out you'll still be too young to remember the house, but we'll show you pictures of it, tell you stories about it. I'd love to tell you the story of this evening, the night you're conceived, but the right time to do that would be when you're ready to have children of your own, and we'll never get that chance.

Telling it to you any earlier wouldn't do any good; for most of your life you won't sit still to hear such a romantic—you'd say sappy—story. I remember the scenario of your origin you'll suggest when you're twelve.

"The only reason you had me was so you could get a maid you wouldn't have to pay," you'll say bitterly, dragging the vacuum cleaner out of the closet.

"That's right," I'll say. "Thirteen years ago I knew the carpets would need vacuuming around now, and having a baby seemed to be the cheapest and easiest way to get the job done. Now kindly get on with it."

"If you weren't my mother, this would be illegal," you'll say, seething as you unwind the power cord and plug it into the wall outlet.

That will be in the house on Belmont Street. I'll live to see strangers occupy both houses: the one you're conceived in and the one you grow up in. Your dad and I will sell the first a couple years after your arrival. I'll sell the second shortly after your departure. By then Nelson and I will have moved into our farmhouse, and your dad will be living with what's-her-name.

I know how this story ends; I think about it a lot. I also think a lot about how it began, just a few years ago, when ships appeared in orbit and artifacts appeared in meadows. The government said next to nothing about them, while the tabloids said every possible thing.

And then I got a phone call, a request for a meeting.

I spotted them waiting in the hallway, outside my office. They made an odd couple; one wore a military uniform and a crewcut, and carried an aluminum briefcase. He seemed to be assessing his surroundings with a critical eye. The other one was easily identifiable as an academic: full beard and mustache, wearing corduroy. He was browsing through the overlapping sheets stapled to a bulletin board nearby.

"Colonel Weber, I presume?" I shook hands with the soldier. "Louise Banks."

"Dr. Banks. Thank you for taking the time to speak with us," he said.

"Not at all; any excuse to avoid the faculty meeting."

Colonel Weber indicated his companion. "This is Dr. Gary Donnelly, the physicist I mentioned when we spoke on the phone."

"Call me Gary," he said as we shook hands. "I'm anxious to hear what you have to say."

We entered my office. I moved a couple of stacks of books off the second guest chair, and we all sat down. "You said you wanted me to listen to a recording. I presume this has something to do with the aliens?"

"All I can offer is the recording," said Colonel Weber.

"Okay, let's hear it."

Colonel Weber took a tape machine out of his briefcase and pressed PLAY. The recording sounded vaguely like that of a wet dog shaking the water out of its fur.

"What do you make of that?" he asked.

I withheld my comparison to a wet dog. "What was the context in which this recording was made?"

"I'm not at liberty to say."

"It would help me interpret those sounds. Could you see the alien while it was speaking? Was it doing anything at the time?"

"The recording is all I can offer."

"You won't be giving anything away if you tell me that you've seen the aliens; the public's assumed you have."

Colonel Weber wasn't budging. "Do you have any opinion about its linguistic properties?" he asked.

"Well, it's clear that their vocal tract is substantially different from a human vocal tract. I assume that these aliens don't look like humans?"

The colonel was about to say something noncommittal when

Gary Donelly asked, “Can you make any guesses based on the tape?”

“Not really. It doesn’t sound like they’re using a larynx to make those sounds, but that doesn’t tell me what they look like.”

“Anything—is there anything else you can tell us?” asked Colonel Weber.

I could see he wasn’t accustomed to consulting a civilian. “Only that establishing communications is going to be really difficult because of the difference in anatomy. They’re almost certainly using sounds that the human vocal tract can’t reproduce, and maybe sounds that the human ear can’t distinguish.”

“You mean infra- or ultrasonic frequencies?” asked Gary Donelly.

“Not specifically. I just mean that the human auditory system isn’t an absolute acoustic instrument; it’s optimized to recognize the sounds that a human larynx makes. With an alien vocal system, all bets are off.” I shrugged. “*Maybe* we’ll be able to hear the difference between alien phonemes, given enough practice, but it’s possible our ears simply can’t recognize the distinctions they consider meaningful. In that case we’d need a sound spectrograph to know what an alien is saying.”

Colonel Weber asked, “Suppose I gave you an hour’s worth of recordings; how long would it take you to determine if we need this sound spectrograph or not?”

“I couldn’t determine that with just a recording no matter how much time I had. I’d need to talk with the aliens directly.”

The colonel shook his head. “Not possible.”

I tried to break it to him gently. “That’s your call, of course. But the only way to learn an unknown language is to interact with a native speaker, and by that I mean asking questions, holding a conversation, that sort of thing. Without that, it’s simply not possible. So if you want to learn the aliens’ language, someone with training in field linguistics—whether it’s me or someone else—will have to talk with an alien. Recordings alone aren’t sufficient.”

Colonel Weber frowned. "You seem to be implying that no alien could have learned human languages by monitoring our broadcasts."

"I doubt it. They'd need instructional material specifically designed to teach human languages to nonhumans. Either that, or interaction with a human. If they had either of those, they could learn a lot from TV, but otherwise, they wouldn't have a starting point."

The colonel clearly found this interesting; evidently his philosophy was, the less the aliens knew, the better. Gary Donnelly read the colonel's expression too and rolled his eyes. I suppressed a smile.

Then Colonel Weber asked, "Suppose you were learning a new language by talking to its speakers; could you do it without teaching them English?"

"That would depend on how cooperative the native speakers were. They'd almost certainly pick up bits and pieces while I'm learning their language, but it wouldn't have to be much if they're willing to teach. On the other hand, if they'd rather learn English than teach us their language, that would make things far more difficult."

The colonel nodded. "I'll get back to you on this matter."

The request for that meeting was perhaps the second most momentous phone call in my life. The first, of course, will be the one from Mountain Rescue. At that point your dad and I will be speaking to each other maybe once a year, tops. After I get that phone call, though, the first thing I'll do will be to call your father.

He and I will drive out together to perform the identification, a long silent car ride. I remember the morgue, all tile and stainless steel, the hum of refrigeration and smell of antiseptic. An orderly will pull the sheet back to reveal your face. Your face will look wrong somehow, but I'll know it's you.

"Yes, that's her," I'll say. "She's mine."

You'll be twenty-five then.

The MP checked my badge, made a notation on his clipboard, and opened the gate; I drove the off-road vehicle into the encampment, a small village of tents pitched by the Army in a farmer's sun-scorched pasture. At the center of the encampment was one of the alien devices, nicknamed "looking glasses."

According to the briefings I'd attended, there were nine of these in the United States, one hundred and twelve in the world. The looking glasses acted as two-way communication devices, presumably with the ships in orbit. No one knew why the aliens wouldn't talk to us in person; fear of cooties, maybe. A team of scientists, including a physicist and a linguist, was assigned to each looking glass; Gary Donnelly and I were on this one.

Gary was waiting for me in the parking area. We navigated a circular maze of concrete barricades until we reached the large tent that covered the looking glass itself. In front of the tent was an equipment cart loaded with goodies borrowed from the school's phonology lab; I had sent it ahead for inspection by the Army.

Also outside the tent were three tripod-mounted video cameras whose lenses peered, through windows in the fabric wall, into the main room. Everything Gary and I did would be reviewed by countless others, including military intelligence. In addition we would each send daily reports, of which mine had to include estimates on how much English I thought the aliens could understand.

Gary held open the tent flap and gestured for me to enter. "Step right up," he said, circus-barker-style. "Marvel at creatures the likes of which have never been seen on God's green earth."

"And all for one slim dime," I murmured, walking through the door. At the moment the looking glass was inactive, resembling a semicircular mirror over ten feet high and twenty feet across. On the brown grass in front of the looking glass, an arc of white spray paint outlined the activation area. Currently the area contained only a table, two folding chairs, and a power strip with a cord leading to a generator outside. The buzz of fluorescent lamps, hung from poles along the edge of the room, commingled with the buzz of flies in the sweltering heat.

Gary and I looked at each other, and then began pushing the cart of equipment up to the table. As we crossed the paint line, the looking glass appeared to grow transparent; it was as if someone was slowly raising the illumination behind tinted glass. The illusion of depth was uncanny; I felt I could walk right into it. Once the looking glass was fully lit it resembled a life-sized diorama of a semicircular room. The room contained a few large objects that might have been furniture, but no aliens. There was a door in the curved rear wall.

We busied ourselves connecting everything together: microphone, sound spectrograph, portable computer, and speaker. As we worked, I frequently glanced at the looking glass, anticipating the aliens' arrival. Even so I jumped when one of them entered.

It looked like a barrel suspended at the intersection of seven limbs. It was radially symmetric, and any of its limbs could serve as an arm or a leg. The one in front of me was walking around on four legs, three non-adjacent arms curled up at its sides. Gary called them "heptapods."

I'd been shown videotapes, but I still gawked. Its limbs had no distinct joints; anatomists guessed they might be supported by vertebral columns. Whatever their underlying structure, the heptapod's limbs conspired to move it in a disconcertingly fluid manner. Its "torso" rode atop the rippling limbs as smoothly as a hovercraft.

Seven lidless eyes ringed the top of the heptapod's body. It walked back to the doorway from which it entered, made a brief sputtering sound, and returned to the center of the room followed by another heptapod; at no point did it ever turn around. Eerie, but logical; with eyes on all sides, any direction might as well be "forward."

Gary had been watching my reaction. "Ready?" he asked.

I took a deep breath. "Ready enough." I'd done plenty of fieldwork before, in the Amazon, but it had always been a bilingual procedure: either my informants knew some Portuguese, which I could use, or I'd previously gotten an introduction to their language from the local missionaries. This would be my first attempt at conducting a true monolingual discovery procedure. It was straightforward enough in theory, though.

I walked up to the looking glass and a heptapod on the other side did the same. The image was so real that my skin crawled. I could see the texture of its gray skin, like corduroy ridges arranged in whorls and loops. There was no smell at all from the looking glass, which somehow made the situation stranger.

I pointed to myself and said slowly, "Human." Then I pointed to Gary. "Human." Then I pointed at each heptapod and said, "What are you?"

No reaction. I tried again, and then again.

One of the heptapods pointed to itself with one limb, the four terminal digits pressed together. That was lucky. In some cultures a person pointed with his chin; if the heptapod hadn't used one of its limbs, I wouldn't have known what gesture to look for. I heard a brief fluttering sound, and saw a puckered orifice at the top of its body vibrate; it was talking. Then it pointed to its companion and fluttered again.

I went back to my computer; on its screen were two virtually identical spectrographs representing the fluttering sounds. I marked a sample for playback. I pointed to myself and said "Human" again, and did the same with Gary. Then I pointed to the heptapod, and played back the flutter on the speaker.

The heptapod fluttered some more. The second half of the spectrograph for this utterance looked like a repetition: call the previous utterances [flutter1], then this one was [flutter2flutter1].

I pointed at something that might have been a heptapod chair. "What is that?"

The heptapod paused, and then pointed at the "chair" and talked some more. The spectrograph for this differed distinctly from that of the earlier sounds: [flutter3]. Once again, I pointed to the "chair" while playing back [flutter3].

The heptapod replied; judging by the spectrograph, it looked like [flutter3flutter2]. Optimistic interpretation: the heptapod was confirming my utterances as correct, which implied compatibility between heptapod and human patterns of discourse. Pessimistic interpretation: it had a nagging cough.

At my computer I delimited certain sections of the spectrograph and typed in a tentative gloss for each: "heptapod" for [flutter1], "yes" for [flutter2], and "chair" for [flutter3]. Then I typed "Language: Heptapod A" as a heading for all the utterances.

Gary watched what I was typing. "What's the 'A' for?"

"It just distinguishes this language from any other ones the heptapods might use," I said. He nodded.

"Now let's try something, just for laughs." I pointed at each heptapod and tried to mimic the sound of [flutter1], "heptapod." After a long pause, the first heptapod said something and then the second one said something else, neither of whose spectrographs resembled anything said before. I couldn't tell if they were speaking to each other or to me since they had no faces to turn. I tried pronouncing [flutter1] again, but there was no reaction.

"Not even close," I grumbled.

"I'm impressed you can make sounds like that at all," said Gary.

"You should hear my moose call. Sends them running."

I tried again a few more times, but neither heptapod responded with anything I could recognize. Only when I replayed the recording of the heptapod's pronunciation did I get a confirmation; the heptapod replied with [flutter2], "yes."

"So we're stuck with using recordings?" asked Gary.

I nodded. "At least temporarily."

"So now what?"

"Now we make sure it hasn't actually been saying 'aren't they cute' or 'look what they're doing now.' Then we see if we can identify any of these words when that other heptapod pronounces them." I gestured for him to have a seat. "Get comfortable; this'll take a while."

In 1770, Captain Cook's ship *Endeavour* ran aground on the coast of Queensland, Australia. While some of his men made repairs, Cook led an exploration party and met the aboriginal people. One of the sailors pointed to the animals that hopped around with their young riding in pouches, and asked an aborigine what they were called. The aborigine replied, "Kanguru." From then on Cook and his sailors referred to the animals by this word. It wasn't until later that they learned it meant "What did you say?"

I tell that story in my introductory course every year. It's almost certainly untrue, and I explain that afterwards, but it's a classic anecdote. Of course, the anecdotes my undergraduates will really want to hear are ones featuring the heptapods; for the rest of my teaching career, that'll be the reason many of them sign up for my courses. So I'll show them the old videotapes of my sessions at the looking glass, and the sessions that the other linguists conducted; the tapes are instructive, and they'll be useful if we're ever visited by aliens again, but they don't generate many good anecdotes.

When it comes to language-learning anecdotes, my favorite source is child language acquisition. I remember one afternoon when you are five years old, after you have come home from kindergarten. You'll be coloring with your crayons while I grade papers.

"Mom," you'll say, using the carefully casual tone reserved for requesting a favor, "can I ask you something?"

"Sure, sweetie. Go ahead."

"Can I be, um, honored?"

I'll look up from the paper I'm grading. "What do you mean?"

"At school Sharon said she got to be honored."

"Really? Did she tell you what for?"

"It was when her big sister got married. She said only one person could be, um, honored, and she was it."

"Ah, I see. You mean Sharon was maid of honor?"

"Yeah, that's it. Can I be made of honor?"

Gary and I entered the prefab building containing the center of operations for the looking glass site. Inside it looked like they were planning an invasion, or perhaps an evacuation: crewcut soldiers worked around a large map of the area, or sat in front of burly electronic gear while speaking into headsets. We were shown into Colonel Weber's office, a room in the back that was cool from air conditioning.

We briefed the colonel on our first day's results. "Doesn't sound like you got very far," he said.

"I have an idea as to how we can make faster progress," I said. "But you'll have to approve the use of more equipment."

"What more do you need?"

"A digital camera, and a big video screen." I showed him a drawing of the setup I imagined. "I want to try conducting the discovery procedure using writing; I'd display words on the screen, and use the camera to record the words they write. I'm hoping the heptapods will do the same."

Weber looked at the drawing dubiously. "What would be the advantage of that?"

"So far I've been proceeding the way I would with speakers of an unwritten language. Then it occurred to me that the heptapods must have writing, too."

"So?"

"If the heptapods have a mechanical way of producing writing, then their writing ought to be very regular, very consistent. That would make it easier for us to identify graphemes instead of phonemes. It's like picking out the letters in a printed sentence instead of trying to hear them when the sentence is spoken aloud."

"I take your point," he admitted. "And how would you respond to them? Show them the words they displayed to you?"

"Basically. And if they put spaces between words, any sentences we write would be a lot more intelligible than any spoken sentence we might splice together from recordings."

He leaned back in his chair. "You know we want to show as little of our technology as possible."

"I understand, but we're using machines as intermediaries already. If we can get them to use writing, I believe progress will go much faster than if we're restricted to the sound spectrographs."

The colonel turned to Gary. "Your opinion?"

"It sounds like a good idea to me. I'm curious whether the heptapods might have difficulty reading our monitors. Their looking glasses are based on a completely different technology than our video screens. As far as we can tell, they don't use pixels or scan lines, and they don't refresh on a frame-by-frame basis."

"You think the scan lines on our video screens might render them unreadable to the heptapods?"

"It's possible," said Gary. "We'll just have to try it and see."

Weber considered it. For me it wasn't even a question, but from his point of view it was a difficult one; like a soldier, though, he made it quickly. "Request granted. Talk to the sergeant outside about bringing in what you need. Have it ready for tomorrow."

I remember one day during the summer when you're sixteen. For once, the person waiting for her date to arrive is me. Of course, you'll be waiting around too, curious to see what he looks like. You'll have a friend of yours, a blond girl with the unlikely name of Roxie, hanging out with you, giggling.

"You may feel the urge to make comments about him," I'll say, checking myself in the hallway mirror. "Just restrain yourselves until we leave."

"Don't worry, Mom," you'll say. "We'll do it so that he won't know. Roxie, you ask me what I think the weather will be like tonight. Then I'll say what I think of Mom's date."

"Right," Roxie will say.

"No, you most definitely will not," I'll say.

"Relax, Mom. He'll never know; we do this all the time."

"What a comfort that is."

A little later on, Nelson will arrive to pick me up. I'll do the introductions, and we'll all engage in a little small talk on the front porch. Nelson is ruggedly handsome, to your evident approval. Just as we're about to leave, Roxie will say to you casually, "So what do you think the weather will be like tonight?"

"I think it's going to be really hot," you'll answer.

Roxie will nod in agreement. Nelson will say, "Really? I thought they said it was going to be cool."

"I have a sixth sense about these things," you'll say. Your face will give nothing away. "I get the feeling it's going to be a scorcher. Good thing you're dressed for it, Mom."

I'll glare at you, and say good night.

As I lead Nelson toward his car, he'll ask me, amused, "I'm missing something here, aren't I?"

"A private joke," I'll mutter. "Don't ask me to explain it."

At our next session at the looking glass, we repeated the procedure we had performed before, this time displaying a printed word on our computer screen at the same time we spoke: showing HUMAN while saying "Human," and so forth. Eventually, the heptapods understood what we wanted, and set up a flat circular screen mounted on a small pedestal. One heptapod spoke, and then inserted a limb into a large socket in the pedestal; a doodle of script, vaguely cursive, popped onto the screen.

We soon settled into a routine, and I compiled two parallel corpora: one of spoken utterances, one of writing samples. Based on first impressions, their writing appeared to be logographic, which was disappointing; I'd been hoping for an alphabetic script to help us learn their speech. Their logograms might include some phonetic information, but finding it would be a lot harder than with an alphabetic script.

By getting up close to the looking glass, I was able to point to various heptapod body parts, such as limbs, digits, and eyes, and elicit terms for each. It turned out that they had an orifice on the underside of their body, lined with articulated bony ridges: probably used for eating, while the one at the top was for respiration and speech. There were no other conspicuous orifices; perhaps their mouth was their anus too. Those sorts of questions would have to wait.

I also tried asking our two informants for terms for addressing each individually; personal names, if they had such things. Their answers were of course unpronounceable, so for Gary's and my purposes, I dubbed them Flapper and Raspberry. I hoped I'd be able to tell them apart.

The next day I conferred with Gary before we entered the looking-glass tent. "I'll need your help with this session," I told him.

"Sure. What do you want me to do?"

"We need to elicit some verbs, and it's easiest with third-person forms. Would you act out a few verbs while I type the written form on the computer? If we're lucky, the heptapods will figure out what we're doing and do the same. I've brought a bunch of props for you to use."

"No problem," said Gary, cracking his knuckles. "Ready when you are."

We began with some simple intransitive verbs: walking, jumping, speaking, writing. Gary demonstrated each one with a charming lack of self-consciousness; the presence of the video cameras didn't inhibit him at all. For the first few actions he performed, I asked the heptapods, "What do you call that?" Before long, the heptapods caught on to what we were trying to do; Raspberry began mimicking Gary, or at least performing the equivalent heptapod action, while Flapper worked their computer, displaying a written description and pronouncing it aloud.

In the spectrographs of their spoken utterances, I could recognize their word I had glossed as "heptapod." The rest of each utterance was presumably the verb phrase; it looked like they had analogs of nouns and verbs, thank goodness.

In their writing, however, things weren't as clear-cut. For each action, they had displayed a single logogram instead of two separate ones. At first I thought they had written something like "walks," with the subject implied. But why would Flapper say "the heptapod walks" while writing "walks," instead of maintaining parallelism? Then I noticed that some of the logograms looked like the logogram for "heptapod" with some extra strokes added to one side or another. Perhaps their verbs could be written as affixes to a noun. If so, why was Flapper writing the noun in some instances but not in others?

I decided to try a transitive verb; substituting object words might clarify things. Among the props I'd brought were an apple and a slice of bread. "Okay," I said to Gary, "show them the food, and then eat some. First the apple, then the bread."

Gary pointed at the Golden Delicious and then he took a bite out of it, while I displayed the "what do you call that?" expression. Then we repeated it with the slice of whole wheat.

Raspberry left the room and returned with some kind of giant nut or gourd and a gelatinous ellipsoid. Raspberry pointed at the gourd while Flapper said a word and displayed a logogram. Then Raspberry brought the gourd down between its legs, a crunching sound resulted, and the gourd reemerged minus a bite; there were corn-like kernels beneath the shell. Flapper talked and displayed a large logogram on their screen. The sound spectrograph for "gourd" changed when it was used in the sentence; possibly a case marker. The logogram was odd: after some study, I could identify graphic elements that resembled the individual logograms for "heptapod" and "gourd." They looked as if they had been melted together, with several extra strokes in the mix that presumably meant "eat." Was it a multiword ligature?

Next we got spoken and written names for the gelatin egg, and descriptions of the act of eating it. The sound spectrograph for "heptapod eats gelatin egg" was analyzable; "gelatin egg" bore a case marker, as expected, though the sentence's word order differed from last time. The written form, another large logogram, was another matter. This time it took much longer for me to recognize anything in it; not only were the individual logograms melted together again, it looked as if the one for "heptapod" was laid on its back, while on top of it the logogram for "gelatin egg" was standing on its head.

"Uh-oh." I took another look at the writing for the simple noun-verb examples, the ones that had seemed inconsistent before. Now I realized all of them actually did contain the logogram for "heptapod"; some were rotated and distorted by being combined with the various verbs, so I hadn't recognized them at first. "You guys have got to be kidding," I muttered.

"What's wrong?" asked Gary.

"Their script isn't word-divided; a sentence is written by joining the logograms for the constituent words. They join the logograms by rotating and modifying them. Take a look." I showed him how the logograms were rotated.

"So they can read a word with equal ease no matter how it's rotated," Gary said. He turned to look at the heptapods, impressed. "I wonder if it's a consequence of their bodies' radial symmetry: their bodies have no 'forward' direction, so maybe their writing doesn't either. Highly neat."

I couldn't believe it; I was working with someone who modified the word "neat" with "highly." "It certainly is interesting," I said, "but it also means there's no easy way for us write our own sentences in their language. We can't simply cut their sentences into individual words and recombine them; we'll have to learn the rules of their script before we can write anything legible. It's the same continuity problem we'd have had splicing together speech fragments, except applied to writing."

I looked at Flapper and Raspberry in the looking glass, who were waiting for us to continue, and sighed. "You aren't going to make this easy for us, are you?"

To be fair, the heptapods were completely cooperative. In the days that followed, they readily taught us their language without requiring us to teach them any more English. Colonel Weber and his cohorts pondered the implications of that, while I and the linguists at the other looking glasses met via video conferencing to share what we had learned about the heptapod language. The videoconferencing made for an incongruous working environment: our video screens were primitive compared to the heptapods' looking glasses, so that my colleagues seemed more remote than the aliens. The familiar was far away, while the bizarre was close at hand.

It would be a while before we'd be ready to ask the heptapods why they had come, or to discuss physics well enough to ask them about their technology. For the time being, we worked on the basics: phonemics/graphemics, vocabulary, syntax. The heptapods at every looking glass were using the same language, so we were able to pool our data and coordinate our efforts.

Our biggest source of confusion was the heptapods' "writing." It didn't appear to be writing at all; it looked more like a bunch of intricate graphic designs. The logograms weren't arranged in rows, or a spiral, or any linear fashion. Instead, Flapper or Raspberry would write a sentence by sticking together as many logograms as needed into a giant conglomeration.

This form of writing was reminiscent of primitive sign systems, which required a reader to know a message's context in order to understand it. Such systems were considered too limited for systematic recording of information. Yet it was unlikely that the heptapods developed their level of technology with only an oral tradition. That implied one of three possibilities: the first was that the heptapods had a true writing system, but they didn't want to use it in front of us; Colonel Weber would identify with that one. The second was that the heptapods hadn't originated the technology they were using; they were illiterates using someone else's technology. The third, and most interesting to me, was that the heptapods were using a nonlinear system of orthography that qualified as true writing.

I remember a conversation we'll have when you're in your junior year of high school. It'll be Sunday morning, and I'll be scrambling some eggs while you set the table for brunch. You'll laugh as you tell me about the party you went to last night.

"Oh man," you'll say, "they're not kidding when they say that body weight makes a difference. I didn't drink any more than the guys did, but I got so much *drunk*er."

I'll try to maintain a neutral, pleasant expression. I'll really try. Then you'll say, "Oh, come on, Mom."

"What?"

"You know you did the exact same things when you were my age."

I did nothing of the sort, but I know that if I were to admit that, you'd lose respect for me completely. "You know never to drive, or get into a car if—"

"God, of course I know that. Do you think I'm an idiot?"

"No, of course not."

What I'll think is that you are clearly, maddeningly not me. It will remind me, again, that you won't be a clone of me; you can be wonderful, a daily delight, but you won't be someone I could have created by myself.

The military had set up a trailer containing our offices at the looking glass site. I saw Gary walking toward the trailer, and ran to catch up with him. "It's a semasiographic writing system," I said when I reached him.

"Excuse me?" said Gary.

"Here, let me show you." I directed Gary into my office. Once we were inside, I went to the chalkboard and drew a circle with a diagonal line bisecting it. "What does this mean?"

" 'Not allowed'?"

"Right." Next I printed the words NOT ALLOWED on the chalkboard. "And so does this. But only one is a representation of speech."

Gary nodded. "Okay."

"Linguists describe writing like this—" I indicated the printed words "—as 'glottographic,' because it represents speech. Every human written language is in this category. However, this symbol—" I indicated the circle and diagonal line "—is 'semasiographic' writing, because it conveys meaning without reference to speech. There's no correspondence between its components and any particular sounds."

"And you think all of heptapod writing is like this?"

"From what I've seen so far, yes. It's not picture writing, it's far more complex. It has its own system of rules for constructing sentences, like a visual syntax that's unrelated to the syntax for their spoken language."

"A visual syntax? Can you show me an example?"

"Coming right up." I sat down at my desk and, using the computer, pulled up a frame from the recording of yesterday's conversation with Raspberry. I turned the monitor so he could see it. "In their spoken language, a noun has a case marker indicating whether it's a subject or object. In their written language, however, a noun is identified as subject or object based on the orientation of its logogram relative to that of the verb. Here, take a look." I pointed at one of the figures. "For instance, when 'heptapod' is integrated with 'hears' this way, with these strokes parallel, it means that the heptapod is doing the hearing." I showed him a different one. "When they're combined this way, with the strokes perpendicular, it means that the heptapod is being heard. This morphology applies to several verbs.

"Another example is the inflection system." I called up another frame from the recording. "In their written language, this logogram means roughly 'hear easily' or 'hear clearly.' See the elements it has in common with the logogram for 'hear'? You can still combine it with 'heptapod' in the same ways as before, to indicate that the heptapod can hear something clearly or that the heptapod is clearly heard. But what's really interesting is that the modulation of 'hear' into 'hear clearly' isn't a special case; you see the transformation they applied?"

Gary nodded, pointing. "It's like they express the idea of 'clearly' by changing the curve of those strokes in the middle."

"Right. That modulation is applicable to lots of verbs. The logogram for 'see' can be modulated in the same way to form 'see clearly,' and so can the logogram for 'read' and others. And changing the curve of those strokes has no parallel in their speech; with the spoken version of these verbs, they add a prefix to the verb to express ease of manner, and the prefixes for 'see' and 'hear' are different.

"There are other examples, but you get the idea. It's essentially a grammar in two dimensions."

He began pacing thoughtfully. "Is there anything like this in human writing systems?"

"Mathematical equations, notations for music and dance. But those are all very specialized; we couldn't record this conversation using them. But I suspect, if we knew it well enough, we could record this conversation in the heptapod writing system. I think it's a full-fledged, general-purpose graphical language."

Gary frowned. "So their writing constitutes a completely separate language from their speech, right?"

"Right. In fact, it'd be more accurate to refer to the writing system as 'Heptapod B,' and use 'Heptapod A' strictly for referring to the spoken language."

"Hold on a second. Why use two languages when one would suffice? That seems unnecessarily hard to learn."

"Like English spelling?" I said. "Ease of learning isn't the primary force in language evolution. For the heptapods, writing and speech may play such different cultural or cognitive roles that using separate languages makes more sense than using different forms of the same one."

He considered it. "I see what you mean. Maybe they think our form of writing is redundant, like we're wasting a second communications channel."

"That's entirely possible. Finding out why they use a second language for writing will tell us a lot about them."

"So I take it this means we won't be able to use their writing to help us learn their spoken language."

I sighed. "Yeah, that's the most immediate implication. But I don't think we should ignore either Heptapod A or B; we need a two-pronged approach." I pointed at the screen. "I'll bet you that learning their two-dimensional grammar will help you when it comes time to learn their mathematical notation."

"You've got a point there. So are we ready to start asking about their mathematics?"

"Not yet. We need a better grasp on this writing system before we begin anything else," I said, and then smiled when he mimed frustration. "Patience, good sir. Patience is a virtue."

You'll be six when your father has a conference to attend in Hawaii, and we'll accompany him. You'll be so excited that you'll make preparations for weeks beforehand. You'll ask me about coconuts and volcanoes and surfing, and practice hula dancing in the mirror. You'll pack a suitcase with the clothes and toys you want to bring, and you'll drag it around the house to see how long you can carry it. You'll ask me if I can carry your Etch-a-Sketch in my bag, since there won't be any more room for it in yours and you simply can't leave without it.

"You won't need all of these," I'll say. "There'll be so many fun things to do there, you won't have time to play with so many toys."

You'll consider that; dimples will appear above your eyebrows when you think hard. Eventually you'll agree to pack fewer toys, but your expectations will, if anything, increase.

"I wanna be in Hawaii now," you'll whine.

"Sometimes it's good to wait," I'll say. "The anticipation makes it more fun when you get there."

You'll just pout.

In the next report I submitted, I suggested that the term "logogram" was a misnomer because it implied that each graph represented a spoken word, when in fact the graphs didn't correspond to our notion of spoken words at all. I didn't want to use the term "ideogram" either because of how it had been used in the past; I suggested the term "semagram" instead.

It appeared that a semagram corresponded roughly to a written word in human languages: it was meaningful on its own, and in combination with other semagrams could form endless statements. We couldn't define it precisely, but then no one had ever satisfactorily defined "word" for human languages either. When it came to sentences in Heptapod B, though, things became much more confusing. The language had no written punctuation: its syntax was indicated in the way the semagrams were combined, and there was no need to indicate the cadence of speech. There was certainly no way to slice out subject-predicate pairings neatly to make sentences. A "sentence" seemed to be whatever number of semagrams a heptapod wanted to join together; the only difference between a sentence and a paragraph, or a page, was size.

When a Heptapod B sentence grew fairly sizable, its visual impact was remarkable. If I wasn't trying to decipher it, the writing looked like fanciful praying mantids drawn in a cursive style, all clinging to each other to form an Escheresque lattice, each slightly different in its stance. And the biggest sentences had an effect similar to that of psychedelic posters: sometimes eye-watering, sometimes hypnotic.

I remember a picture of you taken at your college graduation. In the photo you're striking a pose for the camera, mortarboard stylishly tilted on your head, one hand touching your sunglasses, the other hand on your hip, holding open your gown to reveal the tank top and shorts you're wearing underneath.

I remember your graduation. There will be the distraction of having Nelson and your father and what's-her-name there all at the same time, but that will be minor. That entire weekend, while you're introducing me to your classmates and hugging everyone incessantly, I'll be all but mute with amazement. I can't believe that you, a grown woman taller than me and beautiful enough to make my heart ache, will be the same girl I used to lift off the ground so you could reach the drinking fountain, the same girl who used to trundle out of my bedroom draped in a dress and hat and four scarves from my closet.

And after graduation, you'll be heading for a job as a financial analyst. I won't understand what you do there, I won't even understand your fascination with money, the preeminence you gave to salary when negotiating job offers. I would prefer it if you'd pursue something without regard for its monetary rewards, but I'll have no complaints. My own mother could never understand why I couldn't just be a high school English teacher. You'll do what makes you happy, and that'll be all I ask for.

As time went on, the teams at each looking glass began working in earnest on learning heptapod terminology for elementary mathematics and physics. We worked together on presentations, with the linguists focusing on procedure and the physicists focusing on subject matter. The physicists showed us previously devised systems for communicating with aliens, based on mathematics, but those were intended for use over a radio telescope. We reworked them for face-to-face communication.

Our teams were successful with basic arithmetic, but we hit a road block with geometry and algebra. We tried using a spherical coordinate system instead of a rectangular one, thinking it might be more natural to the heptapods given their anatomy, but that approach wasn't any more fruitful. The heptapods didn't seem to understand what we were getting at.

Likewise, the physics discussions went poorly. Only with the most concrete terms, like the names of the elements, did we have any success; after several attempts at representing the periodic table, the heptapods got the idea. For anything remotely abstract, we might as well have been gibbering. We tried to demonstrate basic physical attributes like mass and acceleration so we could elicit their terms for them, but the heptapods simply responded with requests for clarification. To avoid perceptual problems that might be associated with any particular medium, we tried physical demonstrations as well as line drawings, photos, and animations; none were effective. Days with no progress became weeks, and the physicists were becoming disillusioned.

By contrast, the linguists were having much more success. We made steady progress decoding the grammar of the spoken language, Heptapod A. It didn't follow the pattern of human languages, as expected, but it was comprehensible so far: free word order, even to the extent that there was no preferred order for the clauses in a conditional statement, in defiance of a human language "universal." It also appeared that the heptapods had no objection to many levels of center-embedding of clauses, something that quickly defeated humans. Peculiar, but not impenetrable.

Much more interesting were the newly discovered morphological and grammatical processes in Heptapod B that were uniquely two-dimensional. Depending on a semagram's declension, inflections could be indicated by varying a certain stroke's curvature, or its thickness, or its manner of undulation; or by varying the relative sizes of two radicals, or their relative distance to another radical, or their orientations; or various other means. These were non-segmental graphemes; they couldn't be isolated from the rest of a semagram. And despite how such traits behaved in human writing, these had nothing to do with calligraphic style; their meanings were defined according to a consistent and unambiguous grammar.

We regularly asked the heptapods why they had come. Each time, they answered "to see," or "to observe." Indeed, sometimes they preferred to watch us silently rather than answer our questions. Perhaps they were scientists, perhaps they were tourists. The State Department instructed us to reveal as little as possible about humanity, in case that information could be used as a bargaining chip in subsequent negotiations. We obliged, though it didn't require much effort: the heptapods never asked questions about anything. Whether scientists or tourists, they were an awfully incurious bunch.

I remember once when we'll be driving to the mall to buy some new clothes for you. You'll be thirteen. One moment you'll be sprawled in your seat, completely un-self-conscious, all child; the next, you'll toss your hair with a practiced casualness, like a fashion model in training.

You'll give me some instructions as I'm parking the car. "Okay, Mom, give me one of the credit cards, and we can meet back at the entrance here in two hours."

I'll laugh. "Not a chance. All the credit cards stay with me."

"You're kidding." You'll become the embodiment of exasperation. We'll get out of the car and I will start walking to the mall entrance. After seeing that I won't budge on the matter, you'll quickly reformulate your plans.

"Okay Mom, okay. You can come with me, just walk a little ways behind me, so it doesn't look like we're together. If I see any friends of mine, I'm gonna stop and talk to them, but you just keep walking, okay? I'll come find you later."

I'll stop in my tracks. "Excuse me? I am not the hired help, nor am I some mutant relative for you to be ashamed of."

"But Mom, I can't let anyone see you with me."

"What are you talking about? I've already met your friends; they've been to the house."

"That was different," you'll say, incredulous that you have to explain it. "This is shopping."

"Too bad."

Then the explosion: "You won't do the least thing to make me happy! You don't care about me at all!"

It won't have been that long since you enjoyed going shopping with me; it will forever astonish me how quickly you grow out of one phase and enter another. Living with you will be like aiming for a moving target; you'll always be further along than I expect.

I looked at the sentence in Heptapod B that I had just written, using simple pen and paper. Like all the sentences I generated myself, this one looked misshapen, like a heptapod-written sentence that had been smashed with a hammer and then inexpertly taped back together. I had sheets of such inelegant semagrams covering my desk, fluttering occasionally when the oscillating fan swung past.

It was strange trying to learn a language that had no spoken form. Instead of practicing my pronunciation, I had taken to squeezing my eyes shut and trying to paint semagrams on the insides of my eyelids.

There was a knock at the door and before I could answer Gary came in looking jubilant. "Illinois got a repetition in physics."

"Really? That's great; when did it happen?"

"It happened a few hours ago; we just had the videoconference. Let me show you what it is." He started erasing my blackboard.

"Don't worry, I didn't need any of that."

"Good." He picked up a nub of chalk and drew a diagram:

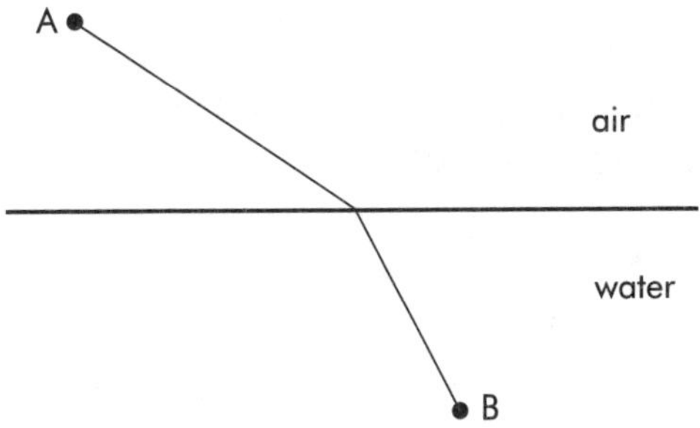

"Okay, here's the path a ray of light takes when crossing from air to water. The light ray travels in a straight line until it hits the water; the water has a different index of refraction, so the light changes direction. You've heard of this before, right?"

I nodded. "Sure."

"Now here's an interesting property about the path the light takes. The path is the fastest possible route between these two points."

"Come again?"

"Imagine, just for grins, that the ray of light traveled along this path." He added a dotted line to his diagram:

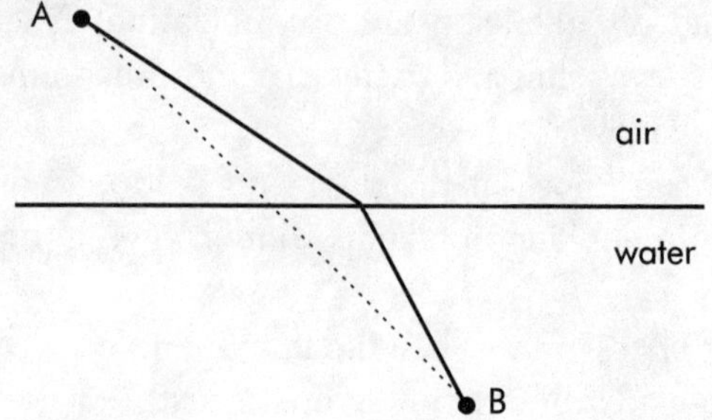

"This hypothetical path is shorter than the path the light actually takes. But light travels more slowly in water than it does in air, and a greater percentage of this path is underwater. So it would take longer for light to travel along this path than it does along the real path."

"Okay, I get it."

"Now imagine if light were to travel along this other path." He drew a second dotted path:

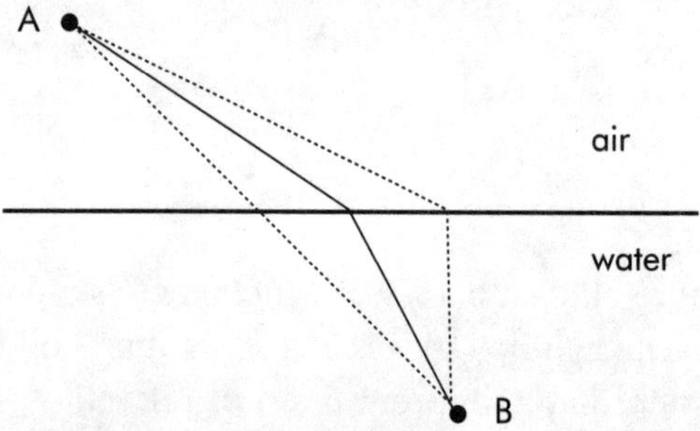

"This path reduces the percentage that's underwater, but the total length is larger. It would also take longer for light to travel along this path than along the actual one."

Gary put down the chalk and gestured at the diagram on the chalkboard with white-tipped fingers. "Any hypothetical path would require more time to traverse than the one actually taken. In other words, the route that the light ray takes is always the fastest possible one. That's Fermat's Principle of Least Time."

"Hmm, interesting. And this is what the heptapods responded to?"

"Exactly. Moorehead gave an animated presentation of Fermat's Principle at the Illinois looking glass, and the heptapods repeated it back. Now he's trying to get a symbolic description." He grinned. "Now is that highly neat, or what?"

"It's neat all right, but how come I haven't heard of Fermat's Principle before?" I picked up a binder and waved it at him; it was a primer on the physics topics suggested for use in communication with the heptapods. "This thing goes on forever about Planck masses and the spin-flip of atomic hydrogen, and not a word about the refraction of light."

"We guessed wrong about what'd be most useful for you to know," Gary said without embarrassment. "In fact, it's curious that Fermat's Principle was the first breakthrough; even though it's easy to explain, you need calculus to describe it mathematically. And not ordinary calculus; you need the calculus of variations. We thought that some simple theorem of geometry or algebra would be the breakthrough."

"Curious indeed. You think the heptapods' idea of what's simple doesn't match ours?"

"Exactly, which is why I'm *dying* to see what their mathematical description of Fermat's Principle looks like." He paced as he talked. "If their version of the calculus of variations is simpler to them than their equivalent of algebra, that might explain why we've had so much trouble talking about physics; their entire system of mathematics may be topsy-turvy compared to ours." He pointed to the physics primer. "You can be sure that we're going to revise that."

"So can you build from Fermat's Principle to other areas of physics?"

"Probably. There are lots of physical principles just like Fermat's."

"What, like Louise's principle of least closet space? When did physics become so minimalist?"

"Well, the word 'least' is misleading. You see, Fermat's Principle of Least Time is incomplete; in certain situations light follows a path that takes *more* time than any of the other possibilities. It's more accurate to say that light always follows an *extreme* path, either one that minimizes the time taken or one that maximizes it. A minimum and a maximum share certain mathematical properties, so both situations can be described with one equation. So to be precise, Fermat's Principle isn't a minimal principle; instead it's what's known as a 'variational' principle."

"And there are more of these variational principles?"

He nodded. "In all branches of physics. Almost every physical law can be restated as a variational principle. The only difference between these principles is in which attribute is minimized or maximized." He gestured as if the different branches of physics were arrayed before him on a table. "In optics, where Fermat's Principle applies, time is the attribute that has to be an extreme. In mechanics, it's a different attribute. In electromagnetism, it's something else again. But all these principles are similar mathematically."

"So once you get their mathematical description of Fermat's Principle, you should be able to decode the other ones."

"God, I hope so. I think this is the wedge that we've been looking for, the one that cracks open their formulation of physics. This calls for a celebration." He stopped his pacing and turned to me. "Hey Louise, want to go out for dinner? My treat."

I was mildly surprised. "Sure," I said.

It'll be when you first learn to walk that I get daily demonstrations of the asymmetry in our relationship. You'll be incessantly running off somewhere, and each time you walk into a door frame or scrape your knee, the pain feels like it's my own. It'll be like growing an errant limb, an extension of myself whose sensory nerves report pain just fine, but whose motor nerves don't convey my commands at all. It's so unfair: I'm going to give birth to an animated voodoo doll of myself. I didn't see this in the contract when I signed up. Was this part of the deal?

And then there will be the times when I see you laughing. Like the time you'll be playing with the neighbor's puppy, poking your hands through the chain-link fence separating our back yards, and you'll be laughing so hard you'll start hiccuping. The puppy will run inside the neighbor's house, and your laughter will gradually subside, letting you catch your breath. Then the puppy will come back to the fence to lick your fingers again, and you'll shriek and start laughing again. It will be the most wonderful sound I could ever imagine, a sound that makes me feel like a fountain, or a wellspring.

Now if only I can remember that sound the next time your blithe disregard for self preservation gives me a heart attack.

After the breakthrough with Fermat's Principle, discussions of scientific concepts became more fruitful. It wasn't as if all of heptapod physics was suddenly rendered transparent, but progress was steady. According to Gary, the heptapods' formulation of physics was indeed topsy-turvy relative to ours. Physical attributes that humans defined using integral calculus were seen as fundamental by the heptapods. As an example, Gary described an attribute that, in physics jargon, bore the deceptively simple name "action," which represented "the difference between kinetic and potential energy, integrated over time," whatever that meant. Calculus for us; elementary to them.

Conversely, to define attributes that humans thought of as fundamental, like velocity, the heptapods employed mathematics that were, Gary assured me, "highly weird." The physicists were ultimately able to prove the equivalence of heptapod mathematics and human mathematics; even though their approaches were almost the reverse of one another, both were systems of describing the same physical universe.

I tried following some of the equations that the physicists were coming up with, but it was no use. I couldn't really grasp the significance of physical attributes like "action"; I couldn't, with any confidence, ponder the significance of treating such an attribute as fundamental. Still, I tried to ponder questions formulated in terms more familiar to me: what kind of world-view did the heptapods have, that they would consider Fermat's Principle the simplest explanation of light refraction? What kind of perception made a minimum or maximum readily apparent to them?

Your eyes will be blue like your dad's, not mud brown like mine. Boys will stare into those eyes the way I did, and do, into your dad's, surprised and enchanted, as I was and am, to find them in combination with black hair. You will have many suitors.

I remember when you are fifteen, coming home after a weekend at your dad's, incredulous over the interrogation he'll have put you through regarding the boy you're currently dating. You'll sprawl on the sofa, recounting your dad's latest breach of common sense: "You know what he said? He said, 'I know what teenage boys are like.' " Roll of the eyes. "Like I don't?"

"Don't hold it against him," I'll say. "He's a father; he can't help it." Having seen you interact with your friends, I won't worry much about a boy taking advantage of you; if anything, the opposite will be more likely. I'll worry about that.

"He wishes I were still a kid. He hasn't known how to act toward me since I grew breasts."

"Well, that development was a shock for him. Give him time to recover."

"It's been *years*, Mom. How long is it gonna take?"

"I'll let you know when my father has come to terms with mine."

During one of the videoconferences for the linguists, Cisneros from the Massachusetts looking glass had raised an interesting question: was there a particular order in which semagrams were written in a Heptapod B sentence? It was clear that word order meant next to nothing when speaking in Heptapod A; when asked to repeat what it had just said, a heptapod would likely as not use a different word order unless we specifically asked them not to. Was word order similarly unimportant when writing in Heptapod B?

Previously, we had only focused our attention on how a sentence in Heptapod B looked once it was complete. As far as anyone could tell, there was no preferred order when reading the semagrams in a sentence; you could start almost anywhere in the nest, then follow the branching clauses until you'd read the whole thing. But that was reading; was the same true about writing?

During my most recent session with Flapper and Raspberry I had asked them if, instead of displaying a semagram only after it was completed, they could show it to us while it was being written. They had agreed. I inserted the videotape of the session into the VCR, and on my computer I consulted the session transcript.

I picked one of the longer utterances from the conversation. What Flapper had said was that the heptapods' planet had two moons, one significantly larger than the other; the three primary constituents of the planet's atmosphere were nitrogen, argon, and oxygen; and fifteen twenty-eighths of the planet's surface was covered by water. The first words of the spoken utterance translated literally as "inequality-of-size rocky-orbiter rocky-orbiters related-as-primary-to-secondary."

Then I rewound the videotape until the time signature matched the one in the transcription. I started playing the tape, and watched the web of semagrams being spun out of inky spider's silk. I rewound it and played it several times. Finally I froze the video right after the first stroke was completed and before the second one was begun; all that was visible onscreen was a single sinuous line.

Comparing that initial stroke with the completed sentence, I realized that the stroke participated in several different clauses of the message. It began in the semagram for 'oxygen,' as the determinant that distinguished it from certain other elements; then it slid down to become the morpheme of comparison in the description of the two moons' sizes; and lastly it flared out as the arched backbone of the semagram for 'ocean.' Yet this stroke was a single continuous line, and it was the first one that Flapper wrote. That meant the heptapod had to know how the entire sentence would be laid out before it could write the very first stroke.

The other strokes in the sentence also traversed several clauses, making them so interconnected that none could be removed without redesigning the entire sentence. The heptapods didn't write a sentence one semagram at a time; they built it out of strokes irrespective of individual semagrams. I had seen a similarly high degree of integration before in calligraphic designs, particularly those employing the Arabic alphabet. But those designs had required careful planning by expert calligraphers. No one could lay out such an intricate design at the speed needed for holding a conversation. At least, no human could.

There's a joke that I once heard a comedienne tell. It goes like this: "I'm not sure if I'm ready to have children. I asked a friend of mine who has children, 'Suppose I do have kids. What if when they grow up, they blame me for everything that's wrong with their lives?' She laughed and said, 'What do you mean, if?' "

That's my favorite joke.

Gary and I were at a little Chinese restaurant, one of the local places we had taken to patronizing to get away from the encampment. We sat eating the appetizers: potstickers, redolent of pork and sesame oil. My favorite.

I dipped one in soy sauce and vinegar. "So how are you doing with your Heptapod B practice?" I asked.

Gary looked obliquely at the ceiling. I tried to meet his gaze, but he kept shifting it.

"You've given up, haven't you?" I said. "You're not even trying any more."

He did a wonderful hangdog expression. "I'm just no good at languages," he confessed. "I thought learning Heptapod B might be more like learning mathematics than trying to speak another language, but it's not. It's too foreign for me."

"It would help you discuss physics with them."

"Probably, but since we had our breakthrough, I can get by with just a few phrases."

I sighed. "I suppose that's fair; I have to admit, I've given up on trying to learn the mathematics."

"So we're even?"

"We're even." I sipped my tea. "Though I did want to ask you about Fermat's Principle. Something about it feels odd to me, but I can't put my finger on it. It just doesn't sound like a law of physics."

A twinkle appeared in Gary's eyes. "I'll bet I know what you're talking about." He snipped a potsticker in half with his chopsticks. "You're used to thinking of refraction in terms of cause and effect: reaching the water's surface is the cause, and the change in direction is the effect. But Fermat's Principle sounds weird because it describes light's behavior in goal-oriented terms. It sounds like a commandment to a light beam: 'Thou shalt minimize or maximize the time taken to reach thy destination.' "

I considered it. "Go on."

"It's an old question in the philosophy of physics. People have been talking about it since Fermat first formulated it in the 1600s; Planck wrote volumes about it. The thing is, while the common formulation of physical laws is causal, a variational principle like Fermat's is purposive, almost teleological."

"Hmm, that's an interesting way to put it. Let me think about that for a minute." I pulled out a felt-tip pen and, on my paper napkin, drew a copy of the diagram that Gary had drawn on my blackboard. "Okay," I said, thinking aloud, "so let's say the goal of a ray of light is to take the fastest path. How does the light go about doing that?"

"Well, if I can speak anthropomorphic-projectionally, the light has to examine the possible paths and compute how long each one would take." He plucked the last potsticker from the serving dish.

"And to do that," I continued, "the ray of light has to know just where its destination is. If the destination were somewhere else, the fastest path would be different."

Gary nodded again. "That's right; the notion of a 'fastest path' is meaningless unless there's a destination specified. And computing how long a given path takes also requires information about what lies along that path, like where the water's surface is."

I kept staring at the diagram on the napkin. "And the light ray has to know all that ahead of time, before it starts moving, right?"

"So to speak," said Gary. "The light can't start traveling in any old direction and make course corrections later on, because the path resulting from such behavior wouldn't be the fastest possible one. The light has to do all its computations at the very beginning."

I thought to myself, *the ray of light has to know where it will ultimately end up before it can choose the direction to begin moving in.* I knew what that reminded me of. I looked up at Gary. "That's what was bugging me."

I remember when you're fourteen. You'll come out of your bedroom, a graffiti-covered notebook computer in hand, working on a report for school.

"Mom, what do you call it when both sides can win?"

I'll look up from my computer and the paper I'll be writing. "What, you mean a win-win situation?"

"There's some technical name for it, some math word. Remember that time Dad was here, and he was talking about the stock market? He used it then."

"Hmm, that sounds familiar, but I can't remember what he called it."

"I need to know. I want to use that phrase in my social studies report. I can't even search for information on it unless I know what it's called."

"I'm sorry, I don't know it either. Why don't you call your dad?"

Judging from your expression, that will be more effort than you want to make. At this point, you and your father won't be getting along well. "Can you call Dad and ask him? But don't tell him it's for me."

"I think you can call him yourself."

You'll fume, "Jesus, Mom, I can never get help with my homework since you and Dad split up."

It's amazing the diverse situations in which you can bring up the divorce. "I've helped you with your homework."

"Like a million years ago, Mom."

I'll let that pass. "I'd help you with this if I could, but I don't remember what it's called."

You'll head back to your bedroom in a huff.

I practiced Heptapod B at every opportunity, both with the other linguists and by myself. The novelty of reading a semasiographic language made it compelling in a way that Heptapod A wasn't, and my improvement in writing it excited me. Over time, the sentences I wrote grew shapelier, more cohesive. I had reached the point where it worked better when I didn't think about it too much. Instead of carefully trying to design a sentence before writing, I could simply begin putting down strokes immediately; my initial strokes almost always turned out to be compatible with an elegant rendition of what I was trying to say. I was developing a faculty like that of the heptapods.

More interesting was the fact that Heptapod B was changing the way I thought. For me, thinking typically meant speaking in an internal voice; as we say in the trade, my thoughts were phonologically coded. My internal voice normally spoke in English, but that wasn't a requirement. The summer after my senior year in high school, I attended a total immersion program for learning Russian; by the end of the summer, I was thinking and even dreaming in Russian. But it was always *spoken* Russian. Different language, same mode: a voice speaking silently aloud.

The idea of thinking in a linguistic yet non-phonological mode always intrigued me. I had a friend born of Deaf parents; he grew up using American Sign Language, and he told me that he often thought in ASL instead of English. I used to wonder what it was like to have one's thoughts be manually coded, to reason using an inner pair of hands instead of an inner voice.

With Heptapod B, I was experiencing something just as foreign: my thoughts were becoming graphically coded. There were trance-like moments during the day when my thoughts weren't expressed with my internal voice; instead, I saw semagrams with my mind's eye, sprouting like frost on a windowpane.

As I grew more fluent, semagraphic designs would appear fully-formed, articulating even complex ideas all at once. My thought processes weren't moving any faster as a result, though. Instead of racing forward, my mind hung balanced on the symmetry underlying the semagrams. The semagrams seemed to be something more than language; they were almost like mandalas. I found myself in a meditative state, contemplating the way in which premises and conclusions were interchangeable. There was no direction inherent in the way propositions were connected, no "train of thought" moving along a particular route; all the components in an act of reasoning were equally powerful, all having identical precedence.

A representative from the State Department named Hossner had the job of briefing the U.S. scientists on our agenda with the heptapods. We sat in the videoconference room, listening to him lecture. Our microphone was turned off, so Gary and I could exchange comments without interrupting Hossner. As we listened, I worried that Gary might harm his vision, rolling his eyes so often.

"They must have had some reason for coming all this way," said the diplomat, his voice tinny through the speakers. "It does not look like their reason was conquest, thank God. But if that's not the reason, what is? Are they prospectors? Anthropologists? Missionaries? Whatever their motives, there must be something we can offer them. Maybe it's mineral rights to our solar system. Maybe it's information about ourselves. Maybe it's the right to deliver sermons to our populations. But we can be sure that there's something.

"My point is this: their motive might not be to trade, but that doesn't mean that we cannot conduct trade. We simply need to know why they're here, and what we have that they want. Once we have that information, we can begin trade negotiations.

"I should emphasize that our relationship with the heptapods need not be adversarial. This is not a situation where every gain on their part is a loss on ours, or vice versa. If we handle ourselves correctly, both we and the heptapods can come out winners."

"You mean it's a non-zero-sum game?" Gary said in mock incredulity. "Oh my gosh."

"A non-zero-sum game."

"What?" You'll reverse course, heading back from your bedroom.

"When both sides can win: I just remembered, it's called a non-zero-sum game."

"That's it!" you'll say, writing it down on your notebook. "Thanks, Mom!"

"I guess I knew it after all," I'll say. "All those years with your father, some of it must have rubbed off."

"I knew you'd know it," you'll say. You'll give me a sudden, brief hug, and your hair will smell of apples. "You're the best."

"Louise?"

"Hmm? Sorry, I was distracted. What did you say?"

"I said, what do you think about our Mr. Hossner here?"

"I prefer not to."

"I've tried that myself: ignoring the government, seeing if it would go away. It hasn't."

As evidence of Gary's assertion, Hossner kept blathering: "Your immediate task is to think back on what you've learned. Look for anything that might help us. Has there been any indication of what the heptapods want? Of what they value?"

"Gee, it never occurred to us to look for things like that," I said. "We'll get right on it, sir."

"The sad thing is, that's just what we'll have to do," said Gary.

"Are there any questions?" asked Hossner.

Burghart, the linguist at the Fort Worth looking glass, spoke up. "We've been through this with the heptapods many times. They maintain that they're here to observe, and they maintain that information is not tradable."

"So they would have us believe," said Hossner. "But consider: how could that be true? I know that the heptapods have occasionally stopped talking to us for brief periods. That may be a tactical maneuver on their part. If we were to stop talking to them tomorrow—"

"Wake me up if he says something interesting," said Gary.

"I was just going to ask you to do the same for me."

That day when Gary first explained Fermat's Principle to me, he had mentioned that almost every physical law could be stated as a variational principle. Yet when humans thought about physical laws, they preferred to work with them in their causal formulation. I could understand that: the physical attributes that humans found intuitive, like kinetic energy or acceleration, were all properties of an object at a given moment in time. And these were conducive to a chronological, causal interpretation of events: one moment growing out of another, causes and effects created a chain reaction that grew from past to future.

In contrast, the physical attributes that the heptapods found intuitive, like "action" or those other things defined by integrals, were meaningful only over a period of time. And these were conducive to a teleological interpretation of events: by viewing events over a period of time, one recognized that there was a requirement that had to be satisfied, a goal of minimizing or maximizing. And one had to know the initial and final states to meet that goal; one needed knowledge of the effects before the causes could be initiated.

I was growing to understand that, too.

"Why?" you'll ask again. You'll be three.

"Because it's your bedtime," I'll say again. We'll have gotten as far as getting you bathed and into your jammies, but no further than that.

"But I'm not sleepy," you'll whine. You'll be standing at the bookshelf, pulling down a video to watch: your latest diversionary tactic to keep away from your bedroom.

"It doesn't matter: you still have to go to bed."

"But why?"

"Because I'm the mom and I said so."

I'm actually going to say that, aren't I? God, somebody please shoot me.

I'll pick you up and carry you under my arm to your bed, you wailing piteously all the while, but my sole concern will be my own distress. All those vows made in childhood that I would give reasonable answers when I became a parent, that I would treat my own child as an intelligent, thinking individual, all for naught: I'm going to turn into my mother. I can fight it as much as I want, but there'll be no stopping my slide down that long, dreadful slope.

Was it actually possible to know the future? Not simply to guess at it; was it possible to *know* what was going to happen, with absolute certainty and in specific detail? Gary once told me that the fundamental laws of physics were time-symmetric, that there was no physical difference between past and future. Given that, some might say, "yes, theoretically." But speaking more concretely, most would answer "no," because of free will.

I liked to imagine the objection as a Borgesian fabulation: consider a person standing before the *Book of Ages*, the chronicle that records every event, past and future. Even though the text has been photoreduced from the full-sized edition, the volume is enormous. With magnifier in hand, she flips through the tissue-thin leaves until she locates the story of her life. She finds the passage that describes her flipping through the *Book of Ages*, and she skips to the next column, where it details what she'll be doing later in the day: acting on information she's read in the *Book*, she'll bet one hundred dollars on the racehorse Devil May Care and win twenty times that much.

The thought of doing just that had crossed her mind, but

being a contrary sort, she now resolves to refrain from betting on the ponies altogether.

There's the rub. The *Book of Ages* cannot be wrong; this scenario is based on the premise that a person is given knowledge of the actual future, not of some possible future. If this were Greek myth, circumstances would conspire to make her enact her fate despite her best efforts, but prophecies in myth are notoriously vague; the *Book of Ages* is quite specific, and there's no way she can be forced to bet on a racehorse in the manner specified. The result is a contradiction: the *Book of Ages* must be right, by definition; yet no matter what the *Book* says she'll do, she can choose to do otherwise. How can these two facts be reconciled?

They can't be, was the common answer. A volume like the *Book of Ages* is a logical impossibility, for the precise reason that its existence would result in the above contradiction. Or, to be generous, some might say that the *Book of Ages* could exist, as long as it wasn't accessible to readers: that volume is housed in a special collection, and no one has viewing privileges.

The existence of free will meant that we couldn't know the future. And we knew free will existed because we had direct experience of it. Volition was an intrinsic part of consciousness.

Or was it? What if the experience of knowing the future changed a person? What if it evoked a sense of urgency, a sense of obligation to act precisely as she knew she would?

I stopped by Gary's office before leaving for the day. "I'm calling it quits. Did you want to grab something to eat?"

"Sure, just wait a second," he said. He shut down his computer and gathered some papers together. Then he looked up at me. "Hey, want to come to my place for dinner tonight? I'll cook."

I looked at him dubiously. "You can cook?"

"Just one dish," he admitted. "But it's a good one."

"Sure," I said. "I'm game."

"Great. We just need to go shopping for the ingredients."

"Don't go to any trouble—"

"There's a market on the way to my house. It won't take a minute."

We took separate cars, me following him. I almost lost him when he abruptly turned in to a parking lot. It was a gourmet market, not large, but fancy; tall glass jars stuffed with imported foods sat next to specialty utensils on the store's stainless-steel shelves.

I accompanied Gary as he collected fresh basil, tomatoes, garlic, linguini. "There's a fish market next door; we can get fresh clams there," he said.

"Sounds good." We walked past the section of kitchen utensils. My gaze wandered over the shelves—peppermills, garlic presses, salad tongs—and stopped on a wooden salad bowl.

When you are three, you'll pull a dishtowel off the kitchen counter and bring that salad bowl down on top of you. I'll make a grab for it, but I'll miss. The edge of the bowl will leave you with a cut, on the upper edge of your forehead, that will require a single stitch. Your father and I will hold you, sobbing and stained with Caesar Salad dressing, as we wait in the emergency room for hours.

I reached out and took the bowl from the shelf. The motion didn't feel like something I was forced to do. Instead it seemed just as urgent as my rushing to catch the bowl when it falls on you: an instinct that I felt right in following.

"I could use a salad bowl like this."

Gary looked at the bowl and nodded approvingly. "See, wasn't it a good thing that I had to stop at the market?"

"Yes it was." We got in line to pay for our purchases.

Consider the sentence "The rabbit is ready to eat." Interpret "rabbit" to be the object of "eat," and the sentence was an announcement that dinner would be served shortly. Interpret "rabbit" to be the subject of "eat," and it was a hint, such as a young girl might give her mother so she'll open a bag of Purina Bunny Chow. Two very different utterances; in fact, they were probably mutually exclusive within a single household. Yet either was a valid interpretation; only context could determine what the sentence meant.

Consider the phenomenon of light hitting water at one angle, and traveling through it at a different angle. Explain it by saying that a difference in the index of refraction caused the light to change direction, and one saw the world as humans saw it. Explain it by saying that light minimized the time needed to travel to its destination, and one saw the world as the heptapods saw it. Two very different interpretations.

The physical universe was a language with a perfectly ambiguous grammar. Every physical event was an utterance that could be parsed in two entirely different ways, one causal and the other teleological, both valid, neither one disqualifiable no matter how much context was available.

When the ancestors of humans and heptapods first acquired the spark of consciousness, they both perceived the same physical world, but they parsed their perceptions differently; the world-views that ultimately arose were the end result of that divergence. Humans had developed a sequential mode of awareness, while heptapods had developed a simultaneous mode of awareness. We experienced events in an order, and perceived their relationship as cause and effect. They experienced all events at once, and perceived a purpose underlying them all. A minimizing, maximizing purpose.

I have a recurring dream about your death. In the dream, I'm the one who's rock climbing—me, can you imagine it?—and you're three years old, riding in some kind of backpack I'm wearing. We're just a few feet below a ledge where we can rest, and you won't wait until I've climbed up to it. You start pulling yourself out of the pack; I order you to stop, but of course you ignore me. I feel your weight alternating from one side of the pack to the other as you climb out; then I feel your left foot on my shoulder, and then your right. I'm screaming at you, but I can't get a hand free to grab you. I can see the wavy design on the soles of your sneakers as you climb, and then I see a flake of stone give way beneath one of them. You slide right past me, and I can't move a muscle. I look down and see you shrink into the distance below me.

Then, all of a sudden, I'm at the morgue. An orderly lifts the sheet from your face, and I see that you're twenty-five.

"You okay?"

I was sitting upright in bed; I'd woken Gary with my movements. "I'm fine. I was just startled; I didn't recognize where I was for a moment."

Sleepily, he said, "We can stay at your place next time."

I kissed him. "Don't worry; your place is fine." We curled up, my back against his chest, and went back to sleep.

When you're three and we're climbing a steep, spiral flight of stairs, I'll hold your hand extra tightly. You'll pull your hand away from me. "I can do it by myself," you'll insist, and then move away from me to prove it, and I'll remember that dream. We'll repeat that scene countless times during your childhood. I can almost believe that, given your contrary nature, my attempts to protect you will be what create your love of climbing: first the jungle gym at the playground, then trees out in the green belt around our neighborhood, the rock walls at the climbing club, and ultimately cliff faces in national parks.

I finished the last radical in the sentence, put down the chalk, and sat down in my desk chair. I leaned back and surveyed the giant Heptapod B sentence I'd written that covered the entire blackboard in my office. It included several complex clauses, and I had managed to integrate all of them rather nicely.

Looking at a sentence like this one, I understood why the heptapods had evolved a semasiographic writing system like Heptapod B; it was better suited for a species with a simultaneous mode of consciousness. For them, speech was a bottleneck because it required that one word follow another sequentially. With writing, on the other hand, every mark on a page was visible simultaneously. Why constrain writing with a glottographic straitjacket, demanding that it be just as sequential as speech? It would never occur to them. Semasiographic writing naturally took advantage of the page's two-dimensionality; instead of doling out morphemes one at a time, it offered an entire page full of them all at once.

And now that Heptapod B had introduced me to a simultaneous mode of consciousness, I understood the rationale behind Heptapod A's grammar: what my sequential mind had perceived as unnecessarily convoluted, I now recognized as an attempt to provide flexibility within the confines of sequential speech. I could use Heptapod A more easily as a result, though it was still a poor substitute for Heptapod B.

There was a knock at the door and then Gary poked his head in. "Colonel Weber'll be here any minute."

I grimaced. "Right." Weber was coming to participate in a session with Flapper and Raspberry; I was to act as translator, a job I wasn't trained for and that I detested.

Gary stepped inside and closed the door. He pulled me out of my chair and kissed me.

I smiled. "You trying to cheer me up before he gets here?"

"No, I'm trying to cheer me up."

"You weren't interested in talking to the heptapods at all, were you? You worked on this project just to get me into bed."

"Ah, you see right through me."

I looked into his eyes. "You better believe it," I said.

I remember when you'll be a month old, and I'll stumble out of bed to give you your 2:00 am feeding. Your nursery will have that "baby smell" of diaper rash cream and talcum powder, with a faint ammoniac whiff coming from the diaper pail in the corner. I'll lean over your crib, lift your squalling form out, and sit in the rocking chair to nurse you.

The word "infant" is derived from the Latin word for "unable to speak," but you'll be perfectly capable of saying one thing: "I suffer," and you'll do it tirelessly and without hesitation. I have to admire your utter commitment to that statement; when you cry, you'll become outrage incarnate, every fiber of your body employed in expressing that emotion. It's funny: when you're tranquil, you will seem to radiate light, and if someone were to paint a portrait of you like that, I'd insist that they include the halo. But when you're unhappy, you will become a klaxon, built for radiating sound; a portrait of you then could simply be a fire alarm bell.

At that stage of your life, there'll be no past or future for you; until I give you my breast, you'll have no memory of contentment in the past nor expectation of relief in the future. Once you begin nursing, everything will reverse, and all will be right with the world. NOW is the only moment you'll perceive; you'll live in the present tense. In many ways, it's an enviable state.

The heptapods are neither free nor bound as we understand those concepts; they don't act according to their will, nor are they helpless automatons. What distinguishes the heptapods' mode of awareness is not just that their actions coincide with history's events; it is also that their motives coincide with history's purposes. They act to create the future, to enact chronology.

Freedom isn't an illusion; it's perfectly real in the context of sequential consciousness. Within the context of simultaneous consciousness, freedom is not meaningful, but neither is coercion; it's simply a different context, no more or less valid than the other. It's like that famous optical illusion, the drawing of either an elegant young woman, face turned away from the viewer, or a wart-nosed crone, chin tucked down on her chest. There's no "correct" interpretation; both are equally valid. But you can't see both at the same time.

Similarly, knowledge of the future was incompatible with free will. What made it possible for me to exercise freedom of choice also made it impossible for me to know the future. Conversely, now that I know the future, I would never act contrary to that future, including telling others what I know: those who know the future don't talk about it. Those who've read the *Book of Ages* never admit to it.

I turned on the VCR and slotted a cassette of a session from the Fort Worth looking glass. A diplomatic negotiator was having a discussion with the heptapods there, with Burghart acting as translator.

The negotiator was describing humans' moral beliefs, trying to lay some groundwork for the concept of altruism. I knew the heptapods were familiar with the conversation's eventual outcome, but they still participated enthusiastically.

If I could have described this to someone who didn't already know, she might ask, if the heptapods already knew everything that they would ever say or hear, what was the point of their using language at all? A reasonable question. But language wasn't only for communication: it was also a form of action. According to speech act theory, statements like "You're under arrest," "I christen this vessel," or "I promise" were all performative: a speaker could perform the action only by uttering the words. For such acts, knowing what would be said didn't change anything. Everyone at a wedding anticipated the words "I now pronounce you husband and wife," but until the minister actually said them, the ceremony didn't count. With performative language, saying equaled doing.

For the heptapods, all language was performative. Instead of using language to inform, they used language to actualize. Sure, heptapods already knew what would be said in any conversation; but in order for their knowledge to be true, the conversation would have to take place.

"First Goldilocks tried the papa bear's bowl of porridge, but it was full of brussels sprouts, which she hated."

You'll laugh. "No, that's wrong!" We'll be sitting side by side on the sofa, the skinny, overpriced hardcover spread open on our laps.

I'll keep reading. "Then Goldilocks tried the mama bear's bowl of porridge, but it was full of spinach, which she also hated."

You'll put your hand on the page of the book to stop me. "You have to read it the right way!"

"I'm reading just what it says here," I'll say, all innocence.

"No you're not. That's not how the story goes."

"Well if you already know how the story goes, why do you need me to read it to you?"

"Cause I wanna hear it!"

The air conditioning in Weber's office almost compensated for having to talk to the man.

"They're willing to engage in a type of exchange," I explained, "but it's not trade. We simply give them something, and they give us something in return. Neither party tells the other what they're giving beforehand."

Colonel Weber's brow furrowed just slightly. "You mean they're willing to exchange gifts?"

I knew what I had to say. "We shouldn't think of it as 'gift-giving.' We don't know if this transaction has the same associations for the heptapods that gift-giving has for us."

"Can we—" he searched for the right wording "—drop hints about the kind of gift we want?"

"They don't do that themselves for this type of transaction. I asked them if we could make a request, and they said we could, but it won't make them tell us what they're giving." I suddenly remembered that a morphological relative of "performative" was "performance," which could describe the sensation of conversing when you knew what would be said: it was like performing in a play.

"But would it make them more likely to give us what we asked for?" Colonel Weber asked. He was perfectly oblivious of the script, yet his responses matched his assigned lines exactly.

"No way of knowing," I said. "I doubt it, given that it's not a custom they engage in."

"If we give our gift first, will the value of our gift influence the value of theirs?" He was improvising, while I had carefully rehearsed for this one and only show.

"No," I said. "As far as we can tell, the value of the exchanged items is irrelevant."

"If only my relatives felt that way," murmured Gary wryly.

I watched Colonel Weber turn to Gary. "Have you discovered anything new in the physics discussions?" he asked, right on cue.

"If you mean, any information new to mankind, no," said Gary. "The heptapods haven't varied from the routine. If we demonstrate something to them, they'll show us their formulation of it, but they won't volunteer anything and they won't answer our questions about what they know."

An utterance that was spontaneous and communicative in the context of human discourse became a ritual recitation when viewed by the light of Heptapod B.

Weber scowled. "All right then, we'll see how the State Department feels about this. Maybe we can arrange some kind of gift-giving ceremony."

Like physical events, with their causal and teleological interpretations, every linguistic event had two possible interpretations: as a transmission of information and as the realization of a plan.

"I think that's a good idea, Colonel," I said.

It was an ambiguity invisible to most. A private joke; don't ask me to explain it.

Even though I'm proficient with Heptapod B, I know I don't experience reality the way a heptapod does. My mind was cast in the mold of human, sequential languages, and no amount of immersion in an alien language can completely reshape it. My world-view is an amalgam of human and heptapod.

Before I learned how to think in Heptapod B, my memories grew like a column of cigarette ash, laid down by the infinitesimal sliver of combustion that was my consciousness, marking the sequential present. After I learned Heptapod B, new memories fell into place like gigantic blocks, each one measuring years in duration, and though they didn't arrive in order or land contiguously, they soon composed a period of five decades. It is the period during which I know Heptapod B well enough to think in it, starting during my interviews with Flapper and Raspberry and ending with my death.

Usually, Heptapod B affects just my memory: my consciousness crawls along as it did before, a glowing sliver crawling forward in time, the difference being that the ash of memory lies ahead as well as behind: there is no real combustion. But occasionally I have glimpses when Heptapod B truly reigns, and I experience past and future all at once; my consciousness becomes a half-century-long ember burning outside time. I perceive—during those glimpses—that entire epoch as a simultaneity. It's a period encompassing the rest of my life, and the entirety of yours.

I wrote out the semagrams for "process create-endpoint inclusive-we," meaning "let's start." Raspberry replied in the affirmative, and the slide shows began. The second display screen that the heptapods had provided began presenting a series of images, composed of semagrams and equations, while one of our video screens did the same.

This was the second "gift exchange" I had been present for, the eighth one overall, and I knew it would be the last. The looking glass tent was crowded with people; Burghart from Fort Worth was here, as were Gary and a nuclear physicist, assorted biologists, anthropologists, military brass, and diplomats. Thankfully they had set up an air conditioner to cool the place off. We would review the tapes of the images later to figure out just what the heptapods' "gift" was. Our own "gift" was a presentation on the Lascaux cave paintings.

We all crowded around the heptapods' second screen, trying to glean some idea of the images' content as they went by. "Preliminary assessments?" asked Colonel Weber.

"It's not a return," said Burghart. In a previous exchange, the heptapods had given us information about ourselves that we had previously told them. This had infuriated the State Department, but we had no reason to think of it as an insult: it probably indicated that trade value really didn't play a role in these exchanges. It didn't exclude the possibility that the heptapods might yet offer us a space drive, or cold fusion, or some other wish-fulfilling miracle.

"That looks like inorganic chemistry," said the nuclear physicist, pointing at an equation before the image was replaced.

Gary nodded. "It could be materials technology," he said.

"Maybe we're finally getting somewhere," said Colonel Weber.

"I wanna see more animal pictures," I whispered, quietly so that only Gary could hear me, and pouted like a child. He smiled and poked me. Truthfully, I wished the heptapods had given another xenobiology lecture, as they had on two previous exchanges; judging from those, humans were more similar to the heptapods than any other species they'd ever encountered. Or another lecture on heptapod history; those had been filled with apparent non-sequiturs, but were interesting nonetheless. I didn't want the heptapods to give us new technology, because I didn't want to see what our governments might do with it.

I watched Raspberry while the information was being exchanged, looking for any anomalous behavior. It stood barely moving as usual; I saw no indications of what would happen shortly.

After a minute, the heptapod's screen went blank, and a minute after that, ours did too. Gary and most of the other scientists clustered around a tiny video screen that was replaying the heptapods' presentation. I could hear them talk about the need to call in a solid-state physicist.

Colonel Weber turned. "You two," he said, pointing to me and then to Burghart, "schedule the time and location for the next exchange." Then he followed the others to the playback screen.

"Coming right up," I said. To Burghart, I asked, "Would you care to do the honors, or shall I?"

I knew Burghart had gained a proficiency in Heptapod B similar to mine. "It's your looking glass," he said. "You drive."

I sat down again at the transmitting computer. "Bet you never figured you'd wind up working as a Army translator back when you were a grad student."

"That's for goddamn sure," he said. "Even now I can hardly believe it." Everything we said to each other felt like the carefully bland exchanges of spies who meet in public, but never break cover.

I wrote out the semagrams for "locus exchange-transaction converse inclusive-we" with the projective aspect modulation.

Raspberry wrote its reply. That was my cue to frown, and for Burghart to ask, "What does it mean by that?" His delivery was perfect.

I wrote a request for clarification; Raspberry's reply was the same as before. Then I watched it glide out of the room. The curtain was about to fall on this act of our performance.

Colonel Weber stepped forward. "What's going on? Where did it go?"

"It said that the heptapods are leaving now," I said. "Not just itself; all of them."

"Call it back here now. Ask it what it means."

"Um, I don't think Raspberry's wearing a pager," I said.

The image of the room in the looking glass disappeared so abruptly that it took a moment for my eyes to register what I was seeing instead: it was the other side of the looking-glass tent. The looking glass had become completely transparent. The conversation around the playback screen fell silent.

"What the hell is going on here?" said Colonel Weber.

Gary walked up to the looking glass, and then around it to the other side. He touched the rear surface with one hand; I could see the pale ovals where his fingertips made contact with the looking glass. "I think," he said, "we just saw a demonstration of transmutation at a distance."

I heard the sounds of heavy footfalls on dry grass. A soldier came in through the tent door, short of breath from sprinting, holding an oversize walkie-talkie. "Colonel, message from—"

Weber grabbed the walkie-talkie from him.

I remember what it'll be like watching you when you are a day old. Your father will have gone for a quick visit to the hospital cafeteria, and you'll be lying in your bassinet, and I'll be leaning over you.

So soon after the delivery, I will still be feeling like a wrung-out towel. You will seem incongruously tiny, given how enormous I felt during the pregnancy; I could swear there was room for someone much larger and more robust than you in there. Your hands and feet will be long and thin, not chubby yet. Your face will still be all red and pinched, puffy eyelids squeezed shut, the gnome-like phase that precedes the cherubic.

I'll run a finger over your belly, marveling at the uncanny softness of your skin, wondering if silk would abrade your body like burlap. Then you'll writhe, twisting your body while poking out your legs one at a time, and I'll recognize the gesture as one I had felt you do inside me, many times. So *that's* what it looks like.

I'll feel elated at this evidence of a unique mother-child bond, this certitude that you're the one I carried. Even if I had never laid eyes on you before, I'd be able to pick you out from a sea of babies: Not that one. No, not her either. Wait, that one over there.

Yes, that's her. She's mine.

That final "gift exchange" was the last we ever saw of the heptapods. All at once, all over the world, their looking glasses became transparent and their ships left orbit. Subsequent analysis of the looking glasses revealed them to be nothing more than sheets of fused silica, completely inert. The information from the final exchange session described a new class of superconducting materials, but it later proved to duplicate the results of research just completed in Japan: nothing that humans didn't already know.

We never did learn why the heptapods left, any more than we learned what brought them here, or why they acted the way they did. My own new awareness didn't provide that type of knowledge; the heptapods' behavior was presumably explicable from a sequential point of view, but we never found that explanation.

I would have liked to experience more of the heptapods'

world-view, to feel the way they feel. Then, perhaps I could immerse myself fully in the necessity of events, as they must, instead of merely wading in its surf for the rest of my life. But that will never come to pass. I will continue to practice the heptapod languages, as will the other linguists on the looking glass teams, but none of us will ever progress any further than we did when the heptapods were here.

Working with the heptapods changed my life. I met your father and learned Heptapod B, both of which make it possible for me to know you now, here on the patio in the moonlight. Eventually, many years from now, I'll be without your father, and without you. All I will have left from this moment is the heptapod language. So I pay close attention, and note every detail.

From the beginning I knew my destination, and I chose my route accordingly. But am I working toward an extreme of joy, or of pain? Will I achieve a minimum, or a maximum?

These questions are in my mind when your father asks me, "Do you want to make a baby?" And I smile and answer, "Yes," and I unwrap his arms from around me, and we hold hands as we walk inside to make love, to make you.

ABOUT THE AUTHORS

ROBERT CHARLES WILSON's first novel, *A Hidden Place* (Bantam), appeared in 1986. He won the Philip K. Dick Award for his 1995 novel *Mysterium* (Bantam) and the Aurora Award for his novelette "The Perseids." His most recent book is *Darwinia* (Tor), and he is currently working on another novel. He lives in Toronto.

SUSANNA CLARKE has so far written short stories about magic, set in seventeenth- and early nineteenth-century England. Her first published story appeared in *Starlight 1* and was picked for the tenth *Year's Best Fantasy and Horror* (St. Martin's Press). Other stories can be found in Neil Gaiman's *The Sandman: Book of Dreams* (HarperCollins) and Ellen Datlow and Terri Windling's fairy-tale anthologies, *White Swan, Black Raven* and the forthcoming *Black Heart, Ivory Bones* (both Avon). She lives in Cambridge, England, and is working on a novel.

M. SHAYNE BELL'S short fiction has been published in a wide variety of magazines and anthologies. His short story "Mrs. Lincoln's China" was a 1995 Hugo Award finalist. He is also the author of the novel *Nicoji* (Baen) and editor of the anthology *Washed by a Wave of Wind: Science Fiction from the Corridor* (Signature Books). In 1991, Bell received a Creative Writing Fellowship from the National Endowment for the Arts. He is an avid hiker, backpacker, and climber.

RAPHAEL CARTER, author of the novel *The Fortunate Fall* (Tor), reports that if you read enough issues of *Nature*, your dreams acquire footnotes that cite other dreams.

MARTHA SOUKUP'S "Waking Beauty" appeared in *Starlight 1*. She won a Nebula for her story "A Defense of the Social Contracts", which can be found along with many of her other stories, in her collection *The Arbitrary Placement of Walls* (DreamHaven). She lives in San Francisco and has no idea what she'll do when she grows up.

DAVID LANGFORD was born in South Wales and now lives in Reading, England. Since 1975 he has published hundreds of magazine columns about sf and several dozen short stories, and has written or co-written some 20 books. His collection of short pieces *The Silence of the Langford* (NESFA Press) was a finalist for the Hugo Award for Best Nonfiction Book, and he and his sf newsletter *Ansible* have accumulated 14 Hugos. He means to get some sleep some time.

CARTER SCHOLZ was a finalist for Nebula, Hugo, and Campbell awards in 1977. His short stories were widely published in the 1980s, and he is the author (with Glenn Harcourt) of the novel *Palimpsests*, one of the latter-day Ace Specials. Now that he is writing again, his recent work has appeared in *Crank!*, Greg Bear's anthology *New Legends* (Tor), and *Starlight 1*. He lives in Berkeley, California.

ELLEN KUSHNER is host, writer and co-producer of *Sound & Spirit*, a national, public radio program which explores the connections between myth, music, art and belief around the world and through the ages. As co-editor (with Delia Sherman and Donald G. Keller) of the 1997 anthology, *The Horns of Elfland* (Roc), she combined her love of music and of fantasy. Her second novel, *Thomas the Rhymer* (Morrow; Tor), won the World Fantasy Award. Her first novel, *Swordspoint* (Morrow; Tor), is set in the same city as "The Death of the Duke." With her partner Delia Sherman, she recently wrote the short story "The Fall of the Kings," published in Steve Pagel and Nicola Griffith's *Bending the Landscape* (White Wolf); they are currently expanding it to novel length. "The Death of the Duke" takes place some forty years after *Swordspoint* and twenty years before "The Fall of the Kings," and involves characters from both works.

ESTHER M. FRIESNER is the author of twenty-nine novels and more than one hundred shorter works. Two of her short stories, "Death and the Librarian" and "A Birthday," won Nebula Awards in 1995 and 1996, respectively. Besides writing, she has edited four anthologies. She lives in Connecticut with her husband, two children, and necessary cats.

JONATHAN LETHEM is the author of *Gun, with Occasional Music* (Harcourt, Brace; Tor), *Amnesia Moon* (Harcourt, Brace; Tor), *As She Climbed Across the Table* (Doubleday), and *Girl in Landscape* (Doubleday). Seven of his stories are collected in *The Wall of the Sky, The Wall of the Eye* (Harcourt, Brace; Tor), which won the 1997 World Fantasy Award for Best Collection. He has recently returned to his native Brooklyn, New York, where he is at work on a new novel.

ANGÉLICA GORODISCHER is from Rosario, Argentina, and is a well-known Argentine novelist. Much of her work is more comic than fantastic. Diana Belessi, Ursula Le Guin's co-poet on the Arte Publico book *The Twins, The Dream*, thinks that *Kalpa Imperial* is Gorodischer's best book. (There are many.) "The End of a Dynasty" is from *Kalpa Imperial*.

URSULA K. LE GUIN, translator of "The End of a Dynasty," is the author of several of the crucial works of science fiction and fantasy of this century, including *A Wizard of Earthsea*, *The Left Hand of Darkness*, *The Dispossessed*, and *Always Coming Home*. Among her many awards are numbered five Hugos, five Nebulas, and the World Fantasy Award.

GEOFFREY A. LANDIS won the Hugo award for Best Short Story in 1992 for "A Walk in the Sun," and the Nebula in 1990 for "Ripples in the Dirac Sea". He is the author of one short-story collection, *Myths, Legends and True History* (Pulphouse). He has a Ph.D in physics, and works for the Ohio Aerospace Institute at NASA Lewis Research Center. He was a member of the science team for the Mars Pathfinder project, and successfully measured dust deposition on the surface of Mars. He is currently working on instruments to be carried by the 2001 Surveyor Lander mission to Mars. He currently lives just west of Cleveland.

TED CHIANG has had fiction published in *Omni*, *Asimov's*, and *Full Spectrum 3* (Bantam). He won the 1990 Nebula Award for Best Novelette ("Tower of Babylon"), the 1991 *Asimov's* Reader's Award for Best Novelette ("Understand"), and the 1992 John W. Campbell Award for Best New Writer. "Story of Your Life" is his fourth published story. He lives in Kirkland, Washington.